Prince of Tanimara

By J.A. Peter

This book is a work of fiction. Any references to historical events, real people, or real places are used fictitiously. Other names, characters, places, events are products of the author's imagination and any resemblance to any person, place, name or event is entirely coincidental.

Copyright © 2023 by J.A. Peter

All rights reserved. No part of this book may be reproduced in any form or by electronic or mechanical means, including information storage and retrieval systems, without written permission from the author, except for the use of brief quotations in a book review.

Cover design J.A. Peter

A heartfelt and special thanks to my team for bringing this work to life.
A.K. Mushfiq - Cover artist @rare_art on fiverr
Mia Hedgie Art - Cover artist on facebook and instagram
Aaron Rakuu - Map artist @aaronrakuu on fiverr
Xann Smith - Line editor
Aaron Gross - Copy editor @Familylyfe on fiverr
Rachael - Formatter
Belle Manuel - Editorial proofreader/Formatter
If you have any questions please contact peterja135rt@gmail.com
Please follow me on Facebook J.A. Peter and Instagram @j.a._peter

I dedicate this work in loving memory of James R. Peters, and to all those who supported me through this amazing journey.

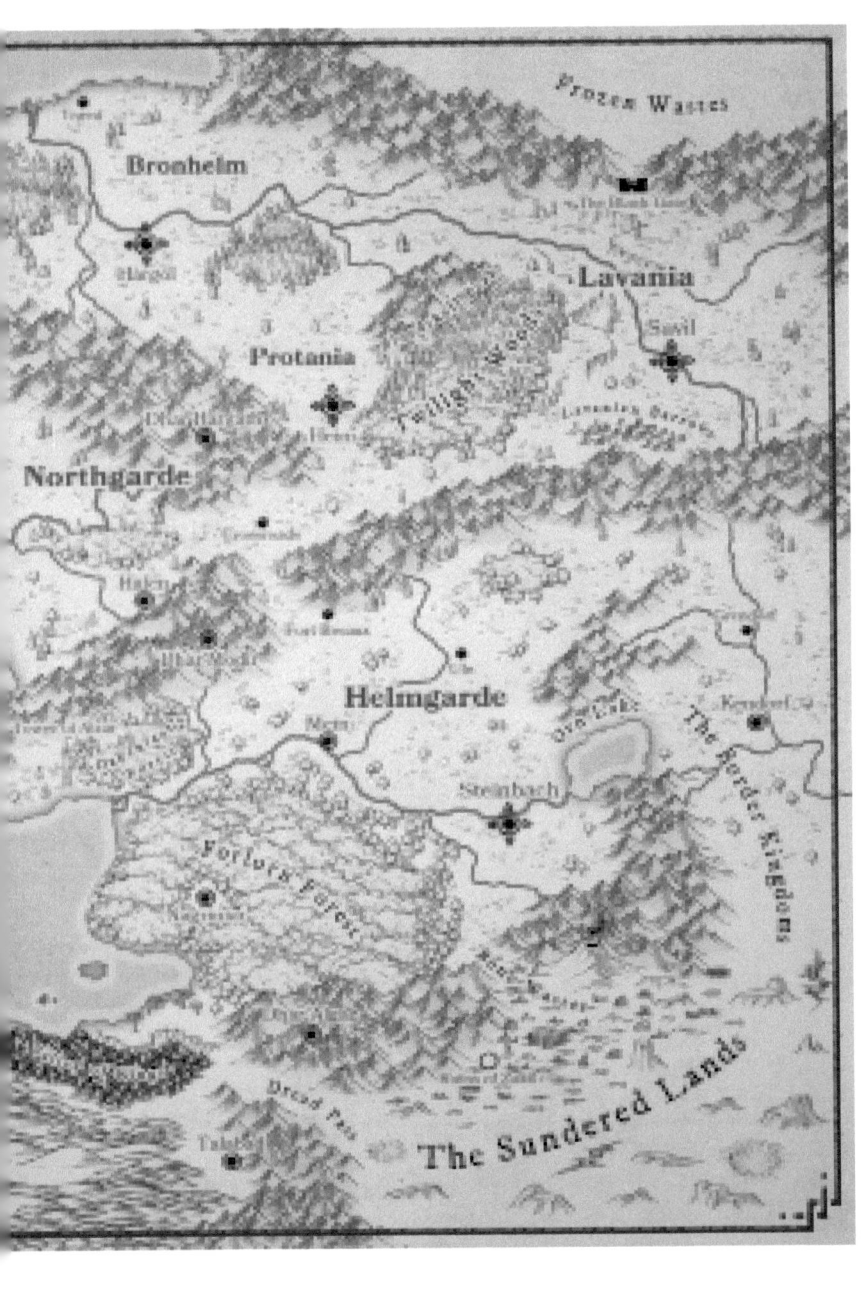

Prologue

Ten thousand years ago, crystals from the corrupted planet Canar, which was shattered by the celestials, made their way across the cosmos and landed on Abrion. The exiled champion of the dragons, Draxus, came across the crystals, which corrupted him into Necrosith. He then forged the crystals into scepters and tempted the kings of the races of the old world, promising power and fortune.

One night, the two moons, Canis and Majoris, eclipsed each other. They powered the arcane lines, and Draxus instructed the kings to raise their Scepters simultaneously. Doing this sundered the area now known as the sundered lands. The sundering corrupted those caught within it. Humans became orcs, dwarves became goblins, and elves became what are known as dark elves.

War broke out between the pure and corrupted races. The pure races captured the scepters and defeated the corrupted, and Necrosith was ultimately imprisoned by the wizard Alzar beneath his tower.

Because of the unsuitability of the sundered lands, the races migrated. The humans were guided by the Celestial, Ata, west to the land of Araba and to the northern regions today known as the human kingdoms. The Celestial Aldir guided the dwarves north to the mountains, which they fortified.

Guided by the celestial Etos, the elves migrated westward and north. They established themselves in The Twilight Grove of the human kingdoms and Tanimara. Of the corrupted races, the orcs and goblins went underground, and the dark elves migrated to the frozen lands beyond the human kingdoms and to the western continent of Abrion.

The Mari, in their native language, or High Elves to men and dwarves, are an enigma. Believing themselves to be superior to the rest of the races of Abrion, they remained reclusive other than when they made war upon the races of the old world.

One hundred years ago, House Melfarin of Atlantin attacked the Thunderforge clan over a resource called electhril. The elves were relentless and defeated the dwarves. In return for sparing them, King Dwoldrumin Brightbelt of the Thunderforge clan presented Lord Ruvyn of Atlantin with the sword, Danar, as a gift.

Peace was observed in Tanimara for 90 years, but then Necrosith escaped the Tower of Alzar, and the drums of war beat once again. Only this time, war comes for Tanimara. An ancient enemy is on the move. Enthralled by their master, Necrosith, the orcs are scouring the world for the Scepters of Canar and will stop at nothing to get them. Unaware that one scepter lies beneath Atlan, the Melfarins are in for the surprise of their lives as Warchief Skroatug of Clan Ragebone has unified most of the clans of the sundered lands and now marches on Atlan!

Chapter 1
And so It Begins

Erlan rolled the dice and moved his units into place, now surrounding Maryl's units.

"It would seem I have you, Maryl," said Erlan smugly.

"It would seem you have, Erlan…once again." Maryl would sigh as this was the fourth time in a row that Erlan defeated him in a game of Dragons&Wizards.

"Do not despair, Maryl; it's almost sunrise, and this will be your last patrol of the shift," said Erlan while giving him a smirk.

Maryl's ears went back, which was a clear sign an elf was irritated. He then grabbed his shield and spear and went outside the post. A moment later, a boulder came smashing through the tower where Erlan had been and knocked Maryl to the ground. He was disoriented and heard a loud ringing.

Slowly bringing himself to his feet, he peered over the edge of the tower, and to his horror, there were hundreds of ships arrayed below. He wiped his eyes to get a clearer look. Again, to his horror, these were not the familiar ships of men or even dwarves. No, these had the iconic crude skull with tusks made of wood planks stuck to their bows. These had to be orc ships.

"Orcs have ships?" he thought.

Once again, another boulder made its way toward the tower, only this one barely missed. He ran back to what was left of the tower and saw that Erlan was dead. The first boulder had crushed him, and the only part of him that Maryl could see was his left arm. The rest of him lay under the boulder.

Maryl grabbed a clear crystal sphere known as a scrying orb and threw it into the air. Its magical properties hurled it out of his sight. He then went back outside of the tower and looked over the edge. The sun had begun to rise, and the orcs had landed. They were raiding the village below. The denizens were getting slaughtered along with the small garrison of soldiers defending them. A moment later, a griffin landed on the tower's balcony, which by some miracle wasn't destroyed.

"By the celestials, thank you," he said as he mounted the griffin and took to the sky. He raced to gain altitude as fast as the griffin would allow. Looking back, he saw the scope of the situation. Tens of thousands of orcs had to be on those ships. This was no raid. This was an invasion!

Maryl went to the command center of the port city of Thalnor. He made his way to Coast Guard Commander Eldrin, his direct superior officer. Maryl approached and stood at attention.

"At ease," said Commander Eldrin. What news do you bring from the tower?"

"Orcs are invading, sir. Tens of thousands have landed on the coast and are making their way through Thalnor as we speak. They made quick work of the garrison posted on the coast, sir. I am the only survivor that I know of."

Commander Eldrin wasted no time. He immediately began writing a letter, and as soon as he was done, he dropped melted wax onto the flap of the letter, binding it shut.

He then stamped it with the commander's seal. "You know what to do, Maryl, fly with haste!" he ordered. Without a word, Maryl gave Commander Eldrin his last crisp salute and left. He mounted his griffin and took to the sky, making his way west.

Maryl landed in Atlan, the capital of the region of Tanimara, known as Atlantin. He ran to the sentry posted at the palace and gave him the grim news. The sentry allowed him access to the palace, and Maryl ran through the halls with haste, panting and sweating while holding a missive bearing the seal of the coast guard commander. As he made his way up and around where he needed to go, the sounds of laughter and banter could be heard getting louder and clearer.

Once he arrived at his destination, he stopped and took a moment to compose himself before showing the guards the seal stamped on the missive. With considerable strength, the two guards clutched the handles and opened the doors, revealing the lord's council chambers. The ceilings were high, and the entire room had pillars, statues of elves holding spherical stones that held the ceiling up. In the middle was the council's table in the shape of Abrion's continents as the elves knew it. The council of the lords of Atlan sat around it, and they were all conversing.

"Many thanks," the messenger then walked briskly straight toward the Lord of Atlantin, Ruvyn Melfarin, bearing a message that could not wait.

He interrupted Lord Melfarin and his council by blurting out, "My Lord Melfarin," in a worried tone.

Ruvyn and his council turned their attention to the messenger, who was now bending the knee in front of them. Meryl figured that the annoyed look on their faces demanded to know the meaning of the intrusion. "My lord," said the messenger nervously, struggling to catch his breath. "My apologies, my lord. Please forgive the interruption."

"All is well, sentry. We are in the middle of something, so out with it, please," Ruvyn politely replied. Maryl promptly handed over the missive to Lord Melfarin, who noticed right away the seal of the coast guard commander. He had an alarmed expression, as this was uncommon unless a threat was too considerable, as the Commanders were usually capable of handling small issues themselves and didn't needlessly bother him. He broke the seal and began reading aloud:

"My lord, I write to inform you that Orcs by the tens of thousands and what appear to be several warbands have invaded the shores of Tanimara through Thalnor. It will not be long before they ravage the countryside, killing everything and everyone, burning everything, and impaling the dead or dying. The scryers reveal that the destructive power of their tide is immense."

Ruvyn set the missive on the table and looked up at those in his council, but before he could say anything, Maryl stated, "I hurried as fast as I could! The heart of my Griffin gave out only moments after we landed." Maryl looked up at Ruvyn and said, "My apologies, I could not get here faster."

Horrified by the news they just heard, the council began to panic.

"I will have silence!" demanded Ruvyn. "Thank you, Maryl, your haste was more than sufficient." He offered Maryl a warm smile. "Take another griffin from my stables and send word to all the houses of Tanimara. Tell them what you have told me today and give to them my seal."

He then dipped a quill in ink and began writing to all the lords. He would hand Maryl letter after letter to keep in his satchel before turning his attention to his council.

"General Krestor, Magris, and Arlen, muster the forces and prepare to march. I want the army ready by nightfall! General Magris, prepare the griffin riders, deploy scrying orbs where the orcs were last observed, and see where they've gone. General Arlen, make ready the transports. We need to move as fast as we can! Tonight, we move, and tomorrow we meet the orcs on the field before they can raid another Atlantin village."

Lord Melfarin turned around and clasped his hands behind his back. He stood tall with long, white straight hair and piercing blue eyes. His shoulders were broad and thick.

He made his way to the balcony overlooking the city of Atlan and thought to himself," *Those green-skinned beasts will learn quickly why no one has ever conquered Tanimara but the elves themselves!"*

The elves rushed to follow orders. Lord Melfarin made his way to his son's chambers. A spitting image of his father with very subtle differences, he stood there as if waiting for his father eagerly.

"Velnir, my son. I have news that requires your attention."

"What is it, Father? Is everything all right?" asked Velnir.

"Now is the time for you to put your martial and tactical leadership to the test. Orcs have invaded our shores, and I can think of no better opportunity for you to hone your skill than to kill those green and black-skinned beasts."

Wide-eyed with excitement and eager to join the fight, Velnir jumped up and said, "Father, the time has come to prove myself worthy, and I will. Give me an army, and I will destroy the orcs. I have learned much from the Academy. My skills are unrivaled."

Lord Melfarin smiled and nodded. "Do not fight them like we fight the dark elves or dwarves. Remember what you have learned about all of the races on Abrion and their combat prowess. The time is now, Velnir. Go," he said, smiling with pride.

Two days passed, and by the dawn of the third, the armies of Atlan set out to meet the orcs in battle. Not long after they arrived, in the outskirts of Thalnor, they came across the first sign of orcish destruction. The army began quietly forming up and getting into position on the hill overlooking the coastal town. Once Lord Melfarin made his way to the top of the hill where his army was posted, he turned his attention to the orc encampment below and was amazed by the sheer number of orcs.

"How could they have gotten here undetected," he wondered.

He pulled from his satchels several scrying orbs, and after muttering a magical incantation, the faces of his son and generals appeared before him within the orbs.

"Father, there must be a hundred thousand orcs here," said Velnir with concern.

"Are your troops in position?" asked Lord Melfarin. "I do believe we have the element of surprise."

All of the commanders nodded in agreement.

"I have levitated scrying orbs into the sky to give you a bird's eye view of the encampment, my lord," said General Arlen.

Lord Melfarin pulled out another scrying orb. They all began circling around him until they came to rest, offering him a view of the whole field. He turned around and looked through each orb to observe the position of his troops. He then turned to peer through the orbs overlooking the orcs and noticed they were in no hurry to counter the elves. They did indeed have the element of surprise.

"Very good," he said. He ordered the generals to prepare their soldiers for battle. Every elf at once lifted their shields and created a massive shield wall. The second line of elves placed their spears through special slots on the front lines' soldiers' shields and awaited further orders. The sound of the clanking shields and spears was remarkably quiet. Once everything seemed in place, Lord Melfarin donned a pleased expression as his army executed the element of surprise with precision and accuracy.

He then gave the order, "Give them hell!"

A few moments later, hundreds of griffin riders in "V" formations took to the sky and flew overhead. The silver armor of the troops and their shields reflected the light of the rising sun, revealing to the orcs that the elves had positioned themselves around the entire tree line on top of the hill overlooking the now-ruined city. It was then that the griffins broke formation and dove toward the orcish ranks as they began to form.

The mages General Magris and Captain Folwin, the commander of the griffins, brought up their staves and began to throw firebolts and conjure firestorms in the orcish ranks. The griffins began attacking the orcs and dug their claws into their shoulders, throwing them around like a child's rag doll and tearing them to shreds, while the warriors that mounted them plunged their lances through whatever part of an orc was available. The carnage was gruesome and seemed to stir the orcs into a frenzy. Several wyverns mounted by orcs with huge axes and serrated spears descended upon the griffins. Chaos ensued as they skirmished. The griffins and wyverns were inflicting heavy casualties upon each other.

"Fall back and regroup," ordered Lord Melfarin. "Send the archers!"

Once the griffins took to the air and were out of harm's way, Lord Melfarin gave the order to let loose. A blanket of fire roared over the hill and descended upon the orcs. By the time the orcish army realized the danger, fire was raining down, and several of them were already set ablaze. The orcs began to huddle together, throwing their shields on top of each other in an effort to block the arrows. This proved effective. Three more volleys were fired but had little effect.

The orcs began to laugh and mock the elves in their guttural language. Several thousand more orcs began running up the lower hill and filling the orcish ranks. They began howling and screeching. A black orc with fiery orange eyes, wielding an enormous black serrated ax and wearing heavy metal plate armor with spikes, appeared on the back of a large wyvern. He began rallying the orcs, who were now smacking their shields in unison. They suddenly stopped. What appeared to be their leader grabbed his ax and pointed it toward the elves. In a blood-furious rage, they began to move up the hill toward the elves at a high rate of speed.

Ruvyn observed the advancing orcs through the scrying orbs. Their numbers seemed endless, but he did not let this deter him. He ordered the archers to fire several more volleys of flaming arrows until they depleted their quivers. This had a devastating effect on the orcs but failed to deter them.

Just as they reached the line of elves, they jumped in the air, axes and spears poised for the attack. The elves, following Velnir's command and with rhythm-like precision, brought their curved blades up to meet the descending orcs. The thunderous clash shook the ground beneath both armies. The elves began tactically moving backward, creating a bulge in their line.

Without thinking, the orcs rushed into the bulge, flailing, howling, and beating the shields of the elves with furious rage. The elves held their line precisely where they intended to. Their shields all connected, spears at the ready, and they began to thrust their spears into the orcish ranks in unison upon the order of Velnir.

Thousands of orcs perished, while only a few elves were lost. Scores of orcs were impaled over and over, and the elvish line began tactically recovering. Where each bulge in the line retracted, elves in the protrusion formed a bulge. From the point of view of Lord Melfarin from his scrying orbs, he could see that his elvish line, some eighteen thousand soldiers, was advancing like an ocean wave's trough and crest. Very pleased with the way the battle was playing out, Ruvyn smiled and ordered General Magris, Captain Folwin, and his griffins to attack the rear of the orcs. The mages once again took to the sky on the backs of their griffins and made their way to the rear of the orcs. They descended upon them, smashing through their ranks and catching them off guard with ferocious precision.

After the shock of their attack waned, the griffins took to the sky once again. This time, they came around the flanks of the orcish ranks and, from both sides, descended, throwing firebolts and conjuring firestorms before once again smashing into their ranks.

The orcish line began to break and the orcs began to run. The griffins made quick work of them before they got too tired to continue.

Now, the orcs were in full retreat. The elves broke the line and began chasing them down and brutally killing every orc they could until they could no longer chase them. Velnir ordered the archers to roam the battlefield littered with wounded orcs and elves and bring the wounded elves to the medics. He then ordered the rest of the army to roam the battlefield and finish off the wounded orcs. The soldiers happily complied, especially those who were singing along with the rest of the victorious elves while thrusting their curved blades and spears into the throats, eyes, or mouths of the wounded orcs.

Ruvyn ordered Velnir, his generals, and lieutenants to the command tent. They arrived, excited over the victory they had won. They entered the tent while the soldiers could still be heard putting the orcs out of their miserable existence. Lord Melfarin would welcome them with delight. After praising them, they began discussing their next plan. The army of House Melfarin began to set up camp and feast.

Idle banter, jokes, and laughter filled the camp as all of the soldiers were overjoyed. The locals even brought them meat, fruits, and vegetables as thanks for their efforts.

The next morning, the Atlantin army was rested and eager to fight more. They packed up their camp and began to march toward the direction the orcs retreated.

Ruvyn ordered Captain Folwin to scout ahead and report what he found. The scouts took off and, after a few hours, returned to inform Lord Melfarin that the orcs had regrouped and more orcs had landed on the shores of Atlantin. They also said there were orcish ships as far as the eye could see off in the horizon. They were either offloading orcs or waiting to do so. Captain Folwin reported that there were too many for an elvish army of this size to defeat on the field and suggested a tactical retreat.

The news alarmed Ruvyn as he mulled over the possible strategies available to him.

He thought to himself, *"What could they want from us? Why are they attacking us?"*

He knew that attempting to get into the mind of an orc was for naught. They do not think the same way elves do. Their reason for attacking Tanimara does not matter. They must be mercilessly punished, or Atlantin would look weak to the other lords and magistrates of Tanimara.

Ruvyn ordered his army to halt. He then summoned his generals and lieutenants. "Our victory yesterday was sound, but I am afraid it was against a smaller force than we anticipated we may face tonight or tomorrow. Captain Folwin has reported that more and more orcs are being offloaded on our shores as of a few hours ago. I fear we do not have enough soldiers to fight this battle on the field. We must not let our excitement cloud our judgment. We will need to retreat back to Atlan and prepare a defensive strategy. If there is one thing our island has proven countless times over thousands of years, it is that its defenses and we elves are well adapted to it. Let us make haste back to Atlan and begin preparations for a siege. In the meantime, I want you to invite every denizen from every town and city to find shelter and safety behind the walls of Atlan. I also need you to conscript everyone capable of fighting into your ranks. Call up the reserves and bring them to Atlan. By now, the messages should have been received by all the other lords of Tanimara. We should expect aid soon."

Ruvyn turned his army around and marched in the direction of Atlan until night fell. Setting up camp, they began to fall asleep.

The night was quiet, and the guards were vigilant; however, a dozen stealthy orcs entered the commander's camp completely by chance and remained unnoticed. They found the commander's tent and confirmed that Ruvyn there asleep. The orc that discovered the commander's tent displayed a disgusting, black-toothed grin as it looked upon the pointy-eared lord fast asleep. Just as fast as it appeared, it silently slipped back into the shadows to inform the others.

Ruvyn awoke to blood-curdled choking and cries. It was clear that they were under attack. He ran out of his tent, and to his horror, discovered his camp was overrun by orcs. They were killing everyone. He became angry and retreated into his tent to grab a weapon. As he grabbed his spear, he took a deep breath and opened the flap of his tent to step outside.

As he took the first step, a serrated blade plunged through his chest and out his back. Ruvyn had a surprised expression on his face. The orc that plunged the blade into him grinned wildly and licked his lips. The orc watched as Ruvyn began to cough up blood, and the orc twisted the blade, finishing Ruvyn off. The orcs tore him to pieces; they ate his limbs and innards, then cut off his head and mounted it atop a stake.

The orcish leader appeared as he and his wyvern landed. The orcs that crafted the stake offered it to him as a trophy, which he gladly took. He attached it to the back of his armor so the elf's head would be above his and the other orcs could see what his clan had accomplished. This would surely strike fear in the hearts of the elves, and the orc relished in what was to come next.

Velnir and the elves he commanded heard the commotion and quickly threw on their armor and formed ranks while he pulled out a jagged-shaped white object known as a scrying crystal, awaiting his father's image to show, but there was only silence.

"Father, what is the commotion?" he asked with an alarmed tone of voice.

Again, he attempted to contact his father and was met with only silence. He threw a scrying orb into the sky and directed it to his father's camp. He could see thousands of orcs raiding it. The ground was soaked in the blood of his fellow Tanimarans. The sight made his stomach turn. He saw the orcs gathering around who appeared to be their leader.

Velnir then directed the scrying orb to get a closer look, and the orc noticed the scrying orb.

The orcish leader reached over his shoulder and grabbed what Velnir thought was a weapon. He then threw it!

Velnir saw it coming toward the orb. He leaned in to get a closer look.

A moment later, the lifeless face of an elf through his ornate silver pointed helmet appeared a second before it collided with the scrying orb, shattering it and making the crystal go blank.

Startled and caught off guard, Velnir jumped back and winced.

"Retreat to Atlan and do so with haste!" he immediately ordered. "Do not stop until we get there. We must hurry!" A short while later, scouts reported that Lord Ruvyn was killed in the fray.

Velnir's troops moved with such grace it was as if they were floating through the air. The sound of their boots hitting the ground in unison surely made for that to only be a stretch of the imagination.

Soon, the tall elven spires synonymous with the city of Atlan were in sight. It was enormous and elegant. The high walls stretched for kilometers and were very tall. They were so thick that quarters were built within and on top of them for soldiers to stay in. The majestic spires towered high above even the walls. The city could easily house two hundred thousand and in times of need, accommodate eight hundred thousand. It could withstand a siege for ten years, assuming they couldn't get food using griffins or other means. It was truly a sight to behold, especially for one who has never been there.

Chapter 2
The Horde Comes

Atlan is one of the largest of the elven cities in Tanimara and surely the crown jewel of house Melfarin culture. Velnir was no stranger to Atlan, however. This was his home, and he paid no attention to its splendor and beauty as he hastily demanded they open the city gates and let them in.

He ordered his troops to man the walls at once. He made his way to the magister's hall to parlay with her. "Kaelina!" he shouted. "Kaelina…Magister Kaelina. It is Velnir, son of Ruvyn Melfarin…Kaelina."

A woman came running out of the Magister's chambers, hastily throwing something on to cover up her naked body. A naked male elf was standing behind her, clutching a pillow over his nethers and had an embarrassed expression but not one greater than the woman whose face was red as a ruby.

"My apologies, Velnir, you caught me at a... rather inconvenient time. What, um, what was it you needed?" she said while curling her hair behind her ear. "You look alarmed. Is everything all right," she asked in a rather disastrous attempt to get the attention off of her. Velnir's facial expression was that of distress and anguish.

"Magister Kaelina, please forgive the intrusion, but this matter cannot wait. We were ambushed by a massive horde of orcs. Lord Ruvyn was killed and we had to retreat. I came here to have you order the city under martial law and assist in getting the city ready for a siege.

"What terrible news, Velnir. Atlantin and all of Tanimara will mourn his passing. I will issue the order at once and make ready the preparations for the siege."

She hurried to a desk which had a quill and bottle of ink at the ready. She began scribbling a missive when she said, "Oh, I forgot. Traevus, Traevus!" She kept calling until her messenger, a scrawny, clumsy young elf, came hastily around the corner. He came immediately from outside and approached the Magister.

"Give this to the town crier at once. It is of great importance!" she said.

He took the missive, trying not to look at what was underneath her haphazardly thrown on gown. Without a word, he hurried off.

"Velnir, I am truly sorry for your loss. You know this now means that you are the lord of Atlantin as you are his eldest son and heir. Atlan belongs to you now."

She leaned against her desk and began to pin her hair up.

"I understand the city is about to be besieged by orcs, but you will need to be properly anointed. We must get that established at once.

Velnir nodded in agreement. His focus was the defense and protection of Atlan.

All the heralds cried the edicts of the Magister. Every Atlan citizen knew what to do. It was as if they had done this before, though the state of the city would suggest otherwise. It was pristine! The city was bustling. The streets were clustered with the people promptly setting the city up for a siege as the denizens from around Atlantin were just starting to enter the city. The reserves showed up and manned the walls with the rest of the army. Able elves of adolescence or older were drafted and began training anywhere they could. The foundry and smiths were hard at work fashioning armor and weapons. Everyone seemed determined to get through what was to come.

The time to begin the ceremonial rite of Etos was to begin shortly. Etos is a celestial being and guardian of the heavenly fortress within the cosmos called the Phatra. The elves of Tanimara perform the rite to receive a blessing of protection and guardianship from the celestial should he listen. Legends of long ago reveal that when catastrophic events happen on Abrion, the celestials do get involved, so performing a rite can, in rare cases, yield some kind of result.

Everyone gathered in the temple of Atlan. It was massive, with tall spires of marble radiating the brilliance of its architect. Inside was a massive hall adorned with drapes bearing the sigil of House Melfarin and of the Celestials, indicating that the

Melfarins worshipped the Celestials. The benches were being populated by many of the city's denizens, praying that the celestials would aid the defenders in protecting Atlan from the orcs. This was, after all, the intention of rites.

The priest of the celestials stood at the opposite end of the temple wearing traditional ceremonial robes. Candles were lit and levitating just above everyone's heads. The ceiling looked as if it were not there at all. But an open view of the stars and cosmos. It was grand and beautiful.

"Are you ready, Velnir?" asked the priest as he began the preparations.

Velnir nodded and spoke quietly, "I am."

The bearers began to come out and form a circle around Velnir. He closed his eyes, and together they all hummed a religious hymn. A moment later, the runes that were inscribed on the temple walls began to glow.

The image of Etos appeared in front of Velnir. Etos looked upon him and around the temple. The image nodded at Velnir before disappearing, indicating that Atlan has his blessing. This, of course, was not actually the Celestial Etos. It was a magical illusion performed by the priest and the bearers. Nonetheless, it served to boost morale as the town criers decreed that Atlan was under the protection of Etos.

Velnir felt empowered and gained confidence. The magister showed up, and everyone, stood then bowed their heads. She was a respected elected member of the magistrate of Tanimara which convened in Tarvana, the capital of Tanimara. She brought with her Danar, the sword of House Melfarin. Ruvyn had received it as a peace offering from High King Dwoldrumin Brightbelt, Dwarf king of the

Thunderforge clan, after the elves overwhelmingly defeated the dwarves in the electhril wars 90 years ago. The sword was forged in the thunderforge of Dhar'Modir, bordering the kingdoms of Nemis and Northgarde.

She walked up to Velnir and presented the sword to him. He took it from her, and by the authority of the high magistrate, she proclaimed him a Prince of Tanimara and High Lord of Atlantin before thousands of witnesses.

Velnir returned to his chambers. Things were ahead of schedule. He took off his ceremonial clothing and put on a robe. His feet hurt, and he could only imagine how his troops felt. "Vetus, come in," he ordered. A servant boy entered his chambers and came to Velnir at once. "Take this missive to Commander Itham on the wall."

Vetus nodded and stated, "At once, my lord." He hurried off to deliver the missive.

Velnir had ordered extra rations of wine, chocolate, and meat to be given to all the soldiers on the wall and in training in the hopes it would boost morale. That was the least he could do, considering what they would soon face.

He rested and thought of his father. Grief started to swell in his heart. The haunting image of the head being thrown at the scrying orb and the crushing feeling of losing his father weighed on him heavily. He knew this burden would not give him the grace to allow time to grieve. Velnir knew what he had to do, and after a short respite, he called to court his generals and council.

The time was now, and he had to prove himself. Remembering his academy training and his involvement in the electhril wars, he needed to reassure himself that he could do this. It was what his father and grandfather did before him. He was no stranger to expectations and knew that his first impression of addressing the court as lord of Atlan could ignite the fire he needed to save his city or otherwise. He put his armor back on with the help of Vetus once he returned.

Velnir stood for a moment, observing his reflection in the mirror. "*It came too soon,*" he thought. He took a deep breath, and a determined expression shown in his reflection. He is now lord of Atlantin, and although sickened with grief, he knew he could not allow it to cloud his judgment. He straightened his shoulders and stood tall as his father did. He was a spitting image of Ruvyn.

He made his way to the court with Vetus. While walking, he laid out his expectations for the servant, who kept nodding instead of speaking. Once he arrived at the court, he saluted the guards. They returned a salute. He stood for a moment, composing himself before giving them the go-ahead to open the doors. Waiting for him were his generals, advisors, and the Magister of Atlan.

It was an emotional moment for Velnir and those present. He moved past his normal seat to that of his fathers at the head of court. He sat down slowly and looked at everyone. "Have we received word from the other Lords of Tanimara?" he asked.

One of his best friends, Arlen, one of the best military Generals of Tanimara was the first to speak.

"We have, my lord, though only from your uncle, Lord Baefric of Madir, and your cousin, Lord Meric of Caphry.

We do not know when to expect their arrival, though. It should be soon."

Magister Kaelina shifted in her seat toward Velnir and said, "At the moment, the city's defenses are at their strongest. We can expect the fortifications to hold. Bolt throwers in each tower are all in working order. I had them tested this morning. The people are well fed and, despite the circumstances, seem to be in good spirits.

"The walls are manned, and the conscripts are being armored and armed. We are ready, My lord," said General Krestor in a somber tone. Krestor was Arlen's father and Ruvyn's best friend. Not only was he a general, but he was an Atlantin noble.

Doubt and fear filled Velnir's head despite the confidence of his generals and magister. He saw firsthand the sheer number of orcs coming and knew, based on the intelligence he gathered, that there were many more to come.

"Double our efforts," ordered Velnir. "We can take no chances. We must make an example out of them, and considering that aid from the other Tanimaran lords is not a guarantee, we need to proceed with caution and expect the worst but hope for the best." He tried to sound as confident as he could in front of them. The last thing he wanted was for them to lose faith in his leadership.

They rose from their chairs and saluted him, each walking gracefully out of the court. Velnir went to his chambers to contemplate what would happen next. He was pleased that his uncle and cousin answered the call to arms but was suspicious as to why the other lords of Tanimara did not. He was well aware of how the politics of Tanimaran princes worked and was looking forward to playing that game perhaps later in his life. Not at this moment when so much was at stake.

A knock on his chamber door startled him. "Come in," he said with a little irritation in his voice. It was his other best friend, Magris, a recently promoted general of the Atlantin forces that his father commanded. "Magris," Velnir said with a gleeful smile. "A pleasure to see you, old friend. How come I missed you at my first council meeting?"

"I am sorry Velnir… I mean Lord Velnir. I did not get the missive in time, so I thought I'd come and see you personally. How are you holding up?" he asked with sincerity.

"My father was killed, and I inherited his land. The first course of action for me is to defend it from an orcish invasion and keep my people from being massacred. The weight of this…Magris, I…," he said before Magris interrupted him.

"Velnir, you are the strongest Tanimaran I know. You are the best with a blade and quite capable in strategy and tactics. You were the most prestigious of our class and easily the most handsome," he joked, trying to lighten the mood.

"Thank you, my friend. I am very much looking forward to fighting the orcs with you," he said in a challenging tone.

"Let the best elf with a blade and, in my case, magic receive the most kills and least injuries." They shared a laugh, and Velnir tucked in for the night after Magris left.

Chapter 3
Dark Tides

Skroatug, warchief of the sundered lands horde and chieftain of Clan Ragebone, reveled in his victory over the pointy ears. "Pile the corpses into the wagons," he ordered one of his grunts. "We will build a pyre of them and ignite it in front of their city. But remove the heads of their fallen first. We will deliver them over their walls. "His grin was wicked, and the grunt nodded in obedience.

The orcs built their camp and began to forage for supplies. The stench of death, dung piles, and orcs filled the air. From all around, the trees and grass began to die. It was as if their presence alone was poisoning the earth itself. Scores and scores of orcs were arriving daily.

Ergog, one of the other warlords, approached Skroatug. "Warlord Skroatug!" he said with a smug, toothy grin. I see you have made quick work of the pointy ears. The dragon wants to know what news you have of the relic the elves keep."

Skroatug turned to face Ergog. Hunched over and draped in a hooded cloak, the warlock's eyes of green fire met Skrotug's. His skin was green and black, and both of his tusks were broken. His jaw was thick and scarred.

"I must sack the city and retrieve it before I can learn of it further, Warlock." Skroatug snapped. He knew Ergog all too well. He was ambitious and always plotting and scheming for more power. Skroatug wished to have his head as a trophy.

"The dragon believes you have enough forces at your disposal to finish taking the city. You best be going, Skroatug," Ergog said in a sinister tone.

He disappeared among the crowd of orcs going about their daily orders. Skroatug, now clearly annoyed, pulled a piked head secured to his back and looked upon the bloody visage of what was once an elven leader to his knowledge. Its cold, dead eyes stared into nothing and were beginning to cloud. "If I could so easily defeat you, then I shall make quick work of your kin." He removed the head from the pike and threw it onto the pile of heads that he ordered the other orcs to cut off the corpses of dead elves.

Skroatug called the rest of the warlords around the bonfire. "Surely you have gotten your fill," he shouted. "Elf flesh is delicious indeed, and there is plenty more to come. Soon, we will be at the gates of their city. We will smash their walls and take everything. We need to prepare for the siege at once."

Orcs roared with excitement, and after a few primitive salutes, they began to work, tirelessly building wagons out of the local timber and creating sacks from the skins of local animals.

The orcs are very efficient at mobilizing large hordes, for they are all nomads of the sundered lands, and most live underground. They use a series of tunnels they either carved themselves or that were formed naturally during the sundering. The sundered lands are located across the ocean, centered east of the great Araban desert. They are no strangers to the rigors of harsh climates, and the climate of the elves was quite comfortable. This allowed them to move with haste, collecting what they needed and building what they needed quickly.

Within a few days, the orcish horde swelled to tens of thousands. There were orcs as far as the eye could see. Skroatug mounted his wyvern and took to the sky. He flew around and inspected the orcs as they began to gather. The land was barren, black, and scorched. The orcs had cut all the trees down for kilometers, trampled the land into mud, and wiped out whole herds of animals in just a few days.

Skroatug was pleased with what he saw. He pulled from his side a horn that appeared to be made of hollowed-out dragon horn. When he blew it, the sound that came out was that of a heavy, low bass tone. It could be heard by all the orcs present, and when heard, they began to move in the direction of Atlan.

Several other warlords mounted their wyverns and accompanied Skroatug in the air. They flew around the horde, observing and scouting. The last thing they wanted was to get outflanked and attacked, for surely, by now, the elves knew they were coming. Several griffin riders were spotted scouting, along with a few scrying orbs.

This was it. The relic was close, and soon Skroatug would have it.

He planned to deliver it to his master personally and hoped he would gain more favor. His thoughts shifted to his mate and his pups. He elected not to bring them because their skills were no match against the elves. Skroatug needed his best clans for such a task. Instead, his pregnant mate and two pups joined the other clans, attacking their traditional and familiar enemy, the humans of Araba. He longed to win glory against such a powerful foe and bring the stories and plunder home with him to his clan and family.

The horde had reached the tree line and could now see the walls of the great elven city of Atlan. They had not known just how massive the walls were or how long they were. The city was enormous and full of tall spires and aqueducts and seemed to be built into a mountain.

Skroatug, as high as he was on his wyvern, still wasn't at the level of the top of the walls. This would require some extensive engineering, and he knew just the goblin for such a monumental task. Once the horde began to dig in around a section of the city, Skroatug called for the master engineer Skeet. A hooded goblin with green skin and no more than three feet tall entered the command hut. He looked up and grinned wickedly as his ugly red eyes and elongated nose met Skroatug's gaze.

"Skeet, as you can see, we have arrived at our destination," Skroatug said confidently. Surely, you've observed their walls by now and know this won't be as simple a task as we had hoped."

"Naw, we always hoping for the best but preparing for the worst, heh?" he said somewhat nervously. "I'll get the crew on the trees immediately and begin building the towers tall enough to reach over the walls. Nothing we cannot handle, boss," Skeet said with a somewhat growly, high-pitched voice. He donned a wicked grin, and beads of sweat rolled down his dark-green complected cheeks.

"We will not only go over the walls, but we are going to go under them, so you must dig tunnels as well. Perhaps they will place most of their forces on top of the walls, and when you and your sappers plant the charges—the soldiers will come crumbling down with the walls." Skroatug said, rather proud of his strategy and with an excited tone. "Battering rams, towers, and catapults. Start with the catapults. I have a gifts to deliver them." Skroatug grinned wickedly.

Skeet ran off and put his goblins to work. They began to chop down all the trees as far as the eye could see, and slowly, the projects came to shape. As per the warlord's orders, the catapults were finished first. Skeet sought out the warchief in his command hut.

"Warchief, the catapults are finished per your request." He then bowed and offered a nervous grin.

"Very good, Skeet. I will have them put in place soon, and in the morning, they will get their gifts," cackled Skroatug. For now, we will feast and make as much noise as possible. I want to be in their nightmares, their heads, and to crush their will before it even begins. I want them to know fear and that they will suffer greatly at the hands of my horde!"

Early the next morning, the warchief summoned all the other warlords into the command tent, Ergog among them.

They came in eagerly, hoping to deliver a blow to the elves. Skroatug announced, "Skeet and his crew have worked tirelessly on creating catapults. I think this morning we will send them a gift. Ergog, I want your coven of warlocks next to the catapults ready to summon earth claws. Let us show the elves a bit of our magic while we roll some heads."

The warlords began to roar and cheer. The sounds of them cheering spurred the horde outside the command tent to begin cheering, and soon, the entire horde was roaring and cheering. Probably not the wakeup call the elves were expecting, but no matter. It was about to get much worse. Skroatug ordered the catapults in place. He ordered the carts of heads to be placed next to them. By now, they were badly decomposed, but most of them still had their easily recognizable pointed helmet of ornate design.

The warlocks took their place next to the catapults and began to chant an ominous hymn. The ground next to each catapult began to shake and the rocks began dancing around. Shortly afterward, a spike of dirt rose high, and the shape of a claw appeared. Trolls and Orcs began to place the heads of the elves into the catapults and claws. Once it was ready, Skroatug blew his horn, and all at once, the catapults and earth claws began to throw the severed heads over the walls.

The cries of horror could be heard, and the Orcs relished. Once the heads were gone, Skroatug ordered the warlocks to launch chaos bolts. This task was very taxing. It required the warlock to concentrate and conjure a massive chaotic ball of green fire powerful enough to take out scores of enemy soldiers or destroy a building. The warlocks gathered together and began to chant. A green spark appeared in the center of their gathering. They chanted louder and with more enthusiasm. The spark turned into a swirling ball of green flame that seemed to grow more unstable as it grew bigger and bigger. It was easy to tell when a chaos bolt was large enough. The swirling of green flames generated a powerful wind, and the warlocks' tangled rat tails and messy hair blew as if they were traveling at a high rate of speed or the wind was fierce.

It was obvious the warlocks had done this many times before. All of the chaos bolts began to rise simultaneously above each gathering. The warlocks were still chanting, and by now they were very loud. Skroatug was pleased and turned his attention to the city walls. He could see the pointy ears panicking on top of them. Skroatug donned a tusky grin, and after a moment, he gave the signal to launch while atop his wyvern.

***

By now, Velnir, the nobles, and generals had moved the people of the city into the safety of the mountain. All that remained were those who were defending the city from the orcs. Velnir observed his army from atop his griffin.

As he had feared, many were visibly nervous and frightened. The elves on the walls and the streets behind the walls had hundreds of years of training for moments just like this. This made them the best soldiers of martial skill the world has ever seen. Many had not seen war in 90 years and for many more, this was their first. They knew some of them would not live to see another day and that hundreds of years of life would end during or after the battle. They also knew they were the best and were confident in their ability to defeat the orcs.

Moments later, the orcs began roaring and shouting in their native language. It was then that Velnir along with the soldiers manning the walls noticed what appeared to be orcish mage's of some sort, conjuring a strange green light. Velnir observed the soldiers beginning to panic.

"Steel yourselves, Atlantins! This is your ancestral home, this is where you have raised your family! You must brace yourselves for what may come, what they may throw at us. Fight to defend what is ours! Let not these green skinned animals destroy everything you have spent centuries working to attain and keep!" The elves began to cheer and hold fast. They all began to stand proud and in ranks almost perfectly.

The orcish catapults began to throw what appeared to be tiny boulders.

One of the generals mounted upon a griffin next to Velnir commented, "They think they can bring down our walls with small rocks?" He scoffed.

Velnir continued to observe and as the tiny objects began to come over the walls and hit the ground, it became obvious that the orcs did not intend to hit the walls with them. Velnir flew down to investigate what they were.

Dismounting, he approached one of them and recognized the helmet right away. When he turned it over, he saw the decomposing face of one of his kin. Rather than strike fear in Velnir, this served to only enrage him. He mounted his griffin and took to the sky once more.

"They throw the severed heads of our kin over our walls in an effort to intimidate and frighten us. These elves were your brothers! Look what they have done to them. They mutilated their corpses and desecrated them! These animals are just that, animals! They have no honor, no dignity! Show no mercy! Kill them all!" Velnir cried in anger and fury. Just then, several of those green balls made their way to the walls.

Velnir ordered his mages to attempt to counter them. Several magical shields were conjured where the fire balls were expected to hit. When they came, some did manage to absorb the impact, sparking cheers from the ranks. Some, however, managed to evade the shields and found their way into the ranks of those on top of the wall.

The green fire completely engulfed them. It was almost like a liquid as it splashed against their armor and beaded off, but when it came into contact with their skin, it ignited it, cooking the elves alive in their armor. The screams were terrible. Some burnt quickly while others seemed to burn slowly. Their comrades rushed to their aid, but it was too hot to get any closer. One elf's screams suddenly turned hoarse and then into nothing more than the sound of gurgling breathing before he finally succumbed to the green fire.

Velnir ordered all the griffin riders to attack and so they took off from the balconies of the tall towers closest to the walls. They descended upon the orcs with haste and conjured firebolts and fire storms. The storms were small chaotic tornadoes of fire conjured from the mage's staff. It moved in random directions. Only a few hit their mark and destroyed the catapults. The firebolts killed several warlocks and destroyed several of the earth claws the orc warlocks had summoned.

***

Skroatug cackled maniacally at the elves' attempt to return the devastation. He hucked a barbed pike into the air, and it met one of the mages atop his griffin killing him instantly. This was nothing more than a sport for Skroatug and his elite orcs. The orcs began to roar, and some even started to move. This caught Skroatug's attention, and he ordered his warlords not to advance. Not yet. The time would come later. For now, it was a show of force. He ordered the continued pounding of the walls with chaos bolts and catapults. He was determined to get a section of the wall down by the next day.

The next morning, Skroatug emerged from his command tent. The orcish ranks were already established, and he could see the massive towers being moved toward the front. His warlords quickly approached him to tell him good news.

"Ha ha excellent," he laughed with excitement.

The clans were all in position and ready to begin the attack. Skroatug ordered that the piles of elven corpses be set ablaze. He and his warlords then mounted their wyverns and took to the air. From his position, he could see the elves were holding fast on top of their walls. It appeared the constant bombardment did not affect this.

Much to his disappointment, the wall hadn't come down either. No matter, he thought, the towers will be sufficient. He descended to Ergog, who was barking orders at the warlocks to keep casting chaos bolts.

Skroatug scolded Ergog for failing to bring down the wall. Skroatug unsheathed a blade made from a single piece of metal. The handle at the base of the blade and the blade's edge—crudely serrated.

He swung it at Ergog, meeting his neck and severing his head from his shoulders. The other warlocks looked stunned but pleased. Skroatug ordered them to stop casting and to get out of the way of the towers. They happily obliged and quickly but exhaustedly ran toward the flank.

Soon, the towers were in place and all the orcs were itching for battle. It was midday, and the sky looked grim. The time was now. Skroatug mounted his wyvern and took to the sky to observe.

He motioned for the other warlords to meet him up there. They too took to the sky.

"We are ready," he exclaimed excitedly, his black tusk dripping spittle. "Order the towers forward first, then the horde! Have the warlocks throw chaos bolts over the walls and into the city. Make them suffer!"

The other warlords gave crude salutes and descended to carry out the orders. The giant towers began to move forward, and soon, the horde followed. Tens of thousands of orcs all marched toward the walls of Atlan, and Skroatug was elated. Soon, the relic would be his, and soon, the dragon would favor him!

***

Velnir hadn't slept. He had been tending to the wounded. He had honed his skill in healing over decades and, like all the others, was able to save many of his kin.

A fellow soldier rushed to him with a pitcher of water. "My lord, you must drink and eat."

Velnir looked up at him and reluctantly nodded. He took the pitcher and what appeared to be salted meat in between two pieces of bread. The food of the common folk for sure, but no matter.

This would be sufficient.

At long last, a break was welcomed. Moments later, another elf came running in. It was one of his generals with urgent news.

"Velnir, the orcs are moving."

Quickly, Velnir got up and ran outside of the infirmary to his griffin. He took to the sky along with his other generals who had been waiting for him there. Velnir turned his attention to the orcish line.

Several tall black towers decorated in spikes and what looked like crude cutouts of orc skulls painted red. Velnir shuttered at the thought of what they could have used to make them red.

Goblins were packed on top of and hanging off the sides of the towers, firing arrows into the ranks of the elves on top of the walls. The hoard was behind the towers, their shields raised to deflect the elves returning arrows.

Velnir looked up to the towers where the ballistae were located. He ordered them to direct their fire toward the towers, and they did so. Several bolts hit their mark but only did minor damage to the armored orcish towers, making the smiling skull they were adorned with all the more menacing.

Once again, Velnir ordered his griffin riders to attack. They descended with haste, hurling the conjured fireballs into the towers. The warlocks were ready for them this time and hurled chaos bolts at the griffin riders.

Several hit their mark, and the riders were forced to retreat. Furious, Velnir descended toward the orcs, much to the dismay of his generals. Some followed him along with their soldiers. They began hurling fireballs and flew with such skill that the orcs did not land a single chaos bolt in their ranks.

Magris hurled a firebolt at a warlock who was about to hurl a chaos bolt over the walls. Right before he was about to let it go, Magris's firebolt smashed into his back, his face donning a surprised expression before exploding into a pink and green mixture of burning brains and guts.

The chaos bolt was hurled; however, it hit one of their own towers, which conveniently had no protection on the back. The orcs were completely exposed with their backs turned, completely unaware of what was about to hit them.

Velnir couldn't help but watch as the chaos bolt smashed into the back of the orcish tower, through the orcish ranks, and out the front of the tower, ironically through the skull decoration. The tower's superstructure failed and collapsed, killing most of the orcs inside and several of the horde around it.

Velnir was shocked that in their haste to build the towers, the orcs hadn't considered their backside's vulnerability.

"The back of the towers," yelled Velnir to Magris and the other elite griffin riders. "Hurl fireballs into the back of the towers. They are unprotected!"

Immediately, the others caught on and began hurling fireballs into the back of the siege towers. One by one, they came crumbling down.

Cheering erupted from the elvish army on top of the walls. Once the towers were burning husks of ruined orcish engineering, Velnir ordered his troops back behind the walls. Not a single one of them fell.

Upon their return, they were met with cheers. The elves' resolve was strengthened, and Velnir took to the sky with his generals once more.

It was obvious that the destruction of their towers did nothing to deter them as the horde, which still numbered in the tens of thousands, still marched forward.

Soon, they would be to the walls.

***

Skroatug roared in fury and cursed the elves atop their griffins as he watched his towers crumble. "SKEET!" yelled Skroatug.

A little green goblin ran toward Skroatug, who grabbed the goblin by the throat and pulled him up to his face.

"The towers, you fool. What have you done?"

Skeet nervously replied in a hoarse and choked voice, "Wee... did not have...time, but I took other actions."

Skroatug tossed him hard to the ground. Skeet squealed in pain as he bounced off the ground.

"What other actions do you speak of, goblin?" Skroatug asked angrily.

Still catching his breath, Skeet replied by pointing toward the walls, and without saying a word, he donned a wicked grin. Skroatug turned his attention toward the walls of Atlan, somewhat confused.

***

The orcs were right outside the walls now, but no ladders or grappling hooks were coming up. Something wasn't right. Velnir approached for a closer look. A large explosion under the walls imploded the section next to a tower. To Velnir's horror, the wall and the tower came crumbling down.

"The walls have been breached. Secure the breach, secure the breach," he ordered.

The elves on the ground quickly filed ranks toward the breach, creating a shield wall linking their shields together and placing their spears through openings between them. They were ready for whatever was to come.

Moments later, the orcs began pouring in through the breach. They climbed over the rubble with ease and made their way toward the elven ranks. They clashed with enraged fury, smashing the elves hard. The elves closed in to form a half circle around the orcs, stopping them in their tracks. The horde on the outside began to place ladders and throw grapples over the walls.

It had begun.

***

Skroatug smiled as he watched the walls of Atlan crumble down. Skeet was still catching his breath, but Skroatug paid him no attention. He mounted his wyvern and took to the sky.

From there he could see the orcs had made it into the city but were surrounded at the breach. He also saw the orcs climbing up the walls on ladders and using grappling hooks. This will not be sufficient, he thought. He then ordered Skeet to bring down several more parts of the walls now that they knew it worked.

"You got it, I am on it," he replied as he scurried off.

Skroatug ordered his wyvern riders to attack the walls and soften up the elves for the ladder boys. He led the wyverns and they dove down smashing into the elven ranks. Several were thrown off the wall, but this did not deter them. Their martial prowess was impressive.

Every time they thrust the spear, they hit exactly where they intended. Skroatug unsheathed two twin blades and began hacking his way through the elves while his wyvern vomited acid upon them. Several minutes had passed, and the fighting was intensifying.

Moments later, several other explosions were heard simultaneously, and whole sections of the Atlan wall crumbled, along with several towers. Skroatug howled, as did thousands of orcs renewing their vigor.

***

Velnir thought about smashing the orcs in the breach with his griffin riders, but just as he was about to ascend, the wyverns landed on the walls and attacked the troops there.

"To the walls," Velnir ordered the griffins.

All at once, they took to the sky and hastily ascended on the wyverns and attacked them viciously. Clashing steel, firebolts, and the screams of orcs and elves drowned out all other sounds. The fighting was tight and cramped in the elves' favor.

Moments later, more explosions were heard, and the walls of Atlan began to crumble. A lump formed in Velnir's throat. He knew that the first district of Atlan would fall to the orcs if the elves retreated to the second district. He also knew that several elves would be killed in the retreat, but having some able to fight in the next stage was better than none, and so the order was given.

"Retreat to the second district." Velnir had thought ahead and had all the districts fortified. He did not expect the orcs to make it this far but was glad he did it anyway.

The front line of the elves kept the shield wall up long enough for the rest of the thousands of elves to retreat to the second district. They backed up slowly, thrusting their spears into the green muscular orcs' throats, faces, and chests.

To Velnir's surprise, most of them made it to the second district which was separated by another equally large wall. Velnir, knowing what the orcs are capable of, did not order any elves on the walls this time. He instead ordered the bolt throwers to fire into their ranks.

Their bolts impaled several orcs at a time, but this couldn't last long as the bolts were now in short supply. He ordered the mages to mount griffins and land on the walls instead so that they could conjure firestorms all over the ranks of the orcs since the wall would provide the elves with protection. They did so to devastating effect.

Thousands of orcs were burned alive, but it seemed that for every one the elves killed, two more took their place, eager to die in such a horrific way.

If it wasn't for their ugly visage, muscular green and black complexion, and terrible tusks, this is what made them all the more terrifying. Their willingness to die like this did not ever cross the mind of Velnir.

***

Skroatug's wyvern had just finished dissolving the elf in front of it. The blood lust invigorated Skroatug's insatiable desire to slaughter. He took a deep breath and closed his eyes.

Thoughts of glory and victory filled his mind, along with those of his mate and pups back home. To his people, this was the pinnacle of glory.

Glory was fleeting, so it had to be done again and again. However, when an orc warlord achieved something that no other orc had before, it was worthy of memory for generations to come. This was Skroatug's moment, conquering an elven land. No other orc in the history of Abrion had ever done so.

Even more satisfying would be to achieve what he had come to do in the first place: retrieve some trinket that a dragon wanted. Skroatug did not care for the trinket.

If he got it, then great. If not, then at this point, if he were to sack the city, he would earn the respect of his people and be able to unite more of the clans of the sundered lands.

The dragon to Skroatug was simply a means to an end, and now, that end was about to become a reality.

Skroatug took to the sky once more and observed the hoard pouring into the first district of Atlan. He had previously given orders to Skeet to sap the next set of walls and to keep doing that until they got to the keep where the trinket was supposedly kept. The fire storms were of no consequence. He understood that to other races, they are more terrifying than effective.

To orcs, it is simply another obstacle to overcome. Skroatug noticed that the warlocks had stopped hurling chaos bolts. He swung his wyvern around and saw that elven griffin riders were attacking the back of his line. The warlocks were being slaughtered. He ordered his wyvern riders to attack the griffins, so they all took to the air from the elven walls and dove straight for them.

Several more explosions were heard within the city; Skroatug smiled as he knew Skeet just successfully sapped more of the walls of Atlan. His orcs were getting closer and closer to their goal.

With renewed vigor, Skroatug and his wyvern riders smashed into the griffins. They didn't stay on the ground for long. The griffins took off without engaging the wyverns for long and did not lose many. This displeased Skroatug. He knew if he were to take to the air, that would leave the warlocks vulnerable to attack again, thus unable to conjure and hurl their chaos bolts.

If he stayed on the ground, the wyverns were vulnerable, too. He ordered the warlocks to mount the wyverns with the other riders, but two to a wyvern. Skroatug and his wyverns took to the sky. However, this proved cumbersome to the wyverns, which slowed them down.

The griffin riders took full advantage of this and began hurling firebolts at them, taking scores of wyverns and their riders down. Skroatug ordered them all into the city but was out-maneuvered by the faster griffins. The fight would be in the air this time—Orc warlock vs elven mage. Green and orange fire began lighting up the darkening sky, offering glimmers of different colors to reflect off the white walls. It was a hellish sight.

***

Velnir ordered the griffin riders to attack the warlocks at the back of the orcish horde and kill as many as they could. They could not afford to take any more damage from those green fireballs. They took off, leaving Velnir and his soldiers to find the goblin sappers. General Krestor, Magris, and Arlen were busy holding off the orcs in the second district.

Velnir flew into the keep to retrieve scrying orbs. He released them, and they did indeed find the sappers. Far too many of them. He couldn't possibly take them on by himself. He was so exhausted…and getting weaker by the moment.

He decided to detonate the scrying orbs once they found the sappers in the hopes of killing them. This only worked to stop a few. Several other explosions were felt, and it was discovered that the orcs had breached the second district.

The generals were given orders to retreat to the third district should this happen. They did so, and with excellent precision. Not many elves had been killed since the warlocks were attacked.

Now that they were distracted fighting the mages in the sky upon their griffins, scores and scores of orcs were being killed. The bodies began to pile up so high, that one may climb above them to get over a wall. The smell was of burnt flesh, dung, and rot. Orcs release their bowels when killed, and it was awful.

Velnir returned to the line, which was now behind the walls of the third district. "General Arlen, I believe I have killed the rest of the sappers."

"Time will tell, my lord," Arlen said nervously.

"All that separates the orcs from the keep is the third district, general. The horde is so massive that not even the entirety of their ranks has entered the city. We are outnumbered, and the walls did little to protect us. You are my senior general. What are your thoughts?"

General Arlen turned to Velnir and said, "Forgo the walls. We must man the keep and fight to the last elf."

They both looked at the griffin riders fighting the wyverns. The green fire became less frequent indicating the orcs were suffering greater losses. "Soon, the griffins will kill those warlocks, and we can recall them to smash the orcs in front of the keep. If we leave the walls, they may remain intact long enough for the griffins to use as a perch. Orcs may not see a need to bring them down if we are not on them." Velnir nodded in agreement. He gave General Arlen the go-ahead and a salute before taking off to tell the others.

The elves were now at the keep. Thousands had formed ranks and were now the last line of defense, but this was what the elves did best. Attrition, precision, and discipline were practiced over thousands of years. Velnir knew that if the orcs couldn't diminish the line here, they wouldn't be able to do so at all. It was bottlenecked in the elves' favor.

***

Skroatug swung his blades all around but missed his target several times. The griffins were too fast. His wyvern took a fire bolt to the chest and began to fall from the sky.

The warlock mounted behind Skroatug began to panic, so Skroatug threw him off the wyvern, and he fell to his death. The wyvern tried desperately to land softly, but it was not in the dice. It hit the ground hard enough to kill it. Skroatug was thrown from its saddle.

When he got back on his feet, he saw the other wyverns falling from the sky. The warlocks were being slaughtered along with his elite wyvern riders. He turned his attention to Atlan and saw the piles of orcish corpses. He estimated that he had lost half his horde by now, which was unexpected. The elves had proven to be a tougher foe than he thought.

Skroatug tracked down another wyvern who was not injured but whose rider had been killed. He mounted it and took to the sky. He flew toward the city with two griffins on his tail. Skroatug hucked a barbed pike at one of the griffins behind him, striking it in the chest. It died instantly and began to fall from the sky along with its rider.

He maneuvered through the city and in between towers, attempting to shake the other griffin off of him, but this was proving difficult. He flew toward the pillars of smoke coming from the burning corpses brought on by the fire storms.

He could not see anything but was willing to take the chance, zig-zagging through. He didn't notice the griffin behind him anymore, so he ascended above the smoke and turned his attention to the ground.

The enemy rider was spotted flying in and out of the pillars, appearing to still be searching for Skroatug.

This pleased him. He drew his blade and dove back down toward the griffin, unbeknownst to the griffin and its rider. Once they reached attacking distance, Skroatug's wyvern unleashed a horrible acid breath, which splashed all over the rider and its griffin.

The elven rider began to scream as he fell from the saddle to his death along with the griffin. Skroatug was free to fly now as the other griffin riders were perched on the walls of the third district, raining fire on the orcs below.

He thought about attacking them, but that would prove futile. He saw the elven line getting hammered by the orcs, but it had held fast for some time now. This was not good. All of a sudden, an explosion was heard under the elven line. The ground imploded, and scores of elves fell through.

Like ants, the orcs poured in and piled themselves up until they formed a bridge for the rest of the horde to infiltrate the keep. Now, the elvish line was divided. Skeet came through, and Skroatug was pleased. He looked upon the elves with murderous eyes and at his horde with pride.

They were going to win!

***

The elves were holding fast. Their training was obvious as the orcs were being slaughtered in droves. Krestor and Magris were down within the ranks defending the keep's entrance. Arlen and Velnir were up in the tower observing and sending orders.

The strategy was proving effective. A bit of confidence returned to Velnir as he was able to sigh in relief. He looked over to the third district's walls and noticed the griffins were beginning to land on it, and the riders were firing fire into the hordes' ranks.

"We will make quick work of them now, my lord," said the general with confidence.

Velnir had learned a lot in the few days fighting these creatures from the sundered lands across the sea. He wasn't as confident as the general. Something in his gut was telling him they had another trick up their sleeve, and not a moment later, an explosion was heard right under the elven line.

The ground beneath them imploded, and scores of elves fell, including Magris and Krestor. Magris appeared to be severely wounded. The orcs wasted no time throwing their dead and themselves into the crater, creating a bridge of bodies. Velnir's jaw dropped in awe.

General Arlen was speechless. Velnir and Arlen immediately jumped on their griffins and flew down to Magris and Krestor. Velnir ordered a medic to take Magris to the hospital. He then went to look for Krestor and saw that Arlen was holding him and weeping.

The General was killed, and Arlen looked at Velnir with sad eyes. Velnir nodded, and Arlen moved his father's body to safety before joining Velnir. The orcs were breaching the keep, and the elves could not push through them.

This made Velnir's heart sink. Velnir landed and joined the ranks on the left while Arlen joined the right, and they attempted, to no avail, to re-secure the line. They were about to lose, the city would surely fall, and all its inhabitants slaughtered.

The ancient city of Atlan and his family's legacy would be lost to history, and he would be the shortest reigning lord ever to serve Atlantin.

The sense of impending doom did not deter Velnir. He was a warrior and would give it his all. He hacked his way through scores of orcs with ease.

It was quite surprising to him just how easy considering orcs appeared to be much bigger and stronger than elves. They were slow and hulky, but if they did land a good hit, he would surely die, so he simply made sure that they could not. If this was his last stand. He would make the most of it.

Chapter 4
Timely Arrival

Skroatug observed the two griffins fly down to join the ranks. One of them wore the same armor as the previous commander he killed.

"Another prize," he said with excitement in his voice.

Just as Skroatug began to fly toward the elven commander, an unfamiliar horn blared to the right of the horde's flanks. Skroatug immediately turned and saw another elven army had formed ranks on the hillside.

Their griffins and cavalry had smashed into the right flank of the horde to devastating effect. Another horn, this time to the left flank of the horde. Another elven army had formed ranks, and their mages were hurling fireballs into the horde ranks. Skroatug's jaw dropped, and his eyes reflected the destruction of his horde.

The line broke and began to retreat. The elves in the city were advancing with ease. Skroatug howled in rage and retreated in the direction the horde was going. The elven reinforcing armies had closed the gap between the city and the orcs but ceased pursuit.

This gave Skroatug a feeling of relief. They retreated into the night until they could not see the smoke from the city or hear the elves. They would attempt to camp here and make their way toward the ships in the early morning.

Skroatug made his way around the encampment and told his horde not to light any fires and to be quiet. The word spread quickly, and not a sound could be heard. This worried Skroatug. It was unlike orcs to be so quiet. He must have lost more of his horde than he thought. He could see the silhouettes of orcs quietly moving around, trying to hide and get comfortable.

"We were so close. I almost had the city and the prize," he thought.

Just then, the sound of clanking metal and jingling chains caught Skroatug's attention. This angered him, and he immediately moved toward the noise. As he got closer, he realized it was Skeet. He had previously thought Skeet was killed, as he was literally right under the elves at the keep.

"Boss," Skeet whispered. "That you, boss?"

Skroatug was slightly happy to see Skeet had made it and was impressed with his cunning in the battle, even though they lost. "I got something for ya boss. Now let me see here." He began fumbling around, and Skeet pulled out an ominous-looking staff from his satchel, which at the end had two black hands holding a glowing purple stone. He handed it to Skroatug, who had no idea what it was.

"What is this?" he asked.

Skroatug was hesitant. The dark purple hue gave him an ominous feeling. This was the relic that the dragon described.

It felt dark and evil but appeared to have no effect on Skeet, who was smiling and eagerly awaiting praise for collecting the prize.

"Very good, Skeet." Skroatug told him to keep them in his satchel and stay close to him from now on. Skeet was happy to oblige.

The next morning, the horde was on the move again, this time in an organized fashion to orcish standards. Skroatug was at the front on his wyvern.

Together, they all moved to the coastline where their ships were waiting. They had sent scouts to see how far the elves were, and they reported they were lagging quite far behind.

Nevertheless, Skroatug ordered they make haste. The ships started to come into view. Hulking floating fortresses adorned in spikes, corpses, and bloody sails. They, too, had the iconic decoration of the orc skull painted in red just off their bows. Pillars of smoke were also observed. It was discovered the local population had killed the garrison of orcs that remained to protect the ships and started setting them ablaze. Skroatug immediately ordered the attack.

With the same fervor as before, the orcs attacked the elves, who clearly weren't soldiers. They started slaughtering them when Skroatug noticed they had only burnt a few ships. He ordered his horde to take them as slaves instead, and so they did.

They boarded the ships and separated the female elves from the male elves. They set across the sea toward the sundered lands. They had gotten away with the prize.

Though Skroatug did not sack the city and get the glory he was hoping for, he did successfully attack an elven city and completed the objective given to him. This would be glory enough. He made his way around his ship and observed it was in good working order.

The orcs seemed to be in high spirits. They were singing and enjoying themselves. This pleased Skroatug, who joined in with them. As he made his way around, he saw a few grunts taunting, bullying, and toying with the elven prisoners.

This pleased Skroatug as he thought elves inferior, ugly, small, and skinny. They had no meat on their bones, and their features were pointy and pink. The elves were sobbing and choking. They were indeed suffering at the hands of their hosts, and Skroatug loved it but understood they still had value.

Once they were finished, Skroatug approached the grunts and said, "No more of that. They will have value at the slave trade since they live long natural lives." One of the grunts began to protest, but Skroatug would have none of it. He eviscerated the orc's belly and threw him overboard. Skroatug ordered the orcs not to bring harm to the slaves and threatened the same fate to any who disobeyed. The elves had confused looks on their faces, as did the orcs. Annoyed, Skroatug returned to his hut to get some shuteye.

***

The sounds of Madiran and Caphiran horns could be heard. Velnir Knew those sounds all too well as they were of his cousin's and uncle's houses. They had answered his call to arms. They came and not a moment too soon. Velnir was so relieved.

The orcs stopped fighting and began what appeared to be a tactical retreat. Velnir would not let them get away so easily. He ordered the elves to advance, and they did with devastating effect. Velnir would punish these monsters. The elves chased the orcs through all three districts, killing as many as possible.

The orcs kept running, seemingly not tired at all. It was strange to Velnir. Once outside the city walls, Velnir noticed the two reinforcing elven armies closing the gap on the retreating orcs. Now, what was left was surrounded, and the slaughter began. Velnir wanted to keep a couple for interrogation, so he ordered General Arlen to capture as many as they could. The rest were viciously slaughtered. The prisoners were bound and carted off into the city. The generals had been able to capture a total of nine hundred and seventy-four orcs.

"Uncle Baefric, Cousin Meric, I was beginning to think you had forgotten about me," said Velnir as he approached the two clad in ornamented elven armor of the highest quality. He moved to embrace both elves, whom he recognized as family.

"Velnir, first and foremost, you have our condolences over the loss of your father. He was my favorite brother," Baefric said with sorrow.

"Uncle Ruvyn will be missed but remembered," said Meric.

Velnir wasted no time on grief and dismissed the heartfelt condolences. He was happy to see his family but unhappy that nobody else came.

"Where are the other houses?" he asked.

Baefric looked at Meric, and then they both looked at Velnir. "They wanted to see how you could handle those savages. To see if you were fit to lead Atlantin, they opted to leave you to your own devices. Meric and I could not stand by and allow the orcs to do anything like this to elven lands, so we chose to come, of course. You are family and now lord of Atlantin. You deserve the respect of the elder magisters, and you have ours, Velnir."

Velnir was disappointed but not surprised. The elven magistrate was greedy and power-hungry. For millennia, the lords of the land had plotted and schemed to turn Tanimara into an elven empire, but none were brave enough to declare open war on their neighbor.

It wasn't worth their precious, long lives to be killed when time was on their side. Why bother when something like an orc invasion would do it for them?

Velnir felt betrayed by his own people. "It has always been like this. Father told me long ago to sleep with one eye open because one day I would rule, and they would try to undermine me. He also said that wealth only means something if you have the power to keep it. The high magistrate clearly had no intention of letting me have my power. I just didn't expect them to blatantly and completely abandon me or my people."

Baefric smiled. "Elves are the strongest race on Abrion. No one could ever defeat an elven army unless it was by another elven army."

Meric chimed in and jovially said, "The dwarves came close…a few thousand years ago."

The polite and seemingly happy demeanor of his uncle and cousin did nothing to quell his anger and frustration. He chose not to wear it, though, and forced a smile. "I'm glad you're here though. We have much work to do, and I think I will put those orcs to it. We have a lot of catching up and planning to do."

The three elves triumphantly marched into the city with thousands of elves marching with precise coordination behind them. They had won the day, and Velnir knew it. This was a great victory and would send a message to the magistrate that he was a capable leader. Though he was unsure he would have been successful had his uncle and cousin not shown up. Never again would Velnir allow these types of shortcomings to interfere with his court.

Chapter 5
Preparations Must Be Made

Velnir woke up from a nightmare he had been reliving from the death of his father and the battle of Atlan. He was sweaty and cold. One of his concubines came to his chambers with warm milk and honey.

"For you, my lord," she said softly.

"Thank you, Mira," said Velnir as he observed her getting his robe ready. He kept quiet, and so did she.

He had his breakfast and allowed her to dress him. She dismissed herself, and Velnir went to the balcony of his chambers, which overlooked the city.

From there, he could see where the battle took place. He could see outside the city where the orcish horde had trampled the ground for days and the scars on the land they left when they were preparing for siege.

Anger filled his heart. He then turned his attention to the city. Atlan was in the process of being rebuilt. The masons and carpenters were masters of their trade, and brought the walls and buildings back up within just a few weeks.

The orcish prisoners were adapting to labor well and proved to be quite capable of lifting big, heavy, and bulky objects elves could not. They were surprisingly cooperative and followed orders well. The language barrier barely hindered productivity. Velnir did not care for them though. These monsters killed so many of his kin. Once they were done, he would have them all killed.

Today was the funeral for Lord Krestor and High Lord Ruvyn. It was a very somber day for everyone in Atlantin. The temple was packed; right outside was a pyre worthy of an Atlantin lord.

Krestor was handsomely dressed and placed on it. Ruvyn's remains were never found, but traditionally, his remains would have been entombed in the ancestral barrow along with all the lords before him. Velnir would have to place a plaque of his memory there instead.

The next day, Velnir met with Meric and Baefric. These three elves were some of the greatest warriors in all of Tanimara. Together, they walked down the streets toward the site of the battle, where all the damage was.

Meric and Baefric were content discussing the rebuilding. They were critiquing the masonry and carpentry and having a good time with it. Velnir had vengeance on his mind. He could not shake the anger toward the magistrate for allowing this to happen. He felt betrayed but all the more grateful that his uncle and cousin came to his aid.

He was not resentful toward them at all, even though he did most of the fighting and knew the magistrate would give them the credit for victory since he would have likely lost had they not arrived. This was frustrating, and he had to come up with a plan to win the magistrate's favor, or they would find excuses to strip him of his title and land and distribute it among themselves.

Velnir looked around silently while his uncle and cousin were still bantering about their ideas of how things should be built in Velnir's city.

He noticed the orcs working together with the elves. They all seemed to be getting along and no fights had been reported. Not one orc out of almost one thousand attempted to flee and or kill an elf. It would appear they have accepted defeat and were content with their new lives… as short as they may be if Velnir has anything to do with it.

Upon his observation, he noticed an orc with a light blue complexion. Next to him was a smaller of the green skins who also had a blue complexion. To Velnir, the orcs he saw all had green, brown, or black skin. The blue ones were the first.

Curious, he approached the two. "You two, come over here this instant," he shouted.

The two turned their attention to him, then glanced at each other, shrugged, and approached Velnir. The big one was muscular but did not have a hunched back like the thousands of others Velnir had seen. His eyes were as blue as his skin and not red or orange like the others. His hair was white, and his clothes were simple robes. He was no warlock, as they were light green-complected, orange, or red eyed, and wore robes made from the skin of their enemies.

The orc was tall and appeared old but was fit. His left tusk was broken, and the right had a gold ring through it. He kept his chin up and looked down on Velnir, though not in arrogance or with pride but curiosity.

The little one was not an orc. He was a goblin. He, too, wore simple robes.

The two said nothing and just stood there looking at him. Baefric and Meric turned their attention to Velnir and saw the orcs within arm's reach of the lord of Atlan.

They drew their swords, and ran toward them ready to attack; as they got closer, they realized the orcs were not attacking Velnir. They just stood there glancing awkwardly at each other and at the two approaching elves.

"Surely by now, if you are intelligent at all, you would have picked up some of our language. Do you understand any elvish?" asked Velnir in a demeaning tone.

The big orc sighed and simply said, "Yes."

The reaction was unexpected. Velnir then asked the orc why he was blue.

The orc said in elvish, "We blue 'cause we have order magics. Warlock green because he has chaos magics."

Velnir was surprised by the orc's ability to speak elven even though it was like that of a child.

He had thought that their bulbous lips, tusks, and thick jaws would make the dialect difficult for them to pick up, but apparently, that was not so. "What do you mean by order magic and chaos magic? You have magic?"

The blue orc nodded. "In my clan, I am shaman." He looked at the smaller one and said, "This goblin, he called Gimit, and he shaman too."

Velnir nodded and asked the orc what his name was.

"I am Dargarok."

Meric started laughing. "You sound like a man but with a deeper voice. Kind of look like them, too, now that I think of it, though just a bit bigger, a bit stronger, with tusks, and…"

"Shut up, Meric," Baefric snapped.

Velnir, clearly annoyed, ignored Meric and continued his conversation with the orc. "What is a shaman, Dargarok?"

Dargarok waited a moment before speaking as if carefully thinking about what to say next. It appeared he knew who Velnir was.

"A shaman… is orc mage," said the orc.

Velnir donned a surprised expression, as did Meric and Baefric. "You mean you have the ability to conjure magic?"

The orc smiled and simply said, "Yes."

Meric was visibly excited, but Baefric was suspicious. Velnir was curious and asked for a demonstration. The orc looked confused by the request and was hesitant.

Velnir ordered some guards to set up a few barrels and told Dargarok to demonstrate some of his magic on those barrels. He then handed the orc a simple staff.

Dargarok nodded and took the staff. He raised it and pointed it at the barrels. Suddenly, several purple magical missiles were ejected from the staff's tip. Their trajectory was a little chaotic, but all of them equally hit their marks and utterly destroyed the barrels.

As the pieces of the barrels were scattered all over the place, the orc turned his hand to face his palm up, and the pieces of the barrel stopped in their tracks. He then clenched his fist and put the barrels back together, as if he never destroyed them, all the while keeping his eyes on Velnir.

The guards took quick action and drew their spears toward the orc. Velnir knew that if Dargarok wanted to kill him, the others, and the guards to make an escape, then he could do so relatively easily.

Velnir wasn't afraid of him, but did wonder why he hadn't tried to escape. "Impressive indeed. You appear to be, at the very least, as skilled as any elven novice mage. I admit, I had not expected that kind of skill to come from an orc. Why have you not tried to escape?"

Dargarok looked at the other two elves and then back to Velnir. "Being slave to elves is better than being slave to mad orcs."

Meric laughed, but for the first time, Velnir felt pity, at least for these two.

He dismissed Dargarok and Gimit back to work and left with Baefric and Meric, but not before telling the guards to keep eyes on those two. The time was for supper, and the feast was unveiled.

Elves were accustomed to such feasts and presented elegant table manners practiced over millennia. The academy had an etiquette class in for such occasions that all elves went through at a very young age. Elves were taught which food category to consume first based on what was presented before them, then the utensil to use.

An elf would know when to speak, when to eat, and how to do it without even looking like they were eating. It was considered rude to be observed chewing food. It was almost like magic. Conversations in the dining hall never ceased.

Tonight, it was about the completion of the rebuilding of Atlan and the healing of the land. The return of the denizens who had fled and things returning to normal. Velnir was not satisfied with simply rebuilding the city and returning Atlantin to normalcy. No, this was not sufficient. The orcs had made him look weak, and now the magistrate plotted against him.

Velnir wanted to make an example out of the orcs, not just the ones he had captured, but their leader. The big ugly black one he saw in the scrying orb who threw a severed head at it and cut so many of his elves to pieces on the battlefield.

Oh, yes, Velnir noticed.

He wanted to find this Orc and do to him what he did to his father. He wanted to employ savage strategy and tactics against the orcs, but knew the logistical challenge of getting an army across the sea and into the sundered lands. His army had suffered many losses in the initial attack because his father severely underestimated the orcs, which, of course, cost him his life. Velnir was a quick learner, and his army, though outnumbered by several to one, held off the orcs for quite some time before his cousin and uncle showed up.

The conversation had been going on for some time, and Velnir hadn't said anything. One of the nobles spoke up and asked Velnir what his thoughts were. Normally, when one is not paying attention, this would catch them off guard, and they would embarrassingly fumble words around, trying to either come up with an answer or simply admit they weren't paying attention in shame.

Not Velnir.

"I do not care for the petty banter of supper conversations lately. I have had nothing on my mind but revenge."

The rest of the elves at the table grew silent, and the jovial atmosphere quickly faded.

Meric smiled and asked, "What would you do then, cousin?"

Velnir peered around the table and stood. "I would invade the sundered lands and bring war to all of the orcs that dwell in that hive of disgust."

The guests began to mutter to themselves, and some donned panicked expressions.

Baefric noticed this and turned his attention to Velnir. "You would take your people to war outside of Tanimara?"

Velnir shot a hateful glance toward Baefric, but they both understood it was not directed at Baefric. "I would," he said coldly. "I would kill every last one of them if I could."

Meric began to clap excitedly. "Wouldn't we all, after what they had done to us, to our people?"

Velnir's glance turned to Meric. "To my people, my land, and my home!" He then looked over to Arlen, who was taking his father's death quite well.

Meric cleared his throat. "Right."

"We deserve a chance to get revenge. We ought to go to their home, burn their villages, and kill their women and children. We ought to eradicate them off the face of Abrion! No house of Tanimara has suffered such a catastrophic loss in over one hundred years. I'll be the first to say, this was an embarrassment. This should never have happened. The second they set foot on Tanimara…Atlantin soil, they should have been stopped. My father underestimated them. He allowed them to get further inland, and by the time he realized his error, it was too late. The orcs must be punished," said Velnir.

The elves had been finishing their meals and excusing themselves from the table and conversation, save for General Arlen and Magris, who was still recovering from his wounds, and now wearing a leather eye patch and sporting a peg leg. Velnir's uncle and cousin stayed as well along with a few nobles. They all began to seriously discuss an invasion of the sundered lands.

To some, this was unthinkable, but it appeared that the majority of the elves in the dining hall, who all happened to be the lords of the land and did have a say in what the elves of this land do, agreed. They, too, wanted revenge. Many of them lost family, countless people, and money. It will take years to recoup their losses in people alone. The magistrate had not lifted the restriction on reproductive intimacy in the region of Atlantin so that the region could repopulate per Velnir's request. It would take years and years.

Baefric and Meric were discussing among themselves while the generals and nobles were arguing over the best strategy, if they could even find one at all.

"Lord Velnir," said Baefric, who was standing next to Meric. "Celestials curse the magistrate. We will commit some of our forces to your invasion."

General Magris chimed in, "The people will follow you, my lord. They want revenge too so we will begin recruiting and training."

Arlen agreed.

The reluctant nobles backed down and said, "If the people want war, then they shall have it. We will overcome the logistical challenges."

The recruiting campaign generated tens of thousands of recruits. Some of whom were former soldiers. They were training hard and eager to fight, which was quite uncharacteristic of elven culture. Elves can live for hundreds and sometimes even thousands of years, hence the reproductive restrictions in Tanimara and the reluctance to fight normally. Supply chains were established directly from Madir to the north and Caphery from the south. The lands which Baefric and Meric were lords of.

All lords sit on the magistrate council. It is a collection of all the lords of Tanimara, and it is there that they decide as a collective the policies and politics of Tanimara. Velnir, Baefric, and Meric were acting outside the Magistrate's wishes and were losing their favor. They seemed not to care.

Velnir issued an edict for the elves of Atlantin to begin sexual reproduction by reason of repopulating, much to the protest of Magister Kaelina. The magistrate sent emissaries to issue the demands of the council, but they were not heeded. Velnir sent a message back to the council stating that if they would not support him in his endeavor, then he would go without them. Velnir would not hear from them again.

Atlantin had begun to look more like a commerce region than an agricultural region. This upset the balance of Tanimara's economy and created some shortages of luxury food and goods, naturally upsetting a lot of people and houses. They were all used to the luxurious lifestyles they had procured over hundreds of years. They had forgotten what it meant to be an elf in this world and what made Tanimara so strong and great in the first place. At least, that was the opinion of Baefric, Velnir, and Meric.

***

The time was fast approaching. The ships Velnir needed were being completed, and in a few months, they would sail toward Araba and then march to the sundered lands. Velnir was staying in Thalnor and went to the docks daily to check on the progress. He observed the soldiers' training and learning. He would not, however, underestimate the orcs in their own land. Velnir was taking every precaution he could think of.

He went to the librarium and studied the orcs and their culture for several hours each night to the best of his ability. When he was not studying, he was training and practicing his swordsmanship. He began to think of Dargarok, and what he said about being a slave to the elves is better than being a slave to mad orcs.

One night, Velnir decided to go to where Dargarok and Gimit were being held. The internment camps were moved outside the port and under guard day and night. The orcs were used to help build the ships, and now that they were almost complete, they were secretly scheduled to be slaughtered the following week.

Velnir had begun to have second thoughts about it, at least for Dargarok and Gimmit. Per his request, Dargarok and Gimit were brought to Velnir.

"By now, you know who I am," Velnir said confidently.

Dargarok and Gimit nodded calmly.

"Feast your eyes upon my war machine. Observe and reflect on what will come to pass to your sundered lands when my army arrives there."

Dargarok and Gimit glanced at each other and were visibly confused.

"Oh, yes, I am going to invade the sundered lands. I am building the largest fleet the world has ever seen. I have almost everything I need to punish the orcs for the insult they have brought upon my people."

Dargarok, now fluent in elvish, looked at Velnir with curiosity. "Almost everything, hmm. I assume that's where we come in? Perhaps you need scouts or spies? I tell you now, we are not interested in bringing war to our people. That is for you and your people."

Perplexed by Dargarok's ability to speak elvish with such fluidity and accuracy, Velnir waited a moment before responding once the weight of his words finally took hold. "The orcs of this internment camp are scheduled to be slaughtered next week," said Velnir.

Dargarok's demeanor changed. "We have done what you asked of us. We did not rebel or disobey. Surely, we are still of use to you."

Velnir smirked. "You are still orcs and have no place in Tanimara and, therefore, must be disposed of."

For the first time, Gimit spoke up, "What if we help? Would you spare us then?"

Velnir looked down upon the blue goblin and replied, "I came here tonight and sought you both out because I do not have everything I need to be as successful as I want. I do understand that you wish not to fight your own kind, and, he sighed, I would not ask that of you. The favor of your situation does lie with me, however, and it would be in your best interest to assist me."

Dargarok responded, "We do not want to die. Could we start there?"

Velnir laughed. "I never thought I'd negotiate with an orc. Perhaps I can show you some elvish hospitality." Dargarok looked perplexed. "You and your companion will come with me tonight and stay in the city. I have made arrangements already. If discussions are favorable for me, perhaps I will spare your lives and much more."

Dargarok and Gimit weren't sure what to say. They were, however, happy to oblige. The orcs in the internment camp were curious and started to get somewhat restless. The commotion sparked a response from the guards.

Dargarok asked Velnir, "If you permit me, I'd like to address my kin so they know where I am going. It will ease them, I assure you."

Velnir furrowed his brow and simply gave Dargarok a nod. Dargarok approached his kin, who had gathered around the entrance but dared not to attempt to walk out the now-open gate. Dargarok began speaking to them in orcish.

Some of them donned curious expressions of what could be interpreted as confusion, worry, and discontent. Their demeanor changed after Dargarok spoke to them, and they dispersed back to their respective places to rest.

Velnir now had questions about Dargarok he had never thought he would have. This orc had taken a role of leadership among the prisoners. Perhaps it was he who quelled their fury.

"Perhaps Dargarok could be much more useful than I had previously thought," Velnir was thinking.

Velnir, his guards, Dargarok, and Gimmit, made their way to Atlan and by nightfall, they had arrived. The orc and goblin were in the carriage hidden from view along with Velnir. The guards were mounted and covered the front, back, and sides of the carriage.

If the people saw an orc being carted through the city, it would cause an uproar. Velnir questioned his actions as he knew how powerful Dargarok was. If he wanted to, he could cause a tremendous amount of damage before being killed. He was a powerful orc.

Velnir turned his attention to him and noticed he was calm. He was too tall to sit upright in the carriage, so he was slouched over a bit. He was gazing out the window, observing elves doing their day-to-day things.

"The fact that he showed interest in our culture at all goes against everything I read about orcs," thought Velnir. "You will find that elves are a peaceful and proud people, Dargarok."

Velnir's expression remained unchanged.

Without taking his eyes off the elven architecture, Dargarok said, "Orcs are warlike and violent. They lust for battle and even fight amongst themselves."

"Tell me something I do not know," retorted Velnir.

Dargarok glanced at Velnir.

The carriage had stopped, and the guards gathered around to shield the orcs. They quickly made their way inside and through the well-lit halls of what appeared to be an elegant building. Dargarok seemed as though he did not expect to be in such a place. Though he felt this was a nice place to look at, it was, in fact, the prison of Atlantin. They were brought to a room where they all sat around a table. The orcs preferred to sit on the floor.

Velnir turned his attention to Dargarok and said, "If you assist me, I will spare your lives. Tell me what I want to know, and I will allow you to leave Tanimara and even arrange to drop you off wherever you want to go."

Gimit lit up with excitement. Dargarok, however, did not and asked, "What of the other orcs? They were obedient as well and do not deserve slaughter."

Velnir thought about it for a moment before replying with a question. "Are you their leader?"

Dargarok's demeanor changed to that of discomfort. "They do look to me to guide them so if that is what you mean, then yes. I would consider myself their leader."

Velnir paused and looked at Dargarok. "You take responsibility for them then?"

Dargarok nodded, and once again, Velnir was surprised.

"I had agreed to spare you and your companion here only, but seeing as you quelled their fury, have not caused any issues, and encouraged obedience, perhaps we can work something out. If you assist me in a way that will be invaluable, I will provide safe passage to wherever you want to go for you and your new clan."

Dargarok leaned back and thought to himself. "My clan?" Dargarok glanced at Gimmit, who was clearly in favor of the elf's offer, and back to Velnir. "Do you expect us to fight orcs on your behalf?"

Velnir scoffed and stated, "We do not need orcs to fight our battles!"

Dargarok nodded. "Very well, we will help you in exchange for freedom." Dargarok proceeded to explain to Velnir that the big black orc on the wyvern was Skroatug, chieftain of clan Ragebone. He was the warchief of a collective of clans who united under the promises of power and glory from an ancient black dragon or enslaved if they refused. He was sent to Tanimara to steal an elven relic for the dragon.

This piqued Velnir's interest as he knew nothing of an ancient relic. The orc proceeded to tell Velnir that the dragon had told Skroatug that the relic was hidden under the keep in what the elves call the 4th district.

It made sense. The orcs knew which side of Atlan to attack. They seemed to know exactly where to go, and when they retreated, they seemed to do so tactfully. Dargarok agreed and stated once they had the relic, the order was to retreat. The fact that the other elves arrived was not anticipated, but that would not deter orcs. They would fight to the death to achieve glory.

Velnir went outside the room for a moment and called General Magris over. "The orc speaks of an ancient elven relic hidden in the keep. Do you know what he is speaking of?"

Magris's face instantly turned pale. "The Scepter of Canar... they were under the keep. The scepter was hidden down there."

Velnir turned to Magris with concern. "Scepter of Canar? Go now and check to see if it is still there. Report to me immediately."

Magris nodded and made haste. Velnir returned to the room and began to question Dargarok more. "If orcs are willing to fight to the death, why did you surrender?"

Dargarok seemed as though he expected the question. "We are not those kinds of orcs. "We prefer to quell our blood lust and convert that energy into magic. My clan was destroyed, and those of us who were not killed were forcibly recruited into Skroatug's horde."

Velnir knew this orc was no ordinary orc. This made sense to him as the "flightiness" did not seem to dwell in the hearts of the orcs that surrendered. "Interesting," he said to Dargarok. "Tell me of this Scepter of Canar."

Dargarok did not hesitate. "All I know is that it possessed strange magic. I know not its purpose or what it is capable of. I do not even know why it was here in the first place or why the dragon desires it."

The truth was neither did Velnir. He wondered if his father even knew of its existence or how long it had been down there. How did Magris know about it?

"In my lifetime, I have only traveled outside of Tanimara a few times. Most elves have not; in fact, I know a handful of elves who still live who have, and that is saying a lot. How do we get to the sundered lands?"

Dargarok looked perplexed but answered the question. "Sail east across the great sea. Make landfall in the region of Araba, and from there, you must travel east into the sundered lands. There is little water and shelter. It is a dry and desolate place."

"We have provisions for all climates on Abrion. My people have traveled around the world, just not recently. Not much has changed since then, but I mean to change that now that new threats are abroad," said Velnir.

The two talked more and Velnir seemed satisfied with what the orc had shared with him. Velnir was now curious about Dargarok himself. "Why did you choose your path, Dargarok?"

He sat there for a moment thinking about the answer. "Fate chose it for me. I did not seek it out. I was part of a hunting party long before the clans united and the dragon came. We would go into human lands and forage for food. We favored two in particular because humans were few and animals were plentiful. They are the regions the humans call Helmgarde and Nemis. Many creatures live there, but to my knowledge, only one man... at least, I think he is a man. He looks like one, but according to the stories, he has lived there for as long as the clans could remember. This one man was able to generate spells that killed all but myself and Gimit. At the time, we were brown like the rest of the orcs of my clan. He brought us back to his tower and kept us there for years. We started as an experiment for him to see if we would be tamed and taught like the humans could."

Velnir interrupted, "It was the wizard who taught you magic?"

Dargarok nodded and stated, "Our stay in the tower turned us blue. It sits on top of an arcane line."

Velnir was familiar with arcane lines. It was what allowed his people to use magic to enchant things ranging from scrying orbs to powerful weapons and trinkets. Enchantments controlled natural magic like pyromancy, allowing it to be channeled through a staff. Otherwise, a mage would catch themselves on fire.

Atlan was built on top of one, but he kept this information from Dargarok.

"We stayed with him for so long that our bloodlust waned, and we learned to channel our anger into magical energy. I believe my magic was as potent as it was because your city is near an arcane line."

Velnir grew curious of this man. "What is the man called?"

Dargarok hesitated for a moment before answering. "He is called Alzar." Dargarok's demeanor changed.

Velnir was hesitant to take such information from an orc, but how could an orc know about arcane lines without the assistance of someone who has knowledge of one? The lines are located at specific places all over Abrion and were believed to have been cataloged thousands of years ago. He knew if this man could teach an orc how to be what Dargarok was, then perhaps he could be of assistance against the orcs.

"Alzar took you and Gimit in but is not an ally of orcs?"

"No, he does make war on some orcish clans. However, once he learned of ours, he leaves us alone."

"How is this wizard so powerful?"

"He is one of three who are called the stewards of Abrion. He has many powerful enchanted trinkets and weapons at his disposal."

Velnir left Atlan and headed to the port town of Thalnor, where the ships were being built. He had invited his uncle and cousin to come with him.

"I think you will have enough ships, Velnir. The resources we have all been bringing in are more than enough to meet your demands," said Baefric.

Velnir nodded in appreciation. "Thank you, Uncle. They will all be put to good use." Baefric could tell that there was something on Velnir's mind. "It is not wise to befriend your enemy."

Velnir turned to him, knowing he meant Dargarok. "I understand the danger of that, and rest assured, uncle, I have no interest in befriending orcs. I do, however, believe he gave me valuable information that could prove helpful in the campaign. He spoke of a man in Nemis. He said the man taught him magic and that…"

Before he could finish, Baefric interrupted, "Alzar."

"You know of him?" Baefric looked away from Velnir and sighed. Of course, the orc would mention Alzar. Take caution, Velnir. I've heard of this wizard, and I have heard he is unpredictable and dangerous, as are all wizards.

Velnir kept listening and did not speak. Baefric had a knack for banter, and this was something, that for once, Velnir was interested in.

"Some say he lives in Nemis in an enormous tower he somehow created by himself. Be warned, though. Wizards are neither good nor evil. They serve themselves, and their magic is powerful indeed, not requiring an arcane line. Celestials created the cosmos, but remember, what can be created can also be destroyed. You cannot contend with a wizard easily, so it is best to stay away. That is my opinion."

Velnir thought about the words of his uncle.

"It is written that elves, men, and dwarves co-existed in the region now known as Araba. It is also written that a dragon was responsible for the destruction of the ancient kingdoms of the mortal races. It was Alzar that banished the dragon, or so it was written." Baefric turned to Velnir. "It was so long ago though, it could be a myth."

Orcs have the same lifespan as humans, and Dargarok proved sufficient in the use of magic, his expertise matched only by a skilled elven mage, though he would never admit it out loud. It could take a mage decades or hundreds of years to achieve such focus and skill as Dargarok has. Velnir let his uncle keep talking, however, he now had more questions than answers.

"Velnir, I do not think he could be of any help to us. I believe your time is better spent here, that is if you are thinking of venturing across the sea to visit this ancient wizard. Such a quest would be a great undertaking and would require much for a prestigious lord such as yourself," said Baefric.

Velnir scoffed but said nothing.

When they arrived, Baefric wandered off. Velnir approached Meric. "Cousin, I need a favor from you."

Meric eyed Velnir up and down. He was suspicious. "What more could you ask of me, cousin? I have given you my army, provisions of my land, and my people for your campaign. I even came to your aid when you almost lost your city." Meric seemed a little upset to be asked for another favor by Velnir.

"I will not attempt to deceive you, Meric. I intend to sail across the great sea to Nemis. I will quest to find this wizard and seek his aid."

Meric turned to look at Velnir, his eyes wide with excitement. "Going to the land of men to seek the assistance of an intriguing wizard, of which we surely suspect helped an orc become adept in the use of magic. Unknown territory, danger all around, and a potential reward that far outweighs the risks. This sounds like a good quest for you, Velnir. Can I come?"

Velnir smiled at Meric, appreciating his support. "Meric, I will need you to stay here to manage my lordship with uncle Baefric while I am gone. This is the favor I would ask of you." Meric looked disappointed, but then his demeanor changed to delight. "I understand, Cousin, your war, your quest." He shrugged and smiled while walking away to find Baefric.

Velnir approached the ship-building guild. They recognized him right away and greeted him as a hero. Velnir felt like no hero, though, for if it weren't for his uncle and cousin, surely he would have lost his city. He forced a smile and asked to see the shipwright.

Velnir was surprised to see not an elf but a man approach him. What is a human doing in Tanimara, he wondered? The man extended out his hand for a shake. Velnir was unsure how to respond but figured he could grab the man's hand, at the very least and so he did. This clearly pleased the man, who donned a smile under his maintained bushy mustache.

Humans were more round and bulbous in their features. This man's arms were very muscular, and he must have been middle-aged for their race. Still, Velnir had only seen humans a handful of times in his long existence, and they were usually of human nobility seeking trade or assistance from his father's court.

"What can I do ya for, lord elf?" said the man with a jovial tone.

Velnir simply replied, "I need a ship that can carry my companions and supplies to Nemis… discreetly."

"Nemis? Why, I can build ya whatever ya want. But, uh, why do ya need it to be discrete?"

Velnir looked down at the man as he was much taller and simply replied, somewhat annoyed, "For reasons, now, are you able or not? I can compensate you handsomely."

The man looked up at the elf and cocked his head slightly. He then looked at the sack of coins that Velnir had produced and smiled gleefully. "Why, I can do just about anything you would ask of me. You want a ship, sir? I can get you a ship. I can get you a large and fast ship well equipped for defense, you know… Just in case."

Velnir tossed the sack to the human with relative ease. The man caught the sack, and it knocked him over, simply demonstrating that elves are deceptively strong.

Chapter 6
Across the Great Sea

Velnir had left his uncle and cousin to manage things in Atlantin. They had sent a scrying orb to confirm they had arrived in Atlan safely and wished Velnir well on his quest. Velnir's ship was indeed fast. Its precise design allowed it to glide across the ocean with ease. The human who commissioned the construction of this had it custom made for Velnir. This pleased the lord of Atlan, and he would not forget the level of craftsmanship the human had.

The others in Velnir's party seemed to be comfortable. They had everything they needed. Several elves were gathered around and singing while Velnir remained in his quarters. Unfortunately, the ship was not big enough to drown out the repetitive and often annoying sound of elves singing. Several days had already passed, and Velnir had not stepped out of his quarters, for he was lost in his thoughts, dwelling on what was to come.

Elves of Tanimara do not often venture outside of its shores. They are proud and view themselves as too superior to parlay with any of what they consider lesser races. They are also typically too embroiled in the politics of Tanimara, plotting and scheming to undermine their neighbors. The relationship between Baefric, Meric, and Velnir was unusual by elven standards. Their family bond was close, and Ruvyn made sure that he and Baefric were always close. He spoke of the bonds between brothers in human culture and mimicked that with Baefric. Ruvyn had spent a considerable amount of time in the human kingdoms long ago.

Velnir did not remember everything his father had taught him about humans. He knew out of all the elven lords of recent history, Ruvyn was the one who maintained diplomatic relations with them. Velnir wished he had listened to his father more and wondered how he would be greeted by the people of Nemis.

A knock struck the door to Velnir's quarters. Velnir snapped out of his thoughts and took a deep breath before saying, "Enter."

A young and beautiful elven woman entered his chambers.

"Ah, Ensign Salin, what is it you need?" She closed the door, approached his desk, and stood at attention.

"I request an audience with the lord," she said confidently. He looked at her and asked her to sit.

"Ensign," he said calmly, "I am in no mood for formality. Speak freely."

She relaxed and turned her attention toward him. She took a deep breath and, with her unusually long fingernails, began to tap on his desk. His eyes met hers, and she waited for what seemed to be a considerable amount of time before speaking.

"What is it?" he asked her as if he were beginning to be annoyed by her presence. "I've got work to do."

"I… well, we were wondering where we are going. Not that we would ever not follow you to even the ends of Abrion if you asked it of us. We are still curious?"

Velnir looked at her in bewilderment. In his haste to discreetly get the ship and crew, plus his companions to leave unseen, he had forgotten to tell them where they were going. He looked at her and furrowed his brow.

"My apologies, Ensign, I had not told anyone where we are going." He clasped his hands, laced his fingers together, and leaned in toward her.

"We are going to Nemis. I have undertaken a quest to seek out a wizard that may dwell there and seek his aid if we are to invade the sundered lands of Araba. He may prove useful, but that remains to be seen."

Her demeanor changed from curious to unsettled. "We are sailing across the great sea to a human kingdom so we can find a mythical wizard?"

Velnir looked at her questioningly.

Before he could tell her more, the ship was rocked hard to the right as if it were hit by something enormous. They jumped up and went outside of his quarters to investigate what was going on. Once they walked out, they noticed large tentacles straddling each side of the ship and its masts.

The elves manning the ship kept yelling. "It is a kraken!"

At that moment, though, the beast held still while still latching onto the ship. The water was silent, and the ship was still. An ominous feeling plagued everyone on the ship.

Most everyone was now holding still themselves, hoping the beast would simply let go and let them be on their way.

Suddenly, the ship was hit from the keel. It didn't split but was brought up out of the water slightly and then back down. The crew made sudden cries. When everything was calm again, they remained still unsure what was to come next.

Velnir noticed something strange immediately. The hit from under the ship felt hard enough to split the ship in half, but it appeared the tentacles were bracing the hull for impact as if it were attempting to be careful. Velnir's heart sank, and a bead of sweat glided down his brow.

"It is trying to get in the ship," he said quietly to himself.

He quickly raced to the lowest deck and was surprised to see that little water had entered. Somewhat relieved, he scoured the lower deck. Ensign Salin was not far behind.

"My lord," she cried as if unsure where he was. She lit a lantern and followed the stairway until she saw the light from Velnir's lantern. "My lord, what is it?"

Velnir said nothing. He simply stood there looking toward the floor. She approached cautiously and turned her attention to the floor as well. Her jaw dropped, and she froze. The ship had quite a large hole in the bottom but wasn't taking on water.

"I saw something under the ship. I think it was trying to get our attention," said Velnir quietly to Salin.

"Perhaps you should attempt to communicate with it," she said without taking her eyes off the hole.

"Greetings," said Velnir in as delightful a tone as he could.

He, of course, did not expect a beast to respond in kind and was unsure if this was the best idea.

"I am Velnir, Captain of this vessel. Why have you stopped us?" Attempting to sound curious and confident, Velnir tried to make it clear that he did not fear the beast.

Suddenly, the water started moving, and a large eye appeared and began looking through the hole. It caught sight of Velnir and Salin standing there with their lanterns fixed on its position. It winced slightly before retreating. The eye was replaced with its beak.

"I was not expecting the Elves of Tanimara," she said with a female voice. "I thought this vessel was full of those green land scum."

Salin and Velnir knew the beast meant the orcs, for they had come through these waters and were presumably sailing back to Araba after their retreat from Atlantin.

"I do apologize to the elves of Tanimara. Oh, what have I done?" she said.

Salin and Velnir looked at each other in bewilderment.

"What are you?" Salin asked the beast in a curious tone.

"Forgive me. I am a kraken—one of many who guard these waters. The green ones attempted to hunt me. You will notice spears sticking out of my tentacles of their design. It rather hurt, and I was offended, so I've been attacking their vessels and feasting on their corpses. I am full of them, and their flesh is quite delicious."

Velnir grimaced at the thought of a kraken eating orcs, but the thought of their ships being destroyed and many of them meeting their deaths was pleasing to him.

"We were also attacked by those green land dwellers. We call them orcs, and we actually plan to pursue them to their homeland and punish them," Velnir said, attempting to establish a common enemy with the kraken to perhaps yield some assistance.

"Orcs, you say? Very well, I have been eating orcs, and the orc flesh is delicious. If they are your enemy, then I assume you don't mind that I hunt them?"

Velnir shook his head. "Eat them to your heart's content. You would be doing many civilizations a great service."

Salin and Velnir heard the crew moving around on the first deck. Velnir motioned Salin to go and tell them what was going on and get them to stop moving. She saluted Velnir and made haste to the first deck.

"We are not your enemy," said Velnir confidently. "We do not hunt your kind and appreciate you protecting these waters. Perhaps we can come to a mutually beneficial agreement?"

Velnir was hoping to charm the kraken but had no idea of its culture. He did know that if he upset the kraken, she could destroy his ship and kill everyone on board. He proceeded with caution.

"Oh, thank you for your appreciation. Kraken have been protecting these waters since the manifestation."

Velnir was unsure of what the Kraken was referring to but kept quiet.

"Our charge was to protect and maintain balance under the seas. The dragons were charged with protecting the land

and maintaining balance, but I assume you know that they have forsaken their charge. We have not! Ours is true, and those vile orcs have tainted these waters with their dark magic. We can work together to preserve balance if you wish."

Velnir understood what the kraken meant after she mentioned the charge of the dragons. He nodded gratefully. "That sounds magnificent. However, our ship is heavily damaged and it appears you are keeping it afloat," said Velnir.

"Ah, yes, I do apologize for that. Once I grabbed it, I realized this vessel was not like the others; before I tore it apart and ate its crew, I wanted to make sure I knew what it was. I know now, and I will make sure to grant you safe passage to…where was it you were going?" said the kraken curiously.

"Nemis, the human kingdom…" Velnir said, realizing he had started to speak before determining whether the kraken was friendly with humans or not.

A long pause ensued, making Velnir nervous. He had noticed the crew had stopped moving around on the first deck.

Not a moment later, the ship began to be pulled. At first, Velnir wasn't sure if the Kraken had been upset and decided to tear his ship apart and eat them, but it soon became clear that the Kraken had seemingly agreed to take them to Nemis without saying a word.

"Thank you, Kraken," he said, not sure what she would like to be called.

He received no reply.

He was unsure and questioned her actions internally before asking, "Would you like us to pull the orc spears out of your tentacles?" He had hoped that if there was any animosity the kraken had toward the humans, this offer and action would help her to forget and perhaps please her.

The ship stopped, and the beak returned to the hole. "That would be appreciated. It makes it hard to swim."

Velnir nodded and rushed to the first deck. Everyone was staring at him in wonder and curiosity. *"They must have been waiting in agony for my return,"* he thought. *"The kraken thought we were orcs. She is taking us to Nemis, and we can repair the ship there. We need to pull the spears out of her tentacles."*

Without hesitation, the crew began to quickly get to work. All hands were on deck, and for every spear they pulled out, the ship would shutter. The kraken's pain could be felt, and so the crew learned to be gentler.

One tentacle was severely injured. The spear was lodged in it in such a way that if it was pulled out, the tentacle may break apart. Velnir ran down to the lower deck to speak with the Kraken.

"It is Velnir once more Kraken. As you can tell, we have removed most of the spears from your tentacles. There is one we are going to have trouble with. It seems as though it will sever your tentacle. What would you like us to do?"

"Kraken can regenerate limbs. If we couldn't, we would have died out long ago."

Velnir nodded and understood what she meant. He ran upstairs and issued the order to pull it. Sure enough, the tentacle was severed and fell into the ocean.

Several sharks began to swarm the severed tentacle. The ship began to move and pick up speed. This surprised Velnir as he had never seen a Kraken. He also didn't know they could move this fast. He was glad he didn't make an enemy out of this one.

The ship was moving faster than the sails could take it with the help of the kraken. The fact the sharks began to eat her tentacle made Velnir feel a bit nervous, so he returned to the lower deck.

"How are you feeling?" he asked the Kraken. The ship stopped, and her beak returned to the hole."

"I feel much better. You have my thanks. I will say, though, that every time you wish to speak with me, I have to stop the vessel. If you could refrain from speaking to me unless it is dire, we will get to Nemis with more haste."

"Very well," Velnir said while nodding.

He returned to the top deck, and the crew looked a little uneasy. Salin approached Velnir, smiling. "Good job, my lord."

He smiled at her and nodded to the crew, indicating everything was all right. This calmed them down, and they began to sigh in relief and donned cheerful attitudes once more.

Velnir returned to his quarters with Salin following.

"I intend to find the wizard in Nemis." He pulled out a map of the human kingdoms and pointed to the geographical location of Nemis. "My uncle said he has a tower here," Velnir pointed to the border of Nemis to a place called the Forlorn Forest. "Baefric said his tower is here. We must dock in the human port town called Taro?"

Salin chuckled, "The humans come up with the strangest of names for their towns and ships."

"We will leave this town and head east until we get to the wizard's tower," said Velnir.

"Have you ever met this wizard, my lord?"

"I have not, but Baefric has. He described him as not a man but only having the visage of one. He did not elaborate. I do know that he is extremely powerful," said Velnir questioningly.

"What do you intend to gain from meeting with him?" asked Salin curiously.

"An ally against the orcs. Though I do wonder. We captured several orcs after the battle of Atlan. One of them was blue in color and seemed to be educated. He learned our language quickly. He claimed this wizard captured him and his companion as prisoners and decided to teach them the ways of magic."

"It could be a trap, Velnir," she said with clear concern.

"I have taken that into account, hence the need for an elite force and all our griffins. If we need to get away quickly, we will be able to. I have a constant line of communication with Meric and Baefric via the scrying orbs. The orc was determined to be very powerful when asked to demonstrate his magical prowess. He could have done considerable damage and killed many while repairing the city."

"You trust the orc," said Salin in a disgusted tone.

He turned his gaze to her and stood. "You are in no place to question me!" She sank in her seat and apologized.

He understood why she felt disgusted and felt compelled to explain why he trusted the orc. "I brought him into the city; we had quite a nice discussion. It was completely uncharacteristic of any orc we have ever encountered before, and he claimed that their leader had enslaved the clans that refused to join his horde. Yes, Salin, I decided to take the orc's word for it and take on this quest. I know it is strange, but you must trust me."

She smiled at him and said, "Of course, my lord. May I be excused?"

Velnir nodded, and without another word, she left. Velnir thought that to be strange, but then again, with everything that had happened within the last few months. Was it really surprising? He thought not.

Velnir awoke from a light slumber to the creaking of the floorboard near his bed. He was not to be disturbed unless it was important, but this was not how his crew would inform him of their presence. Whoever was in his chambers was attempting stealth.

To hide the fact he was awake, he remained still and clenched his dagger. He was lying on his side facing away from the door to his chambers. Whoever it was moved closer. He felt the indentation of the bed on his left side first and then to his right, indicating someone was straddling him. It could only mean one thing.

Velnir threw his arm up, catching the side of the crew member's head. They were thrown off the bed and onto the floor. The moonlight was shining through the window and revealed it to be Salin.

"What are you doing here?" he demanded.

She looked at a kris that she had dropped. He saw it, too, and without a word, she lunged for it. Before she could pick it up, however, his dagger drove itself in between her eyes, killing her instantly. The ruckus could be heard from outside, and a commotion erupted.

Velnir jumped out of bed and cautiously opened the door. His crew were fighting. *"A mutiny,"* he thought.

Velnir joined the fray. He was the most skilled fighter on the ship and made quick work of his crew, leaving those who helped him quite surprised with his skill and those who were against him surrendering and begging for their lives.

"What is the meaning of this?" he demanded.

One of the crew members who had helped Velnir spoke up.

"They had planned to assassinate you, my lord. Ensign Salin said you had lost your mind and were collaborating with orcs. She wanted the crew to kill you and to sail back to Atlantin." The elf indicated by pointing to the crew who helped him. "We thought better of that and only pretended to join her. Once we heard the commotion, we attacked those who followed her."

Velnir looked at the mutineers. "It is true that I have collaborated with an orc. Not the orcs. What I do is of no concern to you. You all took vows to protect me, yet you stand here in the ultimate betrayal."

Velnir went into his quarters, grabbed Salin's lifeless corpse, and dragged her out to the deck. He threw her corpse in front of the mutinous crew.

"Observe the fate that she has met. Unfortunately, I had to act with haste. With you though…I have other plans," he said in a sinister tone. He ordered the crew still loyal to him to bring the mutineers down to the lower deck.

"Kraken," he called out. I must speak with you. The ship stopped, and the kraken's eye appeared. She saw Velnir and several elves with him. Some bound and others with Velnir. She moved her beak to where her eye was and spoke.

"What's wrong, Velnir?" she asked with a tone of concern.

Velnir looked at the bound elves and then spoke to the kraken. These elves had attempted to kill me in my sleep. They must die for their treason."

The kraken stirred a bit. "Treacherous wretches?" she asked.

"Yes," said Velnir. "Are you hungry?" he asked her in a sinister tone before turning his attention to the bound mutineers. They began to squirm and plead even though their mouths were bound. They began to cry and beg for decapitation.

The kraken could hear the pleas of the elves but said nothing right away. Finally, she said, "I could use some sustenance. Pulling this vessel is leaving me quite famished."

"Strip them of their armor and clothes. Start with Salin," Velnir ordered.

They did as they were told. The mutineers knelt on the floor next to Salin's naked body.

Velnir grabbed Salin's corpse by the foot and dragged her to the kraken's beak. The kraken opened her beak wide, revealing her tongue.

It was a disgusting and terrifying sight for the condemned. Velnir tossed Salin's lifeless body into the mouth of the kraken. Her lower half landed in the mouth, and her upper half hung over the kraken mouth's edge.

Immediately, the kraken bit down, dividing Salin's body in half so hard and fast, the force threw Salin's upper half into the air a bit before landing on the deck. The kraken had swallowed Salin's lower half and opened her mouth again.

Velnir picked up what remained of Salin's body by the hair on her head and threw it into the Kraken's mouth. The kraken bit again. Salin's innards were splattered all over the condemned.

The kraken had bitten part of her head off, and her brains began to ooze down the exposed side. The condemned watched in horror. The kraken licked her beak and was pleased to have tried elven flesh.

"Tasty," she said in a seemingly satisfied tone.

Velnir turned his attention to the condemned and paused for a bit. They looked at him longingly, hoping their lord would not feed them to the kraken.

It seemed reasonable to feed Salin's lifeless corpse to it since she was already dead and the leader of the mutiny; however, the kraken opened her mouth again. Velnir pointed to one of the condemned.

"You are next," he exclaimed.

He began to wiggle and squirm. Begging through his gag. Velnir could hear the words, "Please, please no, please."

Velnir's elves tossed him into the mouth of the Kraken. The condemned began to scream, and the moment he landed on her tongue.

She chomped violently. His innards and body parts were strewn all over the place. Velnir ordered his elves to toss the pieces into the mouth of the kraken, who kept eating with pleasure.

The others had to watch as they were slowly, one by one, fed to this beast alive. There was but one left and he was in tears. He knew the fate that awaited him and closed his eyes. The kraken let out an enormous and foul smelling belch.

"That will be enough for now. I need some time to digest if you don't mind." The last of the condemned looked at Velnir and nodded ferociously, crying and begging. "Please, please, I beg of you, please, my lord. Show mercy!"

Velnir looked at him and then at the kraken. "Very well, if you have had your fill."

The kraken removed her beak from the bottom of the ship, and everyone felt the ship move again. Velnir and his crew brought the last mutineer to the top of the deck.

Relief swept his face.

The sun was coming out, and clearly he was glad to be alive. Perhaps he had a second chance. Perhaps his lord would show him mercy and simply take his head. Perhaps he may not even execute him at all. Velnir was known to be merciful back in Atlan, after all.

Velnir was the last to enter the top deck. Everyone stood still. All eyes were fixed on him.

Without saying a word, he made his way over to the side of the ship and peered over. A moment later, he motioned for the crew to bring the last mutineer over to him. All hope faded, and his face turned ghost-white.

Velnir picked up the elf and grabbed his head, forcing him to look over the side of the ship. There were several sharks swimming alongside the ship. Velnir then looked at the last mutineer.

"You deserve no mercy, filth." He then tossed the screaming and begging elf over the ship.

He splashed into the water, still screaming and struggling to swim. The sharks swarmed him and began to feast. His screams turned into gurgles and then to silence. The frenzy had produced quite a lot of blood. All of the crew were watching, and everyone, including Velnir, was silent.

Velnir turned to his crew and noticed that their numbers had seriously diminished. This alarmed him, but he knew what had to be done. Treachery could not be tolerated, and now the crew knew that.

Only a few days separated Velnir from Taro. The crew were relaxing as the kraken continued to pull the ship at a decent rate of speed. The sun was out, and the cook had brought lunch for Velnir and the crew. Velnir decided to eat with the crew members on the deck to show camaraderie and to keep an eye on them.

The crow's nest shouted, "Ship approaching!"

Velnir jumped to his feet and retrieved a scrying orb. He threw it in the direction of the oncoming vessel, which he now knew were vessels. The orb glided through the sky, and Velnir peered through the scrying crystal to see what the orb could see. Suddenly, the ship abruptly slowed down and came to a stop.

Velnir looked into the crystal and shouted, "Orcs!" The crew got to their battle stations. Velnir put the scrying crystal down and ran outside to the deck. He saw that the Kraken's tentacles were hit with orcish spears and began to struggle to hold on to the ship. The crew began to fire its mounted bolt throwers at the orcish vessels, which were fast approaching. The Kraken let go of the ship and went to the depths.

Velnir quickly ordered everyone to gear up in case they had to abandon ship. He then ordered some of the crew to the bottom of the ship to repair the hole the Kraken had made. He then ordered everyone else off their battle stations and manned their posts to get the ship sailing in the direction of land, which he knew was east.

As the ships got closer, Velnir realized that they were not orcs. They were beast men, minotaurs, ogres, and gron. He could tell by their shouting and the language they used.

Suddenly, the kraken emerged under the lead ship. She split it in two, demonstrating her strength. She lunged her tentacles through another ship, splitting it in half. The ships were now leaving Velnir's ship alone and focusing on the kraken. Velnir looked on as his ship sailed away from the fray.

"What brave creatures to take on such a magnificent beast, the kraken," he thought as the gap between them and the other ships began to increase.

Velnir could no longer see the fight. He didn't bother throwing a scrying orb out there. He wanted to focus on getting to land. He ran to the bottom deck and noticed the ship had standing water. The crew had patched the hole for the most part, but by now, there was too much water in the hull. It significantly slowed the ship down. The hole was still leaking by the time the crew ran out of materials to fill it in. Velnir knew he would have to abandon ship soon. He ran back up to the first deck and noticed one of the elite elven soldiers hastily loading the extra griffins with supplies.

He and the elite elf made eye contact. Velnir nodded in gratitude. "Make ready the griffins," he ordered. We will need to abandon ship."

"My lord, we are unsure how far land is from here. The griffins may not make it," said a frantic crewmember.

"The ship will flounder. We have no other option. Make ready the griffins. I will not ask again!" Velnir snapped.

The ship began to list to its port side. The griffins were ready, and Velnir ordered them to take to the sky. One by one, each crew member escaped the sinking ship, avoiding a watery grave.

As they took to the air, Velnir looked back and saw that the ship had completely keeled over and began slipping beneath the waves. Lucky for his companions, there were more griffins than crew to ride them.

They made for great pack animals, so they were, at the very least, not in short supply thanks to the quick thinking of one of the crew members, for which Velnir was very grateful.

Velnir tossed four scrying orbs into the sky. They all scurried in different directions, looking for land, for it wasn't nightfall, and they couldn't wait for the stars to guide them to land. He peered through his scrying crystal, and the orbs were making haste through the air, much faster than the griffins. Soon, he spotted land and ordered everyone to follow him. Together, they flew in formation and seemingly in good spirits. The griffins were in good spirits as well and holding up. The scrying orbs found their way back to Velnir, who tucked them away in his satchel.

Several hours had gone by, and the day was fading into night. Soon, the stars began to appear. The crew were getting tired, and so were the griffins.

"Hold on. We're almost there," said Velnir with confidence. However, he wasn't actually sure how close they were. Soon, the black silhouette of the coastline appeared.

"Land!" cried one of the crew.

Finally over land, all they could see was dense forest. They struggled to find a place where they could land and make camp for the evening, but eventually, they found a clearing revealed to them by the moonlight. All the griffins began touching down in the same area, and their riders dismounted, pleased to be on solid ground once more.

"Make camp here. We need firewood and sustenance," ordered Velnir. He pointed at several members of his entourage. "You, you and you, come with me. We must hunt!" They followed Velnir as the others began to make camp.

Elves were adept at moving silently and quickly, though these forests were much denser than the ones on Tanimara. Nonetheless, they made their way through, looking for anything they could kill for a quick meal.

They came upon a four-legged creature foraging for food. It was dark, and the elves were silent. The animal was completely unaware of their presence.

One of the elves knocked his bow and fired a single arrow. It went straight through the animal, which didn't seem to even notice it. A few moments later, it fell over and died. Such were the skills of elven hunters. They realized it was a stag and dressed the stag before bringing it back to camp, where the rest of the elves waited. The fire was roaring, and the tents were all set up.

They had managed to bring a lot more supplies than Velnir had thought. He would definitely reward the elite elven soldier who was quick to think on his feet to load supplies on the extra griffins for his heroic actions. He sought out the elf and found him quickly.

"Remove your helmet," ordered Velnir.

The elf was quickly compliant and removed his helmet, revealing long white hair, a chiseled jawline, and bright blue but sunken eyes. The elf was older.

"Your actions were heroic. You thought to do what no one else had. For this, when we return to Tanimara, I will be rewarding you handsomely," said Velnir.

"Many thanks, my lord, but I am simply doing my duty. I served with your father during the electhril wars, and we ran into several situations that required quick thinking. Speaking from experience, when you know you have to retreat, you take as much of the essentials as you can," said the elven soldier.

"What is your name?" asked Velnir.

"I am called Garlan, my lord."

Velnir began to chat with the elf for quite some time.

With their stomachs full and the night clear, the elves packed everything in and retired to their quarters. The mutiny was plaguing Velnir's mind, robbing him of sleep. Many things began to flood his mind from the time he lost his mother, and, more recently, his father and many of his countrymen. He had almost failed to protect his city and region from the orcs. Eventually, Velnir did fall asleep, but even his dreams did not spare him the misery.

Chapter 7
Unexpected Visitors

Velnir and his companions had been attempting to navigate through the dense forest for days now. He threw his scrying orbs up to find a clearing but was unsuccessful as they kept returning to him for some reason.

This alarmed Velnir, but his companions were none the wiser. They were lost, and Velnir couldn't see the stars through the thick canopy. The griffins couldn't fly through such a dense forest either, making travel difficult.

Dusk was fast approaching, and Velnir knew they had to make camp soon.

"We stop here and make camp. Clear these trees for firewood and pitch our tents," he ordered.

They did so, and soon night was upon them. They ate their fill and went to bed. Another night in this forest and still no closer to his objective, thought Velnir.

It was beginning to frustrate him. He began to think of home, how Baefric and Meric were doing, how he missed his father, and what he planned to do to the orcs. He was determined to find this wizard, though it would have to wait until the morning, for he was getting tired and fell fast asleep.

"Awake, elf," shouted a female voice in the native elven tongue.

Velnir was startled awake for the first time in his life by the sharp, cold point of a finely crafted spear to his cheek. He had never felt so vulnerable. He opened his eyes to a hoof next to his face.

"Get up slowly," demanded the female.

Velnir did as he was told and raised his hands. When he was able to, he looked at the creature and realized it was none other than a female centaur.

The creature's upper half resembled a muscular female elf as her breasts were visible and uncovered. Her lower half resembled that of a stag. He could hardly believe his eyes. He had never seen one in his life and had only heard tales of them through myths.

"A centaur," he said in awe.

The centaur straightened her back proudly.

"Good, you know of my species. Surely, you understand what you face if you attempt to challenge us!"

Velnir nodded. "We were shipwrecked off the coast of these lands. I assure you, we mean no harm. We are trying to get to Nemis."

The centaur scoffed. "If you mean no harm, why do you hunt our kin?"

Velnir was perplexed, "We have not hunted centaur. We have only hunted the local wildlife. Stags and…" Then it donned on Velnir. She was referring to the wildlife.

In the fables, centaur see themselves as kin to all life within the Forlorn Forest. It was at this moment he knew he had made a terrible mistake. He did not know until now that he was in the Forlorn Forest. He thought he was in Nemis. Regret filled his heart.

Oddly, the centaur could sense it. Her look of hostility changed to pity. "I will not kill you. I must take you to our queen. She will decide what to do with you elves."

Velnir hadn't wanted to reveal who he was out of fear that he would be taken prisoner and a ransom would be demanded, which would ruin his plans. He kept quiet and followed her instructions.

Oddly, the centaurs made sure to take great care of the griffins. They fed them and forced the riders off of their backs. They treated the griffins as equals of the forest, which was far better than the way they treated the elves. All but Velnir were bound to each other and stripped of their weapons.

Velnir had no idea where they were going. He did have an inkling that it was further away from his objective, which annoyed him greatly. He wouldn't dare ask them how long they would be or if they were there yet out of fear of agitating them. Instead, he would observe and listen.

The centaur didn't speak much. Velnir could tell they knew exactly where they were going. They all wore feathers, and used bows and spears. They were different shades of browns, blacks and whites. Velnir observed them as beautiful creatures despite being their prisoner. He noticed a hulking one on the flank of the herd. He wore a crown of feathers, unlike the other ones who wore a single feather. This one was clearly their leader. He kept an eye out for danger as the herd moved. They were surprisingly quiet, considering how big they were. Their stealth, at the very least, matched or perhaps was greater than the elves since they were clearly caught off guard.

Eventually, the forest became less dense, and they made their way to a dirt road. In the distance, Velnir saw what appeared to be a structure resembling a wall made of black stone. As they got closer, he made out spires and a keep of old elven design. Velnir's heart sank. The centaur told him they were taking him and his companions to their queen. He should have known. Darlana!

As the story goes, Darlana was the daughter of a magistrate of Tanimara. It was said that elves and men had a closer bond back then. Darlana took it way too far and seduced an Araban prince, leaving her pregnant.

She gave birth to a half-breed, and this upset the elven courts as they saw themselves as not only superior to humans, but viewed them similar to animals. It was forbidden by law for an elf to lay with any other race, not only because they viewed themselves as superior, but because no one outside of a pure-blooded elf could inherit anything in Tanimara, especially titles and land.

The magistrate of the time ordered her father to kill the child and his daughter, or they would punish him for this abomination. Her father was enraged and did kill the prince and child, but could not find Darlana. It was said that her mother got to her first and sent her to exile.

This started a war with the Araban empire and Tanimara. Many men and elves were killed, but it ended in a stalemate.

Humans were formidable, as they would willingly give their lives to fight for what they believed in.

Elves were more skilled but more reluctant to die for what they believed in. Skirmishes between them were on the high seas or in Araba itself but never in Tanimara. The elves made sure of that. The magistrate blamed Darlana for this. Heartbroken over the loss of her child, her lover, and her home, it is rumored that she vowed vengeance and cursed Tanimara.

It was said that she found refuge in the Forlorn Forest. If this was true, then Velnir had more to contend with than he previously thought.

The centaurs approached the giant black gate. They ordered the gate open in elvish, surprising Velnir and solidifying his belief that this was the home of Darlana. They were brought through the streets, the denizens of which were not centaurs but elves. Some with human features.

This surprised Velnir. The architecture of this city was that of old elven from thousands of years ago. He had forgotten that elves had settled all over Abrion at one time.

They were eventually brought to the palace, which stood very tall and had magnificent spires all around it. They were lined up just outside the door when two centaurs walked up beside them.

Each grabbing one handle, they opened the giant door, revealing the hall inside the keep. It was held up by giant stone pillars all with vines wrapped around them. It looked as though moss had grown through the cracks of the ground. The windows had no glass in them, and the local birds just came and went freely.

Velnir heard a commotion behind them, so he turned to see what it was. The centaurs were encouraging the griffins to be free. They caught on and took to the air.

"Well, this is it," Velnir thought to himself. "The end is nigh, and I have yet to get my revenge. I am sorry, Father, Atlantin, for I have failed you. Forgive me," he said quietly while he waited there with his eyes closed.

"A Tanimaran? How intriguing," said the soft, sweet sound of a woman's voice.

He opened his eyes and saw a thin, pale female elf with long black and purple hair, striking blue eyes, and curvy features. By elven standards, she would be considered a handsome specimen of elvish womanhood.

"I am her prisoner?" he thought.

"Chief Dravon, or king of the centaur, said you were hunting his kin. He is graciously leaving your fate to me, for which you should be grateful. If it were up to him… well, anyhow, what should I do with you?" she asked, looking him up and down and tapping her lips with her well-manicured finger. She did not sound vengeful, evil, or even angry.

Velnir, attempting to explain himself, started by stating who he was. Thinking she would not dare kill him if she knew.

"I am Lord Velnir…" she interrupted.

"Melfarin of Atlantin. I know who you are. I did not know you were Lord of Atlantin, however. What happened to Ruvyn?"

Velnir was visibly surprised.

"He was killed by orcs. If you know who I am, why keep my companions and I in chains? This could have severe repercussions."

"Like I said, you are accused of hunting Chief Dravon's kin."

"We had not realized we were in the Forlorn Forest. We did not mean to cause any harm to your people or his. We thought we were in Nemis," he said without sounding like he was pleading with her.

She curiously glanced at him for a moment, tapping her lip with her finger. "I believe you, Velnir of Atlantin. You are, however, Tanimaran, and as such, are an enemy of my people."

She motioned to the guards to take him and his companions to the prison.

The Tanimarans were dragged to the dungeon below the palace and thrown into separate cells. They were cold, dark and damp. Rats were running out of holes that had been carved by previous prisoners in what appeared to be an attempt to escape before meeting a grisly end. The Tanimarans were wondering when they would meet the same fate.

For several days, they were left down there with nothing but the company of each other and their daily ration until a guard came down from the palace and went over to Velnir in his cell.

"You are coming with me, elf!" he demanded.

Velnir immediately thought this was it. He was to be executed. It was no wonder Darlana hated Tanimarans, given what happened to her. He could not blame her, for he would probably have done the same had a Nagrimaran come to Atlan, even by accident. Velnir felt dread. He would not get his revenge and would fail his people.

To Velnir's surprise, the guard did not grab him or cuff him. He simply led him up to the palace. "This is strange," he thought.

He was brought before the same woman who sent him to the dungeon and then the guard left him with her and what appeared to be servants.

Velnir was unsure.

"You must understand, you are not in Tanimara anymore. You will need to tread carefully going forward. Your ignorance may get you in a lot of trouble," she said with a smile.

He was confused by her demeanor but nodded in agreement.

"We did not mean to cross into your lands. If you would permit us too, we would leave immediately," he said.

"You are my prisoners. Welcome to Nagrimara. The lovely kingdom I have created that other people call the land of the wood elves or your people call, the land of apostates." She walked away from Velnir, and took a seat on her magnificent throne. "They call us apostates because they believe that I tainted our people by having a child with a human, Prince Sampsin of Araba."

"So I have heard," said Velnir.

Everyone in the hall began to leave at the behest of the queen. Soon it was just Velnir and Darlana. Velnir's heart began to race and Darlana could feel it.

"What are you going to do with me as your prisoner?" he finally asked her.

"Whatever I want," she whispered. She began to wave her hand around and without touching him, Velnir's clothes started to fall off and gently glide toward the ground. This made him extremely uncomfortable. She could tell and so she came behind him and put her hands on his shoulders. He did not turn to look at her. He was still unsure what to do.

How could he be so stupid, he thought. Truly, he had only been entertained by concubines. It was not formally customary for a prince to have intimate relationships before he was wed to a suitor of equal status. Since Ruvyn died before he found a suiter for Velnir, Velnir would choose for himself. The thought had not crossed his mind considering everything that had happened immediately following the death of his father. He knew that even though it was not customary, elves of the court did it anyway but discreetly.

Besides, he was never drawn to it and spent most of his free time playing games with his friends, studying enchantments and martial arts. Never had he made time to find love.

Velnir took his vows of lordship more seriously than most, especially Meric and did not want to compromise the legitimacy of his throne or bloodline.

"It is the custom of my people not to engage in interco…"

She placed her finger over his lips in an effort to hush him up, but he gently wrapped his fingers around her wrists and locked eyes with hers.

"Intercourse until I am married."

"Velnir, you are a fool," she said with a laugh. "When in Nagrimar, you ought to dress like a Nagrimaran. You thought that I was trying to… Haha, naive and foolish. Put it on yourself then."

Velnir realized she was removing his Tanimaran armor and thought that was probably because the people would not take kindly to it. She dropped a toga behind him. How could he be so stupid? He was clearly embarrassed. He quickly figured out the toga and put it on. He had no intention of starting trouble.

"So, you found yourself shipwrecked and then ended up within the borders of my kingdom and say you are going to Nemis?" she asked.

"Tanimara was attacked by orcs. Tens of thousands of them sailed across the great sea and invaded my region, Atlantin. They killed my father and placed Atlan under siege. I was able to hold them off long enough for my cousin and uncle to show up and drive them out of Atlantin. They sailed back to Araba, and I intend to bring the war to them."

"Why go to Nemis then?" she asked.

"I learned of a wizard there that may be able to provide aid to the elves of Tanimara."

The mention of a wizard got the full attention of the Queen of Nagrimar. She looked at Velnir with suspicion. "You understand who he is, do you not?" she asked with concern in her voice.

This surprised Velnir.

"I have an idea," he said. "Some say that he is a man with supreme magical power. Others say that he is rumored to be a fallen celestial. I know that he lives in a tower within the borders of Nemis."

Darlana looked at him. "I do not know if he is man or celestial. I do know that in his tower, he has a school of wizardry called the Academy of Higher Arts. Alzar is also very dangerous. In this world, there is to my knowledge, no other with magic as powerful as Alzar. To the denizens of the Forlorn, he is timeless. Men die, but Alzar does not. He has the appearance of an old frail man with a long white beard in a grayish brown robe and pointed hat, but he wields magic you cannot even imagine and he can take on the appearance of whatever he wishes. I speak from experience," she said, frowning.

"How do you know all of this, Darlana?" He had forgotten to call her Queen Darlana but this did not seem to bother her.

"When I was exiled here, he helped me establish Nagrimara. He was sympathetic," she said.

He was once again confused considering everything that had happened since he arrived. He had determined that Darlana was not likely evil, vengeful, or angry but rather lonely.

A few moments passed, then she called for her servants. As they were arriving, they approached him.

Darlana turned to him and said, "You and your elves of Tanimara are my prisoners but we do things differently here. I will treat you as guests in my kingdom though not without limitations. Make yourselves at home and enjoy the hospitality I provide."

Before he could respond with gratitude, she kissed him and walked away. As she turned, he could not help but look at her. Each of her gluteal muscles, bouncing one after the other with each step through the thin silk robes. His thoughts became more and more inappropriate before being interrupted by Garlan.

"This is a very strange place, my lord. I would not mind leaving in a moment's notice… if you wish, of course."

Velnir snapped out of his lustful thoughts and turned his attention to the elf standing next to him. Velnir looked at

Garlan and noticed right away that no harm had come to him and was pleased.

The queen kept her word.

"What of the griffins?" he asked.

The elf responded, "They are enjoying the freedom this city has to offer them. They have not gone far and frequently come back down to receive assurance that it is okay for them to play."

Velnir was pleased to hear that as well. He nodded and let out a sigh of relief. All of the elves were released but placed under the watchful eye of the guards.

They were quite surprised to explore the city of Nagrimar. It was old and did not seem to have been updated but it was well maintained.

The people were strange. Most of them wore minimal clothing. Surprisingly, there were a lot more elves in Nagrimar than he thought. The centaur did not seem to stay in the city itself.

Many Nagrimarans offered their homes for the Tanimarans to stay in. They offered fruit, bread, and meat, which all of Velnir's companions happily indulged in with his blessing, of course.

"What could it hurt?" he thought.

The next morning, there was a gentle knock at the door of Velnir's quarters. There stood a man, tall in stature when compared to the other denizens of Nagrimar. He had semi-pointed ears, though not as pointed as an elf. He was muscular and had a masculinely chiseled jawline. He also had stubble on his face, which was extremely rare among the elves of Tanimara.

"This person must be a half-breed," Velnir thought.

"Her grace requests your presence," said the man in a soft tone before bowing and offering him a scrolled letter with a wax seal of the high court."

"Oh," said Velnir, surprised. "I'll be there at once. Thank you."

The man stood straight and smiled at Velnir. He then mounted a horse with wings and a horn attached to its head and began to stride down the road. This was strange to Velnir indeed. He wondered if it was a good idea to blend in with the people of Nagrimar and wear far less clothing than normal.

He decided that it was in the best interest of himself and his companions if they dressed in the traditional Nagrimaran garb. He dressed himself first and set an example for his companions.

Velnir walked through the city with only two guards. It was early morning, and the city was full of life. The trees were incredibly thick and tall. Birds were coming out of people's houses as though they lived there too. Deer and stags roamed the streets, and a bit of guilt settled in Velnir's heart, thinking of the king of the centaurs and of the stags his companions killed.

"I will make it right for them," he thought.

He looked up and saw the griffins flying with hippogriffs. Velnir had never seen a hippogriff before and was elated. Something about this place gave him a sense of peace and tranquility. Nobody was proud or boastful, as was traditional in Tanimara. Everyone was humble and happy.

Velnir made his way around a corner toward the palace of Nagrimar. He saw one of the denizens holding a device to his mouth and witnessed him placing some type of wadded-up substance inside of a small bowl carved out of the glass. The elf began to suck at the end of it, which produced a strange boiling sound and filled the device with smoke. He inhaled it and when he was done, he simply sat back with glazed-over eyes, and looked as if he was enjoying his life to the fullest. Velnir was curious and approached the denizen of Nagrimar.

"Pardon my intrusion, sir, but I couldn't help but gain curiosity over what you just did. It seems to have made you feel…well, how did it make you feel?" asked Velnir, genuinely curious.

"I feel like I live in paradise. Want to try some?" the denizen asked Velnir.

"What is it?" Velnir wasn't sure he wanted to engage in such an activity before meeting with the queen.

"We call it moss. You wad it up, place it in here, light it up, and smoke it. It will blow your mind," said the denizen before gently leaning back into a pillow shaped in a chair and seemingly falling asleep.

This perplexed Velnir who smiled and said, "Maybe another time," then proceeded to the palace.

The sun's rays began to penetrate the trees. Velnir started thinking of Darlana. Her people seemed so happy and content with their lives, but when he first met her, she did not seem happy. She had mixed emotions and acted strange considering her position here. Velnir began to feel bad for her and thought about what it would be like to be in her shoes.

He made his way up the steps to the giant door to the palace. It was already open to his surprise. Darlana did not seem to have any concern for her safety. No one was guarding the door.

They were left open and there was no one in her palace save for a cleaning maid. He wasn't really sure where he needed to go, so he chose to walk to the end of the hall and went up the left set of steps. These steps had a guard, so Velnir assumed that she must be that way. He approached the guard.

"I have been requested by the queen. I am Velnir," he said, unsure what to expect.

The guard simply pointed up the stairs confirming Velnir's theory. Velnir made his way to a floor of the palace, which was considerably high off the ground.

Looking out through the windows, he could see the city and how beautiful it was. He walked through the hall and up another set of stairs, and this time, to an area where there were many rooms.

Making his way down the hall, not sure which room to go in, Velnir heard some woman speaking around the corner. He approached a large door and assumed this is where Darlana stayed. He decided to knock and wait patiently for someone to answer.

When no one did, he decided to let himself in. The room was large and very spacious. It also had open windows and a balcony with very thin drapes at the entrance. Velnir made his way to the balcony and through the drapes.

Darlana stood there, observing her city with her hand beneath her chin. She wore her hair down. She had on a beautiful silver bracelet, a necklace made of what appeared to be a branch of some sort, and silver earrings decorated her pointy ears. Unlike yesterday, today she wore a strapless red dress made out of some very fine material that was unknown to him. It was elegant, nonetheless.

She turned her attention over to Velnir and smiled. She then motioned for him to come over and sit with her. He obliged and took the appointed seat.

"Good morning, Lord Velnir of Atlantin," she said happily while resting her cheek upon her hand.

He was surprised she called him Lord Velnir. She was very respectful. "Yes, it is, and good morning to you, Queen Darlana of Nagrimar," he said politely.

She did not take her eyes off of him and simply kept her smile up.

"It is strange hearing an elf from Tanimara call me Queen Darlana. No one from Tanimara has ever recognized my legitimacy, let alone visited. You are the first and it is quite exciting for everyone, but I think I am more excited than anyone else. It is a shame it was only by accident. I have attempted many times to establish diplomatic relations with the desire to bring our peoples together. Oftentimes, the severed head of my messenger was sent back to me with a scarlet letter as if I had offended them. They would then send assassins that I would dispatch easily. I do fear though that one of these days, I will not be so fortunate or quick to defend myself. I never had anything worth their time and it is obvious that the Magistrate loathes me for what I did."

Velnir had an idea why her guards were minimal. He felt bad because if the tables were turned, he would likely not have been so kind to her. He now had an idea why she called him into her palace now.

"Being the Lord of Atlantin means you have quite a bit of influence, Velnir." She spoke with confidence and certainty. This was not customary of women in Tanimara and Velnir was guilty of admiring it about her. He simply nodded.

"Perhaps we can come up with a mutually beneficial agreement," she said forcefully and without alternative.

Velnir had barely touched down in a foreign land and already found himself making deals with first the kraken, and now the exiled princess from a time long since passed. All this in her kingdom, a land halfway across Abrion.

This was the life of a prince of Tanimara. Deals had to be made to get things accomplished. Velnir had to be careful, for if he made a bad deal, he could lose his head. He was in her home after all, and was at her mercy. He felt like he had to do whatever she asked of him or at least make her believe he had every intention of doing so. With that in mind, he agreed.

"I am sure we can, especially since you are treating us so well here. After all, you are of elven blood. Personally, I see no issue here. I am sure I can attempt to convince the court of whatever you may need," he said with confidence.

Velnir knew he had no say on issues of the magistrate. He knew he was in dire straits with them just by leaving Tanimara but would not act on it as he had three Tanimaran armies protecting Atlantin at the moment. He wondered if they even knew of his quest by now, or if his uncle and cousin were able to keep it a secret.

Darlana moved herself close to Velnir allowing her leg to touch his. "I will allow you and your companions to go to the wizard."

"And in return?" he asked inquisitively. Statecraft was not his strong suit. He was not as clever with words like the others of the Tanimaran Magistrate. He was a warrior.

"I would like to go to Tanimara whenever I please and do so under your protection. I would of course stay in Atlantin and never go to Tarvana so long as I did not absolutely have to. My father killed my first born and I have no desire to see him."

Velnir looked at her surprised by her request.

"Make no mistake, Velnir, if I return to Tanimara, I intend to spread my influence. The people of Tanimara will know that I am not an evil apostate."

Now she was acting like a Tanimaran who had not forgotten the ways of her people. He now understood what she wanted and knew that the magistrate would absolutely forbid it. She was an exiled princess, who established a kingdom far away from Tanimara.

He has no quarrel with Darlana for what she did. He did not care that she had a half-breed child and thought that it was a silly reason to exile ones daughter, but then again, this was Tanimara. He began to think that if he returned from the sundered lands triumphant, he would have the support of the people, at the very least, but the act of him allowing her to return under his protection against the magistrate's wishes would create an enormous divide in Tanimara.

Velnir knew Raften through his father. He had no idea that the legendary Darlana was his daughter. Raften was now the High Magistrate of all Tanimara. He held the highest rank possible and dwelt in the capital of the so called republic. She knew that now.

"Okay, Darlana." he responded not wanting to say anything before a deal was struck.

"Does he have any other children?" she asked.

"I do not know High Magistrate Raften very well. I only knew him through my father, and the visits to Tarvana were that of state and not pleasure. I do know that he had a daughter other than you, but she was killed in a storm. I went to her funeral. As of now, I am unaware of any other children he may have besides you, Darlana."

"Do you have any children, Velnir?"

"I do not."

She smiled and seemed to be relieved.

"Well then, Velnir, I am an exiled princess and you are a Tanimaran prince. I want to be left alone and live without fear of assassination, so I would respect the traditions of Tanimara and become married to you, and together we would produce a child. This child would be the legal heir to Tarvana and Atlantin making them very powerful and influential, and maybe one day, in exchange, I would offer safe passage to the wizard and..." She paused for a moment and looked at him.

He was dreading the arrangement already, and now this. He honestly felt that safe passage was not enough to justify such an arrangement but he was her guest for now.

If he turned her down, that may change and he could end up back in prison for who knows how long. She was absolutely beautiful, though, and Velnir would certainly be happy with that, but she was a strange elf. They had no chemistry and the marriage as long as it would be, and it would be long, would likely become strained and he knew it.

She continued, "My people have suffered at the hands of orcs for hundreds of years. They would willingly seek retribution if I allowed it. I would offer you myself and my army against the orcs once your invasion commences."

"Your army?" Velnir asked with surprise. He had not seen anyone resembling a soldier outside the guards and centaurs with feathers and spears. Nobody wore armor, and very few actually had weapons.

She donned an offended look. "Yes, Velnir, my army. How do you think I maintain peace in Nagrimar? We captured you and your companions with ease yet could have had you killed. You and your companions would have been none the wiser."

Velnir thought for a moment before giving her a nod. It was true. The centaurs were big and armorless, but perhaps they did not need armor. Their stealth was unmatched even by the elves, and they were obviously a formidable foe. They certainly did not lack conviction.

"The centaurs are formidable indeed, Darlana, but they seem to be only a few," he said.

She smiled and turned her attention to a map on the table that was held down by weights in the shape of mythical creatures… or so he thought. "Not all centaurs live in Nagrimar. Most of them dwell in the forest outside of Nagrimar. They keep the peace throughout the kingdom and the people here keep the peace within Nagrimar."

Velnir nodded as it made sense. "How did you convince the centaurs to fight for you?" he asked.

"I did not convince them. They offered." She smiled at him. "When I arrived here, Alzar and I used magic to create a temperate climate, so the trees would grow larger and thick. It would provide safety for my people. It also served to keep a plentiful harvest as winter does not come here. Fungus, moss, and herbs now grow here whereas they did not before. I used them to treat the ill and wounded. It was their desire so I made it so. The centaurs benefited greatly from the harvest and the medicine because we shared with them. Chief Dravon thinks I deserve their service even though I have told them many times that I would not ever take their freedom. They can come and go as they please. They choose to stay. They offered the kingdom of Nagrimara protection and agreed to stay within its borders to keep invaders out. Dravon swore allegiance to me," she said with a smile and without an ounce of arrogance in her voice.

Velnir was thoroughly impressed. She must be powerful if she was able to persuade Alzar to use his magic for this. This was definitely part of a deal she had with him. He looked at her and smiled. She paid a price so her people could be comfortable and free. "If I agree to marry you and we produce an heir for both Atlantin and Tarvana, this will outrage the Magistrate. I could face exile myself."

"Velnir, do you know how many orcs there are in the sundered lands?"

"I do not know, but I do know that I have one hundred thousand soldiers, several hundred bolt throwers, and a few powerful pyromancers."

"Millions at the very least. You would be overwhelmed and destroyed. Why do you think that no one has ever attempted to destroy those monsters before?" she asked.

Truthfully, the thought never crossed Velnir's mind. He was unsure whether or not Darlana was being truthful though the orcs did bring a sizeable force to Atlantin. There is no way they would have brought their entire force so she could be telling the truth. Not to mention, reports indicate that there are in fact far more orcs in the sundered lands than previously thought.

"Do not underestimate the power of the elves, Darlana. Have you forgotten? We are the most powerful species on Abrion," he said.

"Again, a few centaurs captured you and nearly one hundred of your companions. It is easily calculated then that one centaur is worth thirty elves. I can bring twenty thousand centaurs and twenty thousand Nagrimarans."

"This still does not resolve the issue with the Magistrate and you. If I marry you, I could face exile and lose my titles, my lands."

Darlana was growing impatient. He could tell by the look she was giving him. Still, she exercised a calm demeanor.

"You know Tanimara is a warrior culture. As reclusive and introverted as they are, anger and revenge are rife. If you can successfully kill millions of orcs and eliminate them as a threat, you will win glory enough to gain the respect of your people and several other princes. If you return to Tanimara in triumph, what threat would the Magistrate be to you?" she asked.

Velnir looked at her with a furrowed brow. "You could be right, Darlana. It would be a gamble," he said.

"Revenge for Tanimara and glory for you are more than enough to help the Magistrate forget about me. Help me, Velnir! Marry me, give me a child, and I will help you," she said.

Velnir sat back and thought about it. She was right about the centaur. They are formidable and easily worth that many elves, as embarrassing as that may be to admit; however, they would still need armor if they were to go to the sundered lands. They would be extremely useful. Revenge against millions of orcs would make him a hero of Tanimara. Millions of Tanimarans would respect and support him. Perhaps they wouldn't care or, at the very least, look past the fact he married Darlana. She may not be a legitimate heir, but their child would be because of him. Still, this was a gamble. He was unsure. "And what if I refuse, Darlana?"

She offered him a warm smile. "I do not think I am being at all unreasonable, Velnir, but if you refuse, then I will have you and your companions beheaded and your heads sent to the magistrate. You would bring shame to your house, dying at the hands of the apostate Darlana. It is either death by my hand or glory and respect, assuming you defeat the orcs, and you will with my army," she said with a smirk.

Velnir offered a similar warm smile. It suddenly became worth the risk now that he knew what was at stake. "You are a hard negotiator, Darlana. Such are the ways of lordship and so on. In the interest of Tanimara, my house, my campaign, and…my head, I accept your offer," he said reluctantly.

At least he would have better odds against the orcs and an extremely attractive wife for a while. If Darlana did not take his head, the Magistrate was likely to.

Darlana was elated. She jumped out of her seat and gave him a gentle hug, whispering in his ear, "I thought you might say yes, so I have our betrothal already planned."

Velnir was not at all surprised. He was feeling that he might have divulged too much information, and she simply outsmarted him to get what she wanted. It was admirable but the tactic made him feel like a fool.

"Come, Velnir, let us go for a walk and make sure that the people of Nagrimar see us together."

They made their way out of the palace. She placed her arm in his as they walked down the streets of the city. She liked to talk, and Velnir actually found her pleasant to listen to.

"Tell me of yourself, Velnir," she said, smiling at him.

"Well, I was born in Atlan. I studied at the Atlantin Academy of Military Strategy and Tactics. I ventured all around Tanimara with my father on state business. My first military campaign was against the dwarves during the electhril wars. My father had to come to my rescue as my cousin and uncle did this time. I have only ever left Tanimara a few times."

"Tanimara is a large continent, and the Mari are not known to venture out and explore much. I observed the electhril wars from afar. Do you have family, hobbies, or interests?" asked Darlana.

"My mother died during my birth. I have a cousin and an uncle I am close with. For hobbies, I enjoy alchemy and enchanting. The intricacies of spell components and velum's are fascinating. I also enjoy mounted archery and fencing. I often play Dragons&Wizards with my closest friends Arlen and Magris. Tell me more about you, Darlana."

"I was born in Tarvana. I was quite the rebellious child. My mother and father smothered me and were strict. Back then, the mari and the humans had closer relations. When Maphis was the capital of the Araban Empire, prince Sampsin came to the court of Tarvana. I immediately fell in love, and we met in the twilight grove where the trees of my namesake are. We made love, and I became pregnant. I tried to hide the pregnancy because... Well, you know.

"My son was born with round ears and bulbous features. My father became enraged. He took my son from me and threw him out the window of my chambers. He grabbed me by my hair and dragged me to the dungeons below the palace. I had to hear them execute Prince Sampsin publicly outside my cell. They would have executed me too, but my mother snuck me out of Tarvana and had trusted friends sail me here in secrecy. He branded me an apostate for forsaking our values and purity. He said I tainted our bloodline.

"I sought out the wizard, and he helped me with the Forlorn Forest and turn these ancient elven ruins into Nagrimar. Many other former Tanimarans sought asylum here, and we have been here ever since."

Velnir had heard this story before but it was from other Tanimarans who made her out to be the one who hurt her family, tainted their bloodline, and brought shame to their name. Hearing it from Darlana herself made it sound more like she did it out of love, and it was stolen from her.

"It may please you to know that my father had raised me to know that you were not to blame. He took pity on you, and as I got older, I did too. I cannot see how even a Tanimaran could be so cruel to their own child."

"I met your father during the electhril wars. He was kind to me."

"I never knew you met him," Velnir said with surprise in his voice.

"I was at the Tower of Alzar in Nemis when he asked the king of Nemis for permission to pass through to get to Dhar'Modir. Everyone was struggling with the dwarves there and thought it may be good for everyone if he let him and his army through."

Velnir remembered that his father split their forces, and Velnir and his cousin led their army through Northgarde.

They came around a corner to what looked like some sort of festival, unfamiliar to Velnir. Many people stopped what they were doing and greeted Darlana as if she had done this many times before. It became clear to Velnir that her people really loved her. The fact that she wandered the streets without guards was astonishing. This would never happen in Tanimara. One must always look over their shoulder and sleep with one eye open when in Tanimara, his father would tell him.

***

Several weeks had gone by, and Darlana would constantly request but not force Velnir to go on walks with her throughout the city. It became apparent to Velnir's companions that he was developing feelings for her. When they first started spending time together, he indicated he dreaded it. Now, he was eager to get out first thing in the morning and meet with her. They would taunt him playfully, unbeknownst of his plans to marry her and the circumstances of which they were to be wed, but the time had come for Velnir to tell his companions.

Velnir left the palace and made his way to where his companions were staying. He announced to them that he had planned to be married to the queen in a few days. Several of the elves looked upon him with envy as they, too, had seen Darlana and would want nothing more than a chance with her themselves. Others seemed to be put off, and one was even willing to point out the possible ramifications but swore would follow Velnir to the ends of Abrion if it were asked of him.

The day had come. People throughout Nagrimara came to the palace and brought with them gifts and flowers.

Velnir decided it would be a good idea to show unity now that he knew he had the support of his companions. He and his companions arrived clad in their elegant and ornamented armor of Tanimara. They definitely stood out among the denizens of Nagrimar. Velnir waited at the entrance for Darlana. She arrived with her companions. Velnir looked upon her with wonder. He was beginning to be content with the idea of making her his wife. It couldn't be that bad, he thought.

They locked arms and proceeded down the long hall surrounded by thousands of witnesses. Velnir was unaware of the traditions of Nagrimar as far as marriage goes, but he was prepared to commence them. Once they reached the end, there before them were two bottles of sand each with a different color. Velnir had blue sand, and Darlana had red sand. Velnir immediately recognized the ceremony as that of an ancient elvish traditional style. Darlana was extremely old-fashioned. Blue represented masculinity, and red represented femininity. The purple was the color of the drapes of a house ruled by a married couple. Blue for a single male lord and red for a single female lady.

This certainly came from a time long since passed. Long ago, elvish men and women were seen as equals. That has since changed where the favor went to the males of Tanimara, and the women were subservient to the men. Clearly, Darlana is no longer accustomed to the ways of Tanimara. She would never be welcomed back and most certainly not respected.

Velnir worried as he thought of all of this. They both poured their sand into a larger jar designed to contain the entire contents of each of their jars. He looked at her, and she looked at him. Her blue eyes glistened in the lantern light. She was beautiful, and everyone would agree, but she was not Tanimaran any longer. She was Nagrimaran.

They solidified their unity with a kiss, and everyone cheered. He carried her up to her chambers, but when he entered with her. Several nobles of Nagrimar were standing against the walls of the room. He gently set her down.

"Darlana, what is the meaning of this?" he asked.

"They must bear witness to our consummation. Worry not my husband. They only have to watch once," she said before he realized that he was naked, and so was she.

He was very impressed with her ability to undress him without him even realizing it. He was, however, nervous as these people were watching him with intense looks on their faces.

He lay down, and she threw her left leg over his and straddled him. She decided at that moment to put her hair up. Velnir did not even notice. He had never done this before while others were observing. He had no idea that this was customary back then, but then again, nobody talked about the times of old, and he didn't really pay that much attention to history while attending the academy. The feeling was immense and far different than what he experienced with his concubines.

It no longer mattered that the nobles were observing. He was happy to be there with her. Once they were finished, the nobles left. He lay there looking out the window at the stars while she rolled over and put her arm over him. He truly believed he could come to love Darlana but knew that it would be a gamble to make it work in Tanimara. He dreaded it, as he was unsure what to do.

The next morning, Velnir went to the balcony where some of the griffins had perched. They really seemed to be enjoying themselves, and that pleased Velnir. They didn't get to live like this in Tanimara, but he vowed they would in Atlantin at the very least.

Darlana came up behind him and startled him when she put her arms around his chiseled abs. She began to course her fingers through his long white hair, which did feel very good to him. He could easily forget about his commitments and vows to Tanimara and simply stay here.

However, his conviction was too strong, and he began to loathe that about himself. She was sweet, albeit strange. She was growing on him. She kept bringing him things like wine, fruit, and trinkets. Her servants were not even annoyed. They would do anything for her, for they loved her so much.

It was amazing how her people exalted her. He knew he could not have that kind of respect from his people; if anything, he envied that about his new wife.

The day came for Velnir and his companions to leave Nagrimar. They had spent a considerable amount of time and had come to enjoy it. It would make for a great tourist destination for some elves, but not enough of them to turn it into a lucrative trade. Velnir and his companions mounted their griffins, now armored in a lightweight but thick ornamented armor plating. The denizens who crafted the armor for them were waiting by the griffins to bow to the Tanimarans when they came. Darlana was waiting by Velnir's griffin.

His mount was bonding with Darlana quite nicely. It seemed that everything that came into contact with Darlana grew fond of her. She was old even for an elf, but she didn't look like it. She was almost adolescent in behavior but knew when to do business. She impressed Velnir more than he could imagine. Velnir approached her and his mount.

"I do hope you return soon. I wish I could go with you, my husband." She hugged him and tickled the point of his ear. She knew the right place to touch. Velnir found that he was losing himself again and had to regain his composure.

"My handsome husband," she whispered in his ear.

The day before that, he had stayed with her in the palace doing what anyone could imagine. They hardly left but to go on the occasional walk through the city and greet the denizens. Then, it was right back to their chambers. She was eager to become with child.

Velnir's heart was attached to her. He did not want to go but knew he had to. It was even harder because, secretly, he felt he couldn't stay with her. He looked at her, and a tear almost escaped his eye. He embraced her as if this would be the last time he would see her.

As if it were the final goodbye.

She was really enjoying it, as were the denizens of Nagrimar.

Velnir mounted his griffin along with the other Tanimarans. All at once, they took to the sky and quickly gained formation. As they gained altitude, Velnir looked at the city. It was even beautiful from up here. He looked at his wife, who was waving goodbye with her beautiful blue eyes and wonderful smile. His heart ached for certain.

Once they were above the canopy, he threw a scrying orb into the air, and it darted toward the border of Nemis. They all turned in that direction and headed that way. It soon became clear that Nagrimar was the only part of the Forlorn Forest that was not dense with trees. The forest was thick for as far as the eye could see.

Every now and then, they would pass a peak not covered in so many trees sticking out of the canopy, but they were few and far between. They flew into the night and were getting very tired.

Chapter 8
To the Tower

So far, they had not encountered any trouble, but it was time for them to land for the night. They found the nearest hill to land on and set up camp. Most of the Tanimarans were reluctant to cut down any trees because of what they had learned from the Nagrimarans. They told them the trees were enchanted and alive and could feel the blows from the axes. Not wanting to hurt anything in the place where they were taken such good care of, they went to sleep without any light. The temperature was the same in all of the forest, so they didn't get too hot nor too cold.

The Tanimarans did this for a few days. They were surprised by the vastness of the Forlorn Forest.

"Nobody could invade Nagrimar. Even if the centaur were unable to stop them. To trek this forest would be impossible," thought Velnir.

Midday had approached, and one of his companions spotted a clearing. This was the right direction.

As they got closer, they noticed the forest began to open up. Darlana said this would be the sign that they were in Nemis. Below they spotted a group of centaurs patrolling the border but not going further. It was for sure Nemis.

Now, they had to land and make camp. The trees here were not enchanted, so the Tanimarans were quick to cut firewood. Velnir lay down in his tent, thinking of Darlana. It had been several days, and he already missed her terribly. Her face haunted his memories.

Velnir was stirred from his daydreaming when he heard one of the other Tanimarans screaming. He rushed out of his tent and saw Ardan hanging from a tree upside down with an ax in his hand. He was desperately trying to hit the tree with it.

"What is going on?" Velnir shouted.

It was at that moment he realized that it was no ordinary tree. It had limbs resembling legs and arms, a face, and a beard made of leaves. It was angry and speaking in a deep, slow tone.

"Swing an axe at me, will you pointy ear? I am going to rip you limb from limb," said the tree in a gruff male voice to everyone's bewilderment.

Velnir rushed over to what could be considered the tree's stump and began shouting to get its attention. He had hoped it would simply look at him and attempt to negotiate the release of the elf and not stomp him to his demise.

Velnir successfully got the attention of the tree, and it stopped, even if for a brief moment.

"More of you, hmm?" said the tree, seemingly curious.

"Yes, and if you would hear me for a moment, I can explain everyth…" Velnir could not finish as he had to dodge the attempt by the tree to kick him.

"Please, tree, take me instead." Velnir already regretted offering himself in exchange for Ardan.

The tree stopped and dropped the elf, who scrambled to his feet and fled instantly. The tree then reached to pick up Velnir but he shouted, "Wait, wait." The tree hesitated and looked at him.

Velnir took the opportunity to ask, "Why are you angry with us? What happened and how can we make it right?" Velnir was genuine in his inquiry.

The tree simply looked at Velnir for a moment and replied, "That little imp hit me with an ax!" He then blinked at Velnir.

"Ardan did not think you were alive. If he knew you were alive, he would have never done that." Velnir tried desperately to convince the tree.

The tree looked at him, somewhat confused, and then his demeanor became angry. "We're all alive, you fools!" He then reached for Velnir, who simply stood there and looked at the tree reaching for him. The Tanimarans had formed ranks and lit their arrows on fire, knocked, and aimed at the tree. Luckily for Velnir, the tree noticed and stopped.

"Uh oh," the tree said.

He looked scared and covered his face.

Velnir noticed and ordered the Tanimarans to hold their fire. "We mean you no harm, tree. We clearly," he said with an exasperated tone, "are not from here."

The tree seemed to calm down.

"Yes...well, that is obvious. Your pointy-eared companion hit me with an ax, and I'm rather unhappy about it."

"How can I make it right?" Velnir asked.

"You can start by punishing him, and then you can get out of my forest!"

"Your forest?" said Velnir inquisitively.

"Yes... my forest? It is perfectly maintained and you are disturbing it," said the tree, trying not to let his temper get out of control. Velnir had noticed that he kept eying those fire arrows.

"I do not know what you mean by 'your forest'. Could you elaborate?" Velnir asked.

"Why, it is what you are standing in," said the tree.

Velnir looked at the ground. It was dusk, but he could still see the detail of it. The grass was cut in a fine, detailed pattern. Flowers were arranged with purpose in beautiful patterns. In fact, all of the fauna here was distributed in such a way as to make it appealing to the eye it would seem.

"Oh," said Velnir, now understanding what the tree meant. "I am sorry." Thinking for a moment, he decided to tell the tree why they were there. "Tree," said Velnir before the tree interrupted.

"Please, I am an trebor, and you can call me Oakenleaf. That is my name. I've had it since I was a sapling."

"Oakenleaf then, we did not mean to disturb your forest. We are trying to get to Nemis. We only intended to stay here one night." Velnir turned around. He saw the Tanimarans but did not see the griffins. Velnir assumed they were scared off by the trees. "Now that our griffins seem to have disappeared, we have no way of getting to Nemis with haste."

"Meh," said the tree in his guttural voice. "How is that my problem?"

"Well, it's your problem because you scared them off." Velnir looked to the other Tanimarans and motioned for support.

They caught on and began to agree with Velnir. Oakenleaf glanced at all of them and then turned his attention to Velnir.

"Oh, I see," said Oakenleaf. I do not want you in my forest, and you do not wish to stay but cannot otherwise leave." He looked at the other Tanimarans with fire arrows and then back to Velnir. "I suppose I could give you a lift so long as they put out those fires."

Velnir was not expecting such an offer. The tree really wanted them out of his forest and was willing to take them to Nemis.

"We accept your offer, Oakenleaf," Velnir said with delight as they crawled onto his limbs. Soon, the trebor was walking toward what Velnir assumed was Nemis. The movement seemed very slow and the leaves rustled every time Oakenleaf took a step. This did not stop any of them from sleeping. Somehow, everyone was able to find a comfortable spot to sleep without falling off the trebor.

Velnir had questioned whether or not Oakenleaf would even notice or care to stop and pick them up. Velnir decided it was a good idea to sleep as well. The last thought he remembered having was of Darlana.

"Oh, we forest lords have been around for a long, long time. In fact, we have been around for just about as long as the dragons have. Even before you elves, heh, heh." Velnir woke to the sound of Oakenleaf's voice speaking to one of the other Tanimarans fascinated by him.

All of the Tanimarans seemed to enjoy the tales Oakenleaf had to tell. The trebor was pleased to speak to anyone who would listen. For hours he talked and talked and talked. Velnir decided to speak up.

"Oakenleaf, have you heard of a wizard called Alzar?"

"Hmm, Lazaar, no. However, I do know a wizard named Alzar."

Velnir smiled and said, "We are actually attempting to find him. We understand he lives in Nemis."

"He lives in the region of Nemis, not Nemis the city. He is back that way." Oakenleaf pointed west of where they were headed, which was the opposite direction of where they were heading.

Annoyed, Velnir asked him, "Could you take us to him instead?"

"Why would you want to disturb him? You should leave him alone. He deserves peace for all he has done," said Oakenleaf defensively.

This surprised Velnir because it conflicted with what everyone else said.

"We are seeking his aid against the orcs of the sundered lands."

"Orcs of the sundered lands," said Oakenleaf, his tone becoming angry. "I hate Orcs, always chopping and burning. They make war on us, and we have done nothing to them! I am certain Alzar would not mind helping you fight Orcs. Why, I may even help you. Everyone would help you. Everyone hates Orcs." Oakenleaf rambled on about Orcs for the next few hours.

The sound of grunting and barking could be heard in the distance. It was somewhat muffled by Oakenleaf's deep voice. Oakenleaf did not notice, but Velnir did. He threw a scrying orb into the sky, and it darted toward the direction the sound was coming from. He gazed through his scrying crystal, and figures in the distance appeared and were riding fast toward them.

"We have visitors, make ready, make ready" Velnir shouted. All of the Tanimarans got their bows ready. Oakenleaf seemed confused and was about to throw them off his body when he suddenly noticed the marauders coming toward him.

"Orcs," snarled Oakenleaf.

They were indeed orcs, and when they got close, the Tanimarans noticed they were different. These were not the same type of orcs they fought in Atlantin. These ones had brown skin. They wore their hair in braids, and all of them looked to be females. They were wearing furs and bones.

Some of them were even wearing skulls, presumably of something they killed, clearly much bigger than they were. They began circling Oakenleaf. The trebor began trying to stomp on them but missed every time. They would weave in between his legs and around them. It appeared they knew what they were doing. It was confusing Oakenleaf and making him angry.

The angrier he got, the sloppier he became. Velnir had to act quickly.

The Tanimarans were shooting at the orcs, but their aim was obstructed by Oakenleaf's movements. Velnir saw the orc with the sashimono and noticed the symbol on it was not the same as the one on the siege towers at the battle of Atlan.

"She must be their leader," he thought.

He carefully timed her movement, and when he thought the time was right, he jumped from Oakenleaf's back onto the orc and knocked her off her worg. He drew his sword and faced her.

The other orcs rode around and dismounted while their worgs harassed Oakenleaf distracting him from the quarrel about to unfold. The Tanimarans leaped from Oakenleaf and formed ranks around Velnir.

The orc said something to Velnir, but he was unable to understand it. She motioned for the others to stay back and stared Velnir down. Velnir understood that she wanted to fight him alone, so he motioned for the other Tanimarans to stand back but stay ready.

They began to circle each other. Velnir was surprised by her movements. They were so smooth and much different than those he fought at the siege. As she was moving, she was demonstrating her skill by dancing with her blade against the air. Likely an effort to intimidate Velnir. Velnir held firm and did not bother demonstrating anything he knew to her. She was in for a surprise.

She lunged forward to strike, her sword thrust toward his face. He dodged but just barely. Before he could react, she had done a pirouette and thrust her sword toward his midsection. Velnir was on the defense, but he was no stranger to defensive fighting.

The next time she came around with a blow, he parried with his sword, his strength clearly greater than hers. This served to make her angry. She kicked him and knocked him slightly backward.

She attempted to take advantage of her action and brought her blade up again, but Velnir was ready. He parried her blade and punched her in the face, knocking her back. He lunged forward and brought his sword down, but she rolled out of the way and quickly got to her feet.

Undeterred, she lunged at him again. The two seemed to match in skill, but nobody could be sure. The other orcs were cheering their leader on and speaking in their disgusting orcish language. The Tanimarans waited and said nothing. They simply watched as if they were waiting for him to get it over with.

The female orc was getting tired and sloppy. Velnir gained the upper hand, for he was just getting started. Now, it was simple fun. Velnir was toying with her to demonstrate his superiority.

Velnir had never seen the look of terror on an orc's face before but she was the exception. She realized she could not win. The other orcs did too and stopped cheering her on.

All of a sudden, a massive stump came down and crushed the orc Velnir had been facing. He stepped back and looked up. It was Oakenleaf. He twisted his foot side to side to make sure she was squished into the dirt.

When he stepped off of her, the other orcs had mounted their worgs and took off. The Tanimarans were able to shoot a few of their worgs while they retreated. What was left of Velnir's opponent was a soupy, muddy mess of shards of bone, chunks of unrecognizable flesh, and tufts of hair or whatever she was wearing.

Oakenleaf peeled the rest of her remains off the bottom of his stump and tossed them away.

"Damned orcs!" Oakenleaf shouted.

Velnir felt robbed of his glorious kill. He was no doubt upset with Oakenleaf but decided to let it go. He was in his land after all and the customs were clearly different. No matter. There will be plenty of glory for Velnir later.

"I thought they would have me for firewood," grunted Oakenleaf. "If it wasn't for you, little pointy ear, I may have not survived. You have my thanks," said the trebor, offering a tree-like smile.

"It was my honor, Oakenleaf," said Velnir as he walked toward the other Tanimarans. He did not want to show his irritation with the trebor, especially since the trebor showed him gratitude.

They had traveled for a few more hours listening to Oakenleaf talk about times long since passed. Everyone took turns asking him questions and he seemed to enjoy the company. Soon, they could see a tall black tower in the distance.

"This must be the tower Alzar lives in," thought Velnir.

Oakenleaf stopped. "This is as far as I go, little pointy ears. You must trek the rest of the way on your own. Be warned, though, things beyond this point are likely not what you would expect them to be."

Velnir and the rest of the Tanimarans dismounted the trebor and collected their things. Velnir looked toward the direction they must go before turning to the trebor. "You have my thanks, Oakenleaf. Again, I do apologize for disturbing your forest."

The trebor turned his attention to Velnir. "I am old

and grumpy, small one. You all provided me with quality entertainment over the last few days and saved me from an orc attack. For that, I am eternally grateful," he said with a bow. "Please, if you ever find yourselves in this area, do not hesitate to visit. When you are ready to fight the orcs, we'll be there," said Oakenleaf confidently.

"We?" Velnir inquired.

"I am not the only trebor in the area. Take a look around." He motioned to all the trees scattered throughout the land.

Some were indeed regular trees, but others had details about them that resembled Oakenleaf. There were many, and they were everywhere.

"The forest lords all remain dormant and only awake four times a year or until disturbed. I will wake them when it is time."

Velnir nodded at the trebor and the Tanimarans began making their way toward the tall black tower.

They left the clearing of the land of forest lords, as he thought of it, and entered the forest surrounding the tower. This was nothing like the Forlorn Forest of Nagrimara. It was dark and gloomy. The ground was a black and purplish hue, and vines running all throughout it. The trees were crooked and twisted and looked as though they were in pain. The Tanimarans were careful where they stepped. They were very quiet and somewhat nervous, except for Velnir.

They had found a road which they assumed led to the tower. Hours went by, and they felt no closer. They were getting hungry and decided to stop. They wouldn't cut down any trees or even set up tents. They didn't want to make their presence known in this strange land and garner the wrath of whatever was to come.

Ardan was complaining that he was hungry. The others were grumbling too and Velnir had to act.

"Very well, forage for food, but do not kill anything. Tonight, we eat whatever the land offers. Remember, do not disturb anything that you absolutely do not need to disturb."

Velnir was confident that there was nothing really worth worrying about here. However, he wasn't going to take any chances. He remembered the last time he assumed it was okay to hunt on a foreign land. He ended up with a wife and an accord between his people and hers. Velnir knew his chances of something like that happening again were slim.

"Oooh," said Ardan. "Mushrooms!" Ardan rushed over to an area littered with small brown spotted mushrooms. He licked his lips and picked one up.

It began to scream, which startled the elf.

He dropped it and began to back away.

A moment later, all of the mushrooms stood up. They opened their eyes, and it was then that he realized they too were alive.

"Oh nooo!" he exclaimed.

He got up and ran to the camp, and when he arrived, he looked over his shoulder and didn't see anything following him, so he slowed down and walked toward the other Tanimarans. They asked him if he had found anything, and he simply denied it. Nobody had found anything, and they all came to the conclusion that they were simply going to have to go without for the evening.

The elves started to tuck in for the evening, and many were asleep. Velnir was thinking about Darlana and wondering if she would become pregnant with an heir during his stay with her. If she didn't, he would at least honor their agreement and return to fulfill it, even though it was likely in vain.

Fast asleep, he fell along with all the other elves. Velnir dreamt he was back in Atlan, enjoying time with his father and mother. This was pleasing. He was getting infinitely better at using magic, and Dargarok was there with him and competing with him in a friendly competition.

Dargarok was imprisoned in the internment camp and would remain there until Velnir returned after finishing his quest. In reality, Velnir didn't think he could ever have a friendly relationship with an orc. The sky turned from blue to yellow to orange and then red. It opened up and the face of a celestial appeared and stared at him.

This startled Velnir and he awoke immediately. The other elves also woke up immediately, and began discussing the face they saw in their dreams. It would appear that they all had the same dream in some way.

After a bit of banter, they turned their attention to the front of them. To their bewilderment, a feast was before them. It was elegantly arranged with what appeared to be fruit and vegetables from the forest.

The elves were elated and quickly moved toward it. They prepared to devour it, but Velnir noticed something not too far off in the distance. Little green glowing eyes appeared and began blinking. They were watching the elves. Velnir was immediately suspicious and ordered the men to stop.

"Observe, they are watching us," he quietly exclaimed to the elves.

They looked up and noticed all of the glowing green eyes

watching them. They suddenly lost their appetite and stepped back not sure what to do. Velnir moved in front of them and waited for a moment.

A mushroom suddenly rolled down the slope and stopped in front of Velnir. It jumped up and looked at him. It had glowing green eyes, two arms, two legs, and a mouth. The mushroom cap was its head. It began to speak to him in elvish. Its voice sounded small and frail. Velnir could not tell if it was female or male. Either way, he was bewildered that it not only talked, but speak elvish.

"We have prepared a feast for you, Tanimarans. Please do not eat us. We can be useful in many ways," said the tiny mushroom person.

"We did not know you were alive," exclaimed Velnir. "We're very sorry we have disturbed you."

A moment later, several mushrooms rolled down the slope and landed in front of the prepared feast, which was between the elves and the mushroom folk.

"It is our custom to offer sustenance to travelers so long as they are friendly. We rarely get travelers in these parts. Are you friendly?" asked the same mushroom who was seemingly brave enough to start a dialogue with Velnir.

"Yes, we mean you know harm," said Velnir with a calm and collected tone. "I am Velnir, and these are my companions. We are trying to find the wizard Alzar."

Once he mentioned Alzar, the mushrooms began to act excited and speak to each other quietly in their native language. Velnir looked at the other elves and shrugged.

The mushrooms stopped talking to each other and turned their attention to the elves. Velnir turned his attention toward them.

A mushroom spoke to Velnir and said, "We are myconids—a race of magical mushrooms created by Alzar. My name is Sporepod. You can call me Pod if you wish. Please eat. You all look famished and could use the sustenance. After you are done, we can take you to Alzar."

Sporepod spoke strangely. Velnir was not sure if he could trust the myconid. Never had Velnir heard of such creatures. This was very intriguing to him. He would document their existence and archive it in the great librarium of Tanimara.

Velnir looked at the food once more and noticed he did not recognize any of the exotic fruits or vegetables. None were native to Tanimara.

"What are these? We must know to make sure we do not have an allergy," said Velnir.

The other elves looked at him, confused, as they did not know what an allergy was. Velnir had learned of human allergies and found that they can only eat certain foods. He thought he would try to stall eating and go straight to Alzar.

Then Sporepod moved toward the end of the arrangement which was to Velnir's right and started naming the items before them.

"These are grumbles, and this is a bop. These are muchinis. They are delicious." The other myconids seemed to agree. "That is an oregar, those are chapes, and that is a tree fruit. It is the best we can do, and we did it all for you," said Sporepod gleefully.

They seemed very happy to provide the elves with such

a feast.

"Would you join us then?" asked Velnir, thinking that if they wouldn't, then it must be poisoned, and they would incur his wrath.

Unexpectedly, however, they dove right in without a word as if expecting the visitors to invite them to join. Once the myconids began to devour the food, the elves joined them, and so did Velnir. The myconids spoke the truth. This food was delicious. It was the best that some of them had ever tasted. Velnir wondered why this had never been brought to Tanimara. It would do very well in the local produce markets. Wealthy Tanimaran nobles love exotic things.

The most interesting part about the items at this feast is that once a bite was taken, it seemed to regenerate. Velnir practiced this kind of magic when he was in the academy. He would drink a glass of wine, and it would refill itself. These myconids were magic users and quite adept. Velnir was impressed, to say the least.

Once they were all done, the myconids began to burp. Their small stature made their voices high-pitched. The sound of their belching made the elves laugh. The myconids began to laugh with them. Once again, Velnir and his entourage have stumbled upon a strange group and bonded with them.

Velnir wondered why it was so easy for the Myconids to get along with foreign species. It did not matter to him so much now. He was ever closer to meeting with Alzar. It did surprise him to know that so many creatures knew of Alzar. Some spoke highly, and some not so much. This intrigued Velnir.

The elves and myconids finished their feast

"Was that not delicious, elves?" asked Sporepod.

The elves nodded, and rubbed their tummies in satisfaction.

"If it is Alzar you wish to see, we shall take you to the gate of the tower that bears his name. Come." He motioned the elves to follow him.

The forest seemed to brighten up. No longer did it look and feel dark and gloomy. "Perhaps this was a magical spell to intentionally keep people out," thought Velnir. "If that were so, why would the myconids show so much hospitality? This is a very strange place indeed." Velnir continued to think.

Eventually, they arrived at a large black wall with a large wooden bridge and door. The myconids stopped and Sporepod came forward.

"Here we are Tanimarans. He is on the other side of that door there." Sporepod then chuckled.

Then many small portals opened, and the myconids went through them. As fast as the portals appeared, they disappeared.

"That was impressive, but what could be so funny?" thought Velnir.

As they approached, they noticed a bridge over a seemingly endless ravine. It was so dark down below that no one could see the bottom.

This bothered the other elves, but Velnir moved forward, proceeding with caution. He took his first step onto the bridge when something swung up from under it and landed feet first right in front of Velnir. By this point in his quest, he was used to such surprises, so this did not startle him. He acted fast and drew his sword, ready for combat if necessary.

"The bridge troll will collect its toll, or the bridge troll will not let the elf go," it said in a strange, raspy voice.

The troll was fat and surprisingly agile for its size. It had a round face and bulbous features with a nose that was long and covered in warts. The fingers were more like claws, and its feet were like clubs with three toes. This thing was truly hideous, and the smell was like that of rotten fish being sprayed by a skunk.

Velnir backed off the bridge for he could not stand the stench. "I seek passage past this gate to meet with the wizard, Alzar, troll. What is your toll?"

The troll donned a surprised expression on its face and waited a moment before speaking. It furrowed its eyebrow at Velnir and said, "Oh…well, those who wish to cross the bridge usually prefer fighting me rather than actually paying me. Um…I have not thought of this in ages." The troll's demeanor changed to be more friendly rather than aggressive.

"You do not actually have a toll to charge?" Velnir's tone turned more aggressive than inquisitive. He had waited long enough and had been burdened with many challenges along the way. "I carry with me some gold. Would you like that?" he asked rather impatiently.

"Gold? I have no use for gold." It turned its gaze to one of the elves and licked its lips.

Velnir looked at the elf too, and noticed it was that foolish one, Ardan. He considered it for a moment but decided, as foolish as he is, he is still one of his companions and did not participate in the mutiny against him on the ship. That would bear enough merit to tell the troll, "No."

The troll's tone turned aggressive. "Fine then, I am afraid you have nothing to offer as a toll to the bridge troll, and you may not cross."

Velnir stood there, locking eyes with it. *"Many before them had simply fought the troll to gain access, yet it still lives. Perhaps they all lost, and we would have to take a chance,"* he thought.

He still had his sword sheathed and was combat-ready. He did not want to risk the lives of the other elves, so he motioned them to back up. The troll donned an aggressive expression, baring its black sharp teeth, which oozed some sort of smelly black slime.

"I have tasted elf flesh before, and I'll taste it again," it stated before starting toward Velnir.

The troll swiped at him, and Velnir lunged forward. He dropped to his knees, sliding in between its legs, without hesitation. He thrust his sword up into the troll's groin. The troll howled in pain, stumbling back.

He could not get his sword out and had to hastily retreat out of the way, though the troll's arms weren't long enough to reach under its groin. This amused Velnir, if only for a moment.

"Toss me your spear then shoot at the troll," said Velnir to one of his companions.

Velnir got into a combat position again and faced the troll. He placed his spear through the notch in his shield designed to hold it for precision strike and made his way around to the right of the troll, and it turned to face him.

The other elves began firing at it, making it angry, and it began flailing in a futile attempt to stop the arrows. Velnir took the opportunity to thrust his spear at the troll. This time it pierced its hand, and its green blood spilled.

Once again it howled in pain. Still flailing, it turned and made its way toward the other elves. Velnir acted quickly and ran toward it. He jumped through the air, landing on the troll's back. He then thrust his spear through its neck, and it went all the way through.

Eventually, the troll fell over to its side, and Velnir jumped off. It then disappeared in a poof of purple smoke. He was feeling quite accomplished with himself and turned his attention to his companions—who were all unconscious.

Velnir rushed up to one of them, and kneeled to get a better look. No harm was done to him, and he seemed as though he was simply sleeping soundly. Suddenly, all of the elves began to snore.

"How bizarre," thought Velnir.

One had managed to completely avoid this vile sorcery and of course, it was Ardan, who hit the trebor and plucked the myconid. This time, it was not of his doing.

"My lord, I do not know what happened. I do know that it was not my fault, though," said Ardan.

Velnir was wondering why the dead troll disappeared and why his companions were all asleep except for Ardan when he turned his attention to the door.

He got up and looked at Ardan. Without a word, the two approached the gate. There was a knocker that

Velnir grabbed. The moment he touched it, the door simply opened, revealing a magnificent maze of walls, at the center of which was Alzar's Tower. Discouragement came cloaked the two. The walls were not nearly as tall as Atlan's, but they would be difficult to scale. These types of structures weren't common in Tanimara, so experience was non-existent.

This frustrated Velnir. "ALZAAAAAAAAAR!" he yelled in a desperate attempt to get his attention, which, of course, yielded no result.

A loud squawk could be heard in the distance. Velnir knew that sound. He turned and saw that his griffins had returned. Velnir threw a scrying orb into the sky, and it darted toward the griffins. He would attempt to lure them to him.

It was a success, and they landed shortly afterward. Velnir and the other elf were elated. In total, most had returned. There were enough griffins for everyone, but some had to have two elves mounting them at a time. Relief came to Velnir. Every one of them had damage to their armor that the Nagrimarans gave them and were covered in blood. Velnir was glad to see his griffin again, however.

An idea came to him. "Why not simply fly over the maze and to the tower." He shared his idea with his fellow elf, who nodded in agreement. "You stay here with the other griffins, and I'll go meet with Alzar," he ordered.

Velnir mounted his griffin and took to the sky. It was not until he was a few hundred meters high that he realized the scope of the maze. It was designed to make sure no one reached the tower. It was moving in random directions.

"*How did Baefric, Darlana, and Dargarok all meet this wizard? Surely, they didn't have to endure such hardships along the way,*" he thought.

Chapter 9
Alzar

After what felt like too long of a flight, considering how close the tower was, Velnir finally came to the steps of the tower, which was very large indeed. Bigger than anything in Tanimara.

Velnir was quite impressed with the unique architecture. He dismounted and approached the door, which was no larger than a man. Before he knocked, he had a quick glance around, up and down. He didn't want to be unprepared for any surprises.

A balcony protruding from the left side of the tower very high up caught his attention. This was no ordinary balcony. It stuck out very far and was enormous. This wasn't for a griffin, hippogriff, nor a wyvern. It had to be much, much bigger, but Velnir couldn't think of what was so big it would need to land on that, or why it would in the first place.

"No matter," thought Velnir.

He proceeded to the door and knocked. The door was solid, and his knock barely made any noise. He was disappointed because he thought nobody would ever hear him. He tried to knock again, but there was still no answer.

He thought about mounting his griffin and flying up to the balcony. He started to make his way toward his griffin. Before taking to the sky, the door opened. Velnir stopped and observed.

It was not a man or a woman… or perhaps it was. He was unsure. She looked human, had long blue hair that was decorated with all kinds of chains and jewelry. Her eyes were azure, and from her head protruded two swept horns, which were also decorated with jewelry. She wore a strapless dress that covered her breasts but exposed her belly. It also covered her legs entirely.

"Alzar has been expecting you," she said in the sweet voice of a calm young woman.

Velnir had seen enough strange creatures. This one had no effect on him. He even found her attractive. Even more perplexing was what she said.

"Expecting me?" he said, surprised.

This made Velnir uncomfortable. He did, however, come all this way to meet the wizard that he had only heard rumors about. He wasn't about to stop now that he was so close. She graciously invited him in to meet with Alzar.

Velnir dismounted and she held out her arm for him to take. He did so and they locked arms. This was customary in Tanimara and he appreciated that he was being treated like a noble.

Once inside, Velnir was truly amazed.

From the outside, the tower was intimidating and rather bland.

From the inside, few words could describe it.

The most intriguing thing he noticed right away was what had to be the ceiling. There didn't appear to be one, but there was no sky either. There were stars, and just a moment ago, he was outside and noticed that it was still midday.

The stars moved and a massive round object appeared. It had rings around it. Velnir had no idea what it was but was fascinated by it, nonetheless.

The entire inside walls of the tower were lined with what looked like classrooms and what had to be millions of books. Many of them simply flapped their covers and flew around the inside of the tower. A broom was operating without an operator. Lanterns were floating around, keeping the entire inside of the tower illuminated. He even saw scrying orbs, which were very common in Tanimara.

Before him was a grand staircase. She directed him up the staircase, but instead of walking, she simply levitated and he did as well. Velnir had never experienced such a sensation before. This method seemed to have saved them a lot of time, for they reached the floor they intended to reach in little time.

Velnir noticed they were on the same floor as the large-scale balcony that he observed from the outside. It led into a hall big enough for anything to come in, but the exit was no larger than a doorway designed for a man. The hostess led him to a door and asked him to wait there. She then approached it and it simply opened.

She descended to the ground and stopped levitating. A man was looking through a majestically large telescope, the likes of which Velnir had never seen. He noticed that this room was ornamented with several of those gigantic round objects he saw on the ceiling of the place. Some with rings, and some not. They all seemed to be moving around a centrally located bright round object, Velnir deduced to be the sun.

By now, he understood the round objects must be worlds that he had been taught about during his time in the academy. He had never imagined them to look like this.

The man pulled away from the telescope and greeted the hostess. He wore a brownish-gray robe, several scrolls tied to his waist section next to what appeared to be his spellbook, and a few potions. He was old and frail looking and had a long white beard. The hat he wore had an enormous round brim and was pointed. Of course, this hat was disproportionately larger than the man who wore it.

Velnir recognized the man to be Alzar as he fit the description that everyone told him. The man began conversing with the hostess. He looked at Velnir and nodded at her. He stood there while she came to Velnir.

"The master is ready to see you, Lord Velnir Melfarin of Atlantin, Tanimara," she said while offering a smile.

Velnir simply nodded and took it upon himself to enter without her. He walked right up to Alzar, who was waiting for him. As Velnir got closer, he noticed the man looked very, very old but moved like he was young. He eyed Velnir up and down as he stood there holding his staff.

Once Velnir was within speaking range, where he did not have to yell, he began by stating, "I came across the great sea from Tanimara, as you know. I executed half my crew for mutiny. I was shipwrecked by a Kraken, attacked by beast men, captured by Darlana, almost killed by a tree trebor, attacked by orcs again, and nearly lost the rest of my companions because of your troll at the gate of this celestial forsaken place. I know you have everything to do with what happened to me, wizard. If you knew I was coming to you, why do this to me? Why not use your power to kill me if you did not want to see me?"

Velnir was visibly upset but not aggressive. He genuinely wanted to know why all this happened to him.

The wizard simply looked at him and pursed his lips.

"First of all, welcome to the Tower of Alzar and to the Academy of Higher Arts. You came to me because you think I can help you. Your ship was mistaken for an orc ship by the kraken, which, against its better judgment, helped you get to the shores of the Forlorn Forest. You married Darlana." He chuckled before continuing. "You negotiated a friendship with the forest lords that will last you a lifetime. You befriended one of the only colonies of myconids on the planet, and you defeated the bridge troll. All of which you felt was worth it to get here…to me." He stared at Velnir with conviction.

Velnir was perplexed by the detailed accuracy of Alzar's account of his travels. It seemed he was watching the entire time. Velnir tried to keep his composure and not seem uncomfortable.

"This is all true," admitted Velnir. He wanted to get to the business at hand. "Tanimara was attacked by a massive horde of orcs hailing from the sundered lands of Araba. I wish to sail an army there and destroy them."

"Your father was killed. Skroatug is a formidable foe, Velnir. He nearly defeated you in your own city, and he would have, had Baefric and Meric not shown up. Even though he didn't destroy Atlan, he still completed his objective and retrieved what his master desired."

Velnir was confused for a moment but remembered the mention of the Scepter of Canar.

"Again, this is true, Alzar. I do not believe I can invade the sundered lands and lead a successful campaign without some sort of help," Velnir said, almost as if it were a plea.

"Darlana has committed her forces to your cause, has she not?" Alzar asked, already knowing the answer.

Velnir simply nodded.

"And Oakenleaf has committed the forest lords?"

Again, Velnir nodded.

"You have almost one hundred thousand soldiers waiting for you in Atlantin against the wishes of the high magistrate of Tanimara. So many are willing to follow you, and yet you doubt." Alzar donned a pleased expression.

This bothered Velnir.

"You are right to doubt, Velnir. You are wise enough to know when too much is too much, and yes, going up against the warchief of the sundered lands horde in his territory will only yield you and Nagrimar utter defeat. Darlana and Oakenleaf are no strangers to orcish incursions, as you witnessed in the land of the forest lords."

"I have come here to seek your aid, wizard. What must I do to earn your assistance?" asked Velnir.

Alzar looked at him and shook his head. "This is a fool's errand, Velnir. You do not have enough support to invade the sundered lands and should spare the people of Tanimara and Nagrimara their lives as surely as the day is long. They will all die. I wonder if I can even contend with orcs of that magnitude and their vile master myself. Necrosith is the one you should slay. He was my prisoner for thousands of years until his escape. I will not make that mistake twice."

"It was the orcs that attacked Tanimara. It is the orcs that shall have retribution," said Velnir.

"I am going after Necrosith in due time, Velnir. He is the reason the orcs even attacked Tanimara. The scepter of Canar is one of three. I have the other two here, locked away. It is my tower that he shall attack next. If he has all three scepters, he could create another sundering, or worse.

"If you help us, Alzar, they won't make it to this tower. We will kill them all… together," said Velnir.

"Again, save yourself the trouble, elf, and spare the lives of your kin. Go back to Tanimara and make amends with the magistrate. The celestials know that you stand little chance of retaining your titles and land if you go forward with this," said Alzar.

Velnir was not interested in giving up. He was beginning to grow impatient. "I would be hailed a hero of Tanimara if I defeat the orcs in their own land. I will bring retribution to them for what they have done to my people. They must suffer for the insult against Tanimara and for the lives they stole."

Alzar looked at Velnir and shook his head. "Even if I were to help you with the orcs, Necrosith is the true enemy. I cannot do this, Velnir. I must go after the dragon."

Velnir stood there and said nothing. He did not understand. This wizard had all these powerful trinkets and weapons according to Dargarok. It was then that an idea came to Velnir. "Perhaps I could borrow an enchanted weapon to use against them… Or a trinket. You would not need to be there at all and could take on the dragon. I could use them to get revenge for my people."

Alzar looked at Velnir inquisitively. "Absolutely not. The weapons… the trinkets I have created should never fall into the hands of a mortal. They are only a means to an end. I use them to maintain balance on Abrion, and surely, if I were to recklessly allow you to have anything I have created, it would disrupt that balance I work tirelessly to maintain."

Velnir began to speak when he was interrupted by Alzar. "You may make yourself comfortable and stay in the tower tonight. Tomorrow, you will make your way back home."

Velnir began to protest.

"I have spoken, Velnir." He then looked to the hostess. "Ismi, please take him to the room we prepared for him."

"Very well, master." She then walked over to Velnir, placed her arm around his, and led him out of the room. They were walking silently down the hall of this majestic place. Velnir was upset that he came all this way for nothing. The pair passed a room that two men were carefully bringing a sword into. Velnir stopped to watch, and Ismi stopped with him. The two placed the sword upright on a pedestal and carefully backed away.

"What is that?" inquired Velnir.

"That is Illuminar," said Ismi. "One of many weapons in Alzar's arsenal." She began to give him a history lesson, but he was barely paying attention.

"The sword looked elvish and mighty," he thought.

"It was enchanted to hurl a beam of concentrated fire or conjure a giant wave of fire," she said.

The blade looked white-hot and silver, and it had a red glow on its edge. The hilt was adorned with gold and rubies. Velnir could feel the raw power of the weapon. It was as if it was calling to him.

"If you point it at a target and use your willpower, it will hurl a concentrated beam of fire. If you plunge it into the ground, it will unleash a massive wave of fire," she said.

He knew in his heart that it would be very useful in his campaign.

Ismi stopped talking and nudged Velnir. "Are you all right?" she asked.

Velnir looked at her wide-eyed and confused. "Hmm? Oh, yes I am fine. My apologies. Please proceed," he said.

Ismi did not speak on the sword anymore. She brought Velnir to the room he was staying in and left. Velnir's thoughts shifted to the sword. "Illuminar," he thought.

He sat down on the bed and began to think about what it would take to convince Alzar to let him have it. His mind was blank. Alzar seemed to have made up his mind.

Velnir noticed a stack of vellums and some already prepared enchanting materials. He got up and went to the table they were on and began to sift through them.

He wondered what he could do with them and another idea manifested in his head. He looked at his sword in its sheath. He took it out, placed it on the table, and began going through the materials to see if they were the right ones, and sure enough, they were.

Excitement filled his heart as he jumped and said "yes" aloud. He then realized it was too loud and got quiet, hoping nobody had heard.

After some time had passed, he got to work. He determined that he had just enough materials to make two enchanted vellums of transmogrification.

After a few hours, they were complete, and Velnir was proud of himself. He took a moment to look upon his fine work. He was careful to wrap one vellum around his sword and the other in a cloth. He then cracked open the door ever so slightly and peered into the hall. He stuck his head out and got a good look around, determining there was no one there. He quietly left his room, carefully shut his door, and made his way toward the direction that Illuminar was.

Not a moment sooner, he heard voices around the corner. Velnir quickly hid behind a pillar, praying he would go unnoticed. One man and one woman were walking together and distractedly attracted to each other. It was anyone's guess what they were sneaking off to do. Velnir went completely unnoticed. He sighed in relief. Once the coast was clear, he continued until he heard some footsteps and saw light, which was clearly from a torch. Velnir looked around for a place to hide and could not find one. The steps were getting closer and he was about to be discovered. He looked up and saw that there was just enough space in between a support beam and the archway.

Quietly, he jumped up and, with elf-like precision and stealth, successfully clung to the ceiling. A moment later, a man who was clearly patrolling came around the corner and did not detect Velnir. He was looking at every door. Velnir was glad that he closed his.

The man took an annoyingly long time to get moving, and Velnir was beginning to lose strength. A bead of sweat rolled down his brow and landed on the ground. The man didn't hear it, and he finally got moving.

"Phew," thought Velnir.

Once the man was gone, he quietly got down and continued on his way. He was so impressed by the look of the tower on the inside that he wondered how one wizard could build all of this. The sheer number of books, the lanterns, the ceilings and staircases. It was a sight to behold indeed, but he had other matters to tend to. Now, he was at the gate that barred his entrance into the room that held Illuminar.

"Celestials damn it," he said as he noticed there was a lock. Velnir did not want to break the lock as it would cause alarm, and he didn't know which guard had the key. He grabbed it in frustration and it simply unhatched. Upon further inspection,

Velnir noticed that the guard forgot to latch the lock. Fortune was on his side tonight.

Velnir quietly took the lock off the hinge and let himself in. He took a look around but saw no traps or alarms. He was suspicious, though.

"Why would a wizard of Alzar's stature keep something so powerful unguarded?" he thought.

Velnir pulled out his sword wrapped in a transmogrification enchanted vellum and placed it next to the pedestal then carefully grabbed Illuminar, which was levitating over the pedestal. He quickly wrapped it in the other vellum and crossed the two swords. In his excitement, he struggled to remember the right words and was beginning to get nervous as it was taking too long. He still wasn't sure what the right words were, and suddenly, he heard two people walking in the hall. Velnir had a choice to make and said what he thought would work.

The vellums began to glow, and a moment later, the swords swapped appearances. Velnir could not believe it. Excitement overwhelmed him and he nearly dropped the sword. The two were approaching fast and he had to act. Quickly, he placed his sword where the real Illuminar was. It was impressive to him just how convincing the enchantment was for a moment, and then he quietly went to hide in the corner.

The two men seemed to have stopped, and began conversing with each other. Velnir was getting nervous and realized he still had the padlock. Wide-eyed and terrified, he had to think of something fast. It would appear he had no choice. Velnir had to put the lock back on the gate or he would be discovered.

Velnir took a deep breath, and made his way to the exit. He could not see anything outside but knew the two men were not far. Chances are, they could see the gate open if he were to open it. It might even creek which would surely alert them. He had no choice.

Carefully, Velnir opened the gate, quickly put the padlock on it, and closed it, but closed it a bit too hard, and the sound alerted the two men.

"What was that?" asked one of them.

There was silence for a moment.

"Nothing of consequence. Anyway, as I was saying…"

Now the men were moving past the gate. Velnir realized he did not secure the lock. He could not do it anyway or he would not be able to escape.

The men walked by and appeared not to notice the gate at all. Velnir waited for them to take off and quietly made his escape back to his room.

When he got there, he knew it wouldn't be long before the blade would reveal itself to be a fraud. His enchanting was still at novice level and the quality was lacking. He placed the sword next to his armor and lay in bed.

He began to think of his companions and hoped that they were ok. Ardan's ability to take care of them seemed questionable but Velnir had faith he would pull through. They would be elated to see the sword though. The next morning, Velnir got up and was eager to leave. He put his armor on and sheathed Illuminar which still had the appearance of his sword. He opened the door, and Ismi was already standing there. Velnir was startled.

"Good morning, Lord Velnir Melfarin. The master has asked me to escort you to your companions and then back to Tanimara. For your safety of course."

He did not protest. "All right, let's go on then."

"This way, please." She motioned for him to follow her and he did.

Together, they walked around the tower. He had no idea where they were going. This place was now ever more confusing than before. Staircases were upside down, sideways, and going every which way, and people were still using them. He wondered how.

The pair passed a couple of others in the tower. Velnir wondered why the orc's skin turned blue, but the skin of these humans had not.

As the pair walked by the two, Velnir could overhear the large one say to the small one, "I was in Nemis the other day and I was feeling constipated. I saw a traveling merchant and approached him. He said he had something that would cure my issue, and make my poop sing. Naturally, I was interested. I purchased a vial and drank it, and when it came time to pass, I did so with ease and right when I got up, my plunkies started singing. I was proud of him."

"Singing plunkies? I must see this with my own eyes," said the little one.

"I got more vials. I bought one for you so you don't have to... you know."

The little one was excited. "Ooh, I too shall have singing plun..." The two noticed Velnir and Ismi walking by and jumped at the opportunity to introduce themselves, unaware or uncaring that they had just heard their conversation.

"I am Rubus," said the big one. "I am Lemmi," said the little one.

Rubus was a large man. Significantly taller than any human Velnir had seen and certainly taller than him. The giant was kind of chubby and had a white beard, a round nose, rosy cheeks, and a jolly attitude.

He wore a short, pointed hat, a rucksack, a staff, and a brown wizard's robe. Lemmi was a halfling and was neither a dwarf nor a man. He had a long white beard and curly mustache and wore a very tall hat that something was living in. It was so large that he had to wrap it just to keep it from folding over or perhaps it was to contain whatever he had living in it.

Velnir smiled and nodded. "I am Velnir."

Ismi kept moving, and Velnir was left behind, so he quickly said goodbye and caught up to her. The two continued their crass conversation.

"Those two are interesting. Who are they?" he asked.

"They are Alzar's half-brothers. Also, stewards of Abrion. Those two primarily travel around the world on behalf of the school and offer younglings gifted in the arcane scholarships to attend here and or help Alzar with his wizarding."

"I see… even orcs?"

"Yes, the younglings are naturally gifted by the arcane lines and are not like the rest of their people. They know what they are, and while some do refuse to come here, most do not. We have our own culture here in the Tower of Alzar."

Velnir did not see any elves. He noticed that the other people in the tower were looking at him strangely as well.

"Why are there no elves here?" he asked.

"Halfbreeds have attended in the past, but elves of Tanimara go to the Tanimaran Academy of higher arts. Long ago, Alzar offered to educate elves, but…" she looked at him, "they refused his offer."

Velnir wondered why the elves would refuse. The magic here was much different, and in most cases, better than the magic taught in Tanimara. *"I will absolutely send our young ones here when all this is over,"* he thought.

There had to be millions of volumes of books from top to bottom. It was one giant library with several rooms that served different purposes. Velnir was impressed. The libraries in Tanimara could not even boast such a collection.

"How did he acquire all these books?" he asked.

"Alzar, like everyone, cannot remember everything."

"Did he write all of these?

"Rubus, Lemmi, and Alzar wrote them. These books are a chronicle of Abrion's history, detailed notes of arcane lines left here by the celestials and one of which, the Tower of Alzar was built on, magical spells, enchantments and what have you. It is all a collection of everything the wizards have discovered over the time they have been on Abrion! They live the lives of mortals, and with that comes some less desirable mortal traits, including but not limited to forgetfulness." Ismi chuckled.

"This must have taken them…" Velnir began saying before Ismi interrupted him.

"Roughly fourteen thousand years."

Velnir was bewildered. "Good to know."

"You are welcome to explore the library any time, Velnir. Alzar does not restrict visitors despite what the troll said.

Rubus and Lemmi put that troll there as a joke. Most visitors and students teleport in any way. Nobody has gone through the maze in hundreds of years."

Velnir felt foolish after hearing this. He did not know how to teleport.

"Where are we going?" Velnir finally chimed up.

"We are going to the perch on the balcony." Ismi's demeanor was that of one who did not care. She seemed to be content with everything around her.

"Perhaps dragons do not have the same emotions or facial expression even in their visage form as elves or men do," Velnir thought.

They had finally made their way to the floor of the tower that Velnir recognized as the one he first saw Alzar on. "Why could we not be teleported?" he asked.

"The type of magic used to teleport is very taxing. Using magic can exhaust the user to death if they are not careful. You really should attend Alzar's academy, Velnir," she said while smiling.

They made their way through the hall and through the door large enough to accommodate one of Alzar's or Ismi's heights. Velnir did have to hunch over a bit but it wasn't a problem. The hall they walked into was massive. The pillars that held the dome up were very tall and spread far apart. To the front of them was a large open platform that Velnir recognized as the balcony.

Chapter 10
Homeward Bound

Suddenly, and without warning, Ismi began to morph. A blue mist surrounded her and grew exponentially within a matter of seconds. Once she reached full size, her wings sprouted outward and swept the blue mist away.

She turned her reptilian gaze toward Velnir. Her teeth were sharp-looking, and she had many of them. Her neck was long and scaly. Her snout had a horn at the end of it. Her jaw, cheeks, and the top of her head also had sharp, jagged horns protruding from them.

The horns on her head were swept and seemed to be a larger version of the ones she has in her visage form. Her body was enormous and very long. Her wings were attached to her arms, and her hind legs were thick and large, as if divinely designed for leaping into the air. Her tail was very long and was spiked at the end.

"Dragons were well equipped to defend themselves if they needed to. It was no wonder they strayed from their charge and decided to go their own way. Who could hold them accountable?" Velnir thought as he was climbing up her side and onto her back.

"Ismi, my companions remain at the tower gate with our griffins."

Without a word, Ismi began to make her way to the balcony. She leapt off and fell straight down. When she gained enough momentum, she threw out her wings and glided over the maze. She made her way to the area where Velnir's companions and griffins were. The elves and griffins below were startled when Ismi appeared above them. She buffeted a bit, slowing her descent before she landed. Velnir poked his head around the side of Ismi's and called out to the elves.

"Round up the griffins. She is going to escort us to Atlan," he said with a grin. Flying was a lot of fun.

"You have a dragon?" Garlan asked in complete bewilderment.

"I am not his dragon. I am a friend," said Ismi before winking her reptilian eye at Velnir.

The elves gathered up the rest of the griffins, which took to the air. Once the last of them took off, Ismi leapt up and threw out her wings, and brought them down hard to give herself lift. She did this several times until she could fall again and gain momentum.

"It looked surprisingly easy for Ismi to take off from just about anywhere she wanted," thought Velnir.

By now, they were high above the ground. Much higher than they normally would fly. The griffins seemed to be okay at this altitude and had no trouble keeping up with Ismi, who was clearly going much slower than she had to.

"You know where Atlan is?" Velnir asked, unsure of where they even were.

"I have been there many times, young elf," replied Ismi.

"In three hundred years, I have only seen dragons soar high above Tanimara. Never have I ever spoken to, or been this close to, let alone rode one," he said.

Ismi chuckled, which sounded strange coming from something so big. "We are all around, Velnir. We use our visage form when mingling with mortals. It would be awfully inconvenient and cumbersome to have large dragons roaming your streets, would it not?"

"You mean, you could be there, and we would not even know it?" he asked.

"Yes," she replied simply.

Velnir wondered how many times his family had been visited by dragons in the past. He could not recall ever seeing a strange elf, and he hardly ever saw humans or dwarves. He felt compelled to ask. "Have you ever been to my court?"

"Not that I recall?" she replied. "The affairs of elves are of no interest to me."

He thought that was interesting since, at least to him, elves were the most influential of mortal races. Albeit, over the last few hundred years, they have cut themselves off from the rest of the world. "Why do you help the wizards then?"

"They are no ordinary denizens of Abrion," she replied.

Velnir was taken aback by her reply. *No ordinary denizens of Abrion,* he thought. "What does that mean?" he asked.

"Stay a while and listen while I tell you." She chuckled.

It was obvious that Velnir had nowhere else to go as he was lying upon her back. Her attempt at humor amused him.

"Long ago, the cosmos was only home to the light and the dark. From the dark manifested a hideous amalgamation of nefarious intent. They called it Penumbra. Penumbra began to devour the light, and it was slowly fading. The light manifested the first of the celestials: Thalamon. Thalamon's charge was to defeat Penumbra, and he had trouble, so he created the celestials.

Together, they defeated the darkness by pushing it to the edge of the cosmos. Ata is one of those celestials. She came to Abrion and entered into a romantic relationship with a human after the sundering. Together, they had Alzar. She did the same thing with Rubus and Lemmi's fathers," she said with what he thought was a tone of satisfaction and pride.

Velnir could hardly believe what he was hearing."

A celestial walking among mortals when clearly there are more worlds out there than just Abrion?" he said.

"Oh, yes! In her case, Abrion must always have stewards, and since Dragons failed, she felt it was her duty. Her children naturally inherited immortality and some of her power. They are unique to my knowledge."

Alzar seemed to possess great arcane knowledge and power. The likes of which Velnir had never seen or heard of before. It made sense, he thought.

Velnir's attention turned toward the dragon. "What was the dragon's charge?" he asked.

"We were created to maintain balance on Abrion. Our charge was simple, but one of our kind decided to go his own way," she sighed, "Eventually, he lured most of us into a trap and killed many dragons. Those of us who got away knew we could not contend with him alone. He had power beyond ours that he obtained through unspeakable means. We instead established ourselves in the only place we knew he would not return to."

"Where is that?" asked Velnir.

"The Wyrm isles or Dragon Isles in your tongue," she replied.

"Why did the rest of you abandon your charge?" he asked.

"There weren't enough of us to maintain it. It wasn't until the wizards came that we ventured out seeking allies to contend with Necrosith."

"Necrosith?" Velnir thought. "This must be the dragon that she was referring to as the one that went his own way." Velnir was silent for a few moments, lost in thought. "I wonder if this dragon could have anything to do with the one Dargarok was referring to," he thought.

"I've heard of a dragon commanding the orcs of the sundered lands. Could that be Necrosith?" he asked.

Ismi was silent for a moment as well. Velnir could tell that this conversation was going in an uncomfortable direction for her, and he did not want to upset her.

"Never mind," he said in a friendly voice.

She remained silent for a moment longer before saying, "Yes, we believe Necrosith is behind the creation of the orcs many thousands of years ago and commands them now."

"But you do not know for certain?" he asked.

"No, sixty years after the sundering, Alzar found and imprisoned Necrosith. Since then, he has escaped, and we can be certain it is he who commands the orcs."

Ismi was interrupted by a terrible scream that could be heard in the distance. It was followed by several more. Garlan, leading Velnir's companions on their griffins, motioned to Velnir that something was coming.

"What is it?" Velnir asked Ismi.

"Manticore!" she replied bitterly. "Hold on!"

She took a hard right and dove through the clouds. The manticores were gaining. Velnir looked back and saw several of them. When they believed they were close enough, they breathed a hot purplish orange fire, but Ismi was faster.

Despite her much larger size than a manticore, she easily evaded the beasts. His companions and their griffins were not so lucky. They were forced to contend with the manticore.

"NOOOOOOO!" Velnir cried as the manticore attacked the griffins, and their riders fell to their deaths. "We must help them."

Ismi turned around and gained altitude. She dove on the manticore who were chasing Velnir's companions. She grabbed one, tore it to shreds, then came back around. She bit down on one and crushed it. Velnir's companions began to cheer. Ismi was making quick work of them until two of them landed on Ismi, right behind Velnir. She barrel rolled and tried to shake them off. They dug their claws in.

Velnir thought of using the sword but didn't want to reveal that he had taken Illuminar. Luckily for him, Ismi eventually shook them off. The rest of the manticore retreated, and Velnir could see his companions sighing in relief. Tanimarans have rarely contended with such beasts.

Ismi was gaining altitude again, but it looked like she was tiring.

"Ismi, if you feel like you need to rest, we can land," said Velnir with clear concern in his voice.

"No," she said, "they will be back. We must keep going."

"What are manticore?" Velnir asked.

"Creations of Necrosith. They were meant to hatch into whelps. Instead, Necrosith corrupted them, and they hatched into those things we now call manticore."

Velnir looked at Illuminar. The sword made him feel confident and powerful. He would not let them get to Ismi, even if it meant exposing that he took the sword. She was looking exhausted. She had been flying for hours and they hadn't even reached the great sea yet.

"Surely there must be a cave or someplace for us to hide. At least you in your visage form. My companions and I will protect you," he promised.

Without responding, she turned downward and descended as did his companions. Once below the clouds, she started looking for a place to land and a cave to hide in.

Shortly after, she spotted a cave. "Over there," she said.

She landed softly in a clearing near the cave, and his companions began landing as well. She immediately morphed into her visage form. This surprised Garlan and the others. She looked up and scanned the sky, as did Velnir.

They could see nothing. They hurried into the cave. Ismi had a look around and found a spot where she could rest.

Velnir went to Garlan and said, "Do we have anything to cover her with? She has only a dress on."

Garlan got to work quickly, looking for something he could throw over her. He began to round up the cloaks of a few of the other companions. "This should suffice, my lord. It is all we have," said Garlan.

Velnir took the cloaks and draped them over her as she lay down.

"Thank you," she said quietly.

"Rest, Ismi, we will keep watch," he replied. He made his way to the cave entrance and took a seat. He kept his eye on the sky. Much to his disappointment though, a storm had begun to brew. He could not see the sky, but at least those manticore could not see him either, he thought.

Night fell, and the storm had subsided. Ismi was sound asleep. Velnir and his companions were getting tired. He tried to keep himself awake but failed. Soon, they were asleep too.

He dreamed of Darlana. She was on the balcony as he and his companions took to the sky. Her lovely locks waved in the wind as she waved goodbye to her newlywed husband.

In his dream, she gave birth to a daughter. One he called Paeris. The babe was a girl and she played with both her mother and father. Darlana lifted her and donned the perfect smile. She spun her around several times before setting her down to tickle her. Paeris laughed and giggled. Velnir's heart swelled. Darlana turned her attention toward him. Her mood changed. She scowled at him.

"I know you will betray me, Velnir," she said. He was shocked by her words. Paeris joined in. "You will betray both of us."

Velnir did not know what to say. He just looked at them. He knew in his heart that he would hurt Darlana. He really had no desire to hurt her. His heart began to ache. Darlana and Paeris stood up and began to hiss and growl at him. He backed off and asked them to stop. They pressed on and it got louder.

Suddenly, Velnir awoke. His companions were facing off two manticore meters away from them. He looked over at Ismi, who was still asleep. Velnir and the others began to spread out. He hoped they would feel threatened enough and just take off. They opened their mouths and started to inhale.

Before they could get their fire breath out, Ardan leapt forward and plunged his sword through the head of one of the manticores, interrupting them. The sound the manticore made was like a hideous broken shriek. It threw its head back and knocked Ardan on his backside. Velnir grabbed his sword and got ready to fight.

Ismi had awakened by this time and got their attention. The cave was too small for her to morph into her dragon form. She looked frightened.

Velnir flanked the manticore and plunged his sword into the hind of the closest one. The others began to attack them as well. It appeared that the cave was too small for the manticore to be effective. They hacked, slashed, and stabbed them. Their innards, chunks of flesh, and bone were strewn everywhere.

Velnir could hardly believe how easily they dispatched those manticores. Ismi rushed over to them.

"Are you okay?" she asked. "Are you hurt?"

"I am well," said Velnir. The others seemed okay, too.

Ismi motioned for all of them to go outside. She grabbed Velnir and took him with her. She was surprisingly strong in her visage form.

He did not struggle and followed her of his own volition. She morphed back into a dragon, and he wasted no time mounting her. She leapt up and took to the sky once more, along with everyone else and their griffins. They were racing for altitude. Once she got comfortable and could maintain a good, steady glide, she seemed to calm down.

"Thank you. You all saved my life," she said with genuine gratitude.

"I told you we would look out for you, Ismi. I keep my word," he said, instantly thinking of Darlana.

Guilt once again overcame him.

"I'd like to see them come at me now!" Ismi said in an angry tone. "If they can catch up to me, they will be in for the fight of their lives."

Not long after she made that statement, the shrieks were heard again. The manticore had indeed returned. It was as if Ismi was expecting this. She immediately darted toward them faster than she had previously gone. We were closing in fast.

Suddenly, from Ismi's mouth came a burst of hot fire that streamed several meters ahead of her. It instantly ignited one of the manticores, sending it into shock. It fell from the sky flailing, attempting to put the fire out, to no avail.

Again, Ismi darted around, but this time, she grabbed one with her hind legs and tore it apart. Its innards fell free before she let it go. She again flew up and came to a stop in midair, threw out her wings, and swiveled around to the other manticore chasing her. She buffeted them and maintained her altitude.

Immediately after disorienting them with the buffet, she let out a raging breath that was widespread. It ignited all the manticore and sent them shrieking and howling down toward the ground. This was not enough, though. Ismi gave chase. She caught one in her jaws and bit down, shredding it to pieces.

Velnir was holding on for dear life. There was no way he could grab his sword and help without severely compromising his safety. She went for another one, and this time, she hit it with her wing, sending it to the ground.

It splattered on impact. She turned and hit the last one, blasting it straight into the cliffside. The crash finished it off. Its charred, bloody body peeled off the cliffside, and fell to the rocks below.

"Hrmph," said Ismi. "That'll teach them to mess with dragons. Mess around and find out."

The griffins couldn't fly that fast; she had just finished the manticore off when they arrived. They began to cheer.

Ismi was growing on him. She regained altitude and continued on. Velnir had thought to ask her to pay a visit to Darlana but decided it was against his better judgment. Suddenly, Ismi shuddered. She smiled and kept going.

"What is it, Ismi?" asked Velnir.

"I am with hatchlings, and soon, the eggs will come. I felt them drop into position," she said, smiling.

Velnir was surprised to hear she was pregnant. He didn't know what to say. How do you congratulate a dragon? *"By simply saying congratulations, of course?"* thought Velnir. "Congratulations, Ismi," he said awkwardly.

"Oh, thank you. It is a rare spectacle for a mortal to see a dragon give birth."

Velnir's ears sloped back in embarrassment. He was unaware she planned to have him watch. That did not appeal to Velnir.

"I need to land for a moment. That fight with the manticore was taxing, and I need to rest," said Ismi. She then landed to rest for a moment, along with everyone else. Velnir dismounted. The others did, too, and began to make camp. Ismi had morphed into her visage form again. Velnir went behind some bushes to relieve himself when he heard a commotion. He turned to see what he thought were flowers.

"Those are terrilions," said Ismi, startling Velnir.

He was just finishing up. Ismi did not seem to mind.

"I have never seen one before. Are they speaking?" he asked.

"Yes, they are sentient. They only grow in this part of Abrion, and their fruit is a delicacy to humans. They're not manageable through farming, so Alzar tried to make them manageable with a spell, but it failed."

"So, that made them sentient?" asked Velnir.

"Yes."

The terrilions were cheering and praising toward the sky. Velnir looked up and saw a bird circling. It then dove and casually grabbed one of the terrilions and carried it off. The other terrilion seemed to be pleased with this.

Before he could even ask, Ismi began to tell him, "Alzar told them that birds were spirits of the sky and that they choose a worthy one to spread its seed. That is how those ones got all the way out here."

"How does it spread their seed?" asked Velnir.

"The birds devour them, digest their fruit, and then they defecate their seeds."

Ismi seemed not to mind, but this troubled Velnir to a degree.

"That seems cruel," he said.

"How would you feel if you were in their roots and found out the only way you could populate was by being torn to pieces, devoured, and passed in such a way?" she asked.

Velnir thought about that for a moment. "I see. Unhappy plants do not bear good fruit."

"Precisely, so deceiving them with a half-truth by telling them they are chosen to repopulate and not telling them how they bear good fruit."

"Still seems cruel," said Velnir.

"Mistakes were made. This much is certain. We had to make the best of a terrible situation. No one is happy about it, not counting the terrilions, of course."

The terrilions began to cheer with excitement as another bird came down and casually plucked one from the ground and carried it off. Velnir was uncomfortable and began to question many things.

The next morning, everyone was packed up and ready. They were all waiting on Ismi.

"I think I am good to go," she said.

Velnir mounted Ismi, and they took to the sky once more and made their journey across the great sea.

On the horizon was the coast of Tanimara. He could see the familiar mountains in the distance.

"Finally, I am home," he thought.

As they closed in, Velnir took in all the wonder of Atlantin. He appreciated seeing Atlantin and Atlan from the air like this. It was truly a sight to behold. The region he governed always seemed much larger than he thought it was, and he had been to every part of it.

They approached Atlan. It dawned on Velnir that his people did not know when he was coming back, let alone that he would be taking a dragon back home.

"Oh no," he thought.

"Ismi, watch out!" Just then, many massive bolt throwers from the guard towers aimed at Ismi.

"They do not know we're coming?" she scolded Velnir.

"Fly in between the spires, the bolt throwers cannot turn that far."

She obeyed and flew between the spires.

"Land in that courtyard down there," Velnir said, pointing to a clearing just large enough for Ismi to land. It was in front of his keep.

She landed a little more abruptly than the times before. Velnir dismounted and demanded that everyone hold their fire.

The army was fast approaching from every street. The mages came in on their griffins and surrounded Ismi.

"Stand down!" ordered Velnir.

Generals Arlen and Magris instantly recognized their lord and came running to him.

"My Lord Velnir," they both shouted. By now, the army was retreating, and the mages had taken off. Ismi felt safe enough to morph into her visage to the bewilderment of everyone present. Most of them had not seen a dragon ever do that. Ismi fell to the ground, clutching her belly.

"Ohhh, Velnir, they are coming," she cried.

General Arlen could not believe his eyes. "You got a dragon pregnant, Velnir," he chided.

"Of course not! And you would do well to never question me in such a way again, General," snapped Velnir.

Magris kept quiet. This was a side of Velnir neither of them had ever seen. Velnir went to Ismi.

"Where would be a good place for you to... well, you know."

"A large enough area for me to be in my natural form," she replied.

"I know just the place. The rooftop of the keep has grass up there. It is flat like your balcony at Alzar's Tower. That should be sufficient."

Without a word, she morphed back into her dragon form and immediately made her way up there. Velnir ran over to the stables to mount a griffin. He ordered Arlen and Magris to follow him. Together, the three took to the sky and flew to the top of the keep.

Ismi was squatting over a grassy nest she had created just moments before. The egg was coming. A true sight to behold, for few mortals had ever witnessed such a wonderful event.

Witnessing the birth of a dragon was rumored to bring about good fortune. One egg came out and landed on the grass, which absorbed its impact perfectly. She began to contract back to normal. She stood there for a moment before bringing her hind legs back up to position again.

Another egg was on its way out, and when it finally came, it too had landed in the grass, which absorbed the impact perfectly. Ismi breathed a sigh of relief and morphed back into her visage form.

She had a quick look around and stated, "This will be a nice place for them to rest."

Arlen and Magris were at a loss for words. What they just witnessed made Magris throw up. Arlen just stood there and listened to her. Velnir motioned him over as he walked to her.

"What do you mean, Ismi? You plan to keep them here?" he asked.

"They should not be moved much for several days, so I cannot take them over the great sea with me, Velnir. It will only be a few weeks. I am the consort of Rizim, the patriarch of my brood. I will ask that he come and get them. I must return to Alzar in the meantime. Do care for them for me, and I will reward you."

He was about to retort, but before he could, she morphed back into a dragon and took off. He cursed himself over and over. This could potentially be disastrous for his plans. He looked at the eggs. They were not very big. He could easily carry one on the back of a griffin. He was not going to let them put a hold on his plans. He completed his quest, and now was the time for revenge. He had an army and an armada ready to go, and his commanders were patiently waiting for him back at the port. The people gathered at the base of the keep. He was sure they had questions.

"Arlen, fetch my satchel. I will take the eggs with me and keep them warm. Meet me down there. I must address my people."

"Yes, my lord," Arlen replied.

Velnir mounted his griffin and flew down to the base of the keep.

While Velnir was addressing the people of what just happened, Arlen retrieved a satchel large enough to house two dragon eggs. He stuffed some blankets at the bottom, then wrapped them each in a blanket separately. He then placed another blanket over the top of them. These blankets were enchanted to remain warm. Once the bag was warm to the touch, he mounted his griffin and flew down to Velnir. "My lord, I have your eggs."

Velnir gently took the satchel from Arlen and felt it was warm to the touch. "Good work, General," he said.

Magris just showed up and landed next to Arlen.

"Good," exclaimed Velnir. "Now we can get this invasion going. We will fly to the port and meet my cousin and uncle there."

They took to the sky.

Chapter 11
Preparations Are Complete

Velnir, Arlen, and Magris arrived at the port town, where Baefric and Meric had been overseeing the construction of the ships Velnir needed to take his army across the great sea and into the Araban sundered lands. Meric was waiting for them as they arrived. His hand shielded the sun from his eyes as he watched them come in for a landing.

"Well, hello there, Cousin. I assume you have completed your quest?" Meric said cheerfully.

Arlen and Magris knew nothing about the quest and looked at each other questioningly.

"I have indeed, Meric, and with me, I bring back Illuminar." He pulled his sword from its sheath and showed it to his cousin. The enchantment had worn off by this time.

"It is a sword, Velnir?" He walked over to Velnir with a confused expression and attempted to grab the sword for further inspection.

"It was enchanted by the wizard, and I'm not completely aware of how it works, but I know how to use it. It is known as Illuminar." Velnir turned his attention from his cousin to his blade, "It will win us the war. I am certain of it."

"You went all that way to obtain a sword from a wizard, Velnir? A sword?" Meric said with disappointment in his voice. "You are a brilliant tactician and sword master, Velnir, but you will need a miracle if you wish to defeat the orcs in the sundered lands. A sword... haha." He laughed and walked away to speak with Baefric, who was just arriving to greet his nephew. It was clear Meric was disappointed in Velnir and was filling his uncle in on Velnir's quest. Baefric's expression was anything but disappointing. He looked elated.

"You obtained an enchanted weapon from the wizard, Velnir? How did you manage that?"

Meric was shaking his head.

"Velnir, you did it. Your father would be proud," he said joyfully. "Let's see it, come on now, show me!" he demanded excitedly.

Velnir obliged and held it up, but like his cousin before, Baefric went to take it from him for further inspection. "The magic that this sword has is unlike anything I have witnessed before." Baefric returned Illuminar to Velnir. "The wizard really came through. What does it do exactly, though?"

"If I point it at something, it will manifest a concentrated stream or beam of fire and hurl it toward whatever I am pointing it at. If I plunge it into the ground, a massive wave of fire is said to erupt from the blade and go outward."

"Do you know how to activate the magic?"

"I use willpower." Velnir wasn't sure if any of this was actually true. The more he spoke about it, the more foolish he began to feel. He never bothered testing it out.

"What did he ask in return?"

"I will give him the Scepter of Canar once we defeat the orcs." In truth, he had no intention of giving Alzar the scepter.

"You agreed to give him the Scepter of Canar in exchange for an enchanted sword? I will admit, Velnir, that I do not quite know what the Scepter is capable of, but I would think it is quite dangerous if the orcs came for it and quite valuable if it was stored unbeknownst to any of us under Atlan until recently."

"I was never told of it, and I am not sure if my father knew. I figure it is better to allow the wizard to have it so nothing is incentivized to attack Atlantin again for it. He claims that it is one of three and that he has the other two in his tower. He said that a weapon of that magnitude could do worse than the ancient sundering."

"What makes you think that the wizard has such good intentions with it then?"

"He claims to already have the other two, Uncle." Truly, Velnir was not sure that he could trust the wizard with such weapons.

Baefric looked at Velnir. "You are taking an enormous risk but if you think it was for the best, Velnir, then you have my support. I still think it would have been a good idea to learn what it was for?"

"We do not even currently have it. It is with the orcs, and there is no guarantee we will have it returned. If we were unaware of its existence before, why bother worrying about it now?"

"Simply because of what it is said to be capable of," said Baefric. "Velnir, to my knowledge, such enchantments don't get placed on weapons like the sword you carry just because one has a vendetta against his enemy. If everyone who went to the wizard for help against his enemy got an enchanted weapon as powerful as this, there would be many in existence. The magnitude of power your weapon now holds is going to be legendary. If the wizard was willing to give you this type of dangerous and powerful pyromantic weapon enchantment in the hopes of retrieving the Scepter of Canar. It clearly has some intriguing magic that, at the very least. is equally as powerful, but to say that it combined with the other three could be more devastating than the sundering. That makes it more powerful than any known weapon on Abrion."

"I suppose, Uncle. Still, this weapon will help us achieve victory."

"I do hope it was for the best," said Baefric.

Velnir looked at Baefric. "I needed something now. We are going to be severely outnumbered, and I needed to have a major advantage. When he told me about the scepter, I knew we could not contend. The orcs only have one scepter, though. Now we have evened the odds with Illuminar. Elvish might and this sword will win us this war. Surely you understand."

Now Velnir was feeling trapped in his lies. Of course the wizard didn't give him this sword willingly, but even if he did in exchange for something like the scepter, his uncle, who is old and wise, still thought it was a bad deal.

He only mentioned giving the scepter to Alzar because Alzar expressed a desire to retrieve it. Now, he was thinking it would be a bad idea to allow the wizard to have the third scepter. He neither trusted nor mistrusted him.

Only time would tell.

Baefric looked at Velnir and said, "I understand, and I have faith that you know what you are doing."

Velnir smiled and changed the subject. "I must catch you up on my adventures, Uncle." Velnir placed his arm around his uncle and began walking with him. "So where to start? Let's see, We set sail from here, got attacked by a kraken, which turned out to be helpful, oddly enough. Got attacked by beastmen using orc ships or ships similar to orc ships. Half my crew tried to kill me, so I fed most of them to the kraken. I threw one to the sharks."

Baefric furrowed his brow, but before he could speak, Velnir continued.

"We were eventually shipwrecked and escaped on the griffins, which reminds me, we need to reward Garlan for his quick wit. We might be otherwise dead had he not thought to do what he did. We got lost inland within the Forlorn Forest, unbeknownst to us at the time. We were captured by centaurs and taken to the city of Nagrimar, where their Queen, Darlana, threw us in prison."

"First mutineers, and now Darlana?" interrupted Baefric. "Raften's daughter? Did you tell her?"

"Tell her what, Uncle?" Velnir knew what he was asking but was trying to stall to come up with a lie.

"Did you tell her who he is now, where he is?" he said with a look of concern.

"I did, Uncle. I tell you, her hospitality was magnificent. She desires to come to Tanimara someday," Velnir said before Baefric stopped and looked at him.

"She was declared an apostate and exiled for a reason. To return would mean certain death, Velnir. She had intimate relations with a human as a princess of Tanimara. Her child, the half-breed, would have been entitled to elven land and titles. She broke one of the most sacred of laws by doing this, and she will never be allowed to return," he said. "How did you escape?"

Velnir swallowed hard and kept his mouth shut.

"I can only imagine what you had to do to get out of Nagrimar and return here. Anyway, go on," Baefric said.

"We left Nagrimar and the Forlorn Forest and flew to Nemis. There, we were attacked by a tree trebor, which turned out to be a misunderstanding. He was quite friendly and very talkative."

Baefric looked at Velnir with an odd expression.

"Together, we fought a war band of orcs and made our way to the forest that housed the Tower of Alzar. We met these little mushroom people called myconids. Apparently, they are extremely rare to find on Abrion. They were wonderful little creatures. We came across a toll troll at the bridge into Alzar's tower. It did not want a toll but wanted to fight instead, even after I offered it gold. From there, I met Ismi and Alzar.

"Who is Ismi?" Baefric asked.

"She was the dragon I flew in on," Velnir said nonchalantly.

"You flew into Atlan on the back of a dragon, Velnir?" he said with surprise.

"Yes, I did, Uncle, and it was an amazing ride despite the dangers."

"What, more dangers, Velnir?"

"I'll tell you in a moment. Let me finish, please." Baefric nodded and motioned for Velnir to continue. "Alzar and I made the deal. He gave me Illuminar, and Ismi flew me back. We were attacked by these beasts called manticores and they were defeated. However, not before they killed several of my companions and my griffins. I tell you, Uncle, Ismi utterly destroyed the manticore."

"Did you get a chance to use your sword?"

"I didn't *need* to. A full-sized dragon was more than sufficient, as Ismi demonstrated."

"Sounds like quite the adventure, Velnir. I am sorry you lost your companions. That had to be hard," said Baefric.

"It was, indeed, Uncle. They were brave and will not be forgotten. It pains me to know that only thirty-four came back. I feel guilt for bringing them along only to lose their lives."

"Unfortunately, that is usually how it goes. I cannot say that it went that way for me though, but remember, they went with you knowing full well what risks lie ahead."

"I guess I thought it wouldn't happen to me." He shrugged. "As I said, they will not be forgotten. Anyway, Ismi was pregnant and laid eggs on the roof of the palace in Atlan." Velnir pulled his satchel around. "I have the dragon eggs with me here, Uncle."

Baefric looked bewildered. "Oh my, dragon eggs you say? How many are in there?" he asked.

"Two. She left them with me. I didn't have time to stay here and wait for them to hatch. We have an invasion to commence before the magistrate decides to stop us."

"So, you are bringing them with us? I don't see how having two dragon eggs can help."

"I don't know how they're going to help, Uncle. I couldn't let her down, though. She's my friend. Also, that does beg the question. What to do with them when they hatch? They'll be too small to be effective, right?" Velnir was genuinely unsure.

"You will cross that bridge when we come to it, Velnir," said Baefric, seemingly not worried about it any longer.

"Uncle, there is something I need to take care of before we go. Could you look after the garrison for one more night and sufficiently reward Garlan for his heroism? I will be back in the morning," he asked.

"I will, Velnir. What is one more night?"

Velnir smiled and mounted his griffin, then took to the sky.

Chapter 12
The Armada

He flew back toward Atlan but changed direction toward the internment camp. A few hours later, he arrived. He walked up to the guards and demanded they open the gate. He found Dargarok and Gimit speaking to the other orcs. Velnir interrupted them and asked Dargarok to step outside for a moment. He obliged.

"Dargarok, I cannot believe I am saying this, but it is good to see you," Velnir said in a somewhat sarcastic tone.

Dargarok said nothing.

"I have completed a quest and spoke with the wizard you spoke of. You told me the truth, and it has gained me a great advantage in what is to come. For that, I will honor my word and set you and your people free to go wherever it is you would like to go.

Dargarok folded his arms and looked at Velnir. "We will be slaves no longer. I do not wish to take them back to the sundered lands. I do not wish to take them to that continent at all, and from what I understand, there is no place for us on Tanimara."

Velnir nodded.

"We would like to go east then. You can drop us off in the Mazon jungle. Our people will thrive there."

Velnir was perplexed. "The Mazon jungle is not tamed. It is a frontier of all kinds of dangers. No civilizations outside of trolls have ever been able to survive there. "Are you certain, Dargarok?"

"We have all chosen to go there. We will survive, and we will grow. Do not underestimate us," he said in a friendly tone.

"Very well, to the Mazon jungle with you and the rest of the prisoners. Your ships are waiting at the docks. I have arranged for you to be moved in the cover of night once we have left for the sundered lands. You will have more than enough provisions to get you to the Mazon jungle in the eastern continents. I do not know what orcs eat, so there is a variety."

Dargarok looked delighted. He hadn't expected such hospitality from his captures.

"We will be out of your hair soon, and good luck, Velnir. I hope you complete your objective. Where you are going is a harsh place, and I do not envy you."

Velnir smiled and turned to leave. He gave the guard a nod, who nodded back in understanding of what must be done. Velnir was going to keep his word. He genuinely wanted Dargarok to succeed, as he no longer saw him as his enemy. Velnir mounted his griffin and made his way back to the port. He had a few hours to fly.

In the meantime, the guards at the internment camps entered the camp once Velnir was out of sight.

"Dargarok, over here," said one of the guards. Dargarok came to him outside the gate.

"Yes, guard?" he said inquisitively.

Another guard was waiting behind the gate. He thrust a spear through Dargarok's neck, killing him silently and quickly. The lead guard then motioned for another to come in.

"I do hope this pleases the high magistrate," said the guard.

"You will be rewarded for informing us of Velnir's crimes by brokering a deal with this orc without consulting the magistrate first. In the meantime, say and do nothing. The magistrate is still deciding what measures to take," said the other elf.

"Indeed. What do you plan to do with the rest of the orcs?"

"The magistrate requires me to do what we should have already done to these orcs by now." He then raised his staff and conjured a flame. He grinned wickedly.

He was a pyromancer sent by the high magistrate from Tarvana. The guards locked the gate and gathered around the outside of the camp. The pyromancer began to cast firestorms inside of the camp. The orcs were heard screaming and panicking. The mage conjured more firestorms until nothing was left. The camp and its inhabitants were completely destroyed. All of this was unbeknownst to Velnir, who was now arriving back to Port Thalnor as the sun was coming up.

***

All the soldiers and supplies were loaded onto the ships. There were one thousand ships.

"This is the largest fleet that any lord in Tanimara has ever assembled, Velnir," said Meric.

"We will make history together, cousin!" exclaimed Velnir.

"No, you will make history!" exclaimed Meric with a humble and proud tone.

"I appreciate everything you have done for me, Cousin. I trust you will be comfortable in Atlan?"

"I will be spending all my time in the brothels while Uncle is handling the governance," he said with a cheeky smile.

"I would expect nothing less," said Velnir, followed by a mild chuckle. "Farewell."

They parted ways as Baefric and Meric returned to Atlan to keep his affairs in order. Velnir boarded the flagship with Ismi's eggs, Illuminar, and his griffin. The armada was broken up into ten fleets of one hundred ships and began to sail east toward Araba this time. All the ships were lined up in several rows.

The next day, they were far enough out that they could no longer see land in either direction. This was good; they were making good time. The wind was consistent, and the crew seemed to know what they were doing.

Velnir was content. The other ships all seemed to be in good order. Velnir had his griffin ready at all times in case he needed to travel from ship to ship. It was common for commanders or messengers to send messages this way.

What could be considered a fleet of scrying orbs was far ahead of them, scanning the horizon for potential threats. Velnir was all too aware of the dangers that lurked out here and was taking no chances now that he had some experience on the high seas.

"Sir, a message from General Magris," said the female ensign assigned to Magris' ship.

"Thank you, stay here. I may need you to return with a response." Velnir opened the scroll and read.

"Velnir, I am sailing the Vanguard now, some twenty ships ahead of you. One of the ships received damage to its hull and had to turn around. We are dispersing the soldiers to other ships at the moment. Be advised."

Velnir knew that this would present a logistical challenge. He appreciated that Magris knew what he expected and did the right thing. Velnir was glad that he did not lose any men that day. He sent the ensign back to his ship, mounted his griffin, and took to the sky.

Many mages atop griffins were patrolling the open seas. The mages, the griffins, and the scrying orbs provided the best protection he could imagine. He had a feeling in his gut that something would go wrong again. He looked out his quarters one last time before tucking in. The lights were out, and he fell asleep.

Velnir began to dream of Darlana once again. He made love to her, and they walked the streets of Tarvana together. Paeris, not too far behind and much older now.

High Magistrate Raften welcomed her with open arms. He told her how much he missed her and how it was a mistake to banish her. Surely, this was wishful thinking, but Velnir was dreaming it. They were having a great feast, all of them together.

In the corner stood his father, Ruvyn, smiling at Velnir. He looked proud of his son. Paeris was giggling and enjoying her food. Darlana was laughing with guests and other nobles. Velnir was content.

Suddenly, Paeris's chair cracked, and she fell over. Velnir got up to check on her, but she was no longer Paeris. She was an Orc. His heart sank, and he drew Illuminar and thrust it into her chest. She howled and gurgled her last breath.

Suddenly, he woke up to a commotion. Velnir rushed and hit the door, forgetting that he had a lock installed on it this time. He fumbled around for the key and let himself out. He ran outside and saw that a fleet of ships had attacked their fleet. The mages used their staves to illuminate the sky.

They were bombarding the enemy ships with fire bolts and doing a good amount of damage. Velnir saw that several of his ships were damaged or on fire. This made him angry. They were only a few days into their journey and had already been attacked.

He went back to his quarters, donned his armor, sheathed Illuminar, and went back outside to his griffin. He quickly mounted it and took to the sky.

He decided to take this opportunity to test out the sword, and he flew over to the nearest enemy ship and saw that it was the beastmen again. He looked back and saw that nine out of the one hundred ships in this fleet were destroyed and sinking fast. The other vessels rushed to help the survivors. Velnir flew toward the center ship. He landed and pulled Illuminar from his sheath, making quick work of whatever got in his way.

He raised Illuminar and felt an overwhelming sense of power as he thrust it into the ship. From his sword came a wave of fire. It started small, and as it moved farther out, it ignited the ship he was on in the process. He mounted his griffin and took to the sky. It got wider and taller, much like a tidal wave. It was moving in the direction he was facing.

At that moment, Velnir realized that one of his ships was in the line of fire he had just conjured. The fire wave was moving fast over the water. The friendly ship was desperately trying to get out of the way, but when they realized they couldn't, they abandoned ship. The fire wave ignited the wood and the sails of their vessel, and it burst into flames. Velnir was unsure how many were killed and felt a terrible sense of dread.

This was intriguing, to say the least, and surprised not only Velnir but his entire fleet, who bore witness to it. It set every enemy ship ablaze that was directly in front of him. The others managed to escape and were sailing away from Velnir. He smirked at them, still mounted on his griffin, and flew back to his ship.

Once he landed, he could see the other ships rushing to assist those who fell in the water or escaped their burning ships. Velnir was still upset over his dream. He wore it well too. His crew dared not say anything to him. The ships closest to the combat began to panic again.

Velnir looked over and saw that the beastmen's vessels were being attacked, but not by his fleet. It was the kraken. His heart filled with joy, and it confused his crew.

"Send word to the others not to worry. The kraken is a friend," he ordered his ensign. The jaws of his crew dropped.

Velnir ignored this and went back to his quarters to find rest.

The morning came, and he got up to go check on his fleet. Everything was in good order once again though his fleet was smaller. Still, they pressed on.

Several days went by without a single incident. The kraken was spotted several times after the attack and kept its distance from the elven fleet. Everyone seemed to be at ease. One week had passed without incident.

Velnir thought, "This is quite unusual. By now, something terrible happened."

Right then, he heard something in his quarters. This startled him, but he jumped up and looked to where the sound was coming from. It was the satchel. Velnir rushed over to it and pulled the eggs out. They were hatching.

"Oh no, not now," he said out loud. "Ensign Neia... ENSIGN NEIA," he yelled.

The ensign ran in. "Yes my...whoa...what is that?" she said.

"I need you to get a message to General Arlen. Tell him I need him here now!"

The eggs began to crack. A snout appeared out of one of them. It kept trying to open its mouth. Velnir was frantically tried putting the shell back together, but it was in vain.

"Please, no, not now." He was panicking.

They were coming, nonetheless. The shell of the other egg began to break. Both whelps were now nearly out of their shells.

Finally, they made it, and were both standing in front of Velnir, looking at him. Velnir placed his palms over his face. "Why did I bring them? How could I be so foolish?"

The whelps began to whine. They wanted food. Velnir called for his ensign once again.

"ENSIGN NEIA!" he yelled. Neia rushed in. "They need food."

The ensign went to the mess hall to grab as much food as she could. She brought it to them and threw it in front of them. At first, they weren't sure what to do.

"Well, go on, eat," said Velnir, seemingly frustrated.

At that moment, they began to devour the food, most of which was meat-based. But it wasn't nearly enough. They wanted more. The poor ensign kept bringing everything she could until, finally, the provisions were out.

"What do you mean we're out?" he snapped at her.

"We have no more food, my lord. We must fish!"

Velnir hadn't thought of that. He offered her a quick smile and said, "Good idea, get to it."

She did and got the crew working. They hoisted a net and threw it over the side. An hour later, it was full of fish when they pulled it up.

Velnir motioned for the whelps to go out to the deck to eat, and they did. They devoured every last fish, yet they still whined for more. Velnir was frustrated. The crew threw the net over and began catching more fish as fast as they could.

Other ships were now getting involved, and Arlen coordinated it. The fleet was there to help, and Velnir appreciated that. A few hours later, the whelps seem to have full bellies.

"How could something so small eat so much?" asked Arlen.

"I have no idea," said Velnir.

The whelps were playing with each other on the deck, much to the amusement of the crew. Whenever they wanted something. They came to Velnir as if they knew he was in charge.

"They like you," said Arlen. "They probably think you're their mother."

Truly, Velnir didn't want to hear him repeat it. This was a dreadful thought. Above the ship flew some birds. This was a good sign that land was nearby. Velnir went to prepare for the much-anticipated arrival to Araba. There was a commotion on deck, which hadn't been so uncommon since the whelps hatched.

He went out there and saw that one of the giant birds was attempting to grab one of the whelps. The moment Velnir walked out, the whelps attacked, burning the bird and devouring it with haste.

The little blue whelp looked at Velnir and burped. Velnir closed the door and went back to his business.

"Land ho!" yelled one of the crew.

Velnir was excited now. Revenge was close. Finally, It has been a year since Atlan was attacked. This was it. Time to deliver what the elves are known for. The whelps have grown quite a lot since they hatched a few days ago. They were beginning to weigh the ship down.

They had arrived in Araba. Most of the vessels beached along the northern coast, and the army began to gather their supplies, getting ready to march. The scrying orbs were now farther inland, and no alarms were raised. They had to make haste if they were going to start marching. One thousand ships bringing one hundred thousand elves. This was good.

Arlen and Magris met with Velnir.

"We are ready to march, my lord," said Magris.

"Excellent, then let's get going. Magris, you take the army toward the sundered lands. You know what to do if you find any orcs, but don't take the army into the sundered lands. Arlen, you're with me. I made some friends during my stay here, and they offered to help."

Arlen and Velnir mounted their griffins and headed north while Magris took the army east through the harsh Araban Desert.

"Where are we going?" asked Arlen." His voice was somewhat muffled by the wind.

"To Nagrimar," he replied. Arlen looked bewildered.

"Nagrimar? You cannot be serious. You made friends with the apostate?"

"I married her," Velnir replied. He then looked over to the general's utter bewilderment. "It was going to come out sometime. I figured you should be the first to know since we go way back. I consider you one of my best friends, Arlen."

Arlen looked at him and nodded. "I consider you to be my best friend, Velnir. I'd follow you to the ends of Abrion if you asked it of me. I just wonder what the high magistrate will think of this?"

"They will probably have me executed," replied Velnir, not seeming worried.

"Yeah, they will, and they will take your lands and punish your people. You didn't think of this?"

"Of course I did. I'll figure something out."

"You always do, Velnir. You're one of the boldest, most stupid, most clever elves I have ever had the displeasure of knowing," Arlen said jokingly. He was testing the waters with Velnir to see how far he could go. The incident on top of the keep still bothered him. He never thought he would have an encounter with Velnir like that.

"You know me too well, Arlen," said Velnir, much to the humor of Arlen.

"What is she like?" asked Arlen, genuinely curious.

"I cannot put it into words, General. She is more beautiful than I can describe." The wind was really picking up now, and their words were getting heavily muffled. Several hours had passed, and they were ready to make camp for the evening. They landed in between sand dunes and made camp. They wouldn't have a fire this evening. Instead, they brought out their enchanted blankets.

***

Magris had the army in good spirits. "Elves march with such grace; the world is envious." he said to himself, proud of his fellow soldiers.

Their armor was created to match the color of the desert to provide a degree of camouflage. For as far as the eye could see, there was dust, but from the sky, you couldn't tell what was making the dust right away. The temperature in the desert was extremely hot during the day and very cold during the night.

Elves, while preferring the temperate climate that Tanimara had to offer, were naturally able to adapt to extreme differences. This allowed them to thrive anywhere on Abrion, literally.

This, and the fact they naturally have long lives, created the belief among their kind that they were the superior race of Abrion. Crossbreeding was believed to taint the purity of their race, and was strictly prohibited under pain of death, or in Darlana's case, exile.

***

Velnir and his advisors had chosen a location in Araba that would require the least amount of travel time to get to the sundered lands.

There were, however, no roads nor clear paths to take. They were completely reliant on scrying orbs and the mages mounted on griffins. This proved effective.

After only a week of marching, they finally came to the mountains that separated the Araban desert and the sundered lands. The mountains were desolate and appeared to have no vegetation on them.

As the army marched closer, they confirmed that there was no vegetation. They looked as though they were formed by a large impact or blast long ago and remained in their original condition this whole time. That was not natural.

Magris had never seen anything like this before. He had spent most of his time on Tanimara and in the human kingdoms. He did spend a few years in the western continents simply to explore and familiarize himself with the place. He was a capable general and had served House Melfarin for hundreds of years. He was a great choice to lead the army while Velnir and Arlen went to meet with their allies and bring them to the sundered lands.

The army was marching along the mountain range's base as the Araban side was flat for as far as the eye could see. They were looking for a passageway through the mountains. It didn't take them long to find one, and so they made camp.

***

"You know, scrying orbs can fly much faster than griffin's, Velnir," Arlen said, trying to sound suggestive.

"You are correct. I have not used them for that in a while and failed to think of it. Thank you for the reminder, Arlen," Velnir said before reaching into his pouch and grabbing a scrying orb. "It will get to Nagrimar long before we will." He threw the orb into the air, and it bolted in the direction of Nagrimar.

"You don't have to say it, Velnir." Arlen said with a smirk.

"Say what?"

"Life is significantly better when you have me around to remind you of such trivial things that turn out to be really helpful, hmm." Arlen was trying not to laugh.

Velnir said nothing. He wasn't going to indulge his humor. The pair had been flying for several days by now, stopping every now and then to make camp and collect food.

Velnir was quick to educate Arlen on the risks of such menial tasks here. The land was very magical, but not the same way as Tanimara. Arlen learned quickly.

"The scrying orb is approaching Nagrimar. I can see it through the scrying crystal. Would you like to see it?" Velnir asked, thinking Arlen would be interested.

"I'll wait until we get there, Velnir, if you do not mind," Arlen said with clear disinterest.

This upset Velnir, but he understood. For Tanimaran elves, Nagrimar was like a mockery of what the elves should be. This was the reason Velnir hadn't told anyone else about his marriage agreement with Queen Darlana.

Velnir didn't share the same sentiments as most of the other elves of Tanimara. At a very young age he learned from his father that working with everyone was vital for the survival of life on Abrion. His father took that to heart and provided assistance to the Thunderforge Clan, which gifted Ruvyn, Danar.

It had been in their family for 91 years now. Ruvyn was the first elf to really go out of their way to assist the other races of Abrion. Velnir respected that about him and intended to do the same.

The scrying orb was fast approaching Nagrimar, and as it was zipping around through the city. Velnir got a sense of nostalgia, and was ever more excited to return. It approached the palace, and Velnir decreased its speed to observe. The street leading up to the palace was packed with people.

"What is going on?" he wondered.

Once the orb got to the Palace, he could see his wife. She was standing in front of her advisors. He decided to keep this information to himself since Arlen wasn't interested in Nagrimar anyway.

Darlana and Alzar noticed the scrying orb while they were addressing her people, so Velnir directed it into the hall to wait. He had his scrying crystal at the ready and he could hardly wait to see her face.

Darlana came back into the palace and held her hand out to retrieve the scrying orb so Velnir descended it.

"Darlana," he said with a sigh of relief. Arlen glanced over at the mention of her, seemingly curious. "How I have missed you."

Darlana was smiling and clearly happy to see him. She held the scrying orb up far enough to show him her entire body. He was thrilled to see her figure and was eager to be with her at least once before they traveled back to the sundered lands. Such was the privilege of royalty when on missions such as these. He would not miss the opportunity.

"I have missed you too. We have much to discuss when you get here. I had expected to hear from you for some time now. Why have you not reached out?" she asked.

"We had to overcome several setbacks since I left Nagrimar. I lost several of my companions to a manticore attack."

"You were attacked by manticores? I am so grateful that you are okay, and I'm terribly sorry for the loss of your guard," she said genuinely.

It surprised Arlen that she would have empathy for Tanimarans at all.

"There were many more setbacks that followed but we have overcome them. We will be there in a few days."

Darlana smiled at him. "Keep the scrying orb here in case you need me for anything, Velnir. I'll be here," she said.

Her devotion to him swelled his heart. It made it all the more painful to be constantly reminded of what was to come after the campaign. She set the orb on her mantle and left the room.

"Velnir," said Arlen in a gentle tone. "I am surprised by how devoted she is to you and her empathy for your companions considering you are Tanimaran. Surely she has not forgotten that her father was responsible for all of this."

"She has not forgotten, Arlen," he said with sadness in his voice.

"You know you cannot return to Tanimara with her. You cannot even bring her to Atlantin. The consequences would be dire not only for her but for you and your people. Tanimaran's are not known for forgiveness."

"I know, Arlen, I know," he said with his head bowed. To tell you the truth, I don't know what I am going to do after the campaign."

"Well, you should focus on surviving it first," Arlen said optimistically.

"I am not sure I even want to at this point," Velnir said figuratively. Arlen understood.

"You have an obligation to your people, to Tanimara, and you have already upset the magistrate of which met in Tarvana to discuss the "Atlantin issue," Arlen said with a lack of subtlety.

Velnir shot a glare at him. "Why am I only now hearing of this Arlen? I drag the armies of three houses across the great sea to send a message to orcs and have left Atlantin, Caphery, and Madir vulnerable should Tarvana wish to take advantage of this. I understood they were unhappy but knew nothing of an 'Atlantin Issue.'" He sighed beneath the heavy weight. "At least there is a sizeable garrison left in Atlantin should something happen. Atlan is even more fortified than before since it has been rebuilt. Baefric is a capable commander."

"Velnir, common sense would dictate that if you step on the toes of the magistrate, they will stomp on yours. Also,

I figured Baefric would inform you. I was certain of it," Arlen said.

Velnir was so caught up in getting revenge. He did not take much time to think of the consequences of his actions. "How could I be so foolish?" he thought.

"Father would be so disappointed," said Velnir.

Arlen understood and pondered for a moment before speaking. "Yes, you should have known there would be consequences that may arise in Tarvana because of your recent actions. However, I applaud you for at least leaving one army in Atlantin just in case. Whether that was intended or not is irrelevant."

It was not intended. Velnir only did it because Baefric asked him to. He felt so foolish.

"The fact is you are the Lord of Atlantin now. You have Lord Baefric and Lord Meric as allies clearly. For Tarvana to move against you, that would be a transgression against Baefric and Meric as well. Their value alone would simply make that a fool's errand. But to attack Atlantin. That is simply suicide. The coast is heavily defended now, and they would be spotted long before they could get through the mountains. I wouldn't worry if I were you, Velnir. Press on with your campaign and we will deal with the Darlana issue after." He offered Velnir a warm smile.

Truth be told, this did not make Velnir feel any better. At this moment, the new lord and what many still considered a young elf just wanted to be with his wife in Nagrimar. She had really grown on him and it appeared absence made his heart grow fonder of her.

"You are right, Arlen," he said with confidence even though he secretly did not agree. "We shall make quick work of the orcs to demonstrate my strength and the risks I am willing to take for the safety of Tanimara. That is what this is for. That is what we must do it for, and at the very least, that is what we must convince ourselves," Velnir said with conviction.

Arlen raised a cup of a hot drink he had warmed up over the fire. "Here's to that, my lord." Velnir took the cup that he graciously warmed up for him, and they clinked them together. They both drank and fell fast asleep.

The next morning before dawn, Velnir and Arlen packed up, mounted their griffins, and took to the air as quickly as they could. Even Arlen was somewhat eager to leave, even though only a few hours separated them from Nagrimar.

They would arrive today. Soaring high above the clouds and really pushing their griffins, they moved fast. Velnir's long hair flowed in the wind with elegance and grace despite the high speed. Arlen had braided his own hair for the journey.

Nagrimar was in view. It was only a matter of how fast one could descend at this point. Velnir raced as fast as he could. Arlen, not wanting to be left too far behind, followed suit, but Velnir was moving very fast.

Once they entered the city, Arlen was amazed by its beauty. "She built this?" He wondered. The ancient elven architecture was a style he enjoyed a lot. "This is quite beautiful, Velnir," he yelled.

"What?" replied Velnir.

Neither could hear the other. The wind generated by the high rate of speed was hampering their hearing. They came upon the palace and landed. Waiting for them was Darlana, her advisors and companions.

Velnir hastily went to hug his wife. He picked her up and spun her around, which made her giggle. This did not seem to faze anyone else at all.

"Darlana, it swells my heart with joy to see you again," he said.

"I longed for your return," she said to him before sharing a passionate kiss.

"Well, I am glad you could get reacquainted," said Arlen. "We should get going. Time is of the essence.

Darlana looked over at Arlen and asked, "And you are?"

"I am General Arlen in service to House Melfarin of Tanimara." He reached out to shake the hand of the queen. She simply looked at him and said, "Pleasure, then." Arlen retracted his hand awkwardly.

Darlana locked her arms with Velnir. "Come help me put my armor on," she said suggestively. Everyone knew. Velnir did not hesitate. He even went ahead of her to hold the door open and such. Arlen looked at him with disappointment.

"Why the long face?" asked Dravon to Arlen.

"What?" He was surprised to see a centaur. "Oh, we have traveled long and far. I am a bit weary," he said unconvincingly.

The other two were talking amongst themselves. The centaur had begun marching to the foot of the Palace. Arlen looked at them and could hardly believe his eyes. There were thousands of them.

This was the first time he had seen so many.

He also saw the people coming out of their houses. He was visibly disgusted by them. He knew right away that they were half-breeds, but he corrected his composer quickly. They too had filed in with the centaur at the base of the palace.

She had successfully assembled an army of at least sixty thousand very quickly. Most of which seemed to be centaur. This would prove very helpful as Velnir brought no cavalry.

It seemed like an eternity before Darlana and Velnir had returned. They came out of the palace with locked arms, both clad in heavy armor.

To be honest, Arlen did not expect Darlana to be a fighter. The armor she wore was that of her father's house. He considered it disgraceful for an apostate to wear Tanimaran armor but they were not in Tanimara at the moment, so he kept his mouth shut.

He looked at Velnir and wondered, "She really is more beautiful than you could put into words, you poor son of an ogre."

***

Magris had ordered the camp be set up a distance away from the dread pass for obvious reasons. The way was narrow and the cliffs were high. He did not want to risk an ambush. The longer he stayed there, the more likely the orcs would learn of his presence. Magris was not worried about it. He almost wanted them to know he was there. This was his opportunity for revenge over his leg and eye, and to win glory for his family. Too long had he served the houses of Tanimara. He wanted to make a name for himself. A skilled mage himself, he could join the other mages on the backs of griffins, and go harass the orcs in the passage. That seemed like a good idea.

"Mages, mount up," he said in his raspy voice. "Lieutenants, have the army form ranks. The mages and I are going to soften up the passage. We are no longer waiting. I want glory, and vengeance!"

"Yes, General," said the lieutenants with excitement and enthusiasm.

He had lost an eye on the battle for Atlan and wore a nifty eye patch. He had also received a nice scar across that eye socket really making him look ominous. The long black hair, facial stubble, and raspy voice helped with the intimidation factor. None questioned him. He was probably the greatest practitioner of pyromancy among these mages, at least, but one of the best swords masters. He was second only to Velnir in Atlantin.

"Good, the army is ready to march. Lieutenant Folwin, let's soften up the passageway." They all took to the air and made their way toward what they believed to be an entrance to the sundered lands. The army began to march, kicking up a ton of dust. The mages made it to the passage but did not see any orcs. They swooped down through the ravines and scanned them thoroughly.

"There is nothing here," he said to the other mages. "Keep your eyes peeled. It could be a trap."

They flew considerably far, hoping to lure any fire, but they received none. The army had made it into the passage by now and was moving unimpeded.

"This is unusual," he thought.

They kept up the search and still turned up nothing. One hundred thousand elves and their supplies had made it through the passageway into the sundered lands completely unimpeded. This was totally unexpected.

Magris ordered them into march formation but to remain at the ready. He sent scrying orbs and Folwin ahead to check for orcish encampments or settlements. Most of the elves had unpleasant looks on their faces.

The sundered lands were desolate wastelands. The only vegetation seemed to be pockets of weeds or grass every now and then. The land was gray in color and made up mostly of pebbles. Most of the ground was solid slabs of rock, covering the ground as far as the eye could see.

They were kicking up a lot of dust, and this is just what Magris wanted. He lusted for battle. The scrying orbs picked up an orcish village not too far from the army. Magris didn't hesitate. He ordered the mages to bombard it and leave no survivors. They flew down and conjured fire bolts and fire storms through the village.

Orcish women and children were running rampant as most were now set ablaze, bringing Magris great pleasure. He relished in their screaming and howling. The army wasn't far behind. Their huts were made of hide and bones. They burned very quickly.

"What a stupid race. They have no defenses," he laughed while speaking to another mage. The scrying orbs picked up another village not too far from this one. He flew down to the army and summoned the lieutenants once more.

"These fools have no defenses. We made quick work of them with magic. Have the army pillage and loot whatever they can and kill any survivors. We show them no mercy, not even their children or whatever they are called…beasts. We are going to fly to the next village and light it up. We will pillage until the orcs meet us on a battlefield. Haha, this is going to be glorious," he said to them.

They cheered and hurried to carry out his orders. The army split up and began following orders. Several orcs were still alive but badly burned. Mercy was not given. The elves thought of clever ways to finish them off. They wanted them to suffer.

Some elves nailed a charred orcish child to a piece of a destroyed hut. They began to peel its skin off, causing it to scream and roar. The roar of an orcish child was much less menacing than an adult's. They were disgusting.

An orcish mother grabbed one of her young and started running away from the rubble she had been hiding in. An elf knocked an arrow and shot her in the back. The young one was a babe. It could not even walk and was still wearing a catch cloth. It, too, was not spared.

An elf slowly crushed its head with his boot. Orcish brains were much larger than he had expected them to be.

The mages descended onto the next town. Fire rained down upon the orcs once again. This time, some of the orcs attempted to fight back. They shot at the mages with their crude bows, but it was in vain. The orcish towns weren't that very large and were easily dispatched. The elves conjured more fire storms in the middle of the town and took pleasure in watching most of the orcs and their huts burn. They lobbed firebolts at many of the orcs running away. Most were incinerated.

Throughout the day, the scrying orbs located orcish settlements and towns. The army and the mages were having a blast, raining terror upon them. These towns were mostly home to the females and the young, noticed Magris. This disappointed him. He flew back to his lieutenants with the mages.

"All right. That's enough for today. Let us make camp, and we will pick it back up tomorrow."

Camp was set, and the elves seemed to be enjoying themselves. One hundred thousand elves setting up camp and taking it down was quite the colossal task, yet these soldiers did it every day, sometimes twice.

Magris was proud of his troops. He had hoped he would find a large force of orcs to fight today, but no matter. We will find them tomorrow. Surely, by now, they know we are here. They all tucked in for the night. Sentries were, of course, posted, and the defenses were in place. Many were asleep now.

The night sky was clear, and the stars were visible. The sundered lands didn't look so bad at night. One sentry decided to sit down and take a little break.

Suddenly, he heard a swooping sound, nothing like what he heard before. He got up to investigate but saw nothing. Not thinking much of it, he returned to his post and continued his break. Once again, and only a moment later, he heard another swooping sound, only in a different location. The sentry got up and had a look around.

Then he heard one here, there, and over there. Soon, he was hearing them everywhere. Alarmed, he ran over to one of the tents and peered inside. The lanterns were still lit, but the tent was empty. Whole tents were empty, which bothered him; he looked in another and, to his shock, the same. There were no occupants.

The sentry ran to another, and right then, he opened it up. An orc literally came out of the ground, plunged its dagger into the chest of a sleeping elf, and pulled them underground with him. The sentry was shocked. He backed up in horror and dropped his spear and shield. He was frightened!

A moment later, something grabbed his feet. He saw the black toothed grin of an orc below him, coming from a tunnel underground. He screamed in horror, but the orc quickly pulled him under.

The rest of the camp awoke from the commotion. The elves were coming out of their tents confused. To their bewilderment, elves were simply falling through the ground as if it were caving in. Panic ensued and the elves began to run in all directions. A massive army of orcs appeared to have come up from the ground and began charging the panicking elves. They were carrying torches and howling in rage. They, too, showed no mercy, killing as many elves as they could. Magris came out of his tent and saw what was going on.

"Form ranks! Fight! Fight! Fight!" he yelled.

He was already in his armor and never took it off, seemingly even to sleep. He mounted his griffin and took to the sky along with the mages. They began to counter attack.

Firebolts and fire storms raged across the battlefield. It made it considerably bright. The mages were working hard, conjuring up as much as they could. This allowed the elves they were attacking to get away. The force of orcs was not very large. There were roughly eight hundred to a thousand of them and still more were coming out of the ground.

"How was this possible?" he thought. Still, this could have been a satisfying victory for the elves even though they had been ambushed.

The orcs eventually retreated back underground, and Magris landed. He blew his horn, indicating that it was safe now. The elves began coming back. The lieutenants met with Magris right away.

"Get me a casualty report. I want the army ready to fight immediately. Dawn approaches!" he ordered.

The lieutenants hurried to carry out his orders.

By now, the sun had risen. The elves returned to their camp, which was mostly in shambles. The bulk of the other camps had been left intact.

Magris found the dragons safe and sound, feasting on dead orcs. "They were much bigger now and large enough to be mounted," he thought.

The camps that were not attacked sent word to Magris. They would be arriving shortly.

"Today is the day I get the glory I have been longing for. For my house, for me, for Tanimara," he thought.

The army had come together. The soldiers from the camp that was attacked were still shaken up and allowed a longer respite while the rest of the army was forming up for inspection.

Magris ordered the sentries to investigate the holes the orcs came out of. This proved to be difficult because the type of sand and gravel that was prevalent on the sundered lands would backfill immediately after something fell through it.

"Dig one out and see what is underneath," he ordered.

After digging, one of the sentries bravely stuck their head in, describing a large tunnel. This surprised Magris as he hadn't known the orcs to do such things.

"It makes sense, to live up here in this environment would be harsh. It surprises me that any orc does it at all…animals," said Magris.

Magris ordered the mages to conjure fire within the tunnels anywhere they could penetrate them and drive the orcs out. One of the mages was able to conjure a massive fire underground, blowing out all of the other holes the orcs created within the tunnel network in that area. These areas were only large enough to fit one orc at a time. This left more questions than answers.

The sound of an orcish horn could be heard in the distance. Magris immediately ordered the army at the ready and the mages to their griffins. The bolt throwers were in place, and their bolts were enchanted. Magris mounted his griffin and took to the sky to meet the mages.

He threw several scrying orbs into the sky, and they made their way to where the sound came from. He pulled out his scrying crystal and observed the line of orcs coming around the jagged cliff edge next to the elven camp. Magris ordered the army to position itself between the camp and the orcs. He was ready.

Soon, the orcs were visible to the elves. They simultaneously brought their shields up, and immediately after that, the line behind the first line placed their spears through special notches in the shields. He kept his eye on their movements, and something caught his attention. Within the orcish army were giant creatures made of stone. Their eyes were glowing green, much like the orc warlocks at the battle of Atlan.

As the orcs got closer, it became obvious that they severely outnumbered the elves. At this point, Magris estimated he had about ninety-five thousand soldiers. The orcs easily had twice that many, but Magris wouldn't let that deter him.

"Bolt throwers, fire," he ordered.

Several bolts careened through the air toward the orcish line. About halfway between the elves and the orcs, blades sprung out, and they began to spin very quickly.

Right before they hit their target, they caught fire and exploded on impact, sending shards everywhere. Scores of orcs were vaporized or killed with them. Magris ordered them to fire again and again. He saw firsthand how effective they were against those giant stone creatures, practically pulverizing them.

"Folwin, let's light them up," he said.

The mages descended upon the orcs and began conjuring firestorms and fire bolts. Explosions rocked the orcish lines. This, of course, did not deter them.

Wyverns descended upon the mages and griffins in a surprise attack. Magris drew his sword and engaged them. The fighting was fierce, but the lines hadn't even met at this time in the battle. The elves remained steadfast, and the orcs were still moving.

The bolt throwers were just now running out of bolts, and the mages had stopped conjuring as they were busy fighting for their lives. Magris killed his opponent and made his way to the next.

Another loud horn could be heard, only this time, it came from the cliff. Magris looked up to see what appeared to be their leader on top of the jagged cliff next to the elven line.

"What a prize his head would make," he thought before breaking away from the fight and flying up to the cliff.

The orc simply stood there watching Magris come at him. This went against Magris's better judgment, and he backed off but still ascended. Once he flew above the cliff the orc was standing on. He saw another mighty host of orcs on the cliff overlooking the elves down below.

"No, not my flanks." Magris began to panic. He quickly descended.

The griffins were able to break away and make their way back to the elven line. The orcs were coming hard and fast.

By now, their ugly mugs with their open mouths and drool-dripping tusks could be seen. The elves braced themselves for impact. The archers kept firing as fast as they could. The orcs smashed the elven line.

Orcs in the second wave, leapt on top of the orcs on the first wave and jumped into the elvish line. The lieutenants were shouting orders, desperately trying to keep their ranks in order, when they heard the faint cries of Magris, who was just now reaching them.

"The flanks!" he yelled. "The flanks! Watch the flanks!"

It was too late.

The orcs came down the cliff and were just about to smash the elven flanks. Magris had no cavalry. He had mostly spearmen. His army was quickly surrounded. Magris ordered the mages into the air, and together, they battled wyverns and conjured firestorms whenever they could.

Magris looked all around him and began to despair. His army was surrounded, and his desperate attempt to rectify through magic was failing. He was about to lose Velnir's army.

"Shield wall," he yelled.

He ordered the mages over the elvish line, which now formed a shield wall around itself. The mages began to focus their fire on the stone creatures as they seemed to be the only threat to the army at the moment.

In between pummeling the stone creatures, the mages who were able to conjure fire storms within the orc ranks. This scene was truly hellish. Piles and piles of charred orcish corpses, yet the orcs simply climbed over them, their fury unwavering.

They hacked and slashed at the elves who were still holding the line at this point. Magris began to feel his energy return to him. In desperation, he decided to try a spell that he hadn't practiced but could prove to have dire consequences. He had to fly further away than the rest of the mages, though.

He focused hard, and from his staff, conjured a firestorm. This one started at the expected size of what a mage would normally conjure; however, the more orcs it burned, the larger it grew. It began to make Magris and the other elves nervous.

The psychological effect on the orcs was similar. They began to run. Magris took this opportunity to order a retreat. Captain Folwin, Lieutenant Garlan, and Lieutenant Ardan flew around and sounded the retreat. Now, the elves were tactically retreating in the direction they came. Once the tornado of fire started to die down, the orcs turned around. Magris ordered them to form another shield wall.

To the left of the elven line, a Tanimaran horn was heard, followed by two more unfamiliar horns.

"Velnir," thought Magris.

On the horizon, the centaurs appeared. Thousands of them began to gallop toward the orcish line and smashed into them. They easily made quick work of what remained of this orcish army.

Behind them appeared a strange-looking army of lightly armored elven soldiers he didn't recognize. They began charging the orcs. Magris was not sure who they were exactly. A hippogryph landed, and its rider jumped off and began gracefully cutting down orcs left and right. Magris recognized her black hair and armor immediately.

"Darlana," he whispered.

He began to make his way toward her when the orcish leader landed before him and appeared to be challenging him. Magris drew his sword, as did the orc.

They began exchanging mighty blows. Even with one eye and a peg leg, Magris fought with grace and confidence. The orc was savagely flailing his ax and blurting out what Magris believed to be insults. Magris moved and dodged the orcs' blows, much to his irritation. It was amusing for Magris, who noticed that giant tree men were entering the battlefield.

The orcs were running away as the centaurs and trebors were chasing them. Magris decided to end it quickly. He dodged a few more swings from the orc before shoving his sword through the orc's shoulder and then through his legs, completely immobilizing him.

"You are my prize. Don't go anywhere," Magris said before offering the orc a sinister smile and making his way to the elven line. The battle was over and won. Magris felt relief. He began to look for the hippogryph rider and found her with none other than his Lord Velnir. Nervousness overwhelmed Magris.

Velnir began making his way to Magris.

"My lord, look upon the destruction I have wrought upon our enemies. Glory to our campa…" Magris was interrupted by Velnir's fist to his jaw knocking him out cold.

"Detain this elf at once," Velnir ordered a few soldiers around him. They began to tie the unconscious elf to a bolt thrower's wheel.

"Velnir, come quick," said Darlana in a panic. Velnir rushed to her and saw that Arlen was injured. A medic had already arrived and, at Darlana's behest, was giving him onion water. Velnir looked at Arlen's stomach region and noticed it had been sliced open. The smell of onions through it would indicate a fatal blow, but to everyone's relief, it was not so. Still, the wounds were terrible, and there was no one available to dress them.

"It is all right, my lord, I can make it," said Arlen.

"Absolutely not. You need medical care at once, or your wounds will become infected, and you'll die."

Arlen simply nodded in agreement and rested his head. Velnir knew that several of the ships that came with them were hospital ships for this reason.

Velnir ordered griffins to him immediately. "Captain Eldar, take Arlen to the ships for treatment and make haste," he ordered.

Two soldiers carefully loaded Arlen onto the captain's griffin, and they took to the air, making their way toward the ships.

"I am without words," he told Darlana. "One of my generals foolishly marched my army against my direct orders, and the other grievously wounded. Darlana looked at him and placed her hand on his shoulder. "Such is war, Husband,"

Oakenleaf made his way to Velnir and Darlana.

"Oh, those orcs… those nasty, little, green-skinned savages are on the run. Good riddance. We forest lords can do without them, that is for sure." He began to ramble on, and Velnir was tuning him out. He was instead observing his army… or what was left of it.

Thousands of corpses lined the battlefield, and thousands of wounded were crying for help. The medics were racing to them as fast as they could, Darlana now among them. Velnir saw the centaurs and Darlana's army helping to remove the dead.

Velnir's heart sank. "So much death, so many lives wasted," he thought for the first time since the campaign's inception.

Chapter 13
Commence Punishment

Each army was in its respective camp. The forest lords made it look like there was a miniature forest in this harsh place. It almost brought to it a sense of serenity. The centaurs were bringing back animals they had hunted to restock their supplies. This surprised Velnir.

The fact that there were animals in this harsh place at all was strange. Centaurs hunting them? Perhaps Velnir did not understand them like he thought he did. Velnir made his way into his command tent with Darlana, her lieutenants, Chief Dravon of the Centaurs, and Tanimaran lieutenants. The tent was divided, the Nagrimarans and the Tanimarans on opposite sides of the room. It was clear to Velnir that there was animosity.

Velnir took a deep breath before speaking. "You all know of Princess Darlana," he began saying to the Tanimarans. "You know the stories and the laws that were created as a result of them. This is known by all in this tent."

He then looked to Darlana, who was smiling at him, and then back to the Tanimarans. "She is now Darlana, Queen of Nagrimar and of the centaurs. Her forces captured mine after we were shipwrecked. She gave us shelter and food and treated the wounded. We were her guests in Nagrimar for several weeks. If not for her, the campaign may have already failed before it even started. Everyone on this continent has dealt with orcs. After spending time together, we grew fond of each other."

The Tanimarans began to gasp with disgust.

"She offered to aid our cause if I married her and gave her a child of pure elvish blood." This served to repulse some of the Tanimarans, but most did not react at all.

Velnir continued. "I will do what is best for my people. I care not for what the magistrate mandates. Where were they when Atlantin was invaded? Where were they when Atlan was sieged? Where were they when we requested aid to invade the sundered lands? Darlana answered the call, and all she asked for was something that served to benefit both Atlantin and Nagrimar mutually."

The Tanimarans seemed to be agreeing, much to Velnir's relief.

"He is right," said one of the Tanimarans. "Nagrimar, our sworn enemy, came to our aid when our own magistrate did not. I, for one, am glad that they came. For without Darlana specifically, I could be dead." He turned to look at Darlana. "It was she who dressed my wounds on the battlefield, and it was she who gave me the herbs to quickly heal me. The Nagrimaran Queen, aiding Tanimaran's. Who would have thought?"

The other Tanimarans all agreed that without the help of everyone there, they would all be dead and began to show their gratitude. Darlana was quite delighted with this and began to be social. The word spread among the rest of the Tanimarans, who, over the next few days seemed to accept the Nagrimarans.

Darlana was growing quite popular among the Tanimarans. Many watched her spar and wanted to train with her to learn how to improve their skills.

Velnir welcomed this as he knew just how much experience Darlana had on the battlefield.

"She is the perfect combination of beauty, strength, and lethality, my lord," said Lieutenant Vulas.

Velnir smiled and nodded. "Indeed."

Velnir's thoughts shifted to Magris. He was angry and heartbroken. This distracted him from watching Darlana while everyone else seemed to really enjoy her. He slinked off and made his way to Magris, who was now conscious.

"What have you done with…?" Velnir was unable to complete the question as he was beginning to become angry. He waited a moment to calm down. "My army, Magris?" He looked toward the ground and closed his eyes, trying not to let his anger cloud his judgment. "What have you done to my army?" he repeated with sadness.

Magris looked up and saw Velnir's expression. "I won, my lord," he said in a vain attempt to try and dampen Velnir's emotions.

"A pyrrhic victory at best, Magris," Velnir snapped. "You marched my army against orders for personal glory and revenge." He spoke with anger and disgust. "Your arrogance is responsible for the deaths of over forty thousand Mari, and what if we had not come to your rescue, Magris… what then Hmm? The survivors, the mages, and even you might very well be among the dead. How could you do this to them… to me, Magris? You were my brother! Did you not think that all Atlantins wanted revenge? If you had lost, you would have denied them that."

Magris looked up to Velnir, realizing the weight of his decisions. "I am still your brother, my lord. I severely miscalculated how you would feel, and I take full responsibility for my actions and failures. I will accept any and all judgments against me and will now lay down my life willingly. I regret that I have disappointed you with my negligence." Magris closed his eye and bowed his head. "I regret that I have but one life to give for the thousands I have wasted."

"Magris, you are a fool," he said before briskly walking away. He was unsure what to do with him. Magris was one of his best friends and Atlantin's strongest generals. He was an excellent fighter and had served House Melfarin for two hundred years. He went back to Magris, "I should execute you. If you were anyone else, I would!" Velnir's voice became calm. "I have served with you for hundreds of years. I know you too well, Magris. I fault myself for leaving you in charge of my army."

"My lord, you should execute me. I betrayed your trust and nearly destroyed your campaign. I have no excuse. You are right. I did it for personal glory. I acted out of self-interest and in complete disregard for the army. I do not blame you," Magris said with his head still bowed in shame.

Velnir looked at him and then moved over him. "It was not just I who saved you," he said quietly.

Magris knew what he was speaking of but dared not let his anger about it show. "You allied with the Nagrimarans, centaurs, and what I think may be forest trebors," he said calmly.

Velnir was surprised by his response. He had expected Magris to lash out. This would surely justify a beating at the very least. "I married Darlana and agreed to produce a pure elven child for Nagrimar's aid." He snidely attempted to enrage Magris.

"Oh, I see. I figured it out." He would then quote. "The enemy of my enemy is my friend."

"You misunderstand me, Magris! She is not my enemy. She is my wife, and I do indeed love her. We will have children. I will bring her back to Tanimara, and the Magistrate will accept her."

Magris did not say anything. He instead kept his head bowed. Velnir wanted to know what he was thinking. He wanted badly to justify punishing him without executing him. It would seem Magris would not give Velnir the satisfaction. Magris was truly remorseful and it bothered Velnir.

"Speak freely, Magris," demanded Velnir.

"You know the Magistrate will not allow her to return to Tanimara. Her father is the high Magister. She will be killed along with you, your family, and hundreds of thousands of your people. Your house will be destroyed and lands seized.

You are giving them the perfect excuse to label you an enemy of Tanimara."

"I am showing them that I am sovereign. I do not need their permission, nor do I need them. I have friends inside and now outside of Tanimara."

"Times have changed, Velnir. The magistrate will see this as a threat to their power. Raften is a tyrant, and most of the other princes and princesses bend the knee to him because they are cowards."

Velnir thought about the words of his close friend and general. "You are a better statesman than general, Magris. Perhaps after the campaign, you might consider a career change."

Magris scoffed. "If you do not execute me, I will continue to serve house Melfarin as I have always done in any way I can," he promised.

Velnir waited a moment before speaking again. "Arlen was wounded in the battle. He took an orcish blade to the stomach."

Magris looked up at Velnir with worry in his eyes." Tell me Arlen will live, my lord. Tell me my brother will recover."

Velnir's expression turned sad. "I don't yet know what will become of Arlen. I sent him to the hospital ship. He may need to go back to Tanimara for better treatment." He turned to face Magris. "If it weren't for Darlana, he would have likely died along with several others. She saved many lives with her knowledge of healing and herbal medicine."

Magris waited a moment before responding. He could see in Velnir's eyes his appreciation for Darlana. "I have no quarrel with Darlana, Velnir. If you accept her, then so do I."

Velnir believed him and squatted down to look him eye to eye. "Now that we got that out of the way, We need to discuss your punishment."

Magris looked at Velnir through his one eye. "I need my eye if I am to continue to serve you. Take whatever else. I will give it gladly."

Velnir ordered that Magris be tied to the post, standing him with his armor and clothing off and his back exposed. He had all the soldiers willing to witness come and watch as he sentenced Magris to lashings for his arrogance and negligence.

Magris humbly accepted, and Velnir began lashing at Magris's back. The whip tore the flesh from his back. He received fifteen and never once cried out in pain, though it was clearly visible on his face.

There was no doubt that Magris was tough. He had endured so much, and now he had scars over his left eye, which was still good, and he was missing his right eye and covered it with a menacing patch. The right side of his face was scarred from burning. His back was now scarred, and he was missing his right leg. Velnir could not bring himself to take any more from Magris. "This will have to suffice," he said to himself.

Velnir, Darlana, Dravon, and Magris were now in the command tent. Magris was very surprised by Darlana's pleasant demeanor toward the Tanimarans. He also received medical attention from her after Velnir had lashed him. He still secretly had his reservations about her.

"We are short on supplies. The orcs outnumber us greatly. We have just over one hundred and twenty thousand soldiers, including the forest lords. The centaurs making up for our lack of cavalry is an enormous help. We have two hundred bolt throwers still in service and are stocked with bolts. The mages have recovered, and everyone is eager to continue, though I fear we do not have enough to campaign for long. Surely, by now, the orcs have reached out to all the clans to tell them of our presence."

"May I suggest reaching out to the realms of men and dwarves for assistance?" Darlana asked.

The Tanimarans and Nagrimarans erupted in heated disagreement.

"Enough!" said Darlana. To Velnir's surprise, the Tanimarans complied.

"For millennia, men have been dealing with orcish incursions. Whether it is the Araban kingdoms, or the northern kingdoms. They all have a hatred for orcs. Dwarves, too, have had their treasure stolen, their mountain strongholds raided, and entire clans exterminated by orcs. Velnir, I am sure I can convince the dwarves and humans to come to your aid."

Velnir looked at everyone in the tent, trying to discern whether or not they would accept the help of men and dwarves. He decided he did not care what they thought. "Darlana, we would appreciate any help we can get."

"I'll go at once." Darlana left and mounted her hippogryph. Velnir turned his attention to his lieutenants.

"My lord, what shall we do about the dragons?" asked Garlan.

Velnir had done several things outside the norm of elven culture. "I have grown quite fond of them. I think we can care for them for now. I promised their mother that I would look after them for her."

Everyone in the command center began to laugh and agree. It would seem that they all grew fond of the dragon whelps. They were getting big and were several times larger than when Velnir last saw them.

"Dragons are not like the other species of Abrion. You were the first they saw when they hatched. You are their parent for now, Velnir," said one of the Nagrimarans. "Just remember, they are not animals. You do not own them. If a dragon is loyal, they will do what is in their allies' if it serves their interest as well. Treat them as your equal. You will not regret that, Velnir." said the Nagrimaran.

Truly, he knew nothing about dragons or of their culture. He appreciated her wisdom. "I appreciate you sharing that knowledge with me. What is your name?" he asked her.

"I am Commander Pyra, sir. I have spent years with dragons and am very familiar with their culture."

Velnir took the opportunity to show the Tanimarans and Nagrimarans that he harbored no favoritism. "I would have you advise me regarding dragons then if that is all right with you... until Darlana returns, of course," he suggested.

"It would be my pleasure, sir," she said with a smile.

The others in the tent seemed content with this arrangement.

Darlana had told some of the soldiers outside where she was going. They were very pleased with the plan. The soldiers outside began to cheer and say their goodbyes and give her their gratitude. Those that remained in the command tent were silent for the moment, all looking at Velnir.

Velnir was eager to change the subject. "What information did we gain from the orcish attack that almost cost us our army?"

Garlan spoke up. "They came up from the ground. It would appear that the parts of the ground covered with pebbles can give way if pushed from below. It is rather difficult to dig them out, so I assume it is some sort of sorcery. This is how they killed so many soldiers."

Folwin chimed in. "To Magris' credit, we were able to hold our formation after we stood on solid rock. The orcs were not able to penetrate our ranks and relied on stone giants. The mages made quick work of them."

"Magris also conjured a fire tornado which had to kill tens of thousands instantly and kill tens of thousands more as it roamed over the flat land," said Ardan.

"Excellent, order the soldiers to accommodate themselves based on these new developments. We need to adapt to this harsh environment fast and not allow ourselves to be caught off guard again," said Velnir. He thought about telling them that their leader has a powerful scepter but decided it would not be in the best interest of anyone if he did that. He did not want to sow panic.

Velnir had fortifications built around the camps, which were now built over massive slabs of bedrock that orcs could not penetrate. They had established a stronghold and a supply line from Atlantin to them. The kraken was aiding by escorting the ships safely across the great sea. Things were working out, now they had to wait for the return of Darlana to confirm the assistance of the humans and dwarves if they were to go with their plan or they would have to devise another plan.

Busy in his chambers planning, Velnir was very focused but began to tire. He decided it was time to rest but remembered what his lieutenants said about the orcs coming up from underground.

This was the kind of stuff that parents would tell their children to frighten them if they misbehaved, but this was no tall tale. He placed several blades in the ground under his bed. That way if an orc did attempt to come up, it would be impaled and give Velnir time to react. This helped him sleep. He began to dream, and once again, it was about his wife.

"Love me," she said with her lips and not her voice. He got up and made his way to her. She had returned, and woke him in the best way. He began to kiss her and assist her undressing. Soon, they were both naked, breathing heavily. A few sentries outside could hear the commotion inside the tent. They rushed and saw the two together. The two did not even notice the sentries. One of the sentries, clearly embarrassed, began to retreat quietly while the other one stood and watched in complete awe.

"Come with me, you idiot," the other sentry said before grabbing him by the collar and yanking him out of the tent. They stood guard outside of the tent to ensure no one else would go in. Oakenleaf, approached the two sentries who looked up at the giant forest lord in awe.

"I wish to speak with Velnir," he said, clearing his throat.

Darlana could be heard in the background. Everyone around knew what they were doing. She was loud and did not care who heard. Oakenleaf did not understand, however.

"What is that awful noise? I think someone is getting hurt," he stated with concern.

"Oh…no, no, nope. She is rather enjoying herself," he said, trying to keep a serious expression. The other sentry snickered.

"It sounds like she is crying out. Get out of my way," he would then push over the sentries with ease and peer inside.

"By the celestials," Oakenleaf thought as he watched the two on their cot. "I may have been mistaken. What are they doing?" Oakenleaf said, loud enough for Velnir and Darlana to hear, but he did not care.

They were busy and very much enjoying themselves.

The sentries encouraged the trebor to stop watching so they could explain. Oakenleaf's facial expressions were difficult to define once the sentries explained exactly what Velnir and Darlana were doing. To say the least, it was probably all right to assume Oakenleaf was confused and unsure of what to make of it.

Either way, he lost interest and said he would be back later. Velnir awoke to relieve himself. He cursed his bladder for ruining probably one of the most humorous albeit vivid dreams of his life.

A few days later, Darlana returned. Velnir was out playing with the whelps who were much bigger and obviously stronger than him by now. Darlana had come to play with them as well.

"You must name them, Velnir," Darlana said.

Velnir thought for a moment. "I have no idea what to name dragons, and I do not think it is my place to do so since I am not their mother."

"If they do not like their names, they could always change them," she said.

Velnir thought about it for a moment, "I suppose they could." He looked at the bigger one and thought for a moment before saying, "You are brave and strong. I think I will call you Yzat. It is the ancient elven word for fierce one."

Yzat seemed to accept the name and backed away to allow the other dragon to hear what he would be called.

"I will call you Nythint, the ancient elvish word for strong."

Nythint seemed to accept his name as well.

Yzat came back to Velnir and brought his body down. He did it much like a horse would if it wanted to be mounted. Velnir was reluctant at first. Yzat was still very young but did not believe he could quite understand elvish yet and was quite smaller than Ismi.

"I do not think that is a good idea yet, Yzat."

Yzat bowed his head, seemingly insisting Velnir to climb up.

Velnir patted him on the head and said, "All right then, show me what you can do."

He climbed onto Yzat's back and held on.

Yzat was eager to show Velnir just what he could do, so he immediately leapt up and took to the sky, rapidly going straight up.

Velnir used all his strength to hold on. Yzat was working hard to gain as much altitude as possible before throwing his wings out and halting high above where even a griffin couldn't make it.

Velnir laughed with excitement and had a quick look around. He could see a lot of the sundered lands from here. He noticed what appeared to be a massive sinkhole several kilometers away.

Before he could get a better look, Yzat began to descend very quickly. The wind flowed through Velnir's long white hair and pulled at his cheeks. He could see the ground closing in through his squinted eyes and was unsure whether Yzat could pull up in time with all the weight on his back, but he did to, Velnir's relief.

They soared over the camp, and all the soldiers looked up in bewilderment. Elves and dragons have never been so close, at least in recorded history. This was not natural. The relationship between Yzat and Velnir was strong. For the first time, Yzat spoke elvish.

"Are you pleased with my abilities, Velnir?"

Perplexed and excited, Velnir simply replied, "Absolutely."

They barrel rolled, went up and down, between giant rock pillars, into a cave, and out the other end. It seems Yzat had an endless amount of energy. Eventually, they came back to where they had taken off from. Everyone was clapping excitedly for them. This was monumental for the elves. The dragons seemed content. Velnir had not expected this in his wildest dreams. He dismounted Yzat and asked him, "Would you like some armor like your mother has?"

Yzat started to respond, but Pyra interrupted. "It will need to be enchanted, Velnir. He will not be able to transmorph into his visage and back to his true form with regular armor. I will begin work on the vellums immediately."

"Very good, thank you," Velnir said.

Nythint came up to Velnir and wanted to be ridden, but Velnir wasn't up for it. Magris, though, was eager to try it and volunteered to mount Nythint, who seemed to not mind at all. Up they went, and Magris was having an even harder time than Velnir, as he had never ridden a dragon before. It was amusing to everyone, including Magris, as he was heard, even for a brief moment, laughing as they flew by.

The armorers began crafting armor that could cover the chest and heads of the two dragons. Once complete, Pyra came over and began to enchant them. Many gathered around to watch as they had never seen this kind of magic before. Truly, Pyra was gifted and many wondered how. The armor glowed with a light blue hue. It was beautiful and ornate. The elven armor smiths did a fantastic job. Yzat and Nythint were very pleased.

Velnir had ordered the army to march. He wanted to go investigate the sinkhole he saw while flying around on Yzat. Magris and Velnir both were mounting their dragon allies high in the sky. The mages seemed to be a bit jealous. The griffins did not care. The dragons grew noticeably bigger every day. They were known to be immortal, only claimed by death when killed.

They were fast approaching the sinkhole and decided to descend to get a closer look. It was only a day's march. The army made camp and settled in. Velnir, Drovan, Darlana, Magris, Garlan, Ardan, and Folwin made up the council.

The council approached the sinkhole and peered in. This was in fact no sinkhole. If it was natural, it was done so long ago that a civilization had come to alter it and build an entire city deep down within it. The council quietly peered over the cliff looking in. There were orcs everywhere. The walls were decorated with skulls and crude paintings. Orcs were moving around inside and outside the sunken city in what looked like day-to-day activity. "Orcs could not be civilized," they thought. The original city below was of no architecture known to the elves. It was very ancient and had become a ruin though its walls, and some spires and towers still stood as they seemed to have been repaired by the orcs now dwelling there. It was amazing how deep this hole was, that it could fit a city with such tall towers and spires and still have plenty of space between its tallest structure and the surface. No one had ever seen anything like it.

"Zakil," said Darlana

"What is Zakil?" Magris was first to ask.

"It was one of the first of three kingdoms back when this land was lush and fertile. When one of the planets corrupted by Penumbra was destroyed, a piece of it made its way to Abrion thousands of years ago. Upon entry into Abrion's atmosphere, most of it burned up, but three crystals remained. Their blackish purple glow was rank with the darkness that had plagued the planet they came from." Darlana said.

"Draxus was the first of the dragon kind to be brought to Abrion. It was he who found the crystals, and it was he who was corrupted by them. He became Necrosith and deceived the kings of Zakil, Teth, and Karo to wield scepters that Necrosith had fashioned the crystals into. He promised those fools great power. When Abrion's moons, Canis and Majoris, aligned, the scepters unleashed a great and devastating power that made all life in this area suffer. What once were men were now orcs. What once were dwarves are now goblins, and elves were corrupted into what we know as dark elves or the umbral elves. This once was the fertile kingdoms of three of the first civilizations on Abrion, but is now a wasteland. This is all that remains of that human city; fascinating, I have never been here before," said Darlana.

"How do you know all of this?" asked Magris.

"I attended the academy of Higher Arts over ninety years ago," said Darlana.

"This is how Darlana knew of Ruvyn's expedition during the electhril wars and met him," thought Velnir.

The rest of the council were perplexed as they had not heard this before.

Velnir knew she was speaking of the Scepters of Canar. Now, he saw just how powerful they were and understood what Baefric meant. It made his stomach turn.

"Orcs were men, and goblins were once dwarves? That explains their cunning," Magris said, and everyone agreed.

"They had women and children in several of the villages we incinerated."

"I fought an all-female warband of orcs when I met Oakenleaf on my way to Nemis. They are just as formidable as the males," said Velnir.

"How does this explain why the orcs live down there?" asked Folwin.

"It was once on the surface as we are. It fell below when this land was corrupted. Underneath the surface, magma began to flow and created massive caverns under the whole of the sundered lands. The orcs refer to it as the underway. The dwarves have been known to make use of it within the mountains. This city fell through one, hence, why it seems to be destroyed," said Darlana.

"To think orcs were once capable of creating such monumental structures and now they live in huts made from the bones and skin of their hunts," said Magris.

"It was constructed at the time when they were men," said Garlan.

Velnir stood overlooking the hole. "Make ready the army. We are going to fight them."

The council retreated back to their camp and informed the army to get ready for battle.

"We face a mighty logistical challenge, Velnir. How do we get the army down there?" asked Folwin.

"Leave it to me," said Magris.

The army had formed ranks under the orders of their commanders and got into the position to fight. The bolt throwers and the soldiers stood as if they were about to be attacked. Velnir ordered Magris and Folwin to mount Yzat and Nythint. He then ordered them and the mages who mounted griffins to fly down and attack the city. They took to the sky and flew through the hole. Not long afterward, the army could hear the sound of orcs howling and screaming: dragon's breath attacks, fire storms being conjured, and the clash of fire bolts.

Magris and Folwin caused panic among the orcish ranks, and the dragons were devastating. The orcs that had begun to retreat toward the city center were stopped by firestorms. Velnir tossed several scrying orbs down there. They moved to key locations around the city, and they began to watch it on the scrying crystal.

Soon, it became clear that the orcs were confused. They began to panic and retreat but had nowhere to go. All exits were blocked by the elves and dragons.

The orcs began to go into the houses but were then destroyed by dragon breath. The orcs on the other side of the sunken city managed to break down a part of the wall and escape. They ran for their lives. It was clear that the elves won the day again.

"I have never fought a battle like this before," said Magris.

"Nor have I. Thank you, Nythint, for if it weren't for you, we could not have done this," said Folwin.

"The orcs have dug tunnels like this all over the eastern continent. No one really knows how far they go except the dwarves," said Darlana.

"Let's go and have a look around."

Immediately, the council agreed and made their way down to the city and what could be considered the palace courtyard that now lay in ruin. Ancient pottery, the metal wheels of wagons, and other than the fallen orcs, even the skeletal remains of the inhabitants littered the city. This place was ominous, to say the least.

Magris had used his skill in pyromancy to ignite several torches around the courtyard, illuminating the area. Everyone seemed quite impressed with him. They made their way into the palace but could not get the door open.

Nythint happily smashed it open. Again, corpses littered the hall, but a light appeared over the throne at the very end. It was shining on a skeleton wearing ancient armor and a golden crown. It had several crude arrows stuck in the skull and chest cavity. In its hand was a scroll, for at this time, books hadn't been invented yet.

Velnir carefully removed it and tucked it in his satchel. They looked around and noticed that the room had been decorated with marble statues of humans achieving great things like discovering magic, strength, academics, and astrology. The ceiling was decorated with depictions of the celestials battling the forces of Penumbra. The decorations were unfortunately defamed by the orcs.

"These people had knowledge of science, magic, and religion," stated Darlana. "How intriguing."

They looked around a little longer before taking their leave. Once they left the palace, they could see just how massive the city actually was.

Though it paled in comparison to cities like Atlan and Nagrimar, still for its time, it was enormous. The depth of the hole was astonishing. The city was built so strong that it could fall hundreds of meters and not completely shatter. The architecture was amazing.

"We must get to the surface and send scribes down here to document our findings," stated Velnir.

The council agreed and they mounted up and took to the sky.

Upon their leave, the council noticed that directly in front of the city, the land was flat and led to large tunnels going in various directions. "That must be where the orcs retreated," observed Velnir.

Velnir sent the scribes with his expedition down to the city to document more findings and bring back whatever they could.

Searching below one of the orcish buildings, they discovered many of the Atlantin citizens who were captured and enslaved by the orcs. The survivors were brought to the surface and examined.

It was decided they were too far into the badlands to march back to the coast and take them to the hospital ships. They would stay with the army and receive medical attention from them. Many expressed a desire to fight the orcs and were assimilated into the army.

They had returned to camp, and a messenger was waiting for Velnir.

"Greetings and salutations, my lord. I am Galia. I was sent to you by Arlen to deliver this message." She then handed him a missive with the seal of Atlan. Velnir took it quickly, fearing the worst.

"My Lord Velnir, I write to inform you that the hospital ships were not enough to save me. I requested transport back to Thalnor to receive better medical care. I do apologize for waiting so long to write to you. I was not in a state of mind or physically strong enough to do so. Please, forgive me. I will be recovering in Atlan, but I must inform you that I will be out for quite a long time. Baefric is running things quite well here for you. Meric is enjoying himself as well. Everything seems to be going well, so fear not, my friend. Your land is well kept and cared for. Best regards, General Arlen."

Velnir held the missive to his chest and breathed a sigh of relief. "Thank you, Galia."

The council were all relieved as well, Magris especially, for if Arlen died, he would be responsible.

Velnir had sent the scribes down to Zakil to document their findings. They spent a total of nine days down there making drawings and writing texts about what they found. They had been able to decipher the ancient language of the city and determined it to be human and elvish.

The information they had found so far would be very valuable back home. The Tanimarans were ecstatic about what they found.

The gruff and guttural sound of several individuals conversing was heard outside the command tent. The council stopped talking to listen. They did not speak like elves did. Darlana raised a brow. The sentry informed them that the council was in a meeting and that they would have to come back at a later time.

"We were invited to the meeting, you prancy knife-eared sprite."

The individuals began to direct the strangest anti-elvish insults to them. After a few moments of this, the sentry couldn't take it anymore and interrupted the council.

"My lord, forgive the interruption, but um… you have a visitor," he said, quite irritated. The council stepped outside.

"My my, you pointy ears, how about you show some hospitality," said the dwarf.

Velnir was taken back a bit by the first impression of the stunted one.

Darlana was quite pleased to see him.

"Jokhut," she said with excitement.

"Darlana," said Jokhut with surprise.

Darlana immediately embraced the dwarf who embraced her back.

"You stunties never change, do you?" she said playfully. That sentry was probably going to need a mental health remedy.

"Oh, nothing a big healthy slerp of mead can't fix."

Jokhut laughed with Darlana.

"Come, meet my husband. He is a Tanimaran lord," she said.

"A husband, you say? you finally settled down… Wait, did you say Tanimaran? BWAHAHA! This is interesting," Jokhut said.

"I am quite serious. Come and meet him. He is not like the others," she said.

"You got that right," thought Magris to himself.

"Velnir, this is Jokhut, high king of the Stormanvil Clan."

"Pleased to meet you, pointy ear...err um, Vel...nir?"

"Pleasure to meet you, too, King Jokhut of the Stormanvil Clan. My father received a gift from the king of the thunderfor—"

Jokhut interrupted him. "You got anything to drink?" he asked, seemingly uninterested in formalities. "My brothers and I are thirsty."

"We have Atlantin mead in the mess hall. Help yourselves," Velnir said, trying to be polite.

Darlana was making strange gestures at Velnir, discreetly attempting to warn him. Velnir looked at her, confused, but it was too late. The dwarves made their way to the mess hall and began rummaging through the elven stash until they found what they were looking for. They rudely cleared a table and began drinking and singing very loudly and out of tune.

Velnir placed the open palm of his hand on his forehead and began to shake his head. Other elves began to gather around and started complaining.

"They are our guests. They have come to parlay about..." Truth be told, Velnir figured it had to do with Darlana's visit but was unaware of what they discussed. He understood that they would be attacking somewhere in the northwest.

Magris introduced himself. Immediately, they bonded. The dwarves loved his eyepatch and peg leg. They asked him about his battle scars and began to share war stories. He began to sing and dance with them, and it actually seemed like a lot of fun. Tanimarans began to join them and everyone was having a good time. Despite the mess, Velnir was pleased.

After they got their fill, King Jokhut came into the command tent.

"Darlana here came to me and said a bunch of pointy ears were invading the sundered lands to kick some orc arse. I say, hear hear. It's about damn time you princesses came off your pretty island in your pretty armor with your pretty weapons. The northern peaks of the sundered lands are the ancestral home of my clan. It has been occupied by orcs for hundreds of years, and we cannot afford to pull our forces out of Dhar'Algaz and move them this far south. If we do, we risk all that we have left. What we can do is attack the peaks and distract the orcs there while you take care of the ones down here because I tell you, they multiply like rats, but if you can divide them, you can conquer them. Now, I am a reasonable dwarf. I won't ask for something I'm not willing to work for, and dwarves can dig in for years if they need to. If I attack the peaks and keep those orcs there, you come to my aid to finish them off when you are done here," said Jokhut.

The dwarves smacked the table with their flagons of mead and said, "Hear hear!" startling everyone in the command tent.

Many Tanimarans began to talk amongst themselves.

"I am here to deliver Tanimaran justice to the orcs," said Velnir. "If you are willing to attack the clans that occupy the northern peaks, I will come to your aid, but I will require more than this. We are in need of electhril."

"It is my understanding that the only source of electhril that the Tanimarans have comes from the Thunderforge Clan in Dhar'Modir. What happened?" Jokhut asked.

Velnir was reluctant to tell them. The shipments of supplies stopped coming from Tanimara shortly after they all arrived in the sundered lands, and he wasn't sure why. Electhril ingots were needed to fix or reforge armor and weapons.

"Our supplies are running low," he lied. "War demands more electhril ingots than we can currently be supplied with."

"I see. Very well then, we will ship ingots of electhril from Dhar'Algaz, equal to the weight of mead shipped from Tanimara," said Jokhut with a wide, rosy-cheeked smile along with his companions.

Velnir smiled. He couldn't believe all they wanted was more mead in exchange for electhril. Electhril was very hard for the elves to come by, and they were desperately in need of it. Atlantin produced almost all of the Tanimaran mead and shipped it around Tanimara.

"Agreed, let us begin trading immediately," Velnir said.

"We can begin trading now?" Jokhut asked with excitement in his voice. "Oh, boys, it has been so long since we have had the sweet nectar of the delicious Tanimaran honey mead. I cannot tell you what this will mean for our people. I didn't think you would agree. You have made a friend out of me, Velnir Melfarin," Jokhut said with sincerity.

Velnir was touched. He had no idea that dwarves loved Tanimaran mead so much. He was beginning to think he needed to make a lot of changes to Atlantin's policy when he returned to Tanimara.

"Very well, I'll send word to Atlan to begin production of whatever quota you wish us to meet."

Jokhut had an enormous gold book brought to him by

one of his brothers.

"Sign here," he said.

"What is this? A contract?" asked Velnir.

"This here is my lexicon of agreements and grudges. Now sign."

"Grudges?" Velnir inquired.

"Aye, we don't easily forget who wrongs us or who does right by us. Now sign!"

Velnir signed it and the dwarves left the camp.

"That was very strange," said Magris.

"Dwarves are strange," said Velnir.

The time to find orcs was now.

A few days later, Jokhut sent word they were on the move and it was reported that the humans were also attacking the orcs in Araba near Talabad in the peaks. The elves had to move now.

Velnir and Magris took to the sky atop dragons. The army was marching from the west and deep into the heart of the sundered lands. Their supply lines were dangerously thin and those moving goods have reported that no ships have returned from Tanimara.

This bothered Velnir and now the other council members knew, but a large force of orcs had been gathering several kilometers away and was spotted by scouts. Velnir immediately ordered the army to march toward them. They were well supplied right now and could forage for whatever they needed outside of electhril for the time being.

He did not want it to be a secret that they were coming and it was not. It was impressive just how easy it was for orcs to come together.

Velnir remembered Dargarok say it was 'as easy as the strongest chieftain to defeat other chieftains to absorb their clans into his.'

The three dragon riders threw scrying orbs to get a closer look without risking attack. This army was made up of orcs, trolls, goblins, ogres, and those giants made of stone. The goblins mounted giant black spiders and what seemed like a head with a massive mouth on two legs.

"How could those things be effective mounts?" thought Magris.

They could see that the warlocks were commanding something, and it was pointed out by Magris that it was the stone giants. They flew back to the army.

Velnir had his army form ranks at the base of a jagged cliff. The dragons with Magris and Folwin were perched up there and hidden. The orcish wyverns didn't even think to go that high, which was to the advantage of the elves.

Once again, the elvish front line placed their shields in front of them, creating a massive shield wall. The second line of elves placed their spears in special slots on the front lines' shields. The elves were outnumbered, so they began to form into squares, placing their shields around and above them, forming testudos. Spears were sticking out each side. The elves had perfected the testudo.

It was midday, and the sky was cloudy and dark. The land was barren, and the only life was the opposing forces they were about to face. The orcs were raging, growling, and yelling at the elves. Their spirits appeared to be high.

Velnir immediately recognized the orc leading the wyverns

as being none other than the one they called Skroatug. He was their warchief. The orcs began to charge. Velnir ordered the bolt throwers at the ready. Archers knocked their arrows, and he ordered them to fire.

Row after row of orcs fell, but this didn't deter them. The elves braced for impact and the orcs tried to smash the testudos but were ineffective. They thrust their spears into the faces, throats, and chests of the orcs. The bolt throwers began to fire at the giants.

Several bolts hit the giants, and exploded on impact, creating a colossal mess. The stone giants were vaporized. It seemed to be going well for the elves.

The mages took to the sky and flew over the orcish army. They were engaged by the wyverns but practiced hit-and-run tactics as they knew griffins were faster than wyverns. They began to conjure firestorms within their ranks.

Manticores entered the fray from over the hill in a surprise attack. Their breath attacks killed hundreds of elves and destroyed the first line of testudos. What was left of the testudo tactically fell back into the first line of elves and created a massive shield wall. The manticore were coming back around for another attack.

Velnir signaled for Magris and Folwin to act. They took to the sky and ascended. Both dragons unleashed hellish fire breaths upon the orcs. The stench of charred orc remains filled the air. Again, they made a pass, but this did not deter the orcs. Pass after pass, thousands upon thousands of orcs were incinerated. The same could be said for the elves, as the manticore had been breaking off and strafing the elven line.

They remained undeterred.

Velnir unsheathed Illuminar and moved in front of the front line. This inspired the troops. Velnir was holding his ground well, but Darlana was powering through the orcs. She made it seem easy. Velnir and several of the other troops looked at each other and then at her.

"She really is the perfect combination of beauty, strength, and lethality…" thought Velnir.

She was inspiring. They pressed on.

The dragons made several more breath attacks, but the orcs kept coming. Velnir wanted to put his sword enchantments to the test, so he leaped out of the line.

"Feast your eyes upon me and despair," he shouted.

He then thrust his sword into the ground. From it, expelled a massive wave of fire, and it washed over the entire battlefield of orcs. The orcs began to flail and scream in pain as their flesh began to melt off their body.

This was no ordinary fire, and the elves saw firsthand just how powerful Illuminar was. Darlana even stopped and looked at Velnir. Her face was covered in the blood of orcs, and her armor was covered with their innards.

Her look to him was that of awe and surprise. The orcs began to retreat and the elves in their excitement, began to give chase. Skroatug did not dismount this time and was cursing Velnir.

***

The elves made camp, and the dragons had their fill of dead orcs while the army buried their dead and treated their wounded. The centaur had run down as many retreating orcs as they could and brought back hundreds for the dragons to feast on. Yzat and Nythint were growing fast. They were by now the same size as their mother.

Darlana was assisting in the medical tent. She was in this one by herself, treating twenty wounded elves. It was quite the feat.

Velnir walked up to her. "How are you doing, Darlana?"

"I'm managing."

"You've mastered your skill with blades. You were easily outclassing me, and I'm arguably the best sword master in Tanimara."

"For six hundred years, I have been fighting in the traditional manner. I have never seen such destruction, though I do understand why it was necessary. I've spent a long time in Nagrimar, and war has never come to our doorstep like it has yours. I am a healer and support life. Death is necessary, though, and it will take me some time to get used to it again." She turned her attention to the wounded Tanimaran and applied a healing salve. She was very gentle and skillful, impressive to Velnir.

He stood there and watched her work on his men. They all adored her and seemed to have forgotten that she was known as the apostate of Tarvana.

Velnir left Darlana to her work and sought out Magris and Alzar. They were conversing near the mess tent. Magris was ecstatic over Alzar's skill, and Alzar soaked up all the praise. Ismi was playing with the other dragons and eating the dead orcs. It was quite a grotesque scene.

The ground was covered in the remains of charred dead

orcs. What wasn't charred before was being charred now. The smell was atrocious. The dragons didn't eat the orcs whole, either. They took turns helping each other tear them to pieces, swallowing bit by bit.

The crunch of their bones as the dragons bit into the orc flesh did soothe Velnir. He liked the thought of it. Several hundred orcs were captured. Elves were nailing them to posts and leaving them to starve to death or bleed out. Some were set on fire for the amusement of the soldiers. The Nagrimarans were not part of it.

They were not protesting but instead tended the wounded and helping with food. The centaur, however, took great pleasure in stomping the ones that had not yet been nailed to posts. Their hooves broke the tusks and caved in the faces of the captured orcs.

Chapter 14
Ominous Opportunity

"Hang in there, general. We are almost there," said Eldar.

"Your service and haste are appreciated, captain," said Arlen.

Moments later, they arrived and landed on the hospital ship. Eldar helped Arlen get into bed, along with several nurses and immediately addressed his wounds.

"Whoever dressed your wound before you got here did an immaculate job. I have never seen such delicate work, General. You are very fortunate. Who was able to provide such care?" asked the nurse.

Arlen simply smiled and said, "I cannot remember who it was, but yes, I agree. I am very fortunate."

Eldar knew it was Darlana but chose not to say anything. Arlen had remained in the care of the nurses for several days. It was not long before he was able to get out of his bed and walk around the ship.

The nurse, Arlen's primary caregiver for the last few days, entered his room.

"I brought you some tea, General."

"Thank you, Galia. You are most wonderful," he said as he took a sip.

She was looking at him with longing eyes. It was clear that she had taken a liking to the general. She truly went above and beyond to make him comfortable and take care of him.

"You have done a superb job helping me recover, Galia. I really appreciate your service, and so does Tanimara."

"I live but to serve the Mari," she said.

"Very good," he said while taking another sip of the tea.

"May I ask you something general?"

"You ,can but I may not be able to answer."

"Did lord Velnir really get betrothed to the apostate?" Arlen looked at her, attempting to read her. She looked as though she was in fact curious but sounded quite nervous to ask.

"Between you and me, he did indeed," he said quietly. "Consider this privileged information. I do not think I am supposed to say anything yet, but he married her to secure an alliance with the Nagrimarans."

She showed her disgust. "I've heard stories of her. Any elf that mates with and has a child with a human deserves a fate far worse than hers. I am hardly able to believe that she was only exiled. How can the magistrate be all right with this?"

"They do not yet know, Galia."

"You must tell them. This would bring shame and embarrassment to our people."

He was impressed with Galia's willingness to betray Velnir so quickly. He could not tell if she was so eager to do so because Arlen was there or not. The elves with Velnir did not seem to mind Darlana too much.

"I heard you were going back with captain Eldar to Velnir's encampment."

"Truth be told, I do not want to go back. I despise the idea of fighting alongside a Nagrimaran. Those people are no better than animals. Disgusting apostate's, not at all worthy to even have Mari in their name."

"It pleases me to hear you say this, General," she said while re-filling his tea.

"I have but one problem, Galia. You see, I cannot simply stay here and allow Eldar to leave. He supports Velnir. If he were to return, then…"

She interrupted him. "Say no more. You are both intending to leave tonight while we have supper. Distract him, and I'll do the rest," she said with a smile.

This pleased Arlen greatly.

Arlen saw Eldar speaking with someone on the other side of the ship. Night was approaching, and the two were expected to make their way back to Velnir's army in the sundered lands. The mess hall was beginning to get crowded, and everyone was making their way inside while Arlen and Eldar were about to mount the griffin.

"Eldar, before you go, I'd like to thank you," said Arlen while looking over his shoulders to make sure no one was looking. "You have been paramount in my recovery, and I really cannot thank you enough."

"General, it is an honor to have been the one to carry you to the ship and remain by your side until we return to Velnir."

"Right," said Arlen once again looking over his shoulder. The griffin was at the bow of the ship, and everyone was inside. The ships adjacent from the hospital ship were also having dinner and no one was really around. Both Arlen and Eldar were wearing their armor, which was arguably heavy. "About that. I will not be going back to Velnir and his apostate wife to fight alongside those who call themselves Mari of any kind."

"General, with respect, I understand your sentiment, but we are not bound by our political, ethical code as much as we are by honor and loyalty. We must go back."

"You see captain, I have much to gain if Velnir were to… lose. If there are no Melfarin to take the mantle in Atlantin, it falls to my family, and since I am the only surviving heir, it falls to me. That is why I have been seizing the supplies being sent to Araba from Tanimara. If the orcs do not kill him, what better reason than fraternizing with the enemy, bargaining an alliance with them and building an army, depleting the resources of Tanimara, and sailing it halfway across the world without the approval of the Magistrate?

Lord of Atlantin?" he said with a smug smile.

"How could you even say such things, Arlen? He will be most disappointed. You are his best friend, after all, and to say such things is treason in and of itself. I will report this at…" Eldar's eyes widened in shock. He began to choke on his own blood as his life began to slip out of him. He started to slump over, and behind him stood Galia with a grin ear to ear.

Together, they gently picked him up and tossed his body overboard. The weight of his armor pulled him under with haste. Arlen then quickly tied the griffin down.

"Marvelous work, Galia. He did not even make a sound."

"Many thanks, General," she said with a gleeful smile.

He looked at her as thoughts of his future swam in his head. They made their way to the mess hall and began to enjoy dinner with the other sailors. Afterwords, Arlen requested a meeting with the captain of the ship. He informed him of what Velnir was doing and what had happened to Eldar. He then took command of the fleet and ordered it back to Tanimara, more specifically to Tarvana.

Arlen summoned Galia to his chambers. A knock on his door could be heard. He took a deep breath and got up to let her in. She stood in the doorway with a beautiful smile. She wore her hair down and had on a lovely silk dress.

"Please, come in, Galia," he said. He pulled out a chair for her to sit in, and he sat across from her. "It is with great honor that I promote you to lieutenant. Your healing skills and stealth abilities have proven to be most useful. I will need your help if I am to claim what Velnir is not worthy of. We sail to Tarvana to speak with the Magistrate."

"Thank you for the promotion, General. I am pleased you are taking this to the Magistrate, and I will do whatever I can to assist you," she said, looking at him suggestively, "And please you." He had no objections.

They finally arrived in Tarvana. The city sat atop cliffs and was walled as far as the eye could see. The inlet was below ground level and had bridges over the fissure. Sailing through it was majestic to say the least. Tall spires and massive palaces covered the landscape of Tarvana.

General Arlen only sailed one ship of the fleet into Tarvana and when they docked, he immediately introduced himself and requested an audience with the magistrate. Per the customs of the government, he had to wait in the dockyard until he had approval.

Arlen took the time to look around and take in what he could see. The dockyard was massive and had elegant elven ships loading and unloading what appeared to be trade goods. It was a pretty large hub of the most exquisite that Tanimara had to offer along with the rest of the world.

Arlen looked over and saw a ship from the Ying provinces of the western continent. The merchant was standing on the dock speaking with a Tanimaran. He wore a long golden silk robe with an elegant design woven into it. He had his black hair pinned up and when he turned, Arlen could see that his eyes were almond-shaped and that he had hair on his chin and a thin mustache.

These were not humans or elves, though they somewhat resembled them. They are dragonspawn. Not quite dragons, but the form in which Arlen was witness to was not what they really looked like. This visage was what they chose like other dragons did. Their true form was more of a humanoid drakonid: two legs, two arms, claws, scales, and sharp teeth. They all had slit-shaped pupils. A very strange but intriguing magical race.

A messenger from the Magistrate approached Arlen, granting him permission to speak with the magistrate regarding the matters Arlen wished to discuss immediately. Arlen was pleased, and his escort offered him a carriage ride through the city to the high court, for which he happily accepted.

The roads were lined with elegant darla trees. They had white trunks and purple-blackish leaves. Extremely rare and perplexing. The roads were clean and the townsfolk were happy. Every government building had two guards at each entrance. Such rules were not available in other nations; leave it to the elves to come up with order like this. The dwellings of the regular elves were even ornate and beautiful. They took pride in what they had and it showed.

Eventually, they came up to the palace that towered over the city. Arlen got out and made his way up the steps to check in at the door. He was led inside and up the stairs into the chambers of the Magistrate. The one who escorted him made him wait outside the door and went him by himself presumably to inform the magistrate of Arlen's arrival.

He came back out and informed Arlen that they were ready to see him. Arlen straightened up and made himself as presentable as he could.

"This is it. This is my chance," he thought to himself.

He walked in, and to the sides of the room were rows and rows of seating for the elected magisters to sit in, and directly in front of him was the seat of the high Magister. They all looked at him in complete silence. Anxiety struck Arlen as he walked to the center of the room. The eyes of these elves felt like they pierced his soul as if they knew exactly what his intentions were. This would not deter him.

"Welcome, General Arlen of Atlantin," said the loud, booming voice of High Magistrate Raften. "You come before the Magistrate to inform us of what Lord Velnir of Atlantin is up to in the sundered lands, yes?"

"I do," said Arlen.

"Get on with it then."

"Right, Lord Velnir of Atlantin has sought the alliance of Nagrimar on behalf of Tanimara."

The chamber erupted in shock and awe. Raften had a look of bewilderment.

"Silence!" he demanded. "You witnessed this, General?

"I did. I flew with him to Nagrimar to meet with Darlana."

The magisters began to whisper to each other quietly.

"She has made it to the sundered lands and brought with her an army of elves and centaurs."

Magister Raften peered into Arlen's eyes. "One of your status would not bring these accusations to light so easily. I understand that you and Lord Velnir are the best of friends. Why then would you betray him and come to us?"

"I am loyal to Tanimara, High Magister. If one were to commit treason, it is my duty as a Tanimaran General to report it, especially one of such high regard."

"You are indeed," said Raften before sitting back and smugly, looking at Arlen with his chin perched high. "I charge Velnir with crimes against Tanimara and treason. I move to dismiss him of his lordship, confiscate his lands, and name him an enemy of Tanimara. This disgusting, grotesque representation of the Mari cannot be tolerated, therefore I move to hold a special emergency session to find Velnir Melfarin guilty."

Guards from outside the room flooded in and placed themselves around the chambers with shields and spears in hand. This was a clear show of the tyrannical authority of the High Magister. Tanimara was hardly a republic anymore.

"All in favor of my verdict of guilty, say aye now," demanded Raften.

Everyone in the chamber said Aye. There was no way of telling who was actually in favor or not. Fear gripped most of them, while some clearly stood in favor of the High Magister. Either way, Arlen was pleased. He would be next in line to inherit Atlantin and they did not seem to care.

"Assembly dismissed," said Raften. "General, I will see you in my chambers at once."

Arlen was visibly nervous. The room was clearing, and the High Magister stepped out of his seat and made his way to a room, where he motioned Arlen to follow.

Once inside, Raften closed the door. "Sit," he said.

Arlen obliged and waited for Raften to come around the desk.

"It is an hon…" Arlen began before being interrupted.

"Oh, spare me the niceties. I know what you are up to. The documentation states you are to inherit Atlantin should Velnir, the last of the Melfarins, be killed or removed. You shall have it, but only if you do me a favor."

Arlen was visibly annoyed. He did not need to do anything to receive his rightful status as lord of Atlantin. It was his right by blood! This proved the High Magister's authority was way too high and out of control. Arlen was in no position to disagree, however, and so he nodded and listened.

"I care not how or when you do it, but you will find Velnir and Darlana. You will kill them both and bring me their heads as proof. Once your quest is complete, you will receive your title," he said smugly.

"Very well, I will get started at once."

"Before you do, take your armada and eighty thousand soldiers to capture Atlantin, Madir, and Caphery in the name of Tanimara. Declare martial law, and execute any who oppose you! Dismissed," said the high magistrate in a cold and dismissive tone.

Arlen made his way out of the palace and back to the courtyard where the carriage was awaiting him. He got in and began to think about what had transpired. He was displeased with the arrangement. He felt some remorse for Velnir because he was, after all, his best friend. They grew up together, but Arlen was always in his shadow. Second best and never preferred company over Magris or Meric. He had been jealous of Velnir for hundreds of years now, and finally, he would have his chance to shine, but he wondered now if the cost was too high.

Arlen made his way back to the fleet and brought it into Tarvana to pick up eighty thousand soldiers to march on the treasonous regions. From here, it was a few days sailing to get to Thalnor. Once they arrived, they did not land. Arlen sent a messenger to the port to demand entry, and it was granted.

No blood was shed to take the port of Atlantin. The army offloaded and began to march with haste to the city of Atlan. Arlen knew eighty thousand would not be enough to take the city if they resisted. He would have to place it under siege and request assistance from the other houses. This worried him as it would give sympathizers time to reach Velnir and tell him what was going on.

Velnir could make it back in time to attack and Arlen could not allow this to happen. Wise was the High Magister for only giving him a small army but forcing him to prove himself worthy of Atlantin while protecting Tarvana from any retaliation from Velnir should it come to that.

They marched to the gate of Atlan, and Arlen mounted his griffin. He took to the sky and approached the gatekeeper.

"On behalf of the High Magistrate of Tanimara, I demand that you open the gate and allow this army to enter." Arlen was nervous and started to sweat. The gatekeeper paused for a moment before climbing down into the gate room. There was silence for what seemed to be an enormous amount of time. Arlen was growing more fearful and impatient by the minute.

"The gate should have been open by now!" he yelled. He was becoming anxious.

Suddenly, he saw movement in the archer towers. He raised his shield but held his ground while on top of his armored griffin. If they shot at him, his plans for a peaceful resolution were gone and he would be forced to siege. He could hear his heart pounding in his chest.

He looked back at the army, which was still in column formation. Several minutes had gone by and the gatekeeper was clearly taking his time, but for what? Just then, the gate began to open much to the reprieve of Arlen. Fear turned into anger.

He flew down and landed at the head of the army. He then ordered them to march in.

At the entrance, he ordered several of his troops to retrieve the gatekeeper and bring him to the general at once. While the rest of the army marched through the streets and toward the palace, several guards and Arlan waited at the gate.

A moment later, the soldiers brought the gatekeeper down and placed him on his knees in front of Arlen.

"You took your time opening the gate."

"I was unsure what to do. You have an army with you and Velnir…" Arlen unsheathed his sword, and separated the head from the gatekeeper's shoulders.

Many people around that witnessed were horrified and began to scatter.

"Let this be an example of what happens when you cross me," he yelled. He then remounted his griffin and flew to the magister of Atlan's chambers. Magister Kaelina was waiting there for him. She has a smug look on her face.

"At your service, Arlen…I mean, General Arlen," she said.

"You would do well to show me the respect of a lord, Magister."

"You are not a lord yet," said the magister with a smirk.

"You will come with me to the palace. Baefric and Meric must be removed."

They made their way to the palace. Arlen took the lead and led troops to storm it. They made their way up the stairs and through the halls. Arlen had been here many times and knew exactly where to go. He pounded on the door of the lord's chambers.

"Baefric, the High Magistrate demands your surrender. Surrender to me, and I will spare you and your family."

"Traitor, befouler, monster," Baefric began to shout on the other side of the door. This upset Arlen.

"Open the door, Baefric! You did hear that I would allow you and your family to go free."

"Never, Arlen, you traitor!" said a defiant Baefric.

Arlen looked over his shoulder and motioned for one of the guards to break it down. Once he did, they stormed the chambers. Unbeknownst to the guards, Baefric was holding himself on the ceiling with a dagger in his mouth.

They poured in searching for him. Arlen was rushing guards in by the droves. Suddenly, the cries of injured and dying guardsmen could be heard. This caught Arlen by surprise.

"Guards," he yelled. "We need more guards."

Moments later, several more guards came rushing up the stairs. Arlen motioned them into the chambers, and again, the sounds of elves dying could be heard.

Finally, the guards had subdued Baefric, but not before he killed twenty-one of them. Arlen was sickened by the carnage brought about by one old elf. Baefric was brought before him, beaten and bloodied. He was on his knees, and looked up at Arlen with disgust through the one eye not swollen.

"All you had to do was surrender, you fool," said Arlen with a smug look.

Baefric spit in his face much to the displeasure of Arlen.

"Take him outside. I will make an example out of him." Arlen looked around. "Where is Meric?" A guard approached Arlen and reported he could not be found. Truth be told, Meric was in a brothel having a good time. He heard the troops coming and slipped out the back. He climbed an abandoned tower and watched the crowd assemble below as the guards and Arlen brought Baefric out. Meric could not make out what Arlen was saying, but he saw that Baefric was badly beaten. He knew what was likely to come of this. Moments later, Arlen beheaded Baefric, placed his head atop a pike, and mounted it in the city center for all to see.

Meric waited until nightfall before leaving the tower. He grabbed a cloak and hood and made his way through the alleys of the city. Guards were everywhere.

Martial law had been issued and a curfew was in place. No one but the guards were out right now and he knew he could not get caught. He had some close calls but managed to make his way to the griffin stables. He untied one and mounted it. As quietly as he could, he took to the sky and gained altitude as fast as he could. Much to his surprise, he went unnoticed.

Chapter 15
Skroatug's Revenge

The campaign had been going well. The combination of elves, centaurs, and dragons proved very effective. The army had been bonding well. Some Tanimarans found love within the ranks of the Nagrimarans. Love could be heard in several camps throughout the night. This definitely included that of Velnir and Darlana's.

Reports were coming in that men and dwarves were advancing farther and farther into the northern peaks of the sundered lands. This was good news. "Any word from Atlan, my lord?" said Magris.

"I've heard nothing so far though we are thousands of kilometers away from Atlan and probably from the ships on the coast of Araba as well. The supplies are thinning out, though, and this raises some concern."

Magris nodded and said, "I'll see what I can do, my lord."

"The army packed up as they do every day and marched further inland, combing the sundered lands for orcs. It would seem that the orcs have learned that it was not in their interest to fight the elves in the open as they have lost every time. Scouts are reporting that they are taking refuge in the hills and tunnels underground."

Velnir knew the vastness of the tunnels and wasn't content with them there. As the elves moved further and further inland, the night attacks grew more common. The orcs had mastered the stealth of grab and go of sleeping elves. They would come up from under the elves, grab them, and go back down, the elves never to be heard from again.

The council convened in the command tent. "Reports indicate that the orcs have all moved underground and the attacks are growing more frequent. They think we will not follow them there, but I have a plan. The mages and dragons can wreak havoc with fire and burn them out. I don't know how effective that will be, but it will be worth a try," said Velnir.

"There is an arcane line nearby that we can all tap into," said Magris.

"Very well, let's give it a try and see what we can come up with."

The mages had been practicing pyromancy and had become very proficient. They were even teaching it to some of the Nagrimarans, including Darlana, who was having lots of fun with it. Velnir called them to attention in front of the command tent.

"Today we will be trying a new tactic. I am sure you have noticed the orcs are hiding underground like cowards. Your skills are good with pyromancy, so you and the dragons will burn them out of the tunnels, and we will wait for them up here. Now find a hole, move into position, and on my command, unleash hell," he ordered.

The mages seemed quite excited to follow these orders. They hurried to find any hole that they could determine led to a tunnel. Velnir gave them the order, and all together, they sent fire through the tunnels. The dragons delivered the most damage.

Massive sections of ground were blown up, revealing a cave network below. The orcs scurried as fast as they could, but most of them ended up charred corpses.

"That made quick work of them," said Magris.

"Indeed," said Velnir.

The elves began to march again.

***

The orcs have been retreating for weeks now. Whole families and clans have moved underground out of fear they would be next. A mother held her pup while the father leaned up against the walls of the cave with his bow ready, trying to be as quiet as a mouse. The footsteps of marching elves can be heard above. Rocks and dust fell from the tunnel ceiling. The orcs put out their torches so the smoke didn't penetrate the ground. They went undetected this time but may not be so lucky the next.

"We must go," said Roktuk to his mate Sharma.

"Our pup is only seven days old. We must not rush, or he will get fussy, Roktuk," Sharma protested.

"I was not asking, Sharma," he said with fearfully. "We have to go now if our clan is to survive." They made their way through the tunnels and came out the end of a fork. The area was vast and open. Several thousand orcs had arrived and sought refuge. By now, it was mostly women and children. Skroatug stood atop the back of a stone giant.

"Let not your fear consume you, my brothers and sisters. The dragon will liberate us." Skroatug said, trying to control the crowd.

"The elves have three dragons. They are destroying everything in their wake," said one angry female.

"How can we contend with such power? You promised us glory. You promised us victory if we followed you to the elf land. We did, and now look at what it has wrought," said another.

"Yeah, you got your trinket, but what did we get?" Many were agreeing in anger toward Skroatug. He pulled out the Scepter of Canar, and it emitted a dark, low sound.

The crowd silenced.

"We have experienced setbacks. Once I get this to the dragon, he will use it to liberate us," Skroatug said confidently.

"You are a fool, Skroatug. Why not just use it yourself? Screw the dragon," said a supporter from his clan.

"Yeah, we did the work, not the dragon. Take the power for yourself," said another.

Skroatug thought for a moment. "This is true. We retrieved the Scepter of Canar. Why shouldn't we keep it for ourselves? Why should we not use it to defeat the elves ourselves?" he thought.

"Warlocks, come," he demanded.

The coven of warlocks had a new leader now. Nekros was adept in shadow and chaos magic. He approached Skroatug and turned his attention to the scepter.

"Ah, The Scepter of Canar. It comes from the dark one and has great power. None know how to activate it, not even the dragon. We are all near an arcane line. Let us sacrifice the shamans to enhance its power and see if we cannot commune with the dark one himself," suggested Nekros.

Skroatug was reluctant but desperate and power-hungry. He agreed. "Round up the shamans. This shall be entertaining, at least."

Grunts made their way through the crowds of clans and detained many shamans from several clans–about one hundred in total. Any who resisted were also detained and brought with them. The warlocks gathered around and placed several black candles that emitted a purple and green flame. They placed them in a circle pattern, which had a rune. The shamans were bound along with any who had resisted and placed on the outer ring of the circle.

Nekros was meticulous in the way everything should be placed. He kept looking into a book he carried, trying to find any minor detail he may have missed. "Good, good. The souls of the pure ones should be enough to activate this rune so that we can speak to…the dark one. Coven, gather around and begin," Nekros ordered.

The orcs began to chant an ominous hymn. The shaman's souls were considered pure as they had a connection to the living planet. It was in direct contrast with the warlock's magic, which was that of death and destruction.

The shamans began to wail in agony. Their souls began to be ripped from their bodies. The ghastly images still wailed as they were consumed within the rune.

Soon, the rune consumed enough souls to activate, and a portal appeared to a dark realm. Within, one could see the cosmos and the surface of a corrupted world wrapped in the tendrils of the dark ones. The sound coming from it was low and creepy.

"You must go through the portal, Skroatug, and speak to it," Nekros said schemingly.

Skroatug peered into the portal. His instincts told him not to go in, but his lust for power and desire to learn how to use the Scepter of Canar was more convincing. He stepped in and fell through landing on the other side.

The world was a dark wasteland. The sky was black, and the stars were few. Giant tendrils gripped the planet and an unknown voice penetrated Skroatug's mind.

"You have come for answers, young Abrionling."

Skroatug's mind seared in pain. He would power through it and answer, "Y…yess."

"That which you have is powerful indeed. It can even destroy the wizard. It can even destroy the dragon, should you choose. The price is not much. All I ask in return is for the souls of those most dear to you…and yours when you perish," the unknown voice echoed in Skroatug's mind.

"Very well…the pain…make it stop," Skroatug pleaded.

Of course, it did not stop. Suddenly, he felt the pull, and he was yanked back through the portal. He landed with a thud, and the pain instantly went away.

"What did it say?" demanded Nekros.

Skroatug grabbed Nekros by the throat and tore it out. Nekros slumped over, now a lifeless corpse. The other warlocks backed off and cowered. Skroatug did not say a word. He knew what he must do. He went to find his family. They were hidden away in a cave near the gathering underground. His mate was feeding their pups and breastfeeding one of them. He looked at them longingly.

Skroatug came out of his cave to a crowd of orcs who observed the slaughtered corpses of his mate and pups. In his left hand, the ax which he used to murder his family was still dripping with their blood and in his right hand, the staff that he held high. The crystal was glowing brighter than before. The carving of hands from the wood the staff was made of that held the crystal did not obstruct its glow.

"Behold, the Scepter of Canar. I will use this to crush our enemies and kill the wizard. Then, I will take it to the dragon and negotiate. We will have our glory," he said with a mighty voice.

The orcs cheered and began to send word to the other clans. They started marching through the tunnels at a brisk pace. It was nightfall and they made it to the surface. The wyverns took to the sky to find the position of the elves. They were discovered in a matter of hours and they quickly reported back. Skroatug quietly marched his army to the elvish encampment.

He still wasn't sure how to use the Scepter, but he would figure it out. The army went undetected and was able to form ranks outside the camp. Skroatug raised the Scepter.

Chapter 16
Battle of the Sundered Lands

An elvish sentry spotted a line of shadow appear off in the distance but did not think anything of it. A moment later, an arrow pierced his helmet and went through his head, killing him quietly.

Several other sentries met their fate the same way. Magris heard something fall and left his tent to investigate. Upon further inspection, he noticed the sentry lying on the ground.

"Orcs," he thought. He looked up and saw a tiny little purple object glowing in the distance and could hear the clanking of metal and guttural grunts. He immediately knew what it was.

He turned to yell, "ORCS!"

A massive purple vortex had spawned in the middle of the elvish encampment and began to rampage through it. It was considerably larger than a firestorm.

It sucked the souls of its prey right into it while their bodies simply dropped to the ground and became all shriveled up.

Velnir, Darlana, and Magris immediately went to investigate and, to their horror, saw firsthand the devastation wrought on them.

The dragons had already taken to the sky and began making passes through the orcish line. Thousands of them rushed the elvish camp and began slaughtering everything they could find. The centaurs formed up and charged the orcish flank and smashed into them, giving the Tanimarans and Nagrimarans time to form ranks themselves, but this was not enough. There were so many orcs.

"How could there be this many?" thought Velnir.

They engaged the orcs but stopped their advance. The centaur kept running back and forth, smashing into the orc's flanks, but this did not deter them. They then began galloping in a circle and shooting at the orcs from a distance once they gave chase.

Magris ordered that all of the mages atop griffin riders ignite the tips of their staff to illuminate the battlefield. The elves could now see the full scale of the orcish army and became aware of what they were up against.

Velnir then turned his attention to Skroatug, but before he could react, Skroatug had conjured a massive, dark shadowy purple spike and hurled it toward Velnir, hitting him square in the chest and knocking him back several yards.

Folwin took to the sky. Flaming missiles came barreling out of his staff, hitting several hundred orcs at a time. The shape of a skull that was generated from the pyro missiles created a lot of wind and made it look terrifying. Skroatug again conjured another bolt and threw it at Folwin, knocking him out of the sky. Unfortunately, the griffin was killed, but Folwin was able to get to his feet and retreat back to the elven line.

Yzat saw Skroatug and decided to take the opportunity, so he descended and unleashed a massive breath attack. A purple barrier appeared in front of him and stopped the flames, but it failed to spare any orcs around Skroatug.

They were turned to ash.

Thinking he got the orc, he went back to fighting the manticore along with Nythint and the griffins. The elves began to retreat. Skroatug took this opportunity to press his attack. He used the Scepter to conjure shadowy purple spikes to protrude from the ground in front of the retreating elves.

It broke the ground and made their way toward their line. Several elves were instantly impaled.

"Retreat! Retreat!" yelled Darlana.

Velnir regained consciousness and heard Darlana ordering a retreat. He looked up and saw Skroatug and the orcs advancing on the elves.

They were no match for this and he knew it. He mustered up his strength and thrust Illuminar into the ground. A massive wave of fire went barreling toward the orcish line.

Unfortunately, there were many elves still trying to get away who were also in the path of Illuminar. Skroatug saw this and aimed the Scepter at him. Magris saw this and flew down to grab Velnir in the nick of time. The Scepter's bolt landed right where he was a moment later.

It was daylight. The army was exhausted as they had been running for their lives for hours. The bolt throwers could not be saved. The dragons needed to rest, and the centaurs that had broken their legs were being cared for.

Unfortunately, there was nothing anyone could do for a centaur when they broke their legs. They were too big to move and never fully recover, so the centaurs created a tradition of honorable euthanasia.

Family would gather around the injured centaur and say goodbye. They would pray to the celestials, and the strongest one among them would shoot an arrow through the head of the injured centaur.

It was gruesome and sad.

The centaur thought nothing of it as it was a normal part of their lives. They would grieve in a way not understood well by anyone else there. The elves had suffered a terrible defeat.

"We have no supplies," said Magris.

He was right. Everything had been left back there. They needed to get out of there, and fast. As bad as this looked, it was a fortunate blessing to have such a powerful weapon with them.

Darlana looked around. Many of the soldiers were sitting down and resting. They had started to take off their armor. They were hungry and in need of water. There was no time for respite, however.

"We must get out of here now," Velnir said. "They are coming."

"Where are we?" asked Darlana

"On the other side of the mountain. If they send scouts, they will find us. We need to move."

Velnir quickly got his commanders to order the army to move, and they did reluctantly. This time, Velnir was mounted on Yzat, Magris on Nythint. The orcs found them and began to give chase.

They marched through the sundered lands and into the night. It appeared the orcs had stopped. The elves were on top of a large rock formation and knew the orcs could not come up through it. They were surrounded by mountains and would find themselves trapped.

Velnir saw a pass up ahead that narrowed into a ravine before opening back up at the end. He came up with an idea.

"Let us form ranks halfway down the pass. We can pack enough in there to effectively bottleneck the orcs if they press their attack. The dragons and our griffin riders will pound them from behind. They severely outnumber us now, and we cannot keep running. The only chance we have is to use the terrain."

"What of that orc with his staff? If we are caught in the pass, and he was to unleash it against us, there is nowhere for us to escape," said Magris.

"Leave him to me," said Velnir.

"We need to get them down the pass. I can use Illuminar. The dragons can help as well. We have no choice. Move the army into the pass and form ranks. Get archers on the cliffs. You and Folwin, mount Yzat and Nythint. Darlana and I will be on the front line. Go!"

The elves moved to follow orders. The army had marched down the pass and formed ranks. Archers made their way up the cliffs on either side. The dragons waited on top of the cliffs.

Soon, the orcs could be seen over the horizon. It was late afternoon and cloudy; the elves were exhausted and weary, but still, they brought up their shields and spears. The archers nocked their arrows and they waited.

The horde that approached was the largest they had seen yet. The elves had dwindled substantially. They were coming from as far as the eye could see. Velnir had to defeat them here, or he would lose his army. He was determined. He looked around at his soldiers and realized there were about eighty thousand left or so.

The orcs had to be fielding five hundred thousand or more. He prayed his strategy would work.

The orcs began to make their way down the pass. They smacked their shields with their axes and howled, roared, and spit insults. They knew they had won the day before and seemed rife to win again. The path became narrow, and the line of orcs was the same width as the elves but much, much longer.

The orcs began to charge, and the elves braced themselves. The ugly mugs of the orcs—displaying snotty noses, broken tusks, hunched backs, and drooly mouths. They were in a frenzy. Velnir stepped forward out of the ranks. He pulled Illuminar out and thrust it into the ground right as the orcs began to close in.

From Illuminar, burst a wave of fire that, by now, the orcs had begun to recognize. Those that tried to turn around could not as they were simply trampled by the orcs behind them. The fire wave washed over the entire width of the orcish ranks and began to incinerate them by the tens of thousands. It made its way through them all the way to the mouth of the pass before dissipating.

The orcs remained undeterred. More and more flooded into the pass, and simply ran over the charred corpses of their brethren.

Velnir looked at Illuminar. Its glow had faded and he knew that meant he could not conjure the fire wave again for a bit. He melded back into the front line of the elven formation. The orcs came in quickly. The elves behind threw their shields up above the elves in front of them. The orcish arrows bounced off.

Right as the orcs smashed into the elves, they brought their curved blades up, killing scores of orcs. The elves then thrust their spears into them, some more than once. The groans and moans of the fallen orcs grew louder.

The orcs behind their fallen had begun to climb over them to get to the elves. The elven line had to back up or the orcs would be on top of them. They kept doing this for a while.

Meanwhile, the manticores decided to show up and made their way down the pass. Yzat and Nythint took to the air and swooped in upon them. While the dragons fought the manticore, the mages were conjuring firestorms and fire bolts unleashing tremendous devastation upon the orcs.

Every few minutes, the commander would blow a whistle, indicating the lines were to switch. The front line would move behind the second line and to the back of the army to cycle through. This tactic was used by the elves to prevent their soldiers from becoming too exhausted to continue fighting. The orcs employed no such tactics, and the elves took advantage of their weariness.

The orcs could not penetrate the elven line. By now, the orcs had stopped advancing and simply threw stuff at the elves, unsure what else to do. The dragons had killed the manticores with the help of the mages and begun to make breath attack passes on the orcs. The orcs still outnumbered the elves substantially but had begun to realize they were trapped in the pass. The elven archers were out of arrows by this point and joined the ranks of the spear infantry below.

Velnir looked at Illuminar once again and then to Darlana.

"I'm going to go ahead and then unleash a fire wave. When you see the wave, order the army forward, but do not break ranks."

Darlana nodded, and Velnir moved into position. He thrust Illuminar into the ground, unleashing yet another fire wave. Darlana ordered the army to move forward but not to break ranks.

Slowly, they began to move forward with their shields up and spears out. The wave washed over the orcs and incinerated tens of thousands more. The elves had to march over the corpses of fallen orcs and needed to carefully watch their step.

The orcs that were still alive were met with spears and swords to their vital organs. The wave had dissipated but the orcs got the message. They began to form ranks at the entrance of the pass. Skroatug and his wyverns were flying over them.

When they got to the front of their line, they stopped. He raised the scepter. Velnir looked at Illuminar, and once again, the brightness of its flame had dimmed. He looked at Darlana and the others down the front line. All he could think to do was order the formation of Testudos.

Skroatug decided to dismount and walk out in front of his army. From Velnir's position, he could see the massive black orc's reddish-orange eyes meeting his own gaze. The manticore could be heard screeching from behind the orcish line as they were still fighting the dragons. It was as though he was waiting to unleash the power of the scepter.

Moments went by, and out of the corner of his eye, while the sun was setting over the cliff, Velnir noticed someone up there.

Alzar made his way to the cliff's edge. He peered over and observed the orcs and elves.

"Look at that. The orcs have him backed into a corner, one that not even Illuminar could get him out of. That is good to know." he said.

Ismi walked up next to him and saw Yzat and Nythint fighting manticore.

"I must tend to my whelps, Alzar. They need help," she said.

Alzar turned his attention to the orcs.

***

Velnir was wondering what was taking so long. The orcs have not moved. Who was that on the cliff? He was desperately trying to come up with something.

***

Skroatug was reveling in what was to come. He was about to destroy the elves and liberate the sundered lands. He had big plans. He would eradicate the dwarves and all who resisted him. He would kill the dragon and rule by himself.

***

Alzar raised his staff and began to chant. His voice echoed across the valley for all to hear. Soon, everyone's eyes were upon him. The sky cracked, and a massive hole was now visible. Velnir recognized the backdrop of the hole to be the same one that appeared on the ceiling of the Tower of Alzar. The orcs were unsure what was going on, and not a moment later, a flaming meteor fell through and made its way directly to the middle of the orcish horde.

They had no time to move before it slammed into the ground. The meteor wasn't that big on a cosmic scale, but it was at least the size of a large boulder. The blast wave knocked nearly all the hundreds of thousands of orcs down. The heat generated from it, ignited the ground and all the orcs within the blast wave.

For the first time, the orcs were afraid. They dropped their weapons and began screaming in fear.

Skroatug could not believe it. His horde was destroyed. Millions of orcs perished, and for what, this Scepter? It was the way of orcs to live for war and die the way they lived, but on a scale of this magnitude, it even bothered Skroatug, but he believed there was no way the wizard could do that again. He needed to escape.

"Turn and fight, you cowards! Kill the elves. Fight!" he screamed. No orc would heed his demand.

Alzar mounted Ismi and they descended down to the valley in between the elves and the orcs, who were now in full retreat. Alzar dismounted, and Ismi took to the sky and made her way toward Yzat and Nythint.

Alzar made his way toward Skroatug. Skroatug pulled out the Scepter, but Alzar was quicker, and blasted him with a firebolt. Skroatug grabbed the scepter and tried to use it to no avail. He dropped the scepter, ran to the nearest wyvern, and mounted it. He then left the battlefield.

Alzar approached it. It was the last of three. He picked it up and placed it in his satchel which was significantly smaller than the staff. He then began to make his way over to Velnir.

Ismi was finishing off the manticore with Yzat and Nythint. Magris, Folwin, and the dragons were doing whatever they could to finish off the retreating orcs.

Velnir recognized Alzar and began making his way toward him. His army stayed put. Velnir was smiling. The wizard saved his army, and for that, he was very grateful. He really had no words but was eager to thank him.

As Alzar got closer, though, the look on his face alarmed Velnir. Before Velnir could get a word out, Alzar brought up his staff and conked him on the head. Velnir put his hands on his head to prevent him from doing it again, but this time, Alzar swept his legs and knocked him to the ground. Some of the soldiers, including Darlana, began to rush to Velnir's aid. Alzar shot them a glare with one visible eye from under the brim of his hat.

"You all witnessed a fraction of what I am capable of. Do not test me, for my quarrel is not with you!" Darlana ordered them to stop.

Alzar then looked at Velnir. He tried to get up, but Alzar pressed the tip of his staff under his chin.

"Give back to me what you have stolen, elf!"

Velnir had completely forgotten. "Illuminar," he whispered.

Alzar's eyes glowed gold. It was terrifying. "Hand it over," he demanded, his voice echoing through the valley for all to hear. It was unnaturally loud for a man.

Velnir complied and got to his knees. He pulled Illuminar out, offered it to Alzar, and bowed his head. Alzar snatched the sword out of Velnir's hand and threw it in his satchel. He did not take his eyes off Velnir. He was clearly angry, and rummaging through his satchel for something. He then pulled out Velnir's sword and simply tossed it next to him. Without a word, he made his way over to Darlana. His demeanor changed dramatically.

"Darlana," he said as if happy to see her. She welcomed him and the soldiers rushed over to Velnir. The dragons, Magris, and Folwin were now landing next to the army.

Velnir noticed Alzar talking to Darlana who shot him a glare, arguably more terrifying than Alzar's. The soldiers helped Velnir up from his knees.

"What was that all about?" asked Garlan.

"I have an apology to make," said Velnir. He then made his way to Alzar and Darlana.

Darlana turned and looked at Velnir with disgust. "You lied to me, Velnir. That sword killed many of our own soldiers and I heard you inadvertently destroyed one of your own ships with it on your way here. How could you be so reckless?"

He looked at Alzar who had his staff tucked under his arm and then back to Darlana. "I took the sword because I thought I could control it. I thought it would win the war," he said.

"I warned you, Velnir. You should have listened," said Alzar.

"Please, forgive me, Alzar. My actions are inexcusable," said Velnir sincerely.

"Impressive, a heartfelt apology from a Tanimaran prince. You really aren't like the others, Velnir. I forgive you, but you must make it right. It seems that you have figured out how to use this sword to its full effect. You and I will hunt down Necrosith together and bring him to justice."

Velnir did not protest. "I will go with you, Alzar."

"As will I," said Magris.

"Very good. Continue your campaign if you wish. I will accompany you in the meantime, and when it's time, you and I will go," said Alzar.

Velnir smiled, and they all did what they could to make camp. Darlana wouldn't speak to Velnir. The dragons were becoming acquainted. This was the first time that Yzat and Nythint saw their mother and she would show them things they hadn't learned or couldn't learn from mortals. Now they were using visage forms.

Velnir made his way out of the pass with the rest of the army. The orcs were in full retreat and their leader had gotten away. Velnir approached Alzar.

"What of the scepter?

Alzar looked at him and patted his satchel and then offered a warm smile.

Velnir was relieved. That weapon was too much to contend with.

The army had marched back to where they last set up camp and grabbed all the salvageable supplies they could find. They set up camp and began to stack their dead into large pyres. The dragons did the honors and lit them with their fire. The mood was somber to say the least. The elves had only won a pyrrhic victory once again after suffering a defeat only because Alzar rescued them.

The council convened in the command tent with Alzar and Ismi joining them.

Velnir began, "We won the battle of the Sundered lands. Without you, none of us would…" He was interrupted by Darlana.

"Make no mistake! We only won because Alzar came to our rescue. Without him, we would all be dead," she said.

Everyone in the command tent agreed with her and began to formally thank Alzar, including Velnir. Now he felt as though he should keep his mouth shut.

"The casualty report indicated we lost roughly ninety-one thousand since the campaign started and twelve thousand wounded. Those who were killed by the vortex were found shriveled up like raisins," said Garlan.

"Many who were pounded by the vortex have aged significantly. I don't know what to do for them!" Darlana said.

"The weapon the orc had is known as a Scepter of Canar. It is one of three in existence. This one is now accounted for. However, there is one that is still out there," Alzar said.

"What will happen when they are all together?" asked Velnir.

"They can unleash a cataclysm the world has never seen. When they were first used, they only blighted this land because Necrosith was unaware of their true power. If they can do this unwittingly, imagine what they are capable of to something that knows how to use them," said Alzar.

"How do you know how to use them?" asked Magris.

"I witnessed their destructive power firsthand and began to study the one I had captured from the dwarves," responded Alzar. Magris simply expressed confusion.

The camp ate what they could and began to sleep. It had been an exhausting few days. Many Tanimarans, Nagrimarans, Centaurs, and forest lords had been killed. The next morning, human and dwarven emissaries had found their way to Velnir's camp.

The council gathered in the command tent.

"We have found the orcs, retrieved this Scepter of Canar and they are on the run. We must go after them," said Magris.

"We need time to resupply and collect reinforcements from Tanimara," said Velnir

The human and dwarves requested an audience with the council. The humans were Maphisian and Talabadian—Two Araban kingdoms that neighbored each other. They reported that their armies had been pushed back by the orcs into their lands. The orcs came up from the ground in Araba and out of the mountains in Dhar'Algaz and were laying waste to outlying villages.

"We have come to ask for your aid, seeing as you are now the only army that hasn't been wiped out that borders the sundered lands. Please, come to our aid," pleaded the humans.

"The dwarves were first to answer your call to aid. We attacked when you did and saw mild success until the horde defeated our greatest commander. Now, we are sitting ducks and in need of your help. They already have Dhar'Algaz under siege."

Velnir looked to the Maphisians and Thebians. "Are either of your cities under siege at the moment?"

"I can say that Maphis is not," said one human. The other human said Talabad also was not under siege.

"Very well. The orcs left here are mostly women and children. They are destitute and will pose no threat for the foreseeable future. I suggest we aid the dwarves first and then the humans," said Darlana.

The council agreed. Velnir ordered the army to pack up and make ready to march northwest to the mountain range of the dwarves.

Chapter 17
Fractured Clans

Skroatug and what remained of his horde slipped down into the caverns once more. He had a torch and was leading the way. Not many remained of his horde, and one decided it was time to speak up.

"No longer will I follow you, Skroatug. You have failed us time and time again," he said. Skroatug, enraged, pulled his blade, intending to decapitate the orc. The other orcs pulled their blades and stepped in front of him. Skroatug was alone in this fight.

"I will press on without you fools," he said in spite.

The other orcs turned around and left, likely headed north to join the other numerous clans attacking the humans or dwarves. Skroatug changed his direction.

He came across a cave system big enough for him and his wyvern to fly through. He mounted the wyvern and began to move. The wyvern knew where he was going, so Skroatug did not have to command it. He was lost in his thoughts.

"I sacrifice my family, and for what? This? My mate, my pups. My horde." The wyvern landed, and in a rage, Skroatug unsheathed his ax and beheaded the wyvern.

He made his way down a corridor until he came upon a large cave up against the magma chamber of a volcano. A wall of lava was flowing down into a small reservoir, which illuminated the area, yet there seemed to be nothing there.

"Have you brought what I seek, orc?" The dark and deep guttural sound echoed through the cave.

"I invaded Tanimara. I retrieved the Scepter of Canar and brought it back to the sundered lands, dragon."

"It has been well over two years since I sent you out, orc. Where is it? I cannot sense it on you," said the dragon.

"The elves, they are seeking revenge. They invaded the sundered lands and had allies. My people were being slaughtered. I spoke with the dark one to learn how to use it, so I did. I used it against the elves and did unspeakable damage," Skroatug said, attempting to please the dragon.

"Yet, the princeling still leads them, the wizard lives, and you no longer have the Scepter of Canar," the dragon said calmly. Its tail began to move behind the orc, unbeknownst to him.

Irritated by the dragon pointing out his failure, Skroatug snapped back, "It was I who created the horde. It was I who invaded Tanimara and sacked Atlan. It was I who retrieved the Scepter of Canar. It was my people who suffered and who are all but extinct now. What have you done?" Skroatug said angrily.

The dragon's ugly face appeared from the darkness. He was monstrously large, and his eyes glowed green.

"I have waited ten thousand years to get these scepters back." His voice got louder and deeper." Your kind are useless raging, hulking, savage animals. You do not deserve the air you breathe."

Skroatug was now moving backward as the dragon slowly advanced. "I've done everything you asked and sacrificed everything to do it."

"You failed the objective and only sacrificed everything for personal gain. Do you even know where your family is or where your dead brethren are? Why, they are in the nether, with the dark one, and do you know what happens to souls in the nether, orc?" His voice became dark and loud. Skroatug had his back against the cave wall. He was terrified more than he had ever been in his life. He could not even muster the words to answer the question that he did not even know the answer to.

"They anguish and suffer before the dark one consumes them, and they simply cease to exist. Why not say goodbye to your family one…last…time." The dragon smiled and began to suck in air.

Skroatug attempted to find something to grab onto, but it was in vain. The suction pulled Skroatug down the gullet of the dragon. The dragon did not show mercy by incinerating him first or at least biting down and crushing him to death.

No…he simply swallowed him whole. The lump of Skroatug's soon-to-be lifeless corpse slid down the dragon's long neck and into his belly to be digested slowly.

Skroatug couldn't breathe. He was being constricted by the muscles of the dragon's throat. He felt it squeezing him down the dragon's neck further and further until his head was pressed against the sphincter muscle.

It opened, and he suddenly took a breath. It was not air, though. He couldn't tell what it was because it was pitch black. It smelled and tasted horrible, and finally, he was pushed through the sphincter and splashed into the dragon's stomach acid.

Skroatug flailed, clawed, and punched, trying in vain to get out. He could not breathe, and he felt the flesh melting off his bones. His armor and weapon fell off. His legs collapsed, and he began to sink into the acid.

His last words, "My family," as he slipped beneath the acid into the bottom of the dragon's stomach. Everything went black.

Then, a white light. He could see again, though he was floating in a place unfamiliar to him. He looked around in complete amazement as he saw worlds, stars, and what appeared to be a transparent blue river flowing through the cosmos.

As he got a closer look, the river contained the souls of many fallen orcs among other races he could not recognize. It was the life stream the shaman spoke of. Relief swept over Skroatug.

"The dragon was wrong," he thought.

He saw his mate and his pups float down the stream and to a place that looked like a citadel made out of illuminated gold. He was happy to see them, though they were in a slumbering state. Why was he not in a slumbering state?

Suddenly, A tendril grabbed Skroatug's ankle. It burned him, and he howled in pain, but there was no sound. He looked down and saw a maw with a thousand eyes and a thousand teeth open. Its tongue wriggled around, eager to taste its next meal.

"Noooooo!" he screamed, but again, there was no sound.

He was slowly pulled closer and closer to the gaping maw, its throat black as pitch. He struggled and fought, but it was in vain. The tongues grabbed each of his limbs. His soul was pulled into this maw and disappeared down its black throat.

Meanwhile on Abrion, Skroatug's dissolved corpse would be digested, and a few days later, the dragon would dump what was left of him into a steamy pile of dragon dung on the surface.

All that remained of Skroatug was his skull and bones and his ax, which was now sticking out of the dung pile. Necrosith was now looking for the elves. He was determined to get the scepter back.

Chapter 18
The Dwarves of Dhar'Algaz

The elves had been marching for three weeks. They finally made their way out of the sundered lands and between two giant mountains. The valley was snowy and full of trees. The dwarves were held up in their mountain fortress of Dhar'Algaz, and they were under siege.

A massive orcish army had laid waste to too many dwarves as their frozen corpses littered the path. The army marched through the valley and witnessed the destruction. They could see smoke over the hill, and knew according to the map, that over there was Dhar'Algaz.

Velnir ordered his army to form ranks and march forward. This was to be the dwarves' final stand. Velnir's army approached the back of the orcish army undetected so far. The city was built into the side of the mountain. The orcs were currently trying to bash the gate down with a giant battering ram shaped like a boar's head.

Velnir immediately ordered his archers forward. They began to fire volleys into the backs of the orcs. Half of them turned around and charged the elves.

"Shield wall," Velnir ordered, and his commanders repeated the order.

The army threw their shields up and put their spears out. They braced as the orcs smashed into their ranks.

As they had done before, the elves brought their blades up and cut many of them down in the first wave. They then began to thrust their spears into the orcs. They were used to it by now. The dragons came down and began to strafe the orcs. The elves advanced slowly without breaking ranks, cutting down any orc foolish enough to run into them.

The mages stayed back, and the griffins attacked with their talons. Grabbing orcs with their hind legs, eviscerating them, and raining their bowels all over their ranks.

Velnir, Magris, and Darlana were again at the front line. Darlana was dancing with her blades through the orcs, cutting them down with ease while Velnir and Magris were trying to keep up.

The army stopped. Alzar stepped forward and thrust Illuminar into the ground unleashing a wave of fire into the orcs ranks. They simply fell into the snow and rolled around, only suffering minor burns.

They screamed and howled, then turned their attention to the elves. They smashed into the elven line but could not break it. The elves made quick work of them. What few orcs remained began running uphill and into the mountain.

Velnir ordered the centaur and the dragons to run them down, and they did so with ease.

"Oy," came a voice from the balcony of the keep. It was Jokhut. "Boy, am I happy to see you pointy ears and horsemen. Oh, and you dragons. You came to save our arses from the orcs. I thank you. Come on in."

The elves waited by the giant gate while the dragons began eating the dead orcs. Soon, the gate began to open, the first door slid up, the second and third side to side, and finally the last one went down. The dwarves came rushing out and hugged the elves.

Everyone was happy to see each other. The elves went into the city and saw the glorious architecture of the dwarves for what many would say was the first time they had seen it. Dhar'Algaz, Kingdom of the Stormforged Clan. A city built into the side of an active volcano. Houses and shops were carved out of the side of the mountain. Giant anvils everywhere.

Small dwarves were playing with beads of molten electhril and the stout stunted dwarven woman yelling at them, "Don't burn your eyes out."

The elves were even impressed.

"I have never seen anything like it," said Velnir.

"You really need to get out and see the world then," retorted Darlana with a smile.

They strolled through the city as welcomed guests for the first time.

"To think we were at war with these people at one point," said Magris.

"Their culture is one of pleasure, much like ours," said Darlana.

Velnir looked around as the council was led to the king's chambers. They reached the steps of a dwarven palace or fortress built out of the side of the mountain.

As they went inside, the hall was grand and supported by several pillars. The walls had liquid magma running down either side and flowing under the palace into a reservoir hidden by the floor. It was magnificent.

Jokhut was sitting on his stone throne.

"So, what do you think, you silly pointy ear?" he asked, followed by a light-hearted chuckle.

"It is all right," replied Velnir snidely.

"We have really been enjoying your Atlantin mead only, the shipments stopped. Any idea why?" Jokhut asked.

"I could not tell you why, Jokhut. I will look into it immediately though," replied Velnir.

"In the meantime, I have stopped the production and delivery of electhril ingots until this can be resolved," said Jokhut.

"Fair enough. I will get to the bottom of it," promised Velnir.

Jokhut looked to Darlana.

"I see your soldiers have little to no armor. I will make an exception for them and have them craft some of the finest electhril chain and plates as a gift of appreciation for your timely arrival."

Darlana looked at Velnir for a moment before responding. "They would really appreciate that, Your Grace."

Magris was being pursued by several dwarven women. This was odd to him. He had never been pursued by a woman of any kind before. He would not prefer dwarves even though he was lonely and was trying to gracefully decline and fight them off. They would not relent. While he was occupied, Darlana was making conversation with the nobles. She seemed to know them, and Velnir made his way to her when he was stopped by Alzar.

"Young prince, you may not want to go over there," Alzar said.

"Why not? They are speaking to my wife. Surely, I would be welcome," Velnir retorted.

"They are from the Thunderforge clan. I'd advise you not to go over there, Velnir."

"Oh," Velnir said, thinking of sword Danar.

"Their king gave it to your father as a token of surrender. It was not in the best of circumstances, Velnir. It would be insulting to them if you go over there and bring that sword with you."

Velnir thought for a moment. "You are right, wizard," he said as he walked away, drinking some wine.

The dragons came into the city, though not in dragon form. Yzat and Nythint now had a visage form like Ismi's. They were two dashing young men.

One wore the traditional clothing of a human noble, and the other wore the traditional clothing of an elven noble. They both had long black hair, a dark complexion, and red eyes. They each had the same goatee.

"A bit ominous," Velnir thought as he saw them make their way to the king's chambers.

"Oy… Oy, who might you be? I did not invite you?" the drunken dwarf king stated, but in a questioning tone as if unsure.

Yzat replied in an elegant human voice, "Why, we're dragons."

Jokhut's eyes grew wide. "Oh… well uhm make yourselves at home…hic! And if you can make time, check out our forge. It is magnificent."

The dragons simply walked around and observed.

Velnir and Darlana were given a stateroom. The standards of which actually impressed Velnir. He did not think the dwarves had such good taste: Silk sheets and pillowcases.

The walls were thick stone and soundproof. The floor had rugs from large bear hides. Darlana was quite excited to be there. She began taking her clothes off and invited Velnir into the bed, which he happily obliged.

"I never thought I'd be staying in a dwarven stateroom," he said to his wife.

"Be silent, my husband," said Darlana as she pulled the dwarven silk covers over them…

They had finished doing what loving couples do in silk sheets, and he lay next to her. She rolled over and placed her arm over his chest. He had laced his fingers through her hair and placed his hands behind his head. She looked at him.

"I am six hundred and forty-one years old. How old are you, Velnir?"

"I am three hundred and nineteen years old, Darlana."

"It has been so long since I have been to Tanimara. I am eager to see it again. I know my father will not want to see me, and I do not wish to see him. I am content with visiting Atlan.

"Whether he is or is not, we will live in Atlan and rule Atlantin together. I am prepared to make my case in front of the magistrate. You and your people have been a tremendous asset to the Tanimaran campaign. You saved countless Tanimaran lives. You served Tanimara again, and I will argue in your favor."

Darlana closed her eyes. "I never thought I'd be with someone like you. I am grateful.

Chapter 19
To the Land of Saah's

The army had no time to waste. They liberated the dwarven kingdom of the Stormanvil Clan. It was time to liberate the humans who helped as well, so the dwarves donated all the supplies and then some that they would need for their journey.

They left the city to many farewells and with enough supplies to last them several months. Velnir's army was still roughly seventy thousand strong, and he now had a wizard and three dragons in his ranks. The dwarf king had told him he easily had the most experienced and strongest army the world had ever seen. Velnir was pleased to hear this from him.

The army marched west out of the mountains and then south toward Talabad. From there, they would enter the Araban desert once again. They had traveled for two weeks. The number of supplies they carried with them took longer to haul, but it was worth it.

Darlana had come to Velnir rubbing her belly as she was now with child. Velnir could not be happier. He had an heir, and so did she. Their kingdoms would be united.

The elves marched day and night until they were approached by an emissary from Talabad, who stated that Talabadians were safe from the orcs. The Maphisians, however, lost an army in Araba and were at the mercy of their walls. Velnir ordered the army to turn around and march northwest. In another two weeks, the army approached the city of Maphis, located along the coast of the Araban desert.

The kingdom of Maphis was ruled by Saah Awani. Saah was the Araban word for king. As the elves made their way to the gates of Maphis, they took in all the scenery. The city boasted large stone walls that could rival Atlan's. It too had tall spires and towers.

Hundreds of buildings, temples, and palaces. Maphis was much older than Atlan and had been the trading center of the world for thousands of years. Its harbor was massive. Several hundred ships were docked, and several hundred more were waiting. The ships came from all around the world.

To Velnir's surprise, he saw a ship from East Ying. He had no idea that the trade routes extended to the other side of the world and had a strong desire to get involved. The most prominent features of Maphis, however, were its pyramids. To the east of the city, all the way to the coast, were hundreds of pyramids all right next to each other, blotting out the sun.

It was a true sight to behold but still, Tanimara boasted of being the architectural capital of the world. Tarvana was bigger and better still.

Saah Awani welcomed the elves with open arms. He was a short, chubby man with a large white beard and wore white clothing, including a white turban with a ruby in its center.

"Greetings, friends, and welcome to Maphis, the trade center of all Abrion," he said with pride.

Velnir and Darlana were walking together while Magris and Alzar were walking together. The dragons had not revealed their dragon forms and the people of Maphis were none the wiser. Even Ismi transmorphed without her horns. The people of Maphis were not friends with dragons.

Awani invited them into his palace. It was luxurious even by elven standards. Darlana was impressed with the amount of fauna present, considering they were in a desert. The waterfalls, the mosaics, the statues of kings and queens from long ago littered the courtyard.

Fountains and pillars made of gold were within the palace itself. The king's throne was made to resemble a lion looking over the king and his family. They all sat down to a feast prepared for them by the king. The food was interesting here. Most of it was seafood, but some was of unknown origin.

The elves did not want to be disrespectful so they tried it and rather liked it. Alzar did not eat, and neither did the dragons. They simply sat there and stared at everyone else with their creepy red eyes. The sun was out, and there was a slight breeze. The windows here were glassless like those in Nagrimar, and Darlana could really appreciate that.

Several women came in wearing all kinds of different colored silky transparent gowns. They covered their faces except their eyes. The gowns were transparent enough that their breasts and nether regions were visible. Magris was happy to see that, and he couldn't take his eyes off them.

Velnir ignored it because he knew that Darlana was the most beautiful female in any room he would ever be in. He wasn't the only one who thought that. Saah Awani could not take his eyes off of her. The women did not shave their nethers, and most of the elves were hairless with the exception of their heads, chins, upper lips and eyebrows, so this was not really to their taste. Magris was leaving with six of them, however.

"He is in for a well-deserved good time," Velnir said to Darlana quietly. She simply smiled and nodded.

"I hear you are with child, Queen Darlana," said Saah Awani. He had laced his fingers and placed his elbows on the table. He also placed his chin on his fingers and looked at Darlana with wanting eyes.

"I am. It has been four hundred years since I have been pregnant," she said.

Saah Awani immediately lifted his head from his hands and placed them on his lap. "Did you say four hundred years?"

"Mmhmm," she said with her mouth still full. Velnir noticed and thought, "She will have to get used to Tanimaran etiquette again."

"You look so young. I am but seventy years old and look so old compared to you yet...I am amazed," he said, perplexed. "So, you are Nagrimaran and Velnir is Tanimaran. Tell me. How does that work?" He smiled.

"Simple, you see, she captured my crew and I after we were shipwrecked. She then showed us hospitality and let us stay with her for quite some time. We decided to marry for political reasons, and then we grew fond of each other. Now, we campaign together against the orcs... which, by the way, we did not run into on our way here. I found that interesting," Velnir said, trying to change the subject.

"Yes, they have been skirmishing outside our gates, but as you can see, we do not have settlements outside the gate. We use the wall to keep them out. We did send an army to the sundered lands as you requested, and sadly, none came back. Last I heard, the orcs were seen in my kingdom. This has been a while ago, and scouts have not reported any movement. They seem to be waiting for something, but I do not know what.

Alzar leaned over to Ismi and whispered something. She got up and left. Velnir paid no attention to it, but Darlana thought it was strange.

"Have the orcs ever broken through your walls before?" Velnir asked.

"Never has anyone gotten into Maphis that was not let in. We are a strong people... No offense," said the king.

"None taken, Saah Awani," said Velnir. Truly he did not care. "We will wait for them here then. It will be best to wait for the monsters rather than ride out and meet them in the desert. Orcs are smart and if they can take advantage, they will," said Velnir.

Saah Awani would look Velnir up and down.

"Word has gotten around about you, Velnir. It is said that you wield a sword that can send tides of fire even over water. You, and I assume, Darlana, mount dragons and ride them into battle. Your campaign and success are quite legendary around the world by now, yet I see what appears to be a slightly above-average elven sword." Alzar was smiling at Velnir while chewing his food. "I do not see any dragons, and while you are tall and appear strong, you do not seem very special outside of fancy-looking armor. It appears to me that your success is quite embellished to say the least," said the King of Maphis.

Velnir felt insulted, but Darlana placed her hand gently on his thigh without looking at him. He calmed down and said, "You forgot about the wizard. He alone won the last battle, but do not worry Saah Awani. I promise you that my army has defeated countless orcs. More orcs than you can even imagine." Velnir took a sip of Maphis's finest wine. He actually liked it, or he would have left by now.

"You bring eighty thousand with you? Tell me, how many of them are Tanimari?" Saah Awani asked rather cynically while chewing his food.

Velnir was visibly upset. "Roughly fifty thousand Tanimarans, ten thousand Nagrimarans and twenty thousand Centaurs, and seven hundred or so trebors." Velnir coldly replied before taking another sip of wine.

"So, you started out with one hundred thousand Tanimarans, and now you are down to half? That seems… well, if you do the math… Oh, and not to mention, Darlana came with twenty thousand Nagrimarans and twenty thousand Centaurs. According to those numbers…I would argue that Darlana, and not you, has the strongest army in this world's history. Reports do indicate that your campaign started out rather unsuccessfully until she arrived with her army and some trebors, and of course, the last battle where apparently the wizard single-handedly won victory," Saah Awani said with a smirk.

"The first battle was started by an insubordinate general before Velnir and I arrived to reinforce them, which led to a major loss," said Darlana. "The Tanimarans were unaware of the tactics used by the orcs and took the brunt of the casualties. We have all learned from those mistakes and adapted our tactics and strategies to excel through the sundered lands. A force of eighty thousand, two very skilled pyromancers, and three full-sized dragons, with the help of Alzar, killed millions of orcs over the last year. Velnir led us all. He would never tell you, human, for it is unlike him to boast, but surely you could understand shortcomings. Now, say we decide to leave. You think your walls will stop them? We discovered an unbelievably large tunnel network the orcs would use to simply go under your walls and into your city," Darlana said calmly and with a smile.

Saah Awani sat back in his chair and knew exactly what she was referring to. Just a few weeks earlier, a Maphisian general led an army outside these gates, and to their demise against the orders of the Saah, none survived.

"I do hope that the one responsible was held accountable. You have my apologies, Lord Velnir," said Saah with a lump in his throat.

"We stayed with the dwarves after liberating them long enough to gather the supplies we would need to bring here to help Maphis and Talabad. We did not stay with them long, and I do not think we will be staying with you for long either," said Velnir.

"The orcs will attack again. You will at least stay long enough to assist us against them, yes? That was after all our agreement," asked the Saah.

"We will take our leave now," Velnir stood and so did those in his companions.

As they went to leave the king's dining hall, Saah Awani asked, "By taking your leave, you mean just to the luxurious chambers I have reserved for you and your companions… yes?"

Velnir and Darlana made their way through the city and to the villa that they were staying in. The villa was much more humble than a palace. It too had glassless windows and was located near the ocean. The problem with this location was that it was also near a fishery as well.

The other members of the council had arrived and made it to their respective rooms. They gathered in the courtyard outside which was surrounded by the building. It had a massive wooden table and chairs available with servants to bring them whatever they wanted by order of Saah Awani. The rails had beautiful vines hanging from them, and floral baskets were hung over the doorways. Huge plants marked the corners, and to the left of the table was a fountain featuring a statue of a man urinating on fish.

"It is quite impressive to me that a species that only lives to be one hundred to one hundred and twenty on average could have such architecture," Darlana said, attempting to quell the tension.

"That is long enough to learn manners and respect especially for those who are here to replace your army for its failure," said Velnir.

Magris was making his way downstairs and had a grin ear to ear. "Greetings and salutations, fellow council," he said gleefully. He then pulled up a chair next to the dragons.

"I am glad someone is having a good time," Velnir said, smiling at his general.

"I am indeed. This place stinks and the women do not shave their nethers, but when you look like me, you get what you get and do not throw a fit," Magris said, laughing. Everyone else except the dragons joined him in the humor. The dragons did not appear to understand humor. They were looking at each other, confused.

Velnir appreciated Magris' outlook. The respect for him was returning.

"Saah Awani stated that the army that left the city was completely destroyed by the orcs. The same orcs that are now camped in the desert. I find it unlike them to sit and wait. When they defeated my father in Thalnor, they wasted no time making their way to Atlan. The question here is why do they wait?" Velnir asked the council.

"They could be waiting for reinforcements," said Darlana.

"We killed millions of orcs that covered thousands of square kilometers of the sundered lands. I cannot imagine they would have many reinforcements," argued Magris.

"They could be waiting longer because reinforcements are fewer. I have deployed several scrying orbs to the area so you can regularly check your scrying crystals," added Velnir.

"In our time in the sundered lands, we have not seen Necrosith. Does anyone else find that odd?" Alzar asked. The dragons looked to him and agreed silently. Velnir, Darlana, and Magris were thinking.

"Perhaps these three dragons are frightening enough to keep him away," added Darlana.

"Necrosith is massive and cunning. He could kill any one of us," said Ismi.

"Is there any way to reason with him now that his orcs are all but defeated?" asked Velnir, not wanting to contend with such a dangerous enemy.

"Speaking for the dragons, Necrosith is responsible for almost wiping out our species. We have no interest in reasoning with him. If we could capture him alive, that would be preferred, but this army is not capable of such a task," Ismi said.

"Very well, we will kill him then, but how? We have all seen what you three can do on the battlefield. I shudder to think what Necrosith could do to us," Velnir stated.

"Chances are, he is unhappy over the failure of his orcs collecting the Scepter of Canar," said Alzar. He placed the scepter on the table. "I believe he will come for this. We must bait him, make him vulnerable, and then attack. It will be difficult since he still has an orc army which is gaining reinforcements as we speak," said Alzar.

"Perhaps it is not wise then to stay behind these walls. If Necrosith were to attack this city, many denizens would be killed," said Darlana.

"We cannot simply be out in the open for Necrosith to kill us. We have to have some cover," retorted Magris.

"Dragons have the advantage," Velnir then looked to Ismi, Yzat, and Nythint. How would we best kill you?"

The two younger dragons looked to Ismi, clearly unsure how to answer.

Ismi laced her fingers together and placed her hands on the table. "For a mortal to kill a dragon, they would need either other dragon allies, enchanted items, a lot of magic, or Alzar on their side. All of which you have, Velnir."

"How can we do this without paying such a high price in life?" asked Velnir.

"You cannot," said Alzar.

"The Tanimarans that came with you volunteered, my lord. They believed in your leadership and ability to punish the orcs, and you did. They wanted revenge just as much as you did. Give it to them," said Magris.

"We cannot fight in the open desert and we cannot fight in Maphis. We also cannot leave the orcish army to gather reinforcements to take Maphis. The Scepter is what Necrosith wants; he will come to us. We need to get it to a strategic location and wait for him there while we also destroy the orcish army outside of Maphis," said Velnir.

"We must stay with you and the Scepter," stated Ismi.

"Yes, and Velnir, you agreed to assist me," stated Alzar.

"I did, and I will honor my commitment, Alzar."

"I will lead the army against the orcs, and then we will come to you," said Darlana.

"It is settled then. Now, where do we take the Scepter of Canar?" Velnir looked to Alzar and Ismi for the answer.

Ismi's expression turned into that of an uncomfortable one. "The bone wastes," she suggested. "It sits between the border of Steinbach, the mountains, and the sundered lands. The cliffs are jagged and tall. The ground is black and gray. It is also littered with the bones of my brethren. Not only is it an incredibly dangerous place for dragons to fly, but it is the same place that Necrosith ambushed our dragon army with his orcs and killed damn near all of them. Necrosith will be forced to land there if he needs to fight ground targets. Give the scepter to me, I will lure him there with it. You will be waiting."

"Illuminar is capable of delivering a massive blow to Necrosith. It is a weapon of fire," said Alzar.

"Very well, Darlana. Please inform Saah Awani that we will be departing in the morning. His city is safe. Magris, inform the army not to get too comfortable. Our stay here will be short. Make sure they know that command will be given to Darlana, then hurry back here. We will leave for the bone wastes tonight."

Everyone got up and proceeded to execute their orders. Velnir walked upstairs and looked out the window in the direction of Tanimara. "Father, I hope you are proud of me. I hope you are pleased with the revenge I have taken. I hope that I will be able to, at the very least, live up to your standards as the high lord of Atlantin," he thought.

There was a knock on his chamber door. It was Alzar. "May I come in?"

"Of course, Alzar." Velnir did not bother to sit down.

"You are doing the world a great service. The celestials are watching," Alzar said

"If the celestials know what is going on, why do they not intervene? They are supposed to be all-powerful and the creators of the cosmos," Velnir stated.

Alzar smiled. "The light never intended for the celestials to be able to take care of what would be considered minor tasks on a cosmic scale."

"Minor tasks?" Velnir questioned with an irritated tone.

"Yes, typically when something like this happens and the world is on the verge of major corruption, they would simply destroy the planet. All life would cease to exist. Think of it as being too big to handle something so small. You would break it, so it's best to leave it to something small but powerful to handle. They understand that, and that is why they answer your prayers when you perform rites. There are many other worlds that need their attention as well. Even celestials have limitations," Alzar said.

"Why can they not simply do what you did?"

"They have quite a lot in the history of Abrion. Ata, for instance. Her time here was fruitful as she loved a human, and together, they had my brothers and me. Thalamon called her back to the Phatra, so we inherited the dragon's charge as the steward of this world. I introduced magic to the mortals, hence why the elves are able to use components to enchant vellums or create objects like scrying orbs and learn elemental magics through the use of arcane lines, alchemical potions, elixirs, and such. Ledros and his dominions deliver the souls of the dead to the lifestream which ferries them to the Phatra."

"Ismi told me you are the child of a celestial. Ata is your mother?"

"Yes, she is. She is the Celestial of Magic and created all the arcane lines on Abrion initially for the dragons. Naturally, her children would inherit some of her abilities."

"Then why do you need the help of other mortals to maintain balance?"

"My father was human. I have limits, and unfortunately, there are cosmic forces much greater than my power that can easily contend with me, such as those crystals that the scepters were made from. Splinters, small fragments of a corrupted planet, have immense corruptive power, and it spreads like a disease."

"Why do you have limits?"

"Power is corrupting. I have often found myself being humbled as you have also."

"This is why you are careful whom you assist. Like me with Illuminar. A weapon like this in the wrong hands could be catastrophic."

"Yes, balance refers to equality of power between the races of Abrion and its guardian. They cannot become too powerful and neither can I by order of the Celestials."

"If we were unable to kill such a powerful enemy like the dragon, even with your help, would Ata come down and give others the gift she gave you?"

"Unlikely, though I cannot say for sure. It is more likely that they would simply destroy the planet, but defeating Necrosith will serve the interest of the celestials and the greater good of life on Abrion. It will also fracture the orcish clans and that will create infighting."

"I am already committed to defeating Necrosith, if not for you and for the greater good of Abrion, then for encouraging the orcs to invade Tanimara."

"It pleases me to know that you would use your gifts for good and not self-interest," Alzar said before taking his leave.

Velnir thought it was strange that the wizard would come to his chambers. Why would Alzar care what my intentions are?

Why bother telling me the celestials are watching when they choose to do so little about it. The wizard had acted in his own interests before. Perhaps this is no different. Why mention my interest? Is vengeance not in my interest? What of the Scepter of Canar he took? How will that not make him even more powerful? He is already the most powerful being on the planet. All this about balance, hmm." Velnir thought.

Magris and Darlana had returned to the villa.

"Everything is in order, my lord," stated Magris.

"The Saah is aware," said Darlana.

"Excellent. Magris, Alzar, the dragons and I will leave for the bone wastes tonight. You and Dravon have command of the army.

Chapter 20
Confrontation

The two elves, the wizard and the dragons in their visage forms made their way out of the city.

Once they were far enough away, the dragons transmorphed into their dragonforms.

"Ah, that's much better," said Yzat to Nythint.

"Indeed," replied Nythint.

Velnir mounted Yzat, Magris mounted Nythint, and Alzar mounted Ismi.

"Alzar, Ismi, we will inform you when we are near the bone wastes," said Velnir.

Alzar tossed Velnir Illuminar. "Use it wisely," he said.

"We will bring Necrosith to you," said Ismi before taking to the air and flying toward the sundered lands.

Velnir and Magris took to the air and made their way to the bone wastes.

"Dragons make for good company," Magris said.

"I am glad we can entertain you," said Nythint.

"It is amazing that you can grow to be so large in such a short time. It takes elves and men years to reach adolescence. You pick up language so easily. After spending time with you, Nythint, I only wish I could be a dragon. Or at least transmorph into a dragon the same way you can transmorph into an elf or whatever you like."

"It is nice to want," Nythint replied sarcastically. Yzat and Velnir laughed.

"Not used to befriending a race superior to ours, Magris?" Velnir asked.

"Haha, it is not that at all. It is envy though," Magris said.

"Dragons and elves as allies. I am not sure if this has ever happened in the history of Abrion. Ismi never told us but it is happening now. Velnir, I will remain at your side," said Yzat. "I will as well," said Nythint.

"Me too," said Magris.

Velnir felt humbled. The support of dragons meant a lot to him. The support of the wizard and what the dragons and the wizard were willing to do for his people meant a lot to him.

It did not matter to Velnir what the Tanimarans thought. He would simply do as he saw fit for the greater good of Atlantin. If the Dragons wanted to live there, then so be it. If Darlana wanted to live there, then so be it. It was his land and his sovereign decision.

The magistrate surely has heard by now of all the successes of Velnir with the help of the Nagrimarans, forest lords, and dragons if the Maphisians have.

***

Alzar and Ismi flew high above the ground. They passed where the orcs had been encamped, and they were right. They were waiting for reinforcements, and reinforcements they were getting. The army of orcs was swelling and was swelling fast.

Alzar knew there were many more orcs in the sundered lands underground than on the surface. They multiply like rats. Alzar and Ismi descended upon them. Ismi unleashed a breath attack, destroying supplies the orcs had gathered and killing many others. Alzar had scorched the sand beneath them. Several hundred orcs ignited and burned. Ismi made several more passes, burning and grabbing orcs, among other things in her claws, then dropping them when she gained enough altitude.

"Use the scepter, that will get Necrosith's attention," suggested Ismi.

"I cannot do that. I am not completely aware of its power and do not wish to risk any more destruction or corruption," stated Alzar. "You alone are doing enough damage to the orcs to soften them up for Darlana and Dravon while simultaneously getting Necrosith's attention. As for me, I need to save my strength."

"I understand, Alzar," she said right before another attack. The two were very adept at fighting together. Ismi was an experienced dragon warrior.

"How many do you think we killed?" asked Alzar.

"A few thousand I imagine," said Ismi.

"Let us head to the sundered lands and see if we cannot leave a trail of destruction for Necrosith to follow."

"Sounds good to me," said Ismi.

They flew around burning orcish villages on the surface. Alzar wanted to save his strength for the fight with Necrosith, so he made the ground tremble, which caused some of the caves to collapse.

Dark clouds began to appear overhead. Ismi turned her attention to the sky.

"Necrosith," she said with a hiss.

A giant black dragon burst through the cloud cover and was careening straight for Alzar and Ismi. Ismi spiraled, hurling herself forward at a high rate of speed. She kept low to the ground, weaving in and out of some pillars.

Necrosith was still far behind them, but the pillars were no deterrent. He simply smashed through them. This, of course, slowed him down. Ismi raced toward the sky at a low angle. She could not afford to go straight up. Necrosith was still pretty far behind. Alzar was conjuring lightning bolts from Necrosith's own clouds. They were pounding Necrosith left and right.

It was not doing much damage. It was, however, making him very angry as it obviously still hurt very badly. By now, Ismi had made it above the clouds. Necrosith was now gaining on them. Alzar conjured a blinding light, which did stop Necrosith momentarily, allowing Ismi to get away. She gained speed and was moving as fast as she could go.

Necrosith was maintaining the same speed but was a healthy distance away. They knew that he knew she could only keep it up for a matter of time. She prayed she would be able to make it to the bone wastes in time before exhaustion.

***

Velnir and Magris landed in a small valley within the bone wastes.

"Ismi wasn't exaggerating. There are dragon bones everywhere," said Magris.

The other two dragons seemed uncomfortable as they were looking around and over their shoulders.

"This should be a good location. It should be hard for other dragons to get down here," said Velnir.

The area was covered in enormous, sharp, jagged arched rocks. They stuck out everywhere. It was as if this area was largely volcanic at once and spewed large amounts of molten rock in all directions, and then all at once, it froze or solidified very quickly. It was an ominous sight to behold. The skeletons of dragons, along with orcs and men, littered the floor and the arching rocks. Several dragon skeletons were still impaled against the rocks.

"I understand now what Ismi meant. There is no way that these rocks formed like this naturally," stated Velnir. "It must have happened in an instant to impale dragons midair like that."

"What kind of vile sorcery is this?" Magris asked rhetorically.

The four of them walked around and took in the sight. They were searching for the best place to confront Necrosith. They came upon an area largely open but covered with thick, jagged lava rock.

"This will be sufficient. I will check on Alzar and Ismi," Velnir pulled out his scrying crystal and observed Alzar. He was holding his pointed hat on his head. "They are on their way here. I can only assume they found Necrosith and he has given chase."

"When will they get here?" Magris asked.

"I am not sure. At the rate of speed they are going, it is hard to tell. Dragons are so much faster than griffins."

Loud screeching could be heard echoing through the valley. Velnir and Magris pulled their swords. The dragons morphed into their dragon form.

"Manticore," screamed Magris.

Six of them descended upon the quartet at a high rate of speed. The elves leapt out of the way of their breath attacks and took shelter behind some rocks. The dragons attempted to attack with fire breath but were unsuccessful. Against their better judgment, the dragons both took to the air and gave chase.

"What are they doing?" demanded Magris.

"Trust them, Magris, we must help them."

"I do not have an enchanted weapon like you. I have one eye and one leg. How can I be of any help in this situation?"

"He was right. Magris was pretty useless," thought Velnir. "Stay here and look handsome."

Magris laughed.

Velnir drew his sword and moved into position. The manticore were attempting to make another pass with the two dragons behind them. Velnir pointed his sword at the closest one and shot a stream of fire and light from it.

It cut the manticore in half but also blew a chunk of jagged rock from one of the arches. This sent rocks everywhere and dangerously close to Yzat and Nythint. This did not deter them though. They both caught up to a manticore and chomped their back ends. The manticore screeched and turned their attention to the dragons while their hinds were still in their mouths. They were fighting like hell to get away from the grips of the dragons. This left three more manticore.

"Where are they?" yelled Velnir.

"I cannot see them," replied Magris. "Velnir, behind you!"

Velnir leapt out of the way seconds before the flames from the manticore incinerated the spot where he was standing. Velnir tried again to use his sword's magic, but the dragons were in the way. Another manticore was making its way to Magris. It took a deep breath. Magris stepped out into the open with his sword at the ready.

Velnir used his sword's magic to hurl another bolt of light at the manticore, but he only grazed its mouth. This did serve to interrupt it from performing a breath attack against Magris. However, it plowed into Magris with full force. They both went flying back, but when they came to a stop, the manticore slumped over, and Magris stood and pulled his sword from its head.

"That's one for one, brother," he laughed.

Relieved, Velnir laughed too.

They again took cover behind some rocks. Two more were out there somewhere. The dragons were still shredding the other two manticores.

"Yzat, Nythint, bring them down here," Velnir yelled. The two dragons obliged and brought the two manticores down to them. Velnir and Magris shoved their swords into the necks of the manticore, ending them so the dragon could release them.

"Thank you. Our jaws are not yet strong enough to bite through manticore flesh," said Yzat.

The remaining two manticore descended. The breath attack hit Nythint, who screamed in agony. His tail and left hind leg had been singed. He morphed into his visage and was dragged by Magris to safety behind a rock.

Velnir discharged a beam of fire with his sword, splitting the manticore in half and blasting the jagged rock arch again, sending material raining down upon them. The last manticore was coming in fast. He was aiming for Velnir, and Yzat was poised to attack.

When the manticore was in range, Yzat leapt up from behind a rock and bit down on the head of the manticore, crushing its skull. When Yzat landed, its brains, chunks of its flesh, and blood were oozing through Yzat's teeth. Yzat spit it out. Manticore flesh was grotesque.

They rushed to Nythint.

"Are you all right?" asked Magris.

"I'll be fine. It's just a minor burn," replied Nythint. The burns were deep into the flesh of his thigh and backside. If they stayed long, infection would take hold.

"The manticore has venom. Were you bit?" asked Velnir.

"I do not think so," replied Nythint.

"We need to get you medical aid, and fast," said Velnir. "I wish Darlana were here," he thought. He left to find Alzar and Ismi.

***

Darlana and Dravon marched their army toward the orcish encampment a few kilometers outside Maphis.

"Smoke in the distance over there," Dravon pointed out.

"Ismi and Alzar came through here. Perhaps they softened them up for us," Darlana stated. "Velnir gave me some scrying orbs. Let's see what's going on over there." She threw the scrying orbs into the air and pulled out her scrying crystal as the orbs made their way to the orcish encampment.

"Looks like she did a number on them, and they now know we're coming. They're forming up and making ready for an attack. Dravon, take the centaur around the sand dune and come at them from behind."

"Yes, my queen." Dravon motioned the other centaur to follow him.

"Captain Folwin, take your mages and prepare for battle. The wyverns are just ahead."

"Yes, Queen Darlana. Mages, to the sky, we fly to the wyverns," said Folwin.

Darlana ordered the soldiers to form ranks. The bolt throwers were now in place, and then she took to the sky. The mages had engaged the wyverns, and the battle was fierce.

The griffins were used to fighting wyvern by now and had developed a tactic of attacking with their talons instead of their beaks. Wyvern were heavier and less agile than griffins. This allowed the mages to conjure firebolts and fire storms. The orcs learned too. They were able to start seeing where on the ground the storms were about to start and hastily got out of the way.

"Fire the bolt throwers," she ordered.

Several bolts were shot through the air. Halfway to their target, blades sprung out, and the bolts began to spin at a high rate of speed and exploded on impact. This technology and these tactics were adopted well by Darlana.

The dwarves had crafted these new bolt throwers, and she couldn't tell a difference between elvish ones and dwarven ones. They did so based off what the elves told them and that impressed her. The orcs closed in but not as many as she thought.

"Ismi must have really done some damage to them. I can appreciate that." She dismounted and joined the front line.

The orcs smashed the front line, and the elves brought their blades up, meeting their chests, throats, and faces. Arrows rained upon the orcs that were straggling behind. The elves held the line, and the orcs struggled to break through.

Darlana went through them, slicing and stabbing undetected—the smell of burnt flesh filled the air. The centaur came from around the dune and charged the back of the orcish line. They smashed into them with force and kept driving through, cutting everything down in their path. The mages were done with the wyverns and returned to help the centaur. The orcs began to run away. Darlana stopped and looked around.

"This force matched ours in number," she thought. "Folwin, Captain Folwin!" she called out.

"Yes, Queen Darlana," he said as he landed next to her.

"How many wyvern were there?"

"Not many," he replied.

Darlana remembered that the orcs were growing in reinforcements, but this force seemed to be significantly smaller than what she had expected. Then it donned on her. It was a ruse. Her eyes widened.

"Maphis," she said under her breath. "Dravon, Folwin, we must make haste back to Maphis. The city is under attack. This was a ruse."

Immediately, Folwin and the other lieutenants turned the army around and began marching back toward Maphis.

Darlana threw her scrying orbs into the sky and made their way to Maphis. The army was doing double time. They were still a half a day away.

"How did they get around us?" she wondered.

Then she remembered–orcs live underground. Perhaps their tunnels were deeper and farther outside of the sundered lands than they thought. No matter. She would be there soon.

The army marched through the night. In the distance, there was smoke. Darlana looked through her scrying crystal and saw that there was a massive force of orcs at the walls of Maphis. They were climbing up crude ladders and fighting the humans on the walls. The stone giants were taking chunks of themselves and throwing large stones at the towers with deadly accuracy. Men would get knocked off and thrown several meters before meeting death.

"We have to hurry," said Darlana.

"We cannot move any faster," said Folwin.

The orcs were bashing the gate with a battering ram. The walls were being scaled, and the city looked like it was about to be infiltrated.

The elves finally made it to Maphis. Darlana ordered Dravon to charge the rear of the orcs. Then, the army to follow. She ordered Folwin and his mages to come with her. They flew over the city and saw that the orcs had infiltrated the city. The walls fell, and the human garrison was slowly retreating back to the palace.

"To the palace," she ordered, and they landed behind the human garrison. Saah Awani was barricaded in his palace. He would not let Darlana or any of the other elves in. Darlana looked around. She did not want the mages to use fire spells here. They would destroy the city, but the orcs were already destroying whatever they came into contact with.

"Folwin, take to the sky and attack their rear within the city with fire," she ordered.

"Yes, Queen Darlana." He and his mages took to the sky and began conjuring firestorms and firebolts within the city. The problem with firestorms is that they are somewhat unpredictable, which is why they are usually conjured far away from friendly lines. Unfortunately for the humans, these storms were igniting everything in their path. This did serve to kill many orcs, but Darlana was unsure if the ends justified the means. Dravon had smashed the army into the back of the orcs. They were now surrounded.

With nowhere to go, the orcs began fighting more fiercely than Darlana had ever seen. Buildings and walls stood in between them. Much of it already damaged. Darlana had joined the humans in fighting the orcs. She cut through them with ease while the humans struggled. They were impressed and inspired by her and pressed on.

Several hours went by, and the elves finally scaled the walls from outside the city. The centaurs were pouring in from the broken-down gate and attacking the orcs within the city. This was slow going. The Tanimarans and Nagrimarans were working well together, trying to crush the orcs.

Several more hours of fighting and finally, all the orcs were dispatched. The elves had won many battles and only lost a few in the campaign so far, but the dwarves and the humans suffered defeat left and right.

"Excellent work, Dravon," Darlana said.

"Many of the centaurs were injured or killed in that fight, my queen. They wish to go home to Nagrimar. Normally, we would not stray from a fight, but the desert… it is too taxing on us. Please do not make us stay in the desert any longer," pleaded Dravon.

This was the first time the centaur had asked to leave the campaign or complained about anything.

"You and the centaur have been loyal to me for hundreds of years, Dravon. You came here without question or complaint. You gave your lives for the cause. I cannot, in good faith, demand that you stay longer. If you speak for the rest of the centaur and wish to go home, then you have my blessing."

Dravon bowed. "Thank you, my queen. We will see you at home in Nagrimar."

Chapter 21
The Dragon's Duel

The centaur began to leave the city immediately after the battle for Maphis was won. The Tanimarans and other Nagrimarans were confused. Captain Folwin and Darlana were explaining to them how their bodies couldn't stand the heat of the desert. Elves and even half-elves were more suited to the climate changes.

Saah Awani approached Darlana as she was speaking to her soldiers. "What have you done to my city? The denizens of the first sector are displaced. You burned everything!" he complained.

Darlana did not appreciate getting interrupted. She turned her attention to the arrogant and pompous king of Maphis.

"The orcs did this to your city. Had we not intervened, you and your people would have been slaughtered like sheep. You should be grateful we came to the aid of Maphis, Saah Awani. We liberated you."

The Saah began to laugh with a hint of sarcasm in his voice. "You came here to aid us in accordance with our agreement. You then told me you weren't going to leave the city, and the next day, you did just that, only to allow the orcs to attack us. Your pyromancers were conjuring firestorms, and they destroyed the city. You betrayed us. I should have listened to them. They did warn me about you."

Darlana was perplexed. "Who warned you about what? How could you be complaining after all that had happened? Your army was lost to the orcs. If it weren't for us, your city would be lost too, including your palace, and you and your wives would all be brutally slaughtered. What part of that did you misunderstand?"

The Saah was clearly not interested in what Darlana had to say. His attitude toward the elves had changed significantly, and it didn't make sense.

"The fact is, you came into Maphis and offered your assistance against the orcs and then ruined my city in your so-called liberation attempt. I will not apologize for having higher expectations for elves. I think this was more of a ruse under the guise of liberation to actually destroy. Just look at my city! There is no excuse, Darlana. Guards, arrest her," demanded Saah Awani.

"You cannot be serious?" Darlana protested.

She looked around, and many elves began protesting out loud. Without orders, they quickly formed ranks and prepared to battle if necessary. The Saah shrieked in horror and ran to hide behind one of his big guards. Several of the Nagrimaran commanders began to suggest sacking the city.

"Leave my city at once. If you are the liberators you say you are and not the tyrants we think you are, you will leave." He then whispered to his guard, "Get them out of the city at once!"

Darlana wanted to keep the peace and sort this out diplomatically.

"Nagrimarans, Tanimarans, please lay down your weapons and do what the Saah has demanded. We must not destroy what we have liberated. This is not the fault of the people," she pleaded with them. They reluctantly did so. The army began to march in formation out of the city and made camp just outside Maphis, practically up against the walls.

"I am charging you with unnecessary destruction of Maphisian property and an attack against me, the Saah. You must learn that when in Maphis, I rule here, and the rule of law is me!" he said nervously.

Darlana attempted to reason with Saah Awani. "I did what I had to do to liberate you. We were only equipped to fight in open battlefields. We were not expecting to defend a city from an orcish attack, which is why we met them outside of the city. We were unaware of the orcs attacking Maphis, but we had to act."

"Silence, she-elf! You will have your time to speak when you appear in my court. Until then, you will stay in the dungeon."

The dungeon was underneath the city within the sewer system. It was dark and damp. The smell was awful and there were rats present. Darlana was locked in a cell that did not have anything but four walls and a gate.

She was forced to sleep on the floor; she was to eat whatever slop they gave her, but even though she could easily escape and dispatch the guards, she chose not to. It was not like her to commit violence if she was not in immediate danger. She would plead her case in the court, and if she was seen as a monster, she would then be forced to give them a reason to believe it.

***

Alzar pointed out the location of the bone wastes identified by its large, jagged rock arches. Ismi descended hard and fast. Necrosith was not far behind her, and the dark, ominous cloud followed. She flew through the maze of jagged rocks and was surprisingly good at it. She saw the quartet below and made her way toward them.

"He is right behind us, make ready," demanded Alzar.

The six got ready to face the monstrous dragon. For the moment, it was quiet. They all looked around waiting anxiously. Necrosith barreled through several jagged rock arches and lunged toward them. Velnir held up his sword and attempted to strike him with fire but missed.

Necrosith was fast and agile even though he was enormous. The other dragons took to the sky except for Nythint. Alzar mounted Ismi and took to the sky with her. Velnir and Magris stayed on the ground. Necrosith's scales are very strong. His breath attacks sucked in the air around the area it struck. The power was great and made it very difficult for Velnir and Magris.

Debris was flying all around them. The ground was quaking. The clouds above began to thunder, and the ground cracked, exposing lava. The thundering sounds of dragon roars were deafening. For the moment, Velnir and Magris were useless.

Necrosith was chasing Ismi and Alzar through the air and throughout the valley of the bone wastes. The younger dragon, in pursuit. Alzar was throwing whatever he could at Necrosith, but the dragon was resistant to just about everything and was gaining on them.

Yzat got a little too close to Necrosith's tail and was knocked out of the chase. He regained control and landed with grace but was injured. He cursed Necrosith.

Ismi and Alzar were alone now. The chase was on, and Necrosith was determined to catch up with them.

"I cannot go any longer, Alzar. I am too exhausted!" Ismi said.

"You must, Ismi, you must keep going, or we will perish. I am doing everything I can."

"I have to stop, Alzar, I am sorry, I just cannot." She stopped and turned around. She unleashed a breath attack that stopped the mighty dragon and caused him to panic. Necrosith then slammed into her midair. They both began to fall to the ground.

Alzar was thrown off. The two dragons were fighting, but Ismi was weak. They both hit the ground with Necrosith on top. He bit her neck and twisted, breaking it and killing her instantly. He nudged her with his nose to make sure she was dead. He then took to the sky again in search of Alzar.

Alzar used his magic to slow his fall before he landed and ended up on his two feet. He brought out his staff and examined the location. It was a narrow pass within the bone wastes still covered in jagged rock arches.

The clouds were dark, so Alzar knew Necrosith was close. He made his way down the pass while keeping his eyes peeled. It was quiet. He came to a cliff and saw nothing, so he kept going through the pass until he came to a natural-looking balcony of flat rock with a cliff on the other side. He walked in between two walls of rocks leading to the flat area.

The flapping of wings was heard just below. Necrosith rose from the depths of the cliff to meet Alzar, face to face, light vs darkness.

"Give me the Scepter of Canar wizard, and I shall grant you a painless death!" demanded the dragon.

"If you want it, then come and get it," Alzar challenged.

He then screamed, and from his staff, he conjured a massive bolt of pure light and fire that was instantly directed toward the dragon. It clipped his wing, and he howled in pain. In retaliation, Necrosith unleashed a horrible breath attack.

Despite Alzar's seemingly old-looking demeanor, he was very fast and agile and easily dodged the attack. They exchanged bolts and breaths back and forth. The dragon landed on the platform and swiped at the wizard, who dodged the attacks.

Necrosith used his tail, which only served to smash anything but the wizard. Alzar made his way up higher ground. The dragon followed, biting and swiping. Alzar had the higher ground, and his magic was having an impact.

Every time he hit Necrosith with a bolt of light and fire, he jolted and howled in pain. Finally, he was at the edge of the high ground.

Necrosith swiped at Alzar and knocked him back down to the platform. This would have killed a man, but Alzar was no man. He got up and hid behind a rock.

"For millennia I have been searching for the Scepters of Canar. I will have them in my possession once again! You have no idea what power they can bring. They can destroy, they can create, and they can bring the dead back to life. Give it to me, wizard, and instead of death, I shall use them to grant you untold power, and you will serve me," said the dragon.

"Power is not yours to give Draxus!" said the echo of Alzar.

The dragon was surprised that Alzar used his original name.

"I will not be denied." His tail swiped the area he thought the wizard was in and pulverized the rocks, but Alzar was not there. "How do you know of Draxus, wizard?"

"You were created to protect Abrion and maintain balance. It is because of your failure that I took up the charge."

The dragon roared and swiped another set of rocks he thought the wizard was hiding behind, but yet again, Alzar was not there.

"Your charge was to maintain balance. Because of your failure, Ata gave birth to me. I inherited your charge as steward of Abrion. Did you forget?" the echo of Alzar said calmly.

Once again, the dragon attempted to smash the rocks he thought the wizard was behind. He was getting frustrated, and fear began to penetrate his heart.

"You are celestial then?"

Alzar did not answer, "Now, I am charged with the protection of Abrion."

"Bahh, you need the help of mortals. Celestials should not need mortals." scoffed Necrosith. "Your lies will not convince me."

"You have clearly underestimated mortals, Draxus. You sought to destroy them, yet their will to live was stronger than your will to destroy them, so you used them for yourself, but why?" asked the echo of Alzar.

The dragon was looking around the platform. He saw a shadow just around the corner of the pathway. "It was I who corrupted the humans of Zakil and made them into orcs. I corrupted the dwarves of Dun'Karo and crafted them into goblins. My creations, my masterpiece!" he yelled before unleashing a breath attack around the corner.

He quickly ran over, expecting to see a charred corpse, but he was disappointed.

From behind him, Alzar spoke. "You haven't the power to create. Only the highfather Thalamon does. Your failure is why I was sent here! Unspeakable actions must be punished! We will deliver upon you the justice of the cosmos! Only this time, I will not make the mistake of imprisoning you. This time, you face death instead."

Necrosith turned to face Alzar and Velnir, who were now standing on the platform, pointing their weapons at him. From his staff, Alzar conjured several molten bolts and hurled them toward Necrosith. Velnir pointed his sword at

Necrosith. Fire began to swirl around the blade until it leapt from Illuminar toward Necrosith.

Together, they pierced Necrosith's chest. Alzar stood firm. He threw out his hands with his palms up. He began to lift his hands while muttering intangible words. He was casting a spell that lifted Necrosith into the air and over the cliffs edge. The dragon howled in pain and agony. Velnir was not quite sure what was going on. He was determined to help, though.

Alzar stood there sideways with the brim of his pointed hat over his brow. There was a slight breeze and his robes were waving slightly. He was aiming his staff at Necrosith from his hip. "None shall suffer you to live," Alzar said in a calm and quiet voice.

Fear gripped Necrosith, and he looked at Alzar one last time; his left eye was not covered by the brim of his hat, revealing Alzar's golden eye. "Gift of the highfather," whispered Necrosith.

Velnir looked over and saw it too. It was amazing. Before the spells burst through his back, punching a hole through his chest. Alzar released Necrosith and let him fall to the bone wastes below to be with his fallen ancestors.

Necrosith could feel his life slipping away. When he hit the ground, everything went black. Then light. Then, Necrosith found himself floating through the cosmos. He looked at his wing and saw that it was still there though not black but transparent. He realized he was dead but found it strange as he thought when he was killed, he would go before the celestials. There was no sign of the lifestream or the Phatra. It was dark. A voice entered the mind of Necrosith. It began to sear and cause excruciating pain.

"You have failed!" said the voice.

Necrosith knew what it was. Fear gripped him. Suddenly, several tentacles grabbed and started pulling. Necrosith looked down and saw a maw with a thousand teeth and a thousand eyes. Its tongues were eager to taste him. Try as he might, he could not get away. His soul was about to be consumed and there was no one to save him.

It pulled him ever closer. He would not give up. Every time he looked back, he was getting closer. A moment later, one of its tongues gripped him and pulled him into the mouth. Every time Necrosith moved, the teeth would tear his soul. He kept going down the gullet of this thing. He could see the opening of the maw was getting smaller and smaller. Soon, his consciousness began to fade. Necrosith was no more.

***

Magris and Nythint were making their way to where they last heard the dragons. They came upon Yzat, who was standing over Ismi's body. They gathered around her and bowed their heads in silence.

Alzar and Velnir came around the corner and saw them. They looked at Ismi and rushed to her. Alzar held her head to his chest.

"Ismi," he cried.

The others stood there in quiet contemplation as Alzar grieved over his companion's loss.

"She stood vigil for countless millennia with me. She was a watcher, a protector as much as I ever was. Alzar stood over her and, with a whisper, morphed her into her visage form.

"I will take her to the dragon isles, to her people. The bone waste is no place to leave my Ismi. She deserves a hero's pyre." He choked up and looked at Velnir. "It is over. Necrosith is no longer a threat to Abrion or the mortals. We have all made the world safe and restored…" he choked up again and whispered, "Balance." He then picked her up and began walking down the path until he was out of sight of the others.

Velnir looked at Magris. Words need not describe how Alzar was feeling for them to understand what he was going through, for they both experienced significant loss in the past.

Yzat and Nythint morphed into their dragon form, and the two elves mounted them. They made their way to Maphis.

Chapter 22
Betrayal

Darlana was stuck in her cell for several days now. This was beginning to make her upset. The Saah had arranged for her to appear in court the following day. She could hardly wait to expose the farce.

Surely, the other humans would see reason. The day came for her to face the kingdom of Maphis. She was shackled and brought before the Saah and his council.

"You are guilty of destroying my city. You ordered your soldiers to burn down the first sector and caused significant damage to my walls. Your actions are responsible for hundreds of deaths and the displacement of the people in the sector," he scolded her.

His wives were standing behind him, but they were simply property, as Darlana found out listening to the guards banter back and forth. They were not allowed to speak.

"I was acting in the best interest of the Maphisians under the authority given to me by Lord Velnir Melfarin of

Atlantin, Tanimara. You had an agreement with us to invade the sundered lands and destroy the orcish horde. When you could not, and the tide was turned against you, we answered your call for help," Darlana argued.

The councilors and noblemen called her a liar and taunted her.

She could not believe what was going on. They were denying all of it.

"I never asked the Tanimarans for help. This was an attempted coup. My people could have handled the orcs without your help."

The noblemen agreed with the Saah. Darlana knew better. The people were running for their lives, and when the elves came, they begged them to save Maphis.

"You lie, the people begged us to save your city," she said. Again she was met with boos from the noblemen.

"People of my court, I have a witness from Tanimara who told me in confidence that the elf planned to conquer our kingdom. In the absence of her leader, she would plot against us for her own gain. She would enslave you."

"No! I would never," Darlana pleaded. "Please, listen to me. We were only trying to help."

"Bring the witness," demanded the Saah.

The elf came around from behind the Saah. Darlana's heart sank. She was heartbroken to see that it was none other than Arlen.

"My name is lord Arlen of Atlan. I come before you in the best interests of the magistrate of Tanimara to humbly inform you that this elf is not only a traitor to your people but to ours as well. She was exiled from Tanimara and labeled an apostate by the high magistrate for her lies, which caused the deaths of many."

"Liar, I was exiled for falling in love with an Araban man. The Tanimarans killed my son and Prince Sampsin of Araba. I did nothing wrong."

The noblemen began to whisper amongst themselves. Some of them recalled the story of Prince Sampsin and their war with Tanimara, but that was hundreds of years ago.

"Oh, please, you would have us believe a tall tale such as this?" retorted the Saah. "The war was over trade. Not you!"

"Darlana was in tears. She felt betrayed and angry." Oh, what little you know, Saah Awani. What little you all know and you, Arlen. How could you? I saved your life!"

Arlen smiled as he watched tears roll down her lovely cheeks. "To that, I owe you a debt of gratitude. Perhaps the Saah will grant you a swift death instead of an agonizingly painful one."

Darlana's heart sank. She could easily break through her shackles and kill everyone in this room with her bare hands. She was in despair and broken. All she had done was love a man and was exiled for it. She wanted peace for everyone and to live in harmony together. It became clear to her that the nobles were simply agreeing with whatever the Saah was saying out of fear for their lives. In truth, no one harbored ill will toward her. It was likely that Tanimara had threatened the Saah for allowing Velnir a safe haven and was taking an opportunity to get rid of Darlana once and for all.

"Perhaps I will, if she will confess. Now confess, Darlana. Tell them the truth!" the Saah demanded.

Darlana sat there on her knees with her head bowed and shackled. She said nothing.

"Have it your way." He would turn to the nobles and guard. "Make ready the pyre. We will burn her alive." He then turned his attention toward Arlen. "Would that please the magistrate, lord Arlen?" The Saah asked him somewhat with fear in his voice.

Arlen smugly looked at the king with disgust and simply walked out of the room without saying a word. Darlana was picked up and hauled out of the court and into the courtyard. She was placed in a cage.

The people were ordered to throw rotten fruit at her, but they clearly did not want to. Almost all of them were reluctant at first but began to comply. A mob formed, and the people delighted in pelting her with whatever they could. Darlana cried.

Outside the gates, a few men escaped and made their way to the elves.

"I need to speak with whoever is in charge. It is a matter of urgency," said one of the men. He was then led to Folwin. Right as the man arrived at Folwin, Velnir and Magris arrived. The men proceeded to tell them what had happened to Darlana.

Velnir became enraged. "I will impale that arrogant king atop a golden pike, large and ornate enough befitting his smug sense of self-importance!"

Magris grinned and agreed. They mounted atop their dragons and made their way to the gate.

"Burn it!" Velnir told the two dragons.

Yzat and Nythint unleashed a massive breath attack that knocked down several parts of the Maphisian wall and gate. The elves rushed in and made their way through the city.

Velnir and Magris took to the sky and flew to the courtyard. Velnir could not believe what he was seeing. The people were throwing rotten fruit at his beloved wife.

Enraged, he and Magris descended. The dragons unleashed a breath attack upon the denizens throwing fruit, incinerating them instantly. Velnir dismounted and drew his sword. Magris and Nythint were attacking the human guards trying to stop them.

Velnir smashed the lock and set his wife free. He grabbed her and threw her over his shoulder. She was sobbing. The humans began to retreat from Magris.

"Magris, please take her and keep these animals away from her. I will deal with the Saah."

"Yes, my lord." He took Darlana from Velnir and placed her on a bench next to him. He held her tight as Velnir dismounted Yzat and stormed the palace alone.

Any who got in his way were dispatched with haste. Velnir was enraged and would not waste any time looking for his prize. He kicked the door down to the court and made eye contact with the Saah. Immediately, he made his way to him.

Something caught his attention out of the corner of his eye. From behind the pillar, Arlen appeared. Velnir was stunned; he stopped, and the rage left him. He was thrilled to see Arlen was all right.

"Arlen," he said with a smile.

Arlen smiled and looked him in the eye.

Velnir had let his guard down long enough for Arlen to drive a kris into his side.

Velnir's facial expression went from delight to shock and disbelief as the pain seared through his abdomen. "Why?" he asked while standing there, trying to read Arlen's demeanor.

Arlen gave his former best friend a smug look. "My house is to succeed the Melfarins should they be eradicated or seen as unfit to lead. You know that, Velnir. When you married the apostate, you sealed your fate. You committed the highest of treason, and it would have been much easier for me to take your lands if you were as unsuccessful as everyone thought you would be. Yet here you are…alive and victorious," he said with disappointment. "So, I had to act.

"You were my best friend. You supported me and…"

Arlen twisted the kris, which caused Velnir to howl in pain. He then placed his finger over Velnir's lips. "Shhhh, I was not finished. When I got back to Tanimara, I went to the Magistrate in Tarvana and told them of your betrayal. I am sure by now they have decided your fate though I did not stay long enough to sit through the special trial. I went back to Atlan. I had Baefric arrested and executed. Your cousin Meric got away, but it is only a matter of time before I find him. You left the door wide open for me to slip right on in. It really is too bad you could not simply see through her beauty…" He shook his head in disappointment. "Velnir the fool? Velnir the traitor? Velnir the apostate? Hmmm,

They are all fitting descriptions. I am just wondering which one I will use when I bring your head to High Magistrate Raften in Tarvana."

Velnir still had Illuminar in his hand. Arlen was too busy gloating to notice. Velnir felt betrayed, though he had no time to allow himself to grieve. Instead, he became enraged and ignited Arlen with the flames of Illuminar. Arlen screamed in horror and agony. Velnir watched him flail as he was engulfed in flames. He was empathetic. Not long after, Arlen collapsed. A burning husk is all that remained. He was dead, and while his corpse was smoldering, he turned his attention to the Saah and walked toward him.

"You…you cannot do this. I am the Saah of Maphis. This will bring war to your people. You have no right. Get out. Leave at once!" demanded the Saah, whose expression was that of pure fear.

Velnir grabbed his shoulder and slowly plunged Illuminar into the Saah's chest. Velnir gazed into the Saah's eyes as he choked on his own blood and his life was drained from his body. The wives began to panic and run away.

The Saah was dead.

Velnir turned around and made his way back down to the courtyard. He looked around as the Nagrimarans were kicking in doors and sacking the city to the left, noticing they hadn't made their way to the right. The people were running away from the Nagrimarans. He was furious. He could take it out on all the humans of Maphis. At this moment, they were nothing to him. They were pests that simply needed to be eradicated. He stuck his sword into the ground and was about to unleash a massive wave of fire that could easily and completely destroy half the city of Maphis when Darlana stood in front of him.

Velnir stopped and looked at her. "Move, Darlana!" he demanded. His eyes were red and full of tears.

"My love, do not take your anger out on these people. They only did what they were forced to."

It was then that Velnir realized that she stood between him and a crowd of Maphisian denizens, holding each other as they truly thought this would be their end.

Velnir stood there, the breeze catching his hair. He looked around with hatred in his eyes. He wanted to kill these people for what they had done to his beloved. He wanted them to suffer for their transgression against Atlantin, after all they did for them. He turned his attention back to Darlana. She held out her arms as if asking him to come hold her. He looked at her longingly. The anger left him. He could not resist. He sheathed Illuminar and made his way to her.

They embraced.

"I will never leave you again. We will remain at each other's side from now on," he vowed.

"I would have never let them execute me, Velnir," she smiled at him. "Give me some credit. You have seen me fight."

The denizens backed off and went about their business.

"Did you kill the Saah, Velnir?"

Velnir gave her a look of reluctance. "I did." He took a deep breath. "Arlen too."

"Saah Awani got what he deserved, and as for Arlen, I am sorry you had to do what you did." She placed her hand on his side, which made him wince in pain. She looked down and noticed he was bleeding. "You are injured," she said.

"Arlen caught me off guard."

Darlana called for a medic, who brought her the supplies to dress his wound.

"I need to get cleaned up. Perhaps we can meet everyone back here when I look presentable," suggested Darlana.

Velnir chuckled. "Why are you so forgiving? Why did you stand in the way of me?"

She placed her hand on his cheek and looked him in the eyes. "My nature is to love and care for everyone and everything. It even hurts to see orcs die, albeit not as much."

Velnir chuckled as Darlana walked off and Magris approached.

"The soldiers are kicking in doors and raiding houses," Magris said.

"Order them to cease at once. This is not a coup."

"Yes, my lord."

Velnir watched as Magris took to the sky and began yelling through a horn for the elves to stop sacking Maphis.

Darlana was done getting cleaned up. They all met at the same villa they stayed in when they first arrived.

"Why here, the palace is vacant now?" joked Magris.

Ignoring him, Darlana asked, "Where is Alzar and Ismi?"

Velnir and Magris looked at each other. It was decided when Magris looked away that Velnir was to tell Darlana.

"Ismi fell. Alzar is taking her back to the dragon islands to have a proper pyre."

Darlana's eyes welled up. "Necrosith?" she asked.

"He is dead," confirmed Velnir.

Darlana nodded and looked at the dragons, now in their visage form. "And you? How are you holding up?"

Yzat and Nythint looked at each other and shrugged. "Good, I suppose."

"What do we do about this mess?" asked Magris.

We have to rebuild the city. It is a major global port hub. If we leave it to ruin, this will not bode well for Tanimara," said Velnir. Darlana agreed.

"What about the succession? You killed their king." Magris reminded Velnir.

"Right, well, to be honest, I am not sure how humans do it."

"It goes to the next of kin. But it has to be male," said Darlana.

"Did the Saah have any male heirs?" asked Velnir.

"Not that I saw. I only saw his wives at the trial. One was with child."

"Let's go to the palace then. I have an idea."

The quintet began to make their way through the city. Velnir noticed the streets were littered with rubble.

"Magris, order the army to clean up the city. Once done, they would await further instructions. Each Maphisian household is to house and feed two soldiers. Remind them it is not an occupation. We are here to help. Expect resistance, especially after the army sacked the city, but do not use violence," ordered Velnir.

"Yes, my lord."

Now, Darlana, Velnir, Yzat, and Nythint made it to the palace of Maphis. The dragons stood guard outside while

Velnir and Darlana went in. They searched the palace for the woman. It was fairly large, so it took a while. Finally, they came across a room that smelled of perfume. Upon further inspection, they found twelve women. They were frightened to see Darlana and Velnir before them.

Darlana leaned down and smiled at them. "Do not despair," she said with a calming tone. We aren't here to hurt anyone. We are here to determine who will rule Maphis. The women were stunned except for one. She stood while the others remained seated. This one was the one with child.

"For many years, the Saah ruled as a tyrant. It pleases us to know we are no longer his sex slaves. Maphis is a slave kingdom. Women have no rights. If you intend to rule here, I beg of you to make changes," said the pregnant woman to Darlana.

"What is your name?" Darlana asked the woman.

"Sabreen, my lady."

Darlana looked at Velnir, who nodded to her with his approval. "You spoke up when the others did not." She looked to the others. "Which is fine, I might add." She turned her attention back to Sabreen. "I assume you are with Awani's child?"

"I am."

"Very well then, you will lead Maphis. I will show you how," offered Darlana.

"But I am a woman. Women are not allowed to rule."

"Then make a change," Velnir chimed in.

***

Velnir's wound began to become infected. Darlana was tending to him. Magris and the elven soldiers were working with the Maphisians to rebuild and fix the port as soon as possible. Trade was established again, and now the city was back to what it had been before the orcs attacked. The people were showing gratitude to Velnir and Darlana by bringing them gifts of fruit.

Galia approached Magris. "Lord Magris, I come bearing a message from the High Magistrate of Tarvana. Please, give it to Lord Velnir." She then handed it to Magris and left. Magris made his way through the city admiring his work. Maphis had a bit of an elven architectural touch now. He made sure it would work well with the pyramid theme.

He entered the villa and knocked on Velnir's chambers.

Darlana answered. "Greetings, Magris."

"Greetings, my lady. Is Lord Velnir available? I have a message from the High Magistrate of Tarvana."

Darlana donned an uncomfortable expression. "Come in," she said.

Velnir lay in bed, frustrated by the healing process.

"What has you down, Velnir?" asked Magris.

"Infection, but Darlana is doing well to render aid. I should be up soon."

"I understand, Velnir. I come bearing a message from the High Magistrate in Tarvana. Perhaps it is praise for what we have accomplished. Or a massive reward?" he said with sarcasm. He looked to Darlana." Or perhaps an invitation for the lady Darlana to return home." Magris smiled.

Velnir broke the seal of the magistrate and unfurled the scroll.

"Lord Velnir Melfarin of House Melfarin, Lord of Atlantin and ruler of Atlantin. A special court session was held, and you were found guilty of apostatism, fraternizing with the enemy, treason, murder, and illegally mustering Tanimaran elves to fight a war for personal gain. You are hereby stripped of all titles and land, and declared an enemy of Tanimara. Any and all Tanimarans are ordered to bring you harm. Do not attempt to return, or you will be executed.

Insincerely, High Magistrate Raften"

"What does it say?" asked Darlana.

Magris was interested as well.

Velnir became angry. "The magistrate has declared me an enemy of Tanimara. They have confiscated my lands, executed my uncle, and stripped me of all titles." He said, clenching his fists. "Arlen made me aware of their plans after he stabbed me. I had hoped he was deceiving me, but in my heart, I knew. These are the games of a tyrant and the Magistrate. I let my anger and desire for revenge cloud my judgment…Oh my people, what have I done? We have no home now, and there is no hope of bringing you with me to Tanimara, Darlana."

Darlana and Magris were silent. Darlana leaned over to hug Velnir. "You are all welcome in Nagrimar. I would be honored to make you Prince Consort Velnir, and I will be your Queen. This child will be a prince or princess."

Velnir looked at her and nodded, although reluctantly.

"I swear my oath of allegiance to you then, Darlana, my queen."

Tanimara has been his home since the day he was born, and Atlan is his city. Simply walking away and abandoning his people to the magistrate was a betrayal to his father and his people.

Magris agreed with Darlana

Another knock at the door. This time, Magris answered. It was a messenger from the palace of Maphis, and they looked nervous. He was looking over his shoulder, making sure he was not followed.

"Queen Sabreen asks you to leave Maphis at once. She is humbled and very grateful for everything you have done, but the Tanimarans have threatened her and her people. You and your elves need to leave immediately. It is not personal."

Velnir nodded. "We will leave tomorrow morning. Now shut the door, Magris."

"What do you think they mean by immediately?" asked Magris.

"I am defining it as tomorrow," said Velnir, clearly irritated. "We need our rest." He turned over. Darlana was lying next to him. Magris took his leave and began to get things in order.

The next morning, everything was ready to move. The elves formed marching columns and began marching out of the city. The people were showering them with praise and thank yous as they left. The combination of Tanimarans and Nagrimarans were thrilled to be hailed off in such a way.

Velnir and Darlana were marching with the army while Yzat and Nythint were flying above. The flight was pretty leisurely. They needed to stay near the army for security reasons. Marching through the desert was unpleasant at best. Hot during the day, cold during the night.

The sun was high, and the army was marching in columns. The familiar sound of boots on the round was interrupted by the faint sound of bellowing wind.

"Up there, toward the sun," called out a centurion.

To the horror of the army, many dragons appeared in the sky and began to descend toward them. Yzat and Nythint immediately took off toward the dragons, clearly outnumbered but with loyal resolve. All Velnir, Darlana, and Magris could do was watch, but Velnir did not want to feel helpless. He ordered the army to form testudos.

Just as Yzat and Nythint were about to clash with the overwhelming number of dragons, they all stopped midair. Velnir was perplexed. He shared glances with Darlana and Magris before retrieving a scrying orb and his scrying crystal.

He tossed it in the air, and it began to move toward the dragons high in the sky. They all stood around the scrying crystal as the image began to clear up. It looked as though they were discussing something, and then suddenly, Yzat buffeted the scrying orb and shattered it with his wing. Velnir tried again with another scrying orb, and again, Yzat smashed it, humbling Velnir.

All of the dragons began to descend toward the army. Velnir ordered them to be ready. Yzat and Nythint landed first and turned to face the rest. Several dragons began to land.

"I count thirteen dragons," said Magris.

"Thirteen confirmed," said Velnir

The largest dragon came forward, and he was absolutely massive. It was a wonder that something so big could even fly.

"I am Rizim, patriarch of my brood. Who among you is Velnir?" he asked.

Velnir stepped forward. "I am Lord Velnir Melfarin of Atlantin."

"I was sent to you by the wizard Alzar. I had been looking for Ismi, my consort, when he told me what had happened to her. He spoke of Yzat and Nythint, and I sought them out here. It seems though that my sons wish to stay with you. I must accept their decision of course but as my brood is a wandering brood without ties to those dragons who wish to be governed in the dragon isles," he said before he and the other dragons began to chuckle. "We choose to stay with Yzat and Nythint as we value broodship above all else."

"Why then do you come now?" asked Darlana.

"Ismi chose to work with the wizard. I was not made aware of the hatchlings until I sought out Alzar. We immediately came to you once we were told."

"We are going back to Nagrimar, and I do not think we can provide you with the amount of sustenance you will clearly need," said Velnir.

"For millennia, we have fended for ourselves without the assistance of mortals, and we shall continue," said Rizim.

Darlana had donned a worried expression as she was attached to life in the Forlorn Forest.

"You may not hunt in the Forlorn Forest," she stated with worry.

"You have never seen dragons within trees that are dense like the ones in the Forlorn Forest. Hah, we simply cannot fit, so do not worry. We have our hunting grounds, and they are far enough away from civilization so as not to disturb anyone. I assure you," said Rizim.

Darlana now seemed content. All the elves seemed to relax, and the dragons transmorphed into their visage forms. Many of them adopted the looks of humans, elves, and the drakonid of the ying provinces in the far west. The army began to form columns again and started to march.

It was a welcome sight to see the desert go from sand and dunes, to grasslands to forest and to dense forest. Eventually, Nagrimar came within sight. Dravon was there to welcome them with open arms. They all received a hero's welcome. Darlana and Velnir went to the palace to address the people.

"People of Nagrimar. It is good to be home again. Our campaign was a success, and we should be rid of the orc menace for the foreseeable future. As you can see, I have invited dragons to dwell with us here in Nagrimar. Rizim is the patriarch of this brood and the father of Yzat and Nythint, whom you already know." The people began to cheer. Dragons are formidable allies.

"I have my husband with me, and the Tanimarans who supported him have come back with us. The high magister of Tanimara has named them enemies of Tanimara."

The Nagrimarans began to cheer, much to the confusion of everyone else.

"I invited them all to Nagrimar and accepted Velnir as the Prince Consort of Nagrimar. He has sworn allegiance to me, as have all the Tanimarans who came with him. Let's give them all a Nagrimaran welcome."

The people began to cheer and walk through the ranks of the Tanimaran soldiers, welcoming them as one of them.

"This went well, all things considered," thought Velnir.

A new council is formed with Darlana at the head, Velnir, Magris, Dravon, Rizim, Yzat, and Nythint as members.

***

Velnir had not worn his armor for weeks now. He had only worn the gown of nobility, and it wasn't much. His hair was down, his perfect muscular tone was visible through the robes, and his achievements were known. Many women wished to be with him, and it was customary in Nagrimar to have as many partners as one could want. He respected his wife and chose to only be with her, as he was raised, which was more like Tanimaran culture. Darlana had previously enjoyed many volunteer concubines but had since dismissed them in favor of her husband.

The time for birth was fast approaching. Darlana was nesting in their chambers. Midwives were there around the clock. When Darlana went into labor, she squatted in a tub, and Velnir stood behind her. He reached out as his baby was coming and gently grabbed the child. It was an elf of pure blood.

"What would you like to call her, husband?" asked Darlana.

"Paeris, if you do not mind."

"Why Paeris?"

"It came to me in a dream."

She was Paeris Melfarin. Darlana was fine with her taking Velnir's last name. Paeris would grow up in one of the safest places on the planet. She had no worries.

Chapter 23
Too Good to Be True

Velnir received reports from Tanimara regularly from people he could trust. It seemed that Baefric and Meric's lands were also seized by Tarvana, now the largest and most powerful governing body in all of Tanimara.

This power play angered Velnir, but he was glad not to be part of it. He would never let go of the fact that they robbed his house of everything. Velnir felt he could never truly leave Tanimara behind. It was his desire to one day bring Tanimara and Nagrimara together. He would have liked to go back and negotiate for his land someday, but for now, Nagrimara was fine. He had a family and didn't mind raising them here.

The forest lords had sent a gift. It was a wreath that never died. The dwarves sent baby Paeris a little anvil and a tiny hammer. She drove her parents nuts. The Tanimarans brought with them their skills and technology.

The city was growing and modernized. It had begun to feel more Tanimaran but looked more like Nagrimaran.

They had learned that forging metal with dragon fire made it stronger and gave it magical properties that strengthened whatever was wielding it or wearing it. Industry was booming.

Velnir had established trade with many dwarven clans and human kingdoms, including Maphis, but his requests for trade agreements were denied by any house in Tanimara. He established trade with the Ying provinces of the eastern continent.

No elf had ever been able to do that. Alzar put in a good word for Velnir.

Dragons from the dragon isles paid visits to the throne of Nagrimar, so Velnir had a special platform built at the top of the palace for them to make a landing. This pleased them. Life was great, and the Melfarins were far richer than they could have ever imagined.

"Prince Velnir, you have a visitor," said the gentle voice of Ashera, the chief court servant.

"Send them in." He was going through some paperwork, and someone walked up to him in a brisk fashion. Velnir turned his attention to the visitor and saw that it was Alzar.

"What a pleasant surprise," he said, rising from his chair.

"Likewise, Velnir. I have come to see the Princess of Nagrimara and have brought for her a gift." He held up what appeared to be a plush dragon, however, it was very unique. It resembled Ismi and was enchanted to move, roar, and breathe fire that did not ignite or burn anything.

"Right," he said before motioning Ashera to approach them. "Please, take Alzar to the Chambers of the princess."

"Yes, your grace," said Ashera before she took Alzar to meet with Darlana and Paeris. Paeris loved the dragon, and Darlana thought it was precious.

"Thank you, Alzar," she said.

"I believe that this came to pass exactly as it was intended. For so long, you have desired a child, and now here she is. Worthy of your love and compassion as are your people. It is my hope that truly you have found peace at last Darlana." he offered her a smile.

She looked at the baby and smiled. "With her and Velnir, I believe I truly have found peace, Alzar. Thank you."

Alzar made his way back to Velnir's workspace to find that he was not there. Velnir had made his way to the balcony he had commissioned for Yzat and Nythint at the top of the palace tower. He stood overlooking the city he had been welcomed to live in and grown to love dearly, but the void in his heart for Tanimara and his desire to go home was not filled. He loved his wife and child and would honor his pledge to rule with integrity and honor, but this was not his or Darlana's true home. They belonged in Tanimara.

Alzar found Velnir with Illuminar, overlooking the city as the sun began to set.

"I see that Rizim and his brood found you. I admit. I am only used to seeing this many dragons at the tower. It is quite intriguing to see this many here. Word gets around quickly, and it is said that you host a mighty army and mount dragons into battle."

Velnir smirked. "They do as they please. We are glad to have them. Yzat and Nythint enjoy the company of others like them.

"Not many are as fortunate as you are, Velnir," said Alzar.

Velnir continued to look over the city. "It is not at all as I imagined. For so long, everything was the same. In such a short time, my entire life changed. The decisions I have made, the consequences, and the weight they carry. I thought I was ready to lead but in my heart I knew I never wanted to. Also, I want to give Illuminar back to you."

"I can speak from observation that those who do not wish to lead are better at it than those who seek to. Tarvana is a great example of what a nation should not be. You and Darlana will make Nagrimara great, and I'm proud of you for not taking the fight to Tanimara. Because of this and the fact that you are humble and have helped so many people, I have changed my mind and will allow you to keep Illuminar so long as you use it for the benefit of Abrion. I assure you, in time, things will calm down, and you will be able to return," said Alzar.

"Many thanks, Alzar. I will honor that pledge. Tanimara will not welcome Darlana or I back easily. Many things will have to change," said Velnir.

"I have seen kingdoms and empires rise and fall. I was there when the elves left the eastern continent and discovered Tanimara. I witnessed the rise of Zakil and Karo and their fall. I even witnessed the birth of every race and the death of many," said Alzar.

"Even still, we have built our home here, and here it will remain…for now."

The next morning, Darlana woke up and looked over to Velnir. "Prince Consort, time to get up," she said, rubbing her nose on his cheek.

"I'm up," he said in an annoyed tone. It was clear he did not like being woken up.

Darlana got up to go check on their daughter. She was walking down the hallway toward Paeris's room and heard the people outside going about their daily activities. She was very happy to be home with her new family.

When she got to Paeris's room, she noticed the door was cracked. The guard was nowhere to be found. Darlana rushed into her daughter's room and saw her standing in her crib, happy to see her. Relief swept over Darlana. She picked up her daughter and held her tight.

"Good morning, my precious. Did your father dip you in a bowl of sugar? Because you are so sweet."

Paeris began to giggle and hug her mother.

"Let's go see your father," she said before leaving her room and making her way back to her chambers.

As she entered, she saw Velnir on the floor with a dagger in his back. He was still alive but barely. From behind the curtain, Galia appeared with a Tanimaran crossbow. She shot at Darlana but missed and hit baby Paeris instead. Darlana pulled a throwing dagger from a decoration on a wall while Galia was reloading and threw it at her. It struck Galia in the throat. She fell to the ground and pulled the dagger out. Blood began to gush out of her neck. She collapsed as she gurgled her last breath. Darlana rushed over to Velnir, who now lay unconscious. She began to panic.

"GUARDS," she screamed. "GUARDS!"

One came in and saw the dead assassin and Darlana leaning over her husband. He called for the other guards to sound the alarm. As the alarm sounded, the guard rushed over to Darlana and went to take Paeris. She gave her to the guard and turned her attention toward her husband. She was distraught. Her eyes were welled with tears as he began to choke.

"No, no, no, no, stay with me, Velnir. You cannot leave me. You must not. Please, by the Celestials, stay with me," she cried. She held his head in her lap.

Two guards came in with a stretcher, loaded Velnir onto it, and went on their way to the palace infirmary. Darlana was beside herself. She did not know what to do, so she just stood there, numb. The guard who took Paeris returned and looked at his queen.

"My queen," he said.

She turned her attention to him. Her eyes were red, and she seemed barely coherent.

"The princess is dead."

The memory of her father throwing Prince Sampsin of Araba out the window along with her first baby came to her. She looked at the guard.

As the realization of what just occurred came to her, she wailed loud enough for the entirety of Nagrimar to hear. The agonizing cries of a mother in mourning struck the feelings of everyone who heard.

The guards came in and attempted to help the mourning queen. She was limp and in tears. It was clear she did not want to leave. She said nothing and just cried.

The alarms were ringing, and all of the Nagrimaran guards were quick to patrol the city for any more threats.

Once the city was declared secure, the council convened. Darlana was not present. Everyone was in a very somber mood.

"To our knowledge, there was only one assassin," said Magris.

"She has been identified as Lieutenant Galia Careen of Atlantin," said Dravon.

"She had a letter on her body. It had the names of everyone she was supposed to kill. Darlana, Velnir, and Paeris were among them, of course, but Alzar's name was on there as well."

"There could be more assassins," said Magris.

"We will warn Alzar immediately," said Yzat.

Yzat and Nythint both got up and hurried out of the council chambers.

Darlana entered the council chambers, still wearing the gown from earlier.

It was covered in blood.

She did not make eye contact with anyone and made her way to the head of the table. She sat there and placed her face in her hands.

Everyone was silent. Her pain was felt by everyone present.

Magris got up and went to her. He stood over her for a moment before embracing her. She embraced him back and began to sob. Magris began to cry as well.

Dravon bowed his head as did Rizim. Darlana was shaking and sniffling. She motioned Rizim to pass the snot cloth which he did. She blew her nose and threw it on the floor.

Magris took his seat. Everyone was waiting for her to speak. She sat there, staring at nothing for several minutes, and then spoke.

"The assassin was Tanimaran," she said with a raspy voice and clogged sinuses.

"Indeed, she was the lieutenant of General Arlen," said Magris.

Darlana smiled and scoffed. "I figured. My father has taken everything from me once again. I cannot live in this world so long as he does." she said nonchalantly. Her voice was still raspy and her sinuses were still clogged. Magris, Dravon, and Rizim all looked at each other. Magris turned his attention toward Darlana.

"Are you suggesting we attempt to have him assassinated, my queen?" he asked.

Darlana looked up without bringing her head up entirely. She glared at him. He was unsure if that was the right question to ask at this point but was also unsure just what question to ask. He was thinking he should have just kept his mouth shut.

As Darlana realized she was getting angry, she calmed herself.

"No, that would not be enough. The magistrate, Tanimara, and its people all cheered as he threw my baby and lover out the window in Tarvana. They wanted blood, but my mother snuck me out and sent me to exile. I do not know what became of her."

The three members said nothing and just kept their heads down.

"All I wanted was peace. I wanted everyone to love each other and to come together. By the Celestials, am I not allowed?" she asked rhetorically. She got up and grabbed the snot cloth again. She gave it a good blow and dropped it in the receptacle before returning to her seat. She put her hands on the table and laced her fingers together, now making eye contact with everyone.

"I have never favored war," she said before lowering her

eyes for a moment. She looked at them once more.

"But war, it seems, is unavoidable. They will keep trying to kill me or kill everyone I love unless we stop them. We need to prepare for war!"

Everyone agreed, and so it was decided. Nagrimara would attack Tanimara. Darlana retreated to her chambers. Blood was still on the floor where Velnir was. She had to lay there alone. She grabbed his pillow and buried her face in it to smell his scent. She screamed and began crying. She did not stop until she fell asleep.

The funeral was a few days later. The body of baby Paeris was beautifully dressed and placed on a decorated pyre in the town square. Everyone gathered with lit candles. Darlana, Alzar, and Magris were present, but Velnir could not make it as he was still in recovery. They were standing behind the priest of the celestials as he spoke. Everyone was silent. When the priest was done, he blessed the dead and lit the pyres.

For several days, Darlana did not leave her chambers. Yzat and Nythint had returned from the tower of Alzar and were standing guard outside her chambers, not letting anyone disturb her.

Darlana was sitting on her bed and staring out the window. She prayed for Velnir to recover. She then looked in the direction of Tanimara. Her sad expression had faded into one of anger.

She whispered, "I am coming for you all!"

Epilogue

Meric and thousands of other Tanimarans escaped Tanimara and made their way to Nagrimara. He told her who he was and said the refugees were from the regions of Atlantin, Caphry, and Madir.

They asked for asylum, and she agreed in exchange for their oath of allegiance. She said that when the time came, she would call upon them to attack Tanimara and take their home back.

Meric proved to be a valuable source of information as he still had connections to spies in Tanimara.

Velnir was in a coma, and they don't know how long it will take him to recover. Darlana and her council are preparing for war.

THE END

About the Author

Writing has been a passion of his since he was in third grade when he wrote his first short story about an apocalyptic event forcing people to live in massive submarines. Since then, he has written several short stories and even more backstories for characters he created.

J.A. Peter was introduced to fantasy at a young age by his father who showed him the 1978 animated lord of the rings, collected ceramic statues of wizards and dragons and brought home a game called Asheron's Call. In 2010, he began roleplaying in World Of Warcraft and has loved writing high fantasy ever since.

If you enjoyed the read, please consider reviewing:

www.ingramcontent.com/pod-product-compliance
Ingram Content Group UK Ltd.
Pitfield, Milton Keynes, MK11 3LW, UK
UKHW042003230426
12048UKWH00009B/512